Ancient Civilizations

Book I of Lamentations and Magic

Russell Cowdrey

RPC Novels LLC

Copyright © 2022 by Russell Cowdrey

All rights reserved.

No part of this publication may be reproduced, distributed, or transmitted in any form or by any means, including photocopying, recording, or other electronic or mechanical methods, without the prior written permission of the publisher, except as permitted by U.S. copyright law. For permission requests, contact russellpaulcowdrey@gmail.com.

RPC Novels, LLC - Coppell, TX

The story in this production is fictitious. Some places, events, and people included in this book are based upon actual historical events, places, and people. All characters based on historical figures are deceased, and some details of their lives have been fictionalized. All events portrayed in this book, which include historical persons, have been fictionalized. For other characters, no identification with actual persons (living or deceased) is intended or should be inferred.

The lyrics of three public domain songs were included in this text and are exempted from any copyright claims.

To find out more about this author, go to https://www.russellcowdrey.com.

e-book ISBN: ISBN: 978-1-960300-00-3

paperback book ISBN: 978-1-960300-02-7

hardback book ISBN: 978-1-960300-01-0

Library of Congress Control Number: 2023931308

I would like to thank Diana, my best friend, my wife, and my rock. Without her unwavering support, Ben and Louisa would have never come to life within these pages.

To the members of the North Texas Writers meetup group, I want to say thank you for sharing your love of writing, your knowledge in crafting a great story, and your encouragement along this journey.

To my mother, Karen Pruitt: I want to thank you for inspiring me to read as a young child. It is thanks to your example that I have this love of science fiction, fantasy, and history.

I would also like to thank my two editors, Brandon Purcell, and Patti Waldygo at Desert Sage Editorial Services, along with illustrator Alla Kholodilina for their invaluable contributions.

Chapter 1

Paris, the Louvre, July 1883

What must it have felt like to spend thousands of years of one's afterlife inside the walls of this granite sarcophagus? These and many other thoughts raced through the intruder's mind. How many millennia did this pharaoh, Ramses III, stare with lifeless eyes at the scene on the opposite wall?[1]

To the black-clad figure huddled in the shadows of the ancient coffin, the rest of the hieroglyphics etched into the inside walls of the granite tomb were not as intriguing as this scene: an Egyptian boat that carried a scarab beetle surrounded by a snake eating its tail. Ignoring the discomfort of kneeling on the hard stone, the would-be thief wondered what it meant for the hundredth time since rushing to this hiding place.

As echoes of the night watchman's footsteps receded and his lantern light faded, the thief questioned again whether this had been a wise choice. A few weeks earlier, she had caught a stroke of luck while sipping tea and scouting potential

---

1. The Sarcophagus of Ramses III resides in the Louvre Museum and is covered with scenes from the ancient Egyptian Book of Gates on its exterior and interior. It was moved to the Louvre prior to 1883.

marks at Café de Flore. At a nearby table, she overheard two archaeologists discussing the value of their finds from Egypt.

Her plan had formed in an instant. With her inheritance almost gone, this one heist would provide a comfortable living for the next few years. Best of all, the stolen goods were portable and easy to hide in plain sight. Tonight, would determine which side of the ledger her luck would fall on.

It had taken her days of research and a bit of bribery to locate the largest collection of the targeted Egyptian artifacts. The difficult part of the job required her to break into one of the most well-guarded buildings in Paris. Scouting the location and devising a plan with a reasonable chance of success took her another week.

Tonight, thirty night watchmen roamed the halls of the museum and the government offices of the Louvre. The cost of obtaining that particular information, along with details of the guard rotations, had been a week's worth of breakfast croissants for an off-duty guard.

The day of execution arrived with the robber spending many uneventful hours hiding in a closet. After midnight, she left her initial bolt hole, slinking from shadow to shadow. A harrowing hour later, she reached her most recent hiding place, a lidless sarcophagus.

The burglar peered over the edge of the sarcophagus at the receding steps. Gas-burning wall sconces lit the Sully building, which housed the museum's most treasured antiquities. At 2 a.m., the flickering flames created an eerie scene of light and shadow.

The watchman's back disappeared around a corner, leaving the thief alone in the room with its display cases and stands. She hopped out of the bathtub-shaped sarcophagus. For one brief moment, the wings of a large goddess etched onto the curved end of the coffin framed her. With senses on high alert, she made for the shadows of the far wall. From information gained during an earlier reconnaissance as a museum visitor, she knew she needed to traverse two more large display rooms to reach the corner stairwell.

Peeking into the next room, the thief marked her next hiding spot: the alcove where the Great Sphinx of Tanis lounged.[2] As she sprinted to the darkened alcove, her black, soft-soled shoes were softer than a whisper.

Another watchman's lamp light appeared in the entrance of the next target room. Fighting her sense of urgency, the thief slowly inched to the back of the Sphinx. Her fingers glided along the cool granite flesh of the lion's body until she reached the creature's tail, which curled over its massive haunches. She ignored the thundering sound of her own heartbeat. Her breath fell into a slow rhythm. She averted her eyes away from the watchman's approaching lamp light.

Flashes came to the thief's mind of the hours she'd spent under the tutelage of her uncle, learning the craft of a burglar. "Remember, if you are still and your eyes hidden, you are nothing but a shadow. If you believe you are a shadow, then anyone who looks will see nothing but what you are. The key is to contain your fear and channel it into your breathing until you are still. Now go find a new place to hide. We will continue the game until I can no longer find anything but shadows."

At nine years old, the child knew right from wrong. But from harsh lessons learned, she also knew the world would never make life easy for a bastard. Her decision to do as her uncle said came with no remorse. The child vowed she would take from the world more than the world would take from her.

She didn't flinch at the sound of the guard's loud sneeze. The man's light flashed into the alcove and ran over the intruder's back, then disappeared. A

---

2. Great Sphinx of Tanis is located in the Louvre Museum. It was moved to the Louvre prior to 1883.

suppressed cough and the fading sounds of shambling footsteps signaled the guard's exit.

The thief opened her eyes and peered at the opposite entrance and the retreating guard. She moved along the wall, keeping to the deepest shadows until she was in the last open room. The path, to her relief, proved empty to the closed door in the far corner.

She turned the handle and checked the lock. In a whirl, lock picks once hidden inside a pocket of her special jacket went to work. In mere heartbeats, the door opened. The thief slipped inside the pitch-black stairwell and relocked the door.

Years ago, her uncle implored the blindfolded ten-year-old, "Concentrate. Your life may depend on how quickly you can open or lock a door when you can't see. Ignore the pain and concentrate." The child had winced with every movement of the tools held in her small, blistered, blood-covered fingers. A grim smile formed at these old memories as she headed up the stairs. Two more flights to reach the second floor and the target.

Near the final landing, the sound of keys being juggled penetrated through the door. The thief ran down six steps and bounded over the banister. She dropped without a sound and grasped onto the edge of a marble step. As the door opened, her right hand slipped and left her hanging by the fingers of her left hand.

Adrenaline rushed into her bloodstream. She tightened her left hand on the smooth marble. A lamp lit the stairs above, and once again the thief became a shadow. She fought to control each breath, not daring to move her hand.

As the guard neared the step that acted as the thief's handhold, her childhood memories once again came unbidden. Years before her uncle had begun instructing her on her future profession, the bastard child had avoided the latest gang of bullies.

The youngster had climbed to the one place where she'd found true freedom: the cliffs. That day, a cloudless, light-blue sky contrasted with the deep blue-and-white foam of Ionian waves crashing against rocks at the base of the cliff. A hundred feet above the jagged stones, the child lost her grip and hung by a single hand.

Fear of death gripped the tiny girl. Fighting a burning shoulder and strained muscles, she channeled her pain and seething anger into the will to fight. And, in an act of ultimate defiance, to live.

The child's dangling hand stretched up and fingers found purchase in the crack of a tiny crevice.

With the guard's lamp light two steps farther down, the thief reached up with her free hand. Her well-toned muscles pulled her up and over the banister as the guard turned the landing. She waited at the door for him to unlock the door on the ground floor. At the sound, her lock picks moved too fast to follow.

She walked down a hallway, leaving the stairway door behind. Soon she stood in front of double doors and a sign proclaiming her ultimate destination: "Egyptian Antiquities Receiving Office." Moments later, she opened the doors and squeezed through. With a faint click, she locked the door again.

The room was almost in complete darkness, but its layout filled the intruder's head. "Now close your eyes and visualize Room 401," her uncle's emotionless voice commanded. "What are your exits? What can you use to escape? Where is the dresser? The bed? Where could you hide? Was there a desk or sofa? Were there any valuables visible?"

Accompanied by a maid, the child had visited thirty rooms in a Corfu City hotel that afternoon. Allowed to see each room for a single minute, she had cataloged every key element of the room and its contents using her uncle's techniques.

After closing her eyes, the child visualized a door with 401 hanging as high as she could reach. The door swung open, and she stepped into the room in her mind. She began answering her uncle's questions, knowing that if she missed any detail, it would bring repudiation and even more repetition.

The mandatory exercise might well determine the success or failure of that night's robberies. Failure was not an option. Mama's cough had gotten worse, and the child needed to get her more medicine.

Back in the present, the thief took a tiny kerosine lamp and a match from another pocket. The lamp light beamed out of a pinhole, making it almost impossible to give away her presence. As she moved past the receptionist's desk, the light fell on a stack of unopened packages piled on a worktable.

To each side of the table sat two identical tables. Each held a particular type of artifact. As she moved down the row, thousands of wondrous items being cataloged lay exposed. The last table to the right held what she desired.

Organized chaos would best describe the worktable piled high with papers, scrolls, and a few ancient books. At the near end lay many unopened boxes and envelopes. The thief set the lamp on the table, careful to make no noise, and opened each envelope, looking for ancient papyri.

It took her ten minutes to gather several hundred papyrus documents. She carefully placed them in a leather binder she'd pulled from under her black jacket. Inside the binder she had constructed a special cardboard filing system to lay the documents flat. When she had stowed as many as the binder would hold, she hid the discarded envelopes inside a large urn. Curious, she read the urn's catalog tag. It listed an artifact number, the site where it had been found, a potential dynasty that estimated the artifact's date of creation, and a note on where to archive it.

As she turned away from the urn, her light illuminated something on a nearby table. Lying among small statuettes and jewelry lay a gold necklace with a yellow gem pendant. It was carved in the shape of a man with a bird's head, and she tried to remember the god's name.

Horus. Pretty sure it's Horus.

Next to it lay a ring with a matching yellow gemstone carved in the shape of a sitting cat. Hesitating just a moment before accepting the added risk, she stashed the ring, the necklace, and the pendant in another pocket.

Two hours and a couple of close calls later, she settled into a cleaning closet in a government office wing of the Louvre. With nothing else to do but wait until morning, she took out the Egyptian papyri and began looking them over.

Most of them were unintelligible to her because she had never studied hieroglyphics. Worse, many of the papers used different symbols than those etched on the sarcophagus she had used as a refuge.

Written in ancient Greek, two papyri stood out from the rest. Being educated in the Greek classics and a native speaker, she found it easy enough to understand the contents. The first discussed an interesting trial. An Egyptian high priest had murdered a member of Ptolemy III's royal family.

More compelling, though, the second contained a genuine mystery. It read,

To Basileus Ptolemy, Pharaoh of Egypt, from your brother in arms, Antigenes.[3]

I am filled with joy that we are no longer enemies, but I am overcome with shame, having killed my friend Perdiccas. His defeat at the river and the disappearance of the five thousand were omens he had lost the favor of the Gods.

Before leaving for Macedonia and home, I wished to report on our search for the missing army of Perdiccas. On his command, the troops had pursued what we now understand to be an unknown Egyptian army.

According to the only survivors of the expedition, the army entered a maze of canyons and ravines southeast of Pelusium still in pursuit of the Egyptians. While these men acted as a rear guard, they claim to have witnessed the wrath of the Gods as it destroyed the army.

---

3. Basileus is Greek for "king."

A huge drop of water, like a God's tear, formed over the canyons and burst when a searing beam of light shot into the sky.

Afterward, they followed the trail of their comrades to an empty box canyon and could find no sign of either army, except for their footprints. Thirty men and I followed a survivor to the canyon. Eventually, we stumbled upon a hidden path that led to a strange temple filled with wonders.

Inside the temple, we found people worshiping the living servant of the God Anubis. The creature appeared as a giant wolf walking upright and wore the accouterments of an Egyptian priest.

The wolf priest conducted a strange ceremony on an altar made of gold. At the end, a man with two mangled legs was placed on the altar. I watched the creature heal his legs with magic. The broken bones mended before my very eyes.

The worshipers soon discovered us, and they killed all but three of my men in our escape. You should take a large force to find the cult and understand its secrets. I have left a map inside the tomb of Perdiccas detailing how to find the temple. The Lion of Alexander is the key. The next time we meet, may it again be as brothers.

Strategos Antigenes[4]

The thief wondered, *Where did this letter come from? Did Ptolemy ever investigate? Has anyone found the temple? Has anyone found its gold?*

The promise of an adventure in Egypt chasing riches that could bring financial freedom sounded better than other options she had considered. Besides, that would make it easier to fence the papyri. Her decision was easy because she could also address that personal issue in Cairo. *He* was owed a visit and needed to feel uncomfortable.

With clothes changed and papers packed away, she heard the sounds of office dwellers shuffling into their boring government jobs on the other side of the closet

---

4. Strategos is the Greek equivalent of a brigadier general.

door. No longer an unwanted guest, the office cleaner stepped with confidence out of the cleaning closet. Carrying a large over-the-shoulder bag, she walked with assurance down the hallway, down the stairs, and out the Passage Richelieu.

Many heads turned as she made her way down the Rue de Rivoli. Not at the sight of another cleaning lady leaving work. No, every man and more than a few women paused on catching a glimpse of the confident, graceful, beautiful young woman. Louisa Sophia moved with the purpose of someone who knew what she wanted and how she would get it.

Chapter 2

Nineveh, Mosul Province, Ottoman Empire, July 1883

Abu hated being in the tunnels. Despite their relative coolness compared to the summer sun outside, he was covered in sweat. Holding the kerosene lamp a foot off the ground with his left hand, while a canteen hung from his hip, he crawled forward like a crippled three-legged bear. He reflected on how being with Dr. Ben McGehee these last ten months had opened the possibility of a life he had never dreamed of.

When his parents had died, Abu had lost hope and became despondent. If Dr. Ben hadn't forced him to begin his studies, he might have given up. The grief continued to come and go, but each day he looked forward to soaking up as much knowledge as he could and helping repay the man who had saved his life. Maybe more than once. It still didn't change how he felt about these damn tunnels.

As his leg muscles cramped, Abu fought the conjured thoughts that kept trying to panic him.

The ceiling won't collapse, and I won't suffocate as I claw my hands bloody. Stop it.

After banishing these evil jinn, Abu emerged into a small cavern about fifteen feet long, five feet high, and another fifteen feet wide. Distributed at equal points across the length of the tunnel were wooden beams. They ran up each side of the dirt corridor, holding up similar beams. Together, they not only braced the tunnel itself but also bore the weight of the Tomb of Jonah.

The tomb's rock foundation began some twenty feet above his head. Despite knowing all that, thirteen-year-old Abu felt a deep sense of relief. He brought his five-foot, seven-inch frame from a crawl to a stoop-shouldered stance and rubbed his cramping calf before taking a drink from the canteen hanging at his side.

Dr. Ben knelt with his back to Abu. He directed the light of his kerosene lamp to a stone wall covered in Sumerian cuneiform writing. Dr. Chipiez perched on a short stool to the left of Dr. McGehee. Between the two men sat an upside-down bucket holding another lamp. Its glow aided Dr. Chipiez as he sketched the symbols on the wall.

Abu heard Dr. Ben's unique voice as he whispered to himself. He sounded like any other American, except that every sixth word or so had a distinct "Texas twang." That was how Dr. Ben described his accent because Abu had never met another person from what Dr. Ben called "the Republic of Texas."

Dr. Ben began translating the cuneiform out loud. "After the deluge in the third year of the reign of Enmebaragesi, King of Kish and First King of Sumer, the people of Mari, having sworn fealty to Kish, angered the great god Zababa by worshiping giant, man-like demon-dogs. As punishment for their heresy, Enmebaragesi laid siege to the city and prayed to Zababa for the city's destruction. He promised to offer its people as sacrifice to the great god. On Enmegaragesi's third night of prayer, Zababa spat upon the cursed city, covering the unholy with his sacred water. Zababa then cast a cleansing upon the city before disappearing into the heavens. The next morning, Enmebaragesi found Mari. Hmmm... what is that word?"

Leaning toward the wall, Dr. Ben pointed to a series of lines, slashes, and dot symbols. Dr. Chipiez looked up from his sketch pad and said, "Empty," with a French accent.

Dr. Ben nodded. "The next morning, Enmebaragesi found Mari empty of its people and livestock. To this day, it is said that Zababa feasts upon the wicked of Mari. Well, very interesting, heh, Chipee?"

"Yes, most interesting. It would appear that someone found the city of Mari in the same state as your American brain." Dr. Chipiez's voice had an overtone of snark. "Empty."

"Now, Chipee. I'd expect a better insult from a sophisticated gentleman like yourself."

"Ahem." Abu coughed to cut short the verbal fencing that could go on for several minutes. Sometimes the two adults behaved like schoolboys, playing at archaeology with the city of Nineveh as their playground.

Both men wore round spectacles, but there the similarities ended. The French archaeologist was fair with straight jet-black hair, a well-trimmed beard, and dark brown eyes set into a broad face that matched his shorter, stockier build.

In contrast, the American sported a head of slightly curly brown hair on top of his tall, wiry frame. His tanned complexion contrasted with blue eyes above high cheekbones. Clean shaven, his angular face might have been handsome, except for a noticeable scar. It started just in front of his left ear and ran down his cheek to the tip of his chin.

"Dr. Ben, a postman from Mosul and a group of soldiers have arrived with a large trunk and some letters for you. They insist you sign for them yourself."

Ben smiled, his scar tugging at that side of his mouth. Abu reminded Ben of a drawing he had seen of an Aztec warrior battling Cortez and his men. Like the warrior, Abu had a proud face with a prominent cleft chin and dimpled cheeks, along with a rich brown complexion, black hair, and fierce brown eyes. "Thank you. Please hold up the light for Chipee. He needs all the help he can get."

Ben squeezed past Abu and got down on all fours to enter the smaller tunnel.

Ben heard Chipee fire off one of his favorite French insults. "S'il y avait une taxe sur votre cerveau, vous seriez fauché."[1]

Ben shot back over his shoulder. "Compared to you, I'd still be rich."

More muffled French followed him into the tunnel that would take him out of the human-size rabbit warren.

Emerging into the daylight brought Ben relief and a different type of discomfort. He squinted and took in deep breaths, his lungs working harder to process the hot air. The slight breeze did nothing to stop perspiration from forming on his forehead in the hundred-degree summer weather. The tunnels' one saving grace: they were fifteen degrees cooler than the ruins of the ancient city.

Ben blew out his lamp and set it on the ground. Bending further, he removed a rock and scooped up his faded, dust-covered pork-pie hat with its brim tied up on the right. Using both hands, he positioned it with an ever-so-slight tilt.

A gold-threaded, crossed-sabers patch and a number 7 stood out above the hat's golden tasseled ribbon. He knew the distinctive cavalry hat looked out of place, but he kept it with him like a lucky rabbit's foot. He pulled his Schofield revolver out of its holster and checked its readiness out of habit.

Taking brisk steps, he made a straight line toward the main camp, about half a mile from the tomb. As he approached, he saw six unknown horses tethered to the trough, while several men lounged around a small table in the mess tent. Also new, a large travel chest stood nearby.

Two of the men jumped to their feet and met him beside the trunk. The first, a sergeant in the Ottoman cavalry, wore his dark-blue uniform with its distinctive red cuffs, red collar, and red pant stripes with pride. Topping the ensemble sat a black fez hat with a matching tassel that flopped this way and that as he moved. The sergeant's left hand rested on the hilt of his saber as he extended his right.

---

1. French that translates to "If you taxed your brain, you would be broke."

Shaking hands, he spoke in a thick Turkish accent, "Dr. McGehee, I am Sergeant Chaush Suvari of the Fourth Cavalry, and this is Shahril Tahir. He's a postman from Mosul. We came from the postmaster with some packages for you. One post requested an immediate response via telegram." He disengaged and slapped the satchel on his hip. "There are funds here as well."

The postman handed over a large envelope containing 150 British pounds, a letter from Flinders Petrie, and a book.

"Gentlemen, would you mind putting the trunk in my quarters over there?" Ben nodded toward the tent. "Please rest as long as you need and replenish your supplies. I'll provide you with a reply and a return letter before you head back to town," he added, before walking away.

Ben sat at his small portable desk and read the title of the book, *The Pyramids and Temples of Gizeh by W. M. Flinders Petrie*.[2] He grunted and put the book aside. After opening the accompanying letter, he read:

My Friend Benjamin,

I hope this letter and the accompanying money find you well at Nineveh. Amelia has read me the letters from your expedition.[3] *Your adventures seem lifted from one of the Wild West yarns you Yanks love so much.*

The gunfight with brigands outside Tripoli and your encounter with the ruffians in Aleppo makes me question my choice in careers. Then again, your discovery of the cuneiform tablet library at Nineveh keeps me mad as hops to uncover the secrets of the ancients.

---

2. W. M. Flinders Petrie is considered the father of systematic archaeology. He is famous for a lifetime of work in Egypt.

3. Amelia Edwards was an author and an Egyptologist who helped to fund many archaeology excavations, including some of Flinders Petrie's early expeditions.

On that note, I have very exciting news for the both of us. Hopefully, you will enjoy my new book. As you know, my first. A feat I will now hold over you forever. The book has opened many new doors. Amelia helped me raise the money to lead an expedition to excavate at Tanis starting early next year.

I would like you to act as my second and be my advance man in Cairo. I know how much you have longed to visit and explore Egypt. The money should cover your expenses for getting to Cairo. More money will await you at the Shepeard's Hotel.

I know you will need some time to wrap up the excavations at Nineveh, but I would hope you could be in Cairo in three months' time. If you cannot accept this offer, please let me know as soon as possible. Oh, and keep the money. I still owe you several hundred quid from our last card game. Damfino, how you bushwhacked me so.

I await your response, and I look forward to the adventures we will have together in Egypt. Hopefully, it will not include copping a mouse like your Aleppo fray. Stay on the lookout for the jammiest bits of jam for the two of us in Egypt, will you? Godspeed and, for God's sake, stay alive.

Flinders Petrie

As successful as the current dig had been, Ben knew that if he wanted to leave a legacy as an archaeologist, his destiny lay in Egypt. His heart beat faster as he set the letter down and picked up his pen to reply. "*Wholeheartedly accept stop Thrilled at expedition stop Congrats on book but our tales just beginning stop See you in Cairo with angelica on each arm stop Will avoid waking snakes stop God Bless Ben full-stop.*"

After putting the reply aside, Ben's attention turned to the large travel trunk delivered by two of the Ottoman cavalrymen.

He unstrapped the two belts that secured the trunk. Inside the removable tray on top, an envelope sat on a book labeled *Antiseptic Its Principles Practices and Results*. Next to the tome lay a well-cushioned oblong bundle. He removed the compartment and put it on the ground, then rose to place the letter on his writing desk. He peered into the chest and picked up a holster with a revolver.

Underneath lay a matching gun in a similar holster. After removing it, he admired the bird's eye grip, the metal skull crusher–style handle, and its seven-inch barrel. Below the cylinder he read: "Merwin Hulbert & Co. N.Y. Pocket Army model 3." He turned the revolver over on the opposite side and read: "Caliber Winchester 1873." He pushed the release button on the left side of the gun, rotated the barrel, and pulled the cylinder forward. The entire mechanism moved ahead enough to eject imaginary spent cartridges.

After spinning the cylinder, he slid it back until he heard a solid click. Pointing to the ground, he tightened his finger on the trigger. The hammer raised to the cocked position and slammed back into place. He couldn't help but smile.

He squeezed the trigger two more times, watching the smooth double action of the hammer. Satisfied, he lowered the collapsible hammer before holstering the gun and placing it back in the trunk. With his smile still lingering, Ben reached for the envelope from his brother.

After tearing it open, he found several handwritten pages that read:

1/20/1883

Dear Ben,

"We have missed you back home. I had a lot of difficulty last month, knowing it had been over 20 years since we lost both Mom and Savage.

In an instant, the worst day of his life replayed for the thousandth time. Ben had ridden next to Major Ross and his subordinates in the middle of the cavalry column marching toward Pea Ridge, Arkansas. His brother, Lieutenant Savage McGehee—Ben's older middle brother—had volunteered seventeen-year-old Ben to be a messenger with the command group that morning.

Savage and the rest of his unit rode as the rear guard for the regiment. Without warning, the booming sounds of four or five cannons exploded to their rear. Ben swung in his saddle to see black powder pour out from the woods to the column's right rear. His eyes tracked to where Savage and the rest of his squadron should be. Instead, a dozen horses and their riders lay in crumpled heaps.

It seemed to take forever for Ben's realization of what happened to register, but it must have been a few seconds. Fear froze his heart, and he turned his horse to gallop toward his brother. He would have died that day, except for Major Ross.

Knowing Ben to be the lieutenant's younger brother, the major read the situation and snatched the bridle of Ben's horse. With his free hand, Ross swung a hook, caught Ben on his chin, and dislodged him from his saddle. He fell unconscious before hitting the ground.

It took until the next night for the fighting to subside. Ben and two comrades snuck back to the battlefield and retrieved his mangled brother's remains. He brought the body to his father, who served as a regimental surgeon. Together, they cried in each other's arms after burying Savage in the rocky Arkansas soil. For a while afterward, Ben lost himself to revenge, creating a monster that fed on violence and the rush of battle.

With jaws clenched and his eyes threatening a deluge, Ben turned his focus back to the letter.

It made your absence that much more difficult, little brother, but I understand you are chasing your dreams and hopefully outrunning the ghosts of that damn war.

We were mighty entertained by the latest escapades detailed in your last letter. It also made me worry. I had thought you becoming a doctor would have taken you away from those dangerous paths. Obviously, your need to see the elephant has overridden your common sense.

Since danger seems to follow you like a stray calf, I thought I'd provide you with some help. Hope you don't need to use the two new double action M&H pocket army revolvers, but I know if you do, these will give you an edge over your old single-action Schofield. I made sure they used Winchester 44.40 ammunition to match your rifle.

I'm sending you two in case you need spare parts, and 1500 rounds. It's probably difficult to get Winchester bullets where you are.

You will also find two shorter replacement barrels. That way, you can conceal the guns on your person as needed. I'm sure the engineering degree you received in Georgia will allow you to figure out how to replace the barrels. The mechanisms are really quite ingenious.

And just in case you decide to return to practicing medicine, I have included a book. It may change all of your preconceptions about surgical infections. It's about the new process of using antiseptics during surgery. I have included a bottle of carbolic acid. It's the primary chemical used to kill germs that the theory postulates cause surgical infections. I have been using the new methods for the last six months with outstanding success. Anecdotal, I know, but I conducted eight surgeries with zero deaths from infection.

Both Anne and Harriet send their love. My youngest, William, and Anne's oldest, Savage, are heading down to College Station to attend the new military college. Both of them are ardent admirers of their uncle, the soldier/scholar and now world explorer. Weldon Guthrie's boy, Junior, proposed to Harriet's middle daughter, Lorriene. Her oldest had her 2nd child, a boy, they named Benjamin Ronnie Andrews. I'm sure he will be a little hellion, just like you and Uncle Ronnie. Not sure what she was thinking.

Let us know if there is a potential lady in your future. Especially now that you have taken in the young ward. You don't want to wait too long and end up an old rabble-rouser like Uncle Ronnie.

A tear splattered onto the next paragraph, and Ben looked up, more saltwater pooling in his eyes. The sudden wave of sadness caught him off guard and threatened to overwhelm him. He missed his family, but this was altogether different.

With a sigh, he closed his eyes and grieved.

He grieved for his parents. Incredible role models who loved each other and their children with all they had. He mourned the fact they died without getting to say goodbye to each other.

He grieved for Mahdi and Yara, Abu's loving parents.

And most of all, he grieved for his dream of having a loving family like his mother and father. After the war, his desire to build a family had given him his primary reason to live. His dream went the way of Caesar, an ultimate betrayal perpetrated by those he loved the most.

Teeth clenched, Ben took in a deep breath through his nose and blew it out the same way. His jaws relaxed as he opened his eyes, letting the emotion go. With the back of his sleeve, he wiped away tears.

Maybe Henry's right. I owe it to Abu. But what about me? Do I owe it to myself?

Would he ever be able to give the boy what his own parents had given him? Not alone. Would he ever be able to resurrect that dream for himself? Several times in the last decade he had tried without luck. He expected nothing would work until he was willing to risk experiencing the kind of pain that almost killed him last time.

And there it was, the answer to every problem Ben had ever known. God's able, if you're willing.

Am I willing?

It's not like I have a lot of options out here, anyway.

A rueful grin creased his lips as he rationalized pushing this issue to the back of the queue. With a shake of his head, he returned to reading.

In Texas news, General Ross, now a state senator, may run for governor. We need a firm hand during these turbulent times, and Sul Ross hates injustice as much as any man does. I know you had nothing but admiration for him as your commanding officer while you served in the Texas 6th. Well, we look forward to hearing more about your excavations at Jonah's tomb. It's quite amazing that you are seeing all the places we've read about in the Good Book.

Please write more often and let me know if you need anything else out there on the edge of civilization. I'll get it to you as soon as possible.

Your Loving Brother, Henry

Ben picked up the pen and wrote his reply.

Chapter 3

Ramses Train Station, Cairo, Egypt, September 1883

Ben turned toward the tugging on his arm.

Abu, now certain he had Ben's attention, said, "Dr. Ben, that woman appears to be in trouble. Maybe we should help her."

Abu's dark eyes showed genuine worry and remained locked on the scene unfolding around a beautiful, petite young woman.

At the end of the train platform, she fended off a half-dozen Egyptian men wearing the ubiquitous tunic-and-turban uniform of station porters. With raven-black hair pulled into a bun on her neck under an old-style hat that Ben hadn't seen in ages, she wore a simple light-blue cotton dress. The perplexed woman waved her parasol in menacing circles at the men.

"You're right, Abu. I'll see if I can help. Make sure our baggage gets to the carriage. I'll be along after getting this sorted."

Giving him a disappointed look, Abu turned from the scene and started directing the porters who held their luggage.

Wondering what he'd gotten himself into, Ben lengthened his stride and hurried to what had become a full-blown ruckus. He got closer to the bunched-up porters as a strong, angry woman's voice rose over the din of men.

"Get your bloody hands off. Arrête que tu loutes.[1] Gamísou!"[2]

Plowing through the mob, he reached the young woman and spun around. He cleared an arm's length of space between the young lady, her belongings, and the men who, at best, were looking for work or, at worst, were trying to take advantage of an unwitting victim.

Ben yelled at the men in Arabic, "Enough! We don't want your help! Go! Now!"

Some grumbled, but after a menacing glare from him, the crowd dispersed.

Turning to the young woman, he stared at her old-fashioned, felt postilion hat with its blue ribbons and cloth flowers.[3]

She's short.

He moved his gaze lower as her face tilted up toward his. He assumed that the young woman with the striking facial features was in her mid-twenties. Black curved eyebrows accentuated deep brown eyes full of intense anger. She had a proud, distinguished nose set between high cheekbones.

Finally, he noticed her pursed ruby-red lips and regal chin. An olive-toned oval face with perfect symmetry provided the canvas for this masterpiece. Even buttoned to her neck, her modest blue dress failed to hide her attractive curves. His eyes moved farther down and widened to see the barrel of a small caliber revolver pointed at his gut.

Raising both hands in surrender, he said in his calmest, most casual manner, "Miss, I'm only here to be of assistance. If I help you arrange transportation, will

---

1. French for "Stop that, you lout."

2. Greek that translates to "Fuck you."

3. Postilion hat was an 1860s wool hat that some younger women wore.

you please not shoot me?" He raised his eyebrows and gave her an innocent smile. "I really want to explore the pyramids. It's been a dream of mine since childhood."

The young lady's eyes softened, and her lips relaxed. She put the gun away. Ben exhaled in relief.

The woman took a few heartbeats to inspect him in return. Her gaze paused on his scar before flicking to his hat. From her canny expression, he could have sworn she had taken him apart and knew everything there was to know about him in those few seconds.

Her nostrils flared as she said, "I appreciate you coming to the rescue of those fools. If you hadn't intervened when you did, a few of the scoundrels might never have danced again."

Ben couldn't place her accent. Her almost native English had the British lilt that non-native speakers pick up when learning English from someone, well, English.

Taking the edge out of her voice, she said, "You'll be happy to know I have no intention of endangering your childhood dreams, Mr. . . . ?"

"Benjamin McGehee, ma'am. Pleasure to meet you. I promise, I'll forever endeavor to remain on your good side and out of your gun sights. Miss . . ." Extending his hand, he expected her to offer a dainty handshake. Instead, she used a firm grip and gave as vigorous a shake as any man, while looking him dead in the eye.

"My name is Louisa Sophia. And yes, I could use some help with transportation to my hotel. I speak five languages, but, unfortunately, Arabic is not one of them."

Releasing his hand first, Ben said, "Miss Sophia, I'll be happy to help. Can you tell me your destination and whether you are traveling alone? I need to know what size carriage you'll require."

"Of course. I'm staying at the Shepheard's Hotel by myself. I only have these." She waved toward the suitcases beside her.

"Luckily, Miss Sophia, I'm your Huckleberry. We're staying at the Shepheard's as well. Abu, my ward has already secured a carriage, and you're welcome to ride with us. May I?"

Without waiting for permission, Ben picked up Louisa's two suitcases.

She stepped back, and her eyes narrowed a bit. "I'm unfamiliar with the term *Huckberry*, but I count our meeting fortuitous, Mr. McGehee. Please lead the way."

After turning toward the main entrance, he slowed his pace to walk by Louisa's side and synced up with her shorter steps. He then noticed a messenger bag strapped across her chest, her protective hand gripping the strap.

A reasonable precaution in this place.

As they walked, he asked, "Have you been in Egypt long? We, Abu and myself, just arrived on the train from Port Siad. Until recently, we were in Persia on an archaeological dig at Nineveh. At the site of Jonah's tomb."

Ben caught himself prattling about details that were sure to bore the young lady. He fell into the habit any time he became nervous. Getting back on track, he continued, "We're here to help with a new expedition near Tanis. And you?"

Inscrutable, Louisa responded, "As soon as the boat docked in Alexandria, I grabbed the train here. I'm afraid I'm just another tourist looking for an adventure. Although I also hope to visit a relative who works for the British government here in Cairo."

Ben laughed. "If it's an adventure you're after, then Miss Sophia, you are off to a good start."

She turned her head and shared a smile with him.

As Louisa left the Ramses train station and the scene of her near assault, the smells and sounds of Cairo assailed her senses. Scents of strange spices wafted from nearby street food vendors to mix with the all-too-familiar smells of perspiring men, sweaty horses, and horse dung.

Louisa slowed a step at the aroma, but she came to a complete halt at the sound of the Islamic call to prayer. Its haunting melody prompted her to seek its source amid the busy plaza in front of the station. Ben had taken several steps before he stopped. He looked back as she tilted her head, listening. Her thoughts filled with wonder.

Ben backtracked two steps to stand beside her. "It's really quite beautiful, isn't it? They say the Muslim call to prayer puts a spell on people the first time they hear it. They also say that within a month, you'll welcome it about as much as the cock's crow." He gave her a crooked smile. "Then again, I've heard others say that if you live with it long enough, it'll become the background symphony music for your life's play. Its absence will feel like the songbirds have disappeared on a spring day."

Turning to look into the man's eyes, Louisa wondered what she should make of the American with the strange accent. "It's enchanting, I agree. Shall we?" She waved him ahead.

She followed the rangy man down the line of carriages. A young man, wearing a big grin and waving, sat next to the driver who would take them to their destination.

The teenager jumped down to greet them and held out his hand. "Hello, Miss. I'm Dr. Ben's assistant, Abu. A pleasure to meet you."

She shook his hand. "Nice to meet you, Abu. I'm Louisa Sophia."

"Miss Sophia, are you staying at the Shepheard's hotel as well?"

She gave him a polite smile. "It would appear so."

He broadened his grin and would have continued talking, but Ben handed him the two suitcases. "Let's move along."

Abu passed the suitcases to the driver, who secured them to the roof of the single horse–drawn port chaise carriage. Ben opened the door to the two-person cabin and held his hand out to Louisa. She put her hand in his and bounded up the footboard with the light step of a dancer. He climbed in with much less grace and took the seat next to her.

As they pulled into the stream of traffic, Louisa saw the River Nile crowded with Egyptian dahabeeyah-style sailboats. Standing out among the native vessels were a couple of modern double-decker steamboats. Most boats headed south under full sail or steam. They fought against the wide river's current, seeking its source and many of Egypt's ancient wonders.

"You know," Ben said, "they model the dahabeeyah boats after Egyptian boats built thousands of years ago. There are depictions of the shallow-bottomed boats in tombs, temples, and ruins across Egypt."

Louisa pushed herself into the corner and turned to look at him. He removed his hat and held it in his lap before giving her a sheepish glance.

"You're a font of interesting facts and modest as well, Dr. McGehee." She emphasized his honorific.

"It's nothing, Miss Sophia. I'm no longer a practicing physician. Just another would-be treasure hunter with an obsession for archaeology." Ben gave her another crooked grin.

She smiled. "Louisa, please. I see no need for formalities with someone I almost shot."

"Then Louisa, please call me Ben."

She kept updating her evaluation of the man sitting next to her. When he first came to her aid, she'd taken in his brown tweed suit, spectacles, scar, and strange hat the way she had so many thousands of marks before. If she were to accomplish her goals in Egypt and become a woman of means, it might take her a moment to repress these old habits.

Her evaluation put him in his late thirties, a scholar of some type, with modest wealth but not rich. The scar and the hat screamed former soldier. A soldier, a scholar, and a non-practicing medical doctor added up to more depth and mystery than most.

"I hope you won't think me impolite, but can you tell me the story behind your hat?" Louisa inquired.

Ben held up a finger and leaned out the window. "Abu, how long will it take us to reach the hotel?"

A garbled exchange in Arabic took place above them as Louisa gazed at the crowded streets of Cairo. The carriage's gentle jostling along the hard-packed dirt road added an air of discovery to each new experience. Sweet and pungent smells wafted into the cab, only to be outdone by the cornucopia of humanity filling the thoroughfare.

"The driver said it'll take thirty minutes, Dr. Ben!" Abu yelled.

He turned back to her. "Well, it would appear we have the time for my hat story. I rarely tell it on first meetings. Once solved, the enigma of my hat causes me to lose all mystery. With you learning my sole secret, I think it's only right to trade my story for some information about yourself. Fair?"

"Sure. I'll give you three questions, but I can't promise I'll answer them all. As a lady, I must always maintain an air of unknowability."

Ben paused a moment before pressing on. "I'll keep my questions simple so your secrets remain." He held up a finger. "Miss Louisa, where did you grow up?" A second finger went up. "Second, will you please reciprocate and tell your hat story? I have not seen that style for over ten years." A third. "And last, explain why a beautiful young woman is traveling alone?"

Louisa's brow furrowed at his simple-at-face-value questions. All but one represented an intricacy of challenges. "I've lived in several places, but I was born in Corfu and lived there until I was twelve. You'll get no more for your first question."

She watched him for a moment, daring him to object. "As for the second, I failed to bring a hat on my journey. Some kind strangers helped me rectify this mistake. During the boat ride from Naples, I met the most amusing twins, Alice and Agnes Griffin, from Mobile, Alabama. They were both widows in their sixties who had married the brothers Griffin—not twins, mind you.

"Both their husbands died in recent years, so the pair decided to see the world. Well, for the entire trip, they regaled me with the story of their lives and travels through Europe. A rather handsy fellow from Belgium made listening to the talkative ladies from Alabama a pleasure and a necessity.

"One particularly sunny day on the boat's veranda, the ladies noticed my lack of a hat. They were kind enough to give me two of theirs. This white-and-blue one and I have its twin, a white-and-pink one, in my luggage. As for your third question, I have no one else with whom to share my journey."

Louisa could tell from Ben's slight frown that he found her answers unsatisfying. He apparently decided not to press his luck and replied in accented but almost perfect Greek, "Thank you, Louisa. I owe you a story."

He switched to English. "I received this hat and this scar on my twentieth birthday. The same man gave me both." Ben smiled, but his eyes took on a distant look filled with sadness. "My squadron was scouting ahead of our regiment, the Texas Sixth Cavalry."

His mood darkened. "Well, anyway, we were protecting the right flank and scouting some woods outside of Atlanta. Sherman's army was determined to take the city. We all knew that one more defeat and we would lose the war. We were desperate. Not that it mattered in the end." Ben's voice dripped with regret.

Without thinking, she reached out and touched Ben's arm. The gesture brought him back, and she nodded for him to continue.

"Like I said, we spread out as we rode through the woods when, out of a ravine, charged some cavalry from the Pennsylvania Seventh. I barely had time to draw my Colt before I found one of them on my left, swinging his saber. I lost my hat and some say my good looks in an instant." Ben's left hand touched his scar. "I had no time to aim. I just fired across my saddle. If not for God's great providence, I would not be here today. The shot missed but struck his horse in the eye. Before he could finish me, the horse and rider fell. After our squadron beat back the attack, we discovered a Union officer trapped under his horse."

Ben paused. When he smiled, his scar formed the off-kilter grin she had noted earlier. "Well, this officer turned out to be Major Charles Davis, and he'd broken his leg in the fall. We moved the horse and splinted his leg real quick. He would have surely died if we took him prisoner. Before I sent him back to his lines, I took his hat to replace mine. I also took his Spencer carbine. When we moved his horse, I found his broken saber. I had it shaped into a long knife. I have it in the luggage." Ben pointed to the roof.

Her eyes followed his finger for a moment before drifting down to his face. "Thank you. A story well worth the cost. One question. I would have imagined the scar would be worse, given this happened during a battle. How did you get treated?"

Ben showed a wider, lopsided smile. "My father was the regimental surgeon. I made my way back to him to get stitched up. He was an excellent doctor. Unfortunately, he passed just before the end of the war and never got to go home."

"I'm sorry, Ben."

He gave her a rueful look, and the conversation trailed off as they took in the sights of the busy Cairo streets. Looking but not seeing, Louisa thought more about Ben. After a few moments of daydreaming, she admonished herself for wasting time on the interesting but unneeded man. She had to focus on the plan. Working through it again, she began singing in a low, clear voice.

Her lilting soprano carried the Greek folk song "Ástra Apán' son Ouranón" out into the Cairo street as her mind drifted back to her mother's voice. She pictured herself as little Louisa on one of the last times she had seen her mother strong and healthy. Mama stood at the front of a taverna, singing this very song.

In fact, her mother had sung this song every day since her father had left them, breaking her mother's heart. On her mother's last day, Louisa sang these exact words as she held her mother's hand and watched her slip away.

Ben listened with rapt attention, mesmerized by the beautiful voice next to him. She had held him at pistol-point moments ago, and now she sang as if he didn't exist. The anguish of her song resonated in his bones. Leaning closer, Ben translated the sad Greek song:

Stars in the sky, I have an ache in my heart
and I will tell you about this to relieve my heart.
My smile is gone, my soul is bitter
the person that I loved, has left my world.
Without water, roses and lilies wither
Without you in my soul, I'm burning like them.
Stars in the sky, I'll make a wish
so that becomes a star to see where I'll go.

The carriage pulled up to the Shepeard's Hotel, whose facade could have been lifted off any street in modern-day Vienna. Ben sat in his seat for a protracted moment, lingering in the silence of the carriage as Louisa's song came to an end. Plucked from his trance as they jerked to a stop, he noticed her expectant gaze. He hurried to open the carriage door but paused and asked, "I'm curious. Who is the relative you're visiting?"

Before she could answer, he hopped down and held out his hand for her to descend. She stood in the doorway, looking down at him, her face scrunching up.

"My father," came her terse reply.

She reached the bottom of the steps with her hand still in his. "Thank you for sharing your carriage."

"The pleasure was all mine. I hope we see each other again. If I can be of further assistance while you're in Cairo, just holler. Until the expedition starts in earnest, I'll have more time than I'd like on my hands."

Louisa looked him in the eye, withdrawing her hand before holding it out again. Better prepared for the firm handshake that followed, Ben reciprocated her force as she said, "Thank you again, Ben."

She disengaged, waved goodbye to Abu, and turned to the porter waiting with her luggage.

Ben watched her walk up the steps past the hotel's famous terrace and disappear way too soon into the grand hotel. Abu, now beside him, elbowed Ben in the waist.

Ben shook his head. "Don't say it."

Ignoring him, Abu replied in Arabic, "Dr. Ben, it's great to see you talk to a woman. I thought you might not like them. Miss Sophia sings like a songbird and is beautiful." The teen flashed a mischievous grin. "She's obviously unobtainable for someone like you, but now that I know you like girls, I'll keep an eye out for a more appropriate option." He turned serious. "I worry about you."

Ben disregarded the implied and explicit insults before answering in the same language, "You worry about me? I'm supposed to be looking out for you."

"We both know our relationship doesn't work that way." Abu grinned.

Shaking his head, Ben said, "Let's go check in."

Chapter 4

Shepheard's Hotel, Cairo, Egypt, September 1883

Ben and Abu walked into the grand foyer of Shepheard's Hotel, the rival to any of the top hotels in Europe, the Americas, and the Far East. Nothing could match its grandeur in Africa.

For Abu, outside of a few grand mosques, the luxury of the interior made it the most incredible building he had ever been in. He marveled at the giant granite columns resembling those from Egyptian temples with their ornate carvings. Just as his eyes settled on two bronze topless caryatids stationed on either side of a grand staircase, he bumped into Ben, who stood in front of an enormous marble-topped reception desk.

"Excuse me, Dr. Ben," he apologized in his native Arabic. His view shifted from a large gold-and-crystal chandelier to a stern look from a man in a gray wool suit standing behind the counter.

The man's lip curled in distaste before he focused on Ben. "Checking in?"

"Yes, the reservation is a double room for Dr. McGehee."

Paging through a voluminous book, almost hidden behind the tall counter, the man at last said, "Yes, here you are, Dr. McGehee. We also have a telegram, a package, and some funds that were wired to you from a Mr. Petrie. Please give me a moment to retrieve those, along with your key."

"Please allow two keys for the room. My ward may need to run errands for me." Ben waved toward Abu.

Frowning, the man squinted and replied in a haughty British accent. "We do not allow non-European servants to stay in the hotel. You can find accommodations near the market. Make sure he uses the servants' entrance in the back of the hotel when he needs access to your room."

For Abu, this was the first time anyone had singled him out for such belittling. He remembered watching his father deal with similar mistreatment, always at the hands of some foreign patron visiting their restaurant.

Dr. Ben put both hands on the counter and leaned toward the receptionist. "I believe you misheard me. This is my son, Abu McGehee. You will treat him the same as you would me." Dr. Ben glared at the man. "Is that going to be a problem?"

The man took a step back. "Excuse me for a moment." He turned and walked the short distance to a door behind the counter. After knocking twice, he opened it without waiting. With a glance over his shoulder, he darted through the portal and rushed to close it behind him.

Abu didn't know what he should be feeling. That was the first time Dr. Ben had referred to him as his son. The disrespect the desk clerk had shown him made him feel both small and angry. But his confusion at hearing the word *son* had blunted all that. A simple word, but with so much meaning.

I'm Mahdi and Yara's son.

He liked Dr. Ben and respected him, but he wasn't sure anyone else could ever have that place of honor in his heart. Maybe Dr. Ben only said it because of the situation. He probably didn't even mean it like that.

The hotel clerk disappeared for several minutes, and during his absence, Ben turned to Abu. "I want you to listen to me. Life is not fair. You will have many opportunities to do battle over the unfair prejudices you encounter. Through your studies and personal determination, you need to be prepared to deal with these little evils. But you must choose carefully when and where to do battle."

The teenager stared unblinking, his full attention on Ben.

"Rule number one: Never let others define your worth. Even when you must strategically withdraw, use your intellect and education to let your opponent know they have underestimated you. That you are their equal, if not their better. Number two: Never lose your composure unless they physically threaten you. Three: Never become bitter."

Abu nodded.

Ben placed a hand on Abu's shoulder. "Finally, when all else fails, remember this. God is able, but we are the ones who must be willing. Willing to prepare for situations like this. Willing to educate fools. Willing to forgive. And willing to put these slights behind us." He gave the teen a thin-lipped smile. "If you're willing to do these things, God is able to turn these moments into blessings that help you grow. Don't allow the fools to win."

As Ben finished his lesson, the door opened. The hotel clerk returned to the counter, holding an envelope. "Dr. McGehee, we would be happy to welcome your *son*, ah, Abu, to the Shepheard's Hotel. We just ask that he wear this special pin, so that the staff will know his *special status*." He held up a small bronze brooch shaped like the Great Sphinx. Handing the pin and two large metal keys with long tassels to Ben, he continued, "May I know how many nights you will be staying with us? Our double rooms cost five pounds per week."

Ben handed Abu the pin and a key numbered 220. The cost gave him pause. Ben had never paid fifteen shillings for a single night in a hotel. Then again, he had never stayed in a hotel like the Shepheard. He made a mental note to thank Flinders for sending more funds.

Facing the receptionist, he replied, "We would like to pay for a week in advance. We will inform you toward the end of the week if we'll be staying longer." Ben reached into his pocket, pulled a ten-pound note from his money clip, and placed it on the counter. "Please give the change to my son. Thank you."

Ben dismissed the man with a look and headed for the stairs.

Before he had gone two steps, he heard, "Dr. Ben. Volo mundare!"

Ben beamed at Abu's Latin declaration. *I am willing.*

After freshening up and changing to a cream-colored linen suit, Ben headed downstairs to the Shepheard's bar. He had left Abu with a few math problems and one pound sterling, along with instructions: Explore near the hotel, and be back by dark.

They had discussed the need for Abu to put a cotton tunic over his Western clothes while outside the hotel. Otherwise, he might become a target of the locals who, a year earlier, had rebelled against foreign and British rule.

The high-class saloon, like the rest of what Ben had seen of the hotel's amenities, met his expectations. Its marble-topped bar formed a large, rounded L and took up the first third of the long rectangular room. Tables filled the rest of the open space, with only a few occupied.

Behind the bar, several men in white jackets served the patrons at the counter. A single waiter dressed in a similar uniform moved around the room, serving the tables. High season would not start for another few months because of the scorching heat. Ben figured that accounted for his ease in finding a seat down the longer side of the L-shaped bar.

His closest neighbor sat two bar stools distant, with his back to Ben. The bartender nodded an unspoken question to him.

"I'd like a Sazerac, please."

The bartender acknowledged this and turned to mix the New Orleans classic.

Hearing, "Ah . . ," Ben turned to regard his neighbor, who had closed the distance between them by moving to next stool.

"A fellow American!" bellowed the man with wild gray hair and a matching full beard. He thrust out his hand to Ben. "Charles Edwin Wilbour. Formerly of Rhode Island but now an adopted son of the Nile, at your service. A rare pleasure to meet a Southern gentleman in these parts."

Standing to shake hands, Ben came up a full six inches above the man. The older man might have been the reincarnation of John the Baptist if not for his suit of fine wool.

"Dr. Ben McGehee, of Texas. The honor is mine."

They exchanged a vigorous handshake. From the man's breath, Ben could tell the fellow had already traveled several whiskeys along the road to inebriation.

Charles slapped Ben on the back. "A Texan, you say? Good folk from Texas, good folk. What brings you all the way to Cairo, young man?"

"I'm the advance man for an upcoming excavation at Tanis," Ben explained. "My friend Flinders Petrie is leading it."

The bartender placed a glass filled with ruby red liquid on the bar.

"Allow me. Davis, please put Dr. McGehee's drink on my tab, and bring me another Manhattan as well."

Charles charged on as Davis nodded his understanding. "Ah, Flinders. What a splendid young chap. He did some great work on the survey of the pyramids. Too many make a mess of it. We spent several stimulating afternoons discussing the proper scientific methods for conducting archaeology." The man's beard split into a crazy grin. "As well as a couple of evenings trying to impress the ladies." He scratched his head. "Though I will say those nights are fuzzier."

Ben laughed. "That sounds like the Flinders I know. Scholar and gal-sneaker extraordinaire."

Davis put another glass in front of Charles, who took a sip. "Ben—is it okay if I call you Ben? You're not one of those pretentious prigs who must be addressed by your formal title like Senator Sanctimonious or Major Ass, are you? Anyway, I assume you just got into town. I know pretty much everyone, you see." The crazy, hairy grin returned. "So, let me show you the terrace because I am meeting a friend there. Even if we bore you, the menagerie that is Cairo will entertain you. Follow me."

Without hesitating, Charles marched toward the bar entrance.

Thinking he had nothing better to do, Ben grabbed his drink and hurried to follow. The duo emerged from the quiet foyer onto the hotel's front porch. Countless conversations in a multitude of languages assaulted Ben's ears. Each discussion added volume to drown out the sounds of pedestrian and horse-drawn traffic from Ibraham Pasha Street below.

Underlying the cacophony of sounds came a familiar melody, "Die Schöne Müllerin," by Raff, which sought to tame the dissonance of the street. The raised terrace they stood on extended to the left of the covered landing area and ran some ways along the hotel's facade. A drop-off at the end of the terrace heralded an immaculate garden where a string quartet played. A ten-foot-tall wrought-iron fence topped with small, sharp spear points surrounded the hotel grounds, making Shepheard's a world unto itself.

Charles wasted no time and made for one of the few unoccupied tables. He waved Ben to the favored seat, which had the best view of the street and its kaleidoscope of humanity. When Ben settled into the wide wicker chair, he took a quick inventory of the fast-moving traffic. There were countless Egyptian men attired in earth-tone cotton tunics or wearing Western suits and fez hats in black and red. About half as numerous were Egyptian women wearing darker colors. Most had their faces covered.

A few servants even wore outfits resembling characters in the "Arabian Nights" tale. Mixed in with the Egyptian majority were European men dressed in tweed, wool, or linen suits. Headwear, from derby hats to pith helmets, topped them. A few escorted European ladies in silk or cotton, each sporting a parasol for shade.

Most conspicuous were the occasional British troops, both English and Indian. Their new khaki uniforms stood out on the crowded street. The rarest and, to Ben, the most fascinating were the dark-skinned Nubians dressed in traditional robes.

Ben took a sip of his drink and turned his gaze to Charles, who watched the newcomer soak in the unique atmosphere. "Who says everyday humans can't be more entertaining than any circus? Eh, Ben?"

Ben chuckled at his loquacious companion. "Most of my passions involve observing human activity. Though I'm partial to the people who can no longer change their minds."

Charles ran a hand through his tangle of a beard and appeared about to respond. Then he looked up and smiled. "Émile, you made it."

He stood and Ben followed, taking in a short, thin, very sunburned man with a well-manicured Howie-shaped mustache. A plain-faced woman, several inches taller and with much broader shoulders, stood beside him, holding his arm. Ben would have described her dress as a school marm uniform.

"Émile Brugsch, this is Dr. Ben McGehee—a fellow archaeologist who recently arrived in this magical land. He is helping our common friend Flinders set up his next expedition." Turning to the woman, Charles rushed on. "Now, Émile, who is this enchanting creature you have brought with you? Milady, I am Charles Edwin Wilbour. Any friend of Émile's is a friend of mine."

Charles reached for the woman's free hand and made a small show of giving it a kiss. The woman's pale face flushed at the gesture.

Ben listened to Émile's strong German accent, trying to get familiar with its cadence.

"I am proud to introduce Miss Hermine Hartleben, my fiancée. She arrived in Cairo last week."

Miss Hartleben's face still had a rosy red hue when she said in a refined German accent, "Pleasure to meet you, Mr. Wilbour, and you as well, Dr. McGehee."

Ben shook their hands. "Pleasure to meet you both. Please, call me Ben."

"And Charles, please," interjected the rambunctious rascal.

"Agreed, no need for formalities among friends. Please call me Hermine," she replied as they found their seats around the four-person table.

Not allowing a moment of silence, Charles rushed in. "Hermine, besides Émile, what brings you to Cairo?"

"Émile is the only reason to come to Cairo. I recently secured a job as governess to the children of Khairi Pasha. He's an official with the Turkish viceroy. It has allowed us to finally be together."

Émile reached for Hermine's hand and gave his future bride a proud smile.

"Fantastic. I wish you both the greatest happiness, and I'm pleased you have gainful employment. Of course, if you are to be married in Cairo, you must allow me to attend your nuptials." Charles had no compunction about inviting himself to the couple's happy day.

Émile's mirth grew. "Ja, of course, Charles. It would not be the same without the *Incredible Mr. Wilbour*."

Charles's deep belly laugh had them all smiling. Calming down, he said, "I was just about to tell Ben about my proclivities. Now that you have joined us, Hermine, I can regale both of you with tales of my extraordinary talents." Charles let his laugh die out and continued. "Most days, I am a ne'er-do-well who spends his time plying the Nile River on the *Seven Hathors*, my houseboat, seeking artifacts of interest. Occasionally, I write an article for the papers back home. Of course, I'm always up for helping friends like Émile or Gaston Maspero in their Egyptology endeavors. Gaston's the head of the Egyptian Antiquities Service. If either of you need anything, please ask. You never know where your next adventure will come from, and I love to say yes."

Émile showed his sunburned face to Ben. "If you need any help, I'm the assistant curator of the Bulaq Museum. Do not let Charles's American brashness fool you. He's a wizard in both living and dead languages, as well as the best tour guide in Egypt."

Charles brushed off the compliments and asked, "Tell us what you were working on before coming to Egypt?"

Ben felt excited at the chance to discuss his work. "We were excavating at Nineveh around Jonah's tomb. We found a cuneiform library of several hundred tablets. A few contained segments of the Gilgamesh story."

He leaned over the table in a conspiratorial manner. "The most interesting find was an inscribed stela buried below the tomb. We think it dated to about 2,500 B.C. It told the story of the inhabitants of a Sumerian city named Mari. We think that is the name of their god of storms. Anyway, the stela said that Mari angered another god, and everyone in Mari disappeared after he spat upon the city. It's quite an intriguing mystery. So far, no one has found a Sumerian city by that name . . . " He trailed off in thought. "But enough about me. What have the two of you been working on?"

Émile said, "What incredible finds, Dr. McGehee! Congratulations. Those moments of discovery are infectious and make the tedium of the rest of our work seem a minor nuisance. As for my work, we created an exceptional new exhibit about the Greeks in Egypt called 'Alexander to Cleopatra.' It has been very popular with the tourists."

In the following pause, Charles threw out, "Quite right, a wonderful display, Émile. My most interesting finds lately were some papyri that I purchased from a farmer near Aswan. They seem to be from a settlement of Jews living in Egypt. The documents discussed marriage contracts and much more. I acquired them for a mere ten pounds, but for me, they are priceless bits of social documentation from the era."

Abu turned the problem over for the hundredth time. If he said nothing, he'd be able to keep his word, but then he'd be hiding the truth from Dr. Ben. If he told the truth, Dr. Ben might place him under house arrest. Then he wouldn't be able to keep his promise.

Until after midnight, Abu still struggled with the best route forward when he heard a key being inserted in the hotel room door. Turning in his chair, he raced to open the book to his bookmark. He tried to appear engrossed in reading Samuel Birch's *An Introduction to the Study of the Egyptian Hieroglyphics*.

The book Mr. Petrie had sent to Dr. Ben helped Abu establish a baseline understanding of the alien writing system. He thought how strange it was for the ancient Egyptians to create three distinct ways of writing. Tomb and monument builders used hieroglyphics with its mixture of ideographic and phonetic symbols. The other two versions paraphrased the language. Priests used the cursive-styled hieratic to write on papyrus, while the common people used demotic.

Abu guessed by the way Dr. Ben fumbled with the lock that he was more than a little *drinky*. When Ben finally entered the room, Abu kept pretending to read. Dr. Ben put his gun on the nightstand before shuffling with erratic steps to the armoire to hang up his suit jacket.

41

This might be Abu's chance. He would take advantage of Dr. Ben's current state to accomplish both of his goals. Certainty filled him for the first time all night.

Acknowledging Abu, Dr. Ben said. "Why are you still up? If it's really that interesting, you can start studying after breakfast. The mummies' secrets will be there tomorrow, I promise." Dr. Ben chuckled at his poor joke as he sat on his bed.

Abu turned and grinned to humor him.

It can't hurt.

"I want to finish up this chapter, then I'll go to sleep. What kept you out so late?" Abu said, taking back the initiative.

Dr. Ben's face scrunched up at Abu's line of questioning before he seemed to forget whatever had concerned him.

"Oh, I had a very pleasant evening. I met some delightful people tonight. You would've really liked Mr. Wilbur and his stories about the parties he throws on his riverboat. The *Something Hathor*. What was it called? It'll come to me later. He introduced me to a lovely engaged couple from Germany. Best of all, we're all archaeologists."

Abu raised his eyebrows and assumed a doubtful expression. "Fascinating, I'm sure, but did they share any news about the rest of the world?"

Swaying back and forth, Ben looked up as if trying to remember any other topics. "We discussed the current political climate here in Egypt. Have you heard? There's a cholera outbreak in Alexandria. Oh, and it sounds like the Brits may send troops to Sudan. It's to suppress the locals who, they say, have gotten uppity." He shook his head. "I'm sure those poor sods want nothing more than self-rule. The audacity of those tribal types." Dr. Ben's voice dripped sarcasm.

He took a breath and picked up the pace, along with his excitement. "Nothing as interesting as the finds happening around this incredible country. Émile supervised the exhumation of mummies at Dier El-Bahri, near Luxor. Oh, Émile is the German man I told you about. He's the assistant curator at the Bulaq, the premier museum in Egypt. Would you want to go with me?"

Abu answered, trying to cut Dr. Ben off. "I'd really like that. I had an interesting day, too." If he didn't change subjects, he knew Dr. Ben would tell him more about mummies than he cared to know.

Having lost steam with the interruption, Dr. Ben looked at Abu through heavy eyelids. "That's nice. Anything I should know about?"

Abu knew he would have no better chance than now. He tried to keep his voice unconcerned and to give as few details as possible. "I decided to visit the market, but I was hungry, so I stopped at an Egyptian restaurant between here and there. They have amazing food. You need to try it."

Dr. Ben wobbled.

"The restaurant's called El Fishawi. After that, I wandered around the market. It's so big it'd take days to see it all, and they have everything you could imagine. On my way back, I saw Miss Sophia." One of Dr. Ben's eyebrows shot up. "I didn't get a chance to say hello. She was busy haggling with some peddlers. Anyway, that pretty much sums up all the excitement for me. I came back and began my studies." Abu arched his back and stretched. "You know, I think I *will* go to bed now."

He left out the fact that he had followed Miss Sophia for more than two hours, making sure she was safe as she visited three more antiquities shops.

Having perked up at the mention of Miss Sophia, Dr. Ben now seemed ready to topple. Talking more to himself than to Abu, he said, "I'm glad you had a good time. Next time you see Miss Sophia, say hello. You don't want to be impolite. Since we're awake, let's discuss what we both need to do tomorrow."

He used his fingers to track his list. "In the morning, I need to begin preparations for the expedition's arrival. I'll file the proper paperwork and seek the needed permits." He grabbed another finger between his index and thumb of the other hand. "After that, I'll plan for accommodations in Tanis for the two of us. We'll be conducting the initial survey of the site. While we're there, I'll hire the best local excavators for Flinders." He pinched the next finger.

Ben paused, confusion settling on his face. Then, with order restored in his eyes, he said, "Before I leave, I'll assign you some Greek, Latin, and some more geometry lessons. It looks like you're learning hieroglyphics on your own, so there's no need to discuss that unless you have questions." He moved on to the next finger. "I'll be back by four and work with you until dinner."

Dr. Ben lowered his hands. "If you complete your lessons in the morning, you can spend the afternoon on your own. I don't want you eating at the hotel alone, so grab lunch outside. Just be back by four. How does that sound?"

Abu had to cloak the huge grin threatening to give him away. He deadpanned his answer. "Sounds good. I promise to be back on time."

As Ben shambled away, Abu's smile broadened. He had told Dr. Ben the truth. Most of it, anyway. He'd be able to keep his promise to Nashwa by spending lunchtime at her family's restaurant.

If I'm lucky, the next time Dr. Ben goes out with his new friends, I'll sneak out and meet Nashwa for that kiss she promised me.

It would be his first.

Chapter 5

The Khan El-Khalili Bazaar, Cairo, Egypt, October 1883

Louisa's frustration mounted. Since arriving in the city, she had spoken to twelve artifact dealers, seeking the best prices to sell the papyri. The previous day, she had come to an agreement with this particular vendor of Egyptian antiquities.

The large, hairy, and extra-sweaty man in front of her had promised to buy each papyrus for five pounds. She agreed to sell him twenty. She knew from her time in the market that eager tourists would pay ten to twenty pounds per papyrus, hoping to take home such a unique artifact.

But now, this fool had decided that the papyri had no market value, and he would pass. Louisa cursed the man in four languages and even used the bit of Arabic she'd picked up in her six days in Cairo. The reek of his perfume and body odor upset her stomach. She noticed the hint of a smile on the store owner's sweat-drenched face as she made for the exit.

Instinct kicked in, and she made herself settle down. She took several deep breaths. Stepping outside of the store, she realized her intuition was proven right.

Ta matia sou dekatessera.[1]

As she walked away from the shop, warning bells louder than old Notre Dame on Sunday morning rang in her head. Acting nonchalant for the outside world, she walked for twenty more yards before stopping to open her parasol. She peeked back the way she had come. Three men had slowed and come to a stop, purposely not looking at her.

What a fine mess.

She should have hired some muscle-bound idiot to be her bodyguard while she sold the papyri. Stubborn pride had overridden her common sense, as she'd told herself she needed no man. She put away such thoughts. Outnumbered three to one, even the best of men would be in danger.

Louisa began her stroll, trying to appear oblivious. She used her peripheral vision to seek each robber's location. Now and again, she'd scan the faces coming toward her, looking for a soldier or a policeman. Each time, her frantic search came up empty. Instead, everyday Egyptians filled the road, going about their business.

Having walked another block from the shop, she noticed an alley coming up on her right. A quick glance over her right shoulder caught the man farthest from the street suddenly accelerating. Their plan was now obvious. The gang of thugs intended to rob her in the alley.

She looked back to see whether she could make a break for the street. Instead, she found thug number four angling to cut off that escape route. Her only hope lay in decisive action. Her uncle had drilled into her that in times of danger, the decisive ones gave themselves a chance to survive.

---

1. Ta matia sou dekatessera is Greek for "my fourteen eyes." It represents someone in a dodgy situation or dealing with a deceitful person and needing fourteen eyes to watch his back.

She didn't like it, but her best chance to escape with her life and the papyri would be to get a head start. With luck, she could find a place to climb to safety. Without giving a hint of warning, Louisa sprinted toward the shaded entrance to the alley.

Ben contemplated the unusual architecture of the Al-Hussein Mosque as he made his way toward the bazaar. The mosque, reconstructed after a recent fire, seemed to be a strange mix of styles. A Gothic Revival basilica had grown the ubiquitous minarets representative of Islamic houses of worship.

His mind wandered back to work. For the last six days, Ben had spent his time bogged down in the convoluted double bureaucracy of the British Empire and Egyptian civil service. He gave a small thanks for his new friends. They had helped grease the wheels with Egyptian Antiquities officials.

It might take only another week before they could leave for Tanis. Ben hoped to do an initial site survey and send notes to Flinders months ahead of his arrival.

A young man brushed past him, bringing Ben's thoughts to Abu. The teenager had been acting a little strange of late. A thread of melancholy seemed to lie just below the surface of the meticulous young man. Abu was a voracious learner, but even that seemed to have waned in the week they had been in Cairo. Ben couldn't put a finger on what had caused his sudden shift in attitude.

Abu had not slackened in his studies. If anything, the teenager had grown more vested, even learning how to translate Egyptian hieroglyphics on his own. Ben knew the boy worked so hard to forget the horrific day he'd lost his parents. It was a defense mechanism Ben understood all too well. But for the last few days, Abu had been different. His sadness had given way to boundless energy.

Pondering the strangeness of being a parent and trying to puzzle out how he could best help Abu, Ben topped a small hill. He looked down the street from the slight incline and had a decent view for five or six blocks.

Most of Cairo's streets were dirt causeways. Lined with stone or stucco-covered brick buildings, they had no sidewalks. Some of the newer areas, like the location of the Shepheard's Hotel, had both sidewalks and buildings with European facades. Ben enjoyed the dichotomy of old and new.

In an unconscious agreement, the current street's travelers adhered to an invisible boundary separating horse and pedestrian traffic on the dirt road. Peering over the throngs, Ben located the entrance to the famous market of Cairo. The crowds were densest there. A brief feeling of déjà vu overcame him, as if he'd seen this same scene in a lifetime a thousand years ago.

Snapping back to the present, he calculated how much farther he had to go when a familiar object caught his eye. A white felt hat topped with pink ribbon and cloth flowers bobbed in and out of sight. The last hat he'd seen like that had been adorned in blue.

Through a break in the crowd, he saw the hat's owner. He had not been mistaken. Louisa was walking away from a shop about forty yards ahead of him. She wore a light pink dress that almost matched her hat's ribbons. With her parasol in one hand, she carried her messenger bag strapped across her body. After stopping, she opened the parasol and leaned it against her left shoulder.

Without thinking, Ben quickened his pace. With his eyes locked on Louisa, he couldn't help but notice that four Egyptian men had their eyes trained on the woman as well. They stopped when she stopped. As she started again, they set their strides to maintain a certain distance from her.

Ben pushed aside other pedestrians, not even bothering to excuse himself. He angled toward the less crowded part of the street and the invisible barrier.

Coming to the imaginary curb, he saw Louisa nearing the entrance to an alley. As if the side passage were a signal, the four tunic- and turban-clad men closed the distance with her. Somehow aware of her danger, Louisa sped up and raced into the darkened corridor.

Adrenaline shot through his veins as he quickened his pace, trying to reach her in time. The open street would be his best chance to get past the crowd and close the gap. Stepping free, he jumped into the equestrian traffic. He didn't dare look back at the carriage driver, who cursed him for startling the horses. Ben sprinted ahead, focused on the passageway where Louisa had disappeared.

Calculating the most straightforward path through the pedestrians, he heard the report of a small caliber pistol. His heart pounded from a second boost of adrenaline, and his instincts took over. He shouted in Arabic for pedestrians to move and shoved past one dawdling man. Leaving the sunny street behind, he ran into the shaded alley.

Not seeing Louisa or the four men, he kept running and reached inside his jacket pocket. As he rounded the L-shaped intersection, the three-inch barrel of his M&H Pocket Army led the way. He almost tripped over a tunic-clad body at his feet, then leaped at the last second to clear the man.

As he ran full out, time seemed to slow. Ben evaluated the scene. Twenty yards ahead, a man had gripped Louisa's wrist, keeping her revolver at bay. With their arms straight up in the air, the thick man struggled to get control of her other hand as well.

Closer to Ben, the two remaining robbers ran to either side of the grappling pair. The man on the right raised a long curved knife. Even in the shadows, Ben saw murder written on the man's face.

Ten yards away, Ben raised his gun and fired. The knife and the man spun to the side, then crumpled in slow motion to the ground.

Charging onward, Ben twisted the gun to get a bead on the other man. The robber, his face covered by cloth from his turban, had fled at the sound of Ben's first discharge. Running in the opposite direction, Ben squeezed off a shot from his hip. Splinters of brick exploded off the wall where the thief had been a moment ago.

Ben slowed, looking for Louisa and her attacker. Without warning, a man rammed his muscled shoulder into Ben and sent him flying into the wall. The bull of a man followed his partner back toward the street.

Ignoring the throbbing pain in both shoulders, Ben righted himself with his free hand. He aimed and fired. The shot struck the corner of the intersection just as the last attacker disappeared out of sight. Ben spun on his heels to find Louisa lying on her side. Several yellowed sheets of paper had spilled out of her messenger bag and scattered around her.

Before going to her, Ben looked over at the robber he had shot. The fallen man lay in an awkward position, a low, pained moan escaping his mouth. The monster within, the one Ben had fought for decades, shook its cage. It tempted him with the thrill that would come with its release. He shoved the beast back into the darkness.

Once again in control of his emotions, he thought of being merciful until the face of a dead young soldier filled his vision. He'd spent years trying to forget that face but knew he never would. Risking another glance at Louisa, he set his jaw and fired his fourth shot, silencing the man forever.

Ben reached Louisa's side and knelt, facing the direction the robbers had fled. He checked her back and then rolled her over, inspecting her body for blood. She had a welt on her cheek, growing darker by the moment. Ben turned to stare back down the passage.

Without moving his eyes, he retrieved four bullets from his pocket. Using both hands, he undid the latch in front of the trigger, then twisted the barrel over and forward. Four empty cases clattered to the ground. With a jiggle of the gun, the two unfired bullets found their seating as he closed the cylinder and barrel back in place. While watching for returning robbers, he opened the reload plate and filled the empty chambers.

He needed to get Louisa to safety. They had little time before the men returned. Odds were, if they did, they'd bring guns, friends, or both. For the first time, Ben focused on the papers lying around Louisa and sticking out of her messenger bag: Egyptian papyri.

About a foot above her head, he saw a nickel-plated Bulldog revolver. As Ben leaned over her and grabbed the revolver with his free hand, he smelled the scents of lemon and lavender. Glancing down, he found his face six inches from the white felt hat.

At that very moment, her head whipped up and caught him under the chin. Ben went sprawling backward with hands flailing, a revolver in each. He ended up on his back, trying to ignore the pain shooting up his jaw and the cut on his bitten tongue.

He mumbled, "Louisa, it's me, Ben," as the blurred image of pink ribbon and fierce eyes came into focus. She had straddled him, and Ben could feel cold steel on his neck.

"I'm starting to think you don't like me, Miss Sophia," he slurred, his mouth filling with blood.

Merriment spread across Louisa's face, joining the fierceness in her eyes. She laughed like someone who had just seen the most hilarious of happenings or who had just survived a brush with death.

He'd never seen a smile so beautiful. If it weren't for choking on his own blood, he would have stayed in that moment forever.

As soon as the pressure lifted from his neck, Ben tried to sit up. Louisa hopped to her feet with more agility than a woman recovering from such a blow should have been able to muster. She stood above him with a mischievous grin, taking his measure as he pushed himself up by his elbows.

"I didn't recognize you without your hat, Dr. McGehee." She laughed and spun away, taking her exuberance with her.

Damn, that girl's bricky.

He rolled over and spat out a mouthful of blood mixed with saliva. Regardless of the moment's levity, he had to get them moving. The consequences of delaying might be dire, and his gut told him they needed to run. As he stood, he saw Louisa gather the papyri. He pocketed her revolver and picked up the papyrus that had fallen near him.

He was surprised to see it written in Ancient Greek. His scholar's curiosity piqued, Ben couldn't help but read the first paragraph.

"*To Basileus Ptolemy, Pharaoh of Egypt, from your brother in arms, Antigenes. I am filled with joy that we are no longer enemies, but I am overcome with shame, having killed my friend Perdiccas. His defeat at the river and the disappearance of the five thousand were omens he had lost the favor of the Gods.*"

"Ben, we need to get going," brought him out of his intense studying.

Louisa held out a hand. He gave her the papyrus, and she placed it in the messenger bag with care. She tried to close the clasp, but it had broken during the struggle. Shrugging, she left it unbuckled and walked toward the entrance of the alley.

He pulled her revolver from his pocket and gave it to her, handle first. "I hope you won't need this again, but just in case."

Louisa took the revolver and moved it out of sight. "Thank you."

He retrieved her parasol lying close to the dead man and a growing pool of blood, then rushed to catch up with her. As they reached the intersection with the first body, he peeked around the corner, revolver in one hand and a lady's parasol in the other. He sensed Louisa's absence. She stood staring at the crumpled body of the man on the ground.

Remembering the first time he'd killed a man to survive, Ben stepped next to her. In a firm voice, he said, "Louisa, it's best you don't stop to think about it, or you and I might join him. Be willing to push it aside until we're safe. I promise that if you do, God's able to get us out of this mess."

Her eyes misted with sadness. She gave a single terse nod and marched around the corner toward the light of the sidewalk and the flow of people.

At the alley exit, she held out her hand. "Let me take that. We look strange enough without you carrying that around."

A second later, he understood and handed over her parasol. "Good idea." He placed his revolver back into his jacket pocket.

He looked back up the street. Near the shop where he'd first seen Louisa, a group had gathered. Several participants appeared agitated, waving their arms and pointing.

"Do you see anything?" she asked. "I can't see over the crowd."

Ben enveloped her hand holding the parasol and looked her in the eye. "We have to go." He paused and added, "Take off your hat. It'll make it easier for them to find you."

Louisa broke free of his grip and removed several pins that kept her hat in place. Holding the hat and the parasol with one hand, she clasped Ben's wrist and pulled him onto the sidewalk. They walked fast, stifling the urge to run. They paused at a store's outdoor displays every fifty yards so Ben could look for pursuers.

On the third stop, he looked back. Sixty yards away, he locked eyes with the stocky man who'd bruised his shoulder. If Ben could have died from a look, he would have turned to salt where he stood. The man pointed, and six or seven men ran in their direction.

"They found us. Run!"

Together, they sprinted through the crowd. Nearing the next intersection, they were at the entrance of the bazaar. They turned toward the market's medieval-era arch and raced to reach the maze inside.

As they ran past the stone entrance, Ben heard the crack of a pistol. Shards of stone and dust rained down on his head. A spike of fear drove them to run faster past the first street of merchants who waved them toward stalls filled with spices, vegetables, and housewares. Ben soon lost count of their twists and turns before the turbaned posse disappeared from sight.

With a moment's respite, she looked around. "I have an idea."

She pulled him into a clothing shop off the narrow stone street. From floor to ceiling, it was filled with fabrics, tunics, scarves, and every style of Egyptian clothing. At the front stood a slender, balding man of about fifty wearing a bright blue tunic.

He bowed his head, speaking in halting English, "Welcome esteemed patrons to the house of Hasani. If you cannot find it at Hasani's, it does not exist."

Louisa grabbed Hasani's hand, who attempted to pull away with shock in his eyes. Before he could break free, Louisa pushed a five-pound note into his fist. A grin replaced the shock.

"We need to hide. Now!" Louisa demanded.

Hasani grinned wider. "Your demands are my wishes. Especially for such a beautiful lady." He waved them toward the back of the store. "There is small room past curtain. You will be safe there," he said while taking quick steps.

Hasani pulled open dark red curtains to reveal a small dressing area and a door in the wall behind. She went into the dressing area while Ben moved next to Hasani. His eyes widened as Ben poked his belly with the revolver barrel.

With a grim frown, he said, "Honey so much sweeter than sting. Please, Hasani keeps promises."

In a stern tone, Ben told Hasani in Arabic, "My friend Hasani, I want to trust you. In case the money didn't convince you to stay quiet, you will stand in front of the curtains. I will be here with this pointed at your back. If I hear or see anything I don't like, you will soon be with Allah. Do you understand?"

Hasani, his mouth twitching from nervous anxiety, nodded twice.

"Good. As-salamu Alaykum," Ben said. Stepping next to Louisa, he pulled the curtain closed, except for an inch-wide gap.

Hasani took a few steps toward the front of the store before glancing back and locking eyes on the barrel. He began sorting and folding clothes on several nearby shelves. After many minutes of nothing but the faint rustling sounds of cloth, three men rushed into the store.

Ben held his breath and stood as still as possible, watching the scene unfold. Hasani regaled the men about his incredible clothes made from the richest fabrics. The nearest one addressed Hasani in a loud voice, "Be quiet, old man. Have you seen a British man and woman?"

Hasani shook his head. "I've been taking inventory and have seen no one."

The men turned and ran out of the store.

Hasani took a deep breath and leaned against the shelves. He said nothing for a good minute. With a sigh, he straightened. "I think safe, but I cannot promise they not return. You go."

Ben felt a shoulder tap. He looked at Louisa, who said, "Do you trust me? I have another idea."

"Will you shoot or stab me if I say no? I'm open to any suggestions that don't include either of those outcomes." Ben gave her his best roguish grin.

She smirked and pulled open the curtain.

"Mr. Hasani, we would like to buy some clothes." She held up another five-pound note.

"Don't you feel like a cliche?" asked Louisa, leaning close to Ben's cloth-covered ears.

The pair walked side by side down the narrow market street. Both had their faces covered while their eyes darted everywhere. To help them go unnoticed, Ben hunched over and walked with a slight limp to appear shorter.

Louisa had hidden the messenger bag, now filled with her dress and squashed hat, under the black robes of the burqa she wore. Despite the ruse being her idea, she still complained about having to leave her parasol behind. She also appeared forty pounds heavier than her usual slender self.

Ben wore a rich brown, full-length tunic made from good-quality Egyptian cotton, along with a matching turban and loose-fitting pants. The outfit covered his suit and hid all but the tips of his boots. Despite the quality of the clothing, Louisa let him know Hasani had charged them double. It had been worth every shilling.

"What do you mean?" he whispered while knowing quite well what she meant.

"In every adventure book, when the good guys get chased by the bad guys, they use a disguise to escape. You wearing the dress would be the only thing that's more cliché."

"Sorry, I forgot my me-sized burqa back at the hotel. I usually keep it just for these run-for-your-life occasions. If I had only known I would see the infamous Louisa Sophia, I would have brought it along." Picturing them in each other's clothes, he fought back laughter. He would be the tallest woman in Cairo with the shortest husband.

"Infamous?" she huffed before growing quiet.

Ben continued his limping stroll, and the two neared the arched entrance to the market where they had first sought sanctuary. One of their assailants leaned against the left side of the arch. His head swiveled back and forth, inspecting each person who entered and exited the market.

Ben looked down to hide his eyes. His hand tightened on the revolver's grip inside the sleeve of his tunic. Slowing down, Louisa forced herself to walk a little behind him. Ben watched the man from the corner of his eye as they passed through the arch. He fought the urge to look back. They made it to the corner and turned in the hotel's direction without incident.

From behind, she whispered, "Keep it up. There may be more on the street."

Ten minutes later, they were halfway to the hotel. Ben noticed a sign hanging above the entrance of a restaurant. The name tickled his memory, and as they got close, it hit him. Abu said he'd eaten here and bragged about the quality of the food.

Ben reasoned that the longer they avoided their pursuers, the better the chances they might give up. The robbers might also watch the hotel, as it was the one place Europeans were sure to stay. Without telling Louisa his thoughts, he turned toward the door under the sign. He paused and waited for her to follow.

The smell of roast lamb greeted the pair as they stepped over the threshold. "As-salamu Alaykum. Welcome to El Fishawi," came the high-pitched Arabic greeting from a teenage girl behind a counter.

She wore an orange cotton dress and had tied her hair up in a brown scarf. From her few visible locks, Ben deduced she had shoulder-length hair with a slight curl. The scarf and a few strands of hair framed a full face with large, brown, almond-shaped eyes. Her curved lips were the color of rich mocha mixed with pink.

"Wa-alaikum As-salaam. We would like a private room if possible," came Ben's answer in Arabic.

"Of course, follow me," replied the teen.

The group wove their way through a smoky room filled with low tables occupied by lounging customers in deep conversation. The patrons enjoyed hookahs and a mixture of honey and tobacco or used their fingers to sample the dishes in front of them.

On the far side of the room, the girl pulled open a curtain and went into a room with a long low table. She walked around the empty table toward an open door on the far wall.

They entered a smaller room with two drapery-covered windows. At the center sat a low square table of dark red-stained wood and inlays of shells or ivory. Scattered around the table were about twenty large cushions decorated in reds and browns.

After heading to the far side, Ben sat on a cushion in a casual lounging pose while facing the door. He motioned Louisa to the pillows on his left with a dismissive wave. The position would keep her halfway hidden if anyone entered the room. She paused a step, her eyes narrowing at his insulting directions and lack of politeness. With a cluck of her tongue, she moved to the cushions.

Ben looked up at the teenager. "Please bring us plates of ful medames, baba ghanoush, and fatteh. Also, some karkade. One other request: before anyone enters the room, please have them knock. Thank you."

"Yes, sir, might I suggest having some om ali for dessert? My mother's om ali is famous throughout Cairo. Also, would you like to smoke?"

"No smoking. But we'll give the dessert a try," he said through the piece of turban covering part of his face.

"Very well. I'll bring your drinks shortly." The girl left, closing the door behind her.

Ben and Louisa waited for her footsteps to fade away before removing their face coverings.

"Why did you bring us here?" she demanded.

He smiled, placing his pocket army on the floor under the table. "I was afraid they might be waiting for us at the hotel. The longer we're out, the better. They might think we're staying somewhere else. Also, I'm starving and wanted to discuss what just happened."

"Obviously, I was being robbed. What else is there to discuss?" she said, her tone final.

He stared for a long time, trying to get a reading on the riddle that was Louisa Sophia. After letting the silence go on longer than was comfortable, he said, "I don't believe you."

Looking straight into her brown eyes, he waited until certain that he had lit a spark. "Where did you get all the papyri? Abu said he'd seen you haggling over some documents the first day we arrived."

Louisa's spark became a small flame. "Were you spying on me, Dr. McGehee? I suppose you'll tell me that your being there at just the right time today was merely a coincidence."

"You're damn right. I've been busy doing my job. By pure luck, I planned to visit the market after dealing with my daily dose of bureaucracy. Lucky for you, I saw the men shadowing you, or you would be robbed, dead, or worse. A woman as beautiful as you would fetch a high price!" Ben took a deep breath and saw that the last shot had gotten her attention.

She leaned back. Her fire dampened a little before turning icy hot. "I don't need a man to save me or your approval of what I'm doing," came the frigid reply.

He snorted. "I take it back—"

"What!"

"How much you'd fetch!"

"You . . . You . . ."

"You what?"

"Kólos!"

He smirked. "I've been called worse." Much worse, in fact. *Asshole* was a term of endearment in some of the company he'd kept.

A soft knock caused Ben to reach for the revolver. "Come in," he said, switching to Arabic.

The door opened, and the young woman entered, carrying a tray with a filigreed silver teapot and matching cups. She paused a step to take in Louisa's uncovered face.

Louisa appeared to be very different from what her clothes suggested, and her bruised cheek had continued to redden. Ben knew his light-colored eyes and his less-than-perfect Arabic had already given away his foreign origin. He could do little about any of that now.

Behind her came an older woman carrying a plate with flatbread ringing a large bowl of baba ganoush. The women set the platters on the table, and the young lady filled their cups with a cinnamon-colored drink that smelled of hibiscus. The older woman stepped outside and retrieved another platter. This one contained bread, hard-boiled eggs cut in half, sliced tomatoes, and a paste made from fava beans.

As the two women retreated, Ben said, "Thank you. Can I speak to you for a moment?" He had directed his comment to the teenager, and she turned with an expectant look. "I would appreciate your discretion. If anyone comes looking for a man and a woman, please tell them you have seen no one. Let me know as quickly as possible." He held up a ten-shilling coin and motioned for her to take it. "There will be another when we leave."

She took the coin. "You can count on our discretion." The young lady gave a bright smile and winked. "I, too, understand you cannot deny your heart." She closed the door as she exited.

He laughed to himself, but Louisa brought him back. "What did she just say?"

He turned to see that the interruption had done nothing to thaw Louisa's ice or quench the fire. "She thinks we're illicit lovers." He put on his best crooked smirk.

"Agh. As if."

The disgust on her face caused his smile to evaporate.

Calming himself, he took a deep breath. "What, you can't picture us as a couple?"

She wrinkled her nose. "That picture only exists in your dreams."

He fired back, "Well, at least there's one thing we can both agree on. You don't need a man . . ."

He paused, stirring the innuendo of the comment before finishing, "to save you." Then he softened his tone. "But maybe you could use a friend."

He let the last statement sink in for a few seconds. "Louisa, I know we've had one brief conversation until now, but actions speak louder than words. I've proven myself as someone you can rely on. It would seem my only reward for helping you is almost being shot, almost getting my throat slit, and being chased by murderous thugs." He waited a long moment, trying to gauge her reaction, but he read none. "I'm showing you I'm someone to be trusted. Don't you think you can at least tell me the truth?"

Louisa watched Ben for any sign of an angle. The men in her past were not to be trusted. She had a bastard for a father who had abandoned her and her mother. Her thief of an uncle had manipulated her for his own gain, even if he'd taught her the skills she used to survive.

Then there were boys and later the men who wanted her looks and body. To them, she was nothing but a possession they could use for their pleasure. Could this man be so different? Did it matter? She needed help. Today's near disaster made that obvious. Without thinking, she reached up to touch her bruised cheek.

Wincing, she looked back at Ben lying against a large cushion and dressed as an Egyptian in his Friday best. She'd tried to read those romance novels that the other boarding school girls were always gossiping about but found them trite and unrealistic. There had been no Prince Charming in her life, and she had assumed there never would be.

But Ben *had* saved her life or, as he reminded her, rescued her from a fate worse than death. Did the spectacled Arabian knight next to her just want to be friends? Did he have no other expectations? Maybe. She wouldn't rule it out. Until she was confident, she would see if she could come to an arrangement with him. One that benefited them both. Those were the dealings she understood.

Pushing out a deep breath, she let the anger go. "You're right. The least I can do is to be truthful with you."

But only enough to get what I need.

"As I told you, I came to see the country and my father. I don't have a good relationship with him, but since I have no other family, I came to seek his financial help. I spent what little money I had on my education, and the thought of marrying for money repulses me."

Ben's face softened, and he nodded along. He appeared to be buying it all.

"As for the documents, I won the papyri in a game of chance from an unlucky Frenchman on the train from Alexandria."

Ben's eyebrows rose.

"It's true. Of course, when I won, he was very drunk." She grinned. "We'd been playing beggar-my-neighbor for several hours, and he drank the entire time." She shrugged. "The stakes were small at first but kept growing. For the last hand, I bet twenty pounds, and, to his misfortune, he countered with the papyri."

"What was the name of this Frenchman?"

"I don't recall, Corduroy, or some such." Louisa continued her bald-faced lies. "It surprised me how many documents there were. I'm not wealthy, so I thought I'd sell a few before I'm forced to get a job as a governess or a teacher at an international school." She turned both hands palms up and sighed. "And there is still the matter of working up the courage to confront my father."

Ben interjected, "What's so wrong with being a teacher? You'd have a place to stay. If you're as educated as you appear, you could demand four to five pounds a month from a well-to-do expatriate."

Louisa saw the opening and went to bait the hook. "You're right. There's nothing wrong with it. I just want to explore the mystery first," she said, leaving the mystery unexplained.

Ben mulled over what she'd said. His instincts were telling him not to trust much of it. Then again, what were these other feelings? It had been more than ten years since he'd felt this sense of excitement at being near a woman.

As he considered the mystery of Louisa, along with the one she'd hinted at, he said, "Let's eat before it gets cold."

Grabbing a piece of flatbread, he scooped up some of the eggplant-based dip and held it out for her. She took it from him using two hands, sending a small jolt of electricity up his fingers where they touched. He got some for himself, took a bite, and then winced as the spicy food set off painful explosions from his wounded tongue.

They continued eating in silence for several minutes. Ben fought the discomfort of each bite, but the day's dangerous encounters had made him famished enough to struggle through the pain. Judging by her hearty appetite, Louisa probably felt the same. Another knock came, and the young lady brought in the main dish: a platter covered with rice mixed with roast lamb. She gave them a conspiratorial smile as she left.

Ben took up the question Louisa had posed. "The mystery you're referring to is the letter from Antigenes to Ptolemy. Correct? I read the first part of the letter. If legitimate, it could be very valuable."

She gave him a knowing nod. "Very good, Doctor, but the real value lies in the information the letter contains." Lifting her robes, she uncovered the messenger bag. She retrieved the Greek papyrus and handed it to him.

He felt her eyes on him as he read. As his eyes moved down the letter, he muttered, "It can't be." Shaking his head, he read the letter a second time, muttering under his breath the entire time.

After several minutes, she asked, "What do you think? Is it real? The temple, I mean? What can you tell me about Perdiccas?"

Ben raised his head, his excitement growing as he pondered what the passage might mean for his legacy as an archaeologist.

What are the odds? Must be providential.

He felt a tug at his mouth as his enthusiasm grew. "Do you think a god's tear and a god's spit could be seen as the same thing?"

Louisa's forehead wrinkled, and her eyes narrowed. "What?"

With a raised hand, Ben said, "Sorry. You couldn't possibly understand unless you had read what I read before I came to Egypt." He took a breath. "Do you remember that when we first met, I said I had been excavating at Nineveh, near the tomb of Jonah?"

She gave a half-nod. "I think so, but what could that possibly have to do with this?"

"Maybe everything. Maybe nothing." He shrugged. "When I was there, I uncovered a monument buried under the tomb. It spoke about a city that worshiped man-like demon-dogs and enraged the god Zababa. As punishment, the god spat upon the city, and then a beam of light shot into the heavens. The next day the city was empty."

Louisa's eyes went wide. "That's a lot of coincidences. When did that happen?"

"More than two thousand years before the Greek army disappeared and almost a thousand miles apart." Ben licked his lips, and his voice grew urgent. "We have to find that tomb. If we can prove that the two events are related." His voice trailed off, and his vision blurred as he stared at the Greek text on the papyrus. His mind raced again to what it would mean if he could tie the two events together.

"Will we be rich?" Louisa asked, her cheeks full of pita and hummus.

His eyes darted to her mouth, which had closed as she began to chew. Smacking had to be one of the pet peeves his parents had drilled into him. It never failed to grate on his nerves, and, thankfully, she didn't do it. "No. Not rich, but famous. Well, at least in the circles I run."

She frowned and tore off another piece of bread. "Perdiccas? The temple?"

Ben thought about the letter's contents, getting his answers in order. "When Alexander died, his top generals divided his empire among themselves. Ptolemy became governor of Egypt, and Perdiccas became the acting regent for Alexander's child heir. When Perdiccas sent the body of Alexander back to Macedonia for burial, Ptolemy intercepted it and sent it to Egypt. The Macedonians had a tradition where the man who buries the king becomes his successor. At least symbolically. Ptolemy didn't want Perdiccas to have that honor, so he stole it for himself."

Leaning back on the big cushion, Ben went into professor mode. "When Perdiccas came to take the body back from Ptolemy, he lost the first battle, trying to cross the river near Pelusium. From the letter, we know that another part of his army disappeared near this mysterious temple. After all that misfortune, the top officers in Perdiccas's army assassinated him. Afterward, they sued for peace with Ptolemy. Antigenes was one of the assassins who betrayed and killed Perdiccas." He raised his eyebrows, asking for questions.

She wet her lips and asked, "Do you think the temple is real?"

He took a sip of his herbal drink and did a one-shoulder shrug. "Maybe. I know someone who can help authenticate the letter. If it's real, he may provide us with more information about Perdiccas and the location of the tomb. But I warn you, even if he authenticates the letter, locating the tomb—much less the temple—may be impossible."

"Where do we find the man who can help us?"

"Before I give his name, I have a question for you."

She tilted her head, waiting.

"Would you be willing to partner with me to solve the mystery?" With an expectant look, he watched as she contemplated his question.

Partners?

Of course, Louisa would accept a partner if they could come to an arrangement. Like all men, he thought he would do all the heavy lifting. No matter what he thought, she'd prove her usefulness and pull her weight.

Hopefully, in gold.

She answered by holding out her hand. "Yes, partners. Fifty-fifty."

Ben looked from her eyes to her right hand, then back to her eyes. "On one condition."

"What would that be?" Her eyebrow shot up. "I won't take a lesser share."

"You won't have to. I'm fine with the split. I've had less than happy experiences in my business partnerships, but I still believe that if two people are working toward the same goal, they need to be more than coworkers. If we're going to be partners, we also need to be friends. That means you have to trust me, and you have to always tell me the truth. In return, I promise to be a good friend to you with no other expectations."

Ben held his hand out next to hers but not gripping it. "Can you do that?"

Louisa had yet to meet a man like Ben. Oh, she knew there were so-called *nice men* out there, but the ones she'd met lacked ambition or the intellect to keep her interest. Shaking his hand, she put everything into her grip. "Yes, I can. From this point forward, we're partners and friends."

Louisa meant for the lie to sound believable, but when she looked him in the eyes, she wasn't sure if she had just lied to him or to herself.

The two enjoyed another half-hour of small talk as they ate. As Ben finished his second bowl of om ali, he licked his lips, thinking it was the best he'd ever eaten. Of course, it was also the first he'd ever eaten. The baked pastry made him think of bread pudding, but he doubted anyone could top this rendition.

Wiping his hands on a cloth napkin, Ben noticed the afternoon shadows getting longer. He would be late for his tutoring time with Abu if they didn't hurry. When the young lady came in with some flower-scented water for washing, he paid for the meal and gave her an even bigger tip than he'd promised.

Standing to get their disguises in order, they heard talking and laughing outside a window. Louisa peeked between the curtains. Her soft laughter brought him over to peer outside. The young lady who had helped them all evening held the hands of a young man with his back to them.

Ben whispered to Louisa, "She didn't lie when she said she knew about love."

With quiet laughter, Ben watched the young woman draw her beau toward her. The couple's lips came together, gentle at first, then with more passion as they twisted in their embrace.

Louisa said, "We should leave them alone."

At that moment, the pair separated, and Ben saw the enraptured face of Abu.

"Isn't that . . . Abu?" Louisa started giggling.

Ben felt the blood drain from his face before clenching his jaw.

A soft hand touched his shoulder. "As your new friend, I'm going to offer you some advice. Let them be. We'll be leaving soon, so let him enjoy this moment."

The tension eased as he looked into Louisa's half-serious eyes. "I'll think about it. Let's go. We can sneak into the hotel using the servants' entrance."

Ben took one more glance outside at the couple, who were kissing again. He shook his head and closed the drapes.

Chapter 6

Shepheard's Hotel and Bulaq Museum, Cairo, Egypt, October 1883

"Dr. Ben! Wake up!" Abu shouted, shaking him. The doctor had been yelling and moaning while he tossed in his sleep. Abu felt the sweat through the man's nightshirt. He jumped away from the bed as Dr. Ben shot bolt upright. He sat with his eyes wide open, fear and anguish distorting his face.

"What, huh?" Dr. Ben mumbled, swiveling his head until his gaze rested on Abu. He stared for a moment before recognition came, and the anguish eased. "I'm sorry, Abu. Just another bad dream. Are you okay?"

"I'm fine. You haven't had those dreams for a long time. Are you sure nothing happened yesterday?"

After Abu's parents died and Dr. Ben took him in, the doctor had experienced many dreams just like this. They scared Abu. He thought Dr. Ben had something very wrong with him, but after a month, the dreams disappeared. Dr. Ben's explanation never changed. Just a bad dream.

When Abu talked with Dr. Chipiez about it, the Frenchman told him the dreams were one reason Dr. Ben stopped practicing medicine. He conjectured that the dreams were terrible memories from the war, and a violent event might cause them to come back.

The circumstances of his parents' deaths still kept Abu awake whenever his mind wandered back to that terrible day. Abu figured that day had triggered Dr. Ben's first episode, but now? Dr. Ben said he'd seen Miss Sophia, and they'd shared a meal by the market, but he suspected there might be more to the story.

Dr. Ben looked down. "Don't worry, Abu. I'm sure it's a one-time thing. As for yesterday, there's nothing you need to worry about. Are you sure you don't want to go with Louisa and me to see the museum?"

Abu raised an eyebrow at the redirection. His imagination leaped to the conclusion he wanted. "So, you and Miss Sophia—"

Dr. Ben chuckled. "Not by a long shot, but we've agreed to be friends and business partners."

Abu tried to keep his disappointment from showing.

"Anyway, I promised to take you to the museum if you wanted." Before Abu could answer, Dr. Ben put his bare feet on the floor and said, "Can you light the gas heater for the tub? I'm going to the privy."

"Sure, but I don't want to go to the museum. I want to see some things near the market," he said, keeping his tone neutral.

A slight grin registered on Dr. Ben's face. "Oh. Something near the market, eh? Well, you're probably right. Your *something* will probably be more interesting than seeing some old artifacts." Dr. Ben grew serious again. "Anyway, stay out of trouble. I need to hurry if I'm going to meet Louisa on time." Ben paused. A panicked look passed over his face. "Come to think about it . . . You and I need to have a chat later tonight. Until then, be careful."

Unable to read Dr. Ben's intentions, Abu nodded. "Okay. Make sure the two of you stay out of trouble as well."

The carriage pulled to the curb of a broad, sidewalk-lined street in the Boulaq district of Cairo. Stepping out of the carriage, Ben held his hand out to Louisa. Her white gloved hand brushed his as she floated down the two carriage steps. Once again, Ben was struck by the petite woman's dexterity.

Today, Louisa had eschewed a hat and wore her long onyx hair in a braid with a cream-colored shirt and a brown skirt. She wore makeup for the first time to cover yesterday's bruise. In his opinion, she looked even more striking without it.

They entered a large courtyard filled with ancient Egyptian statues. The stone monuments ranged from a throne-sitting pharaoh with huge legs and missing his top half to several sphinxes of different sizes and in various states of disrepair. The grandeur of the artifacts lay in stark contrast to the rest of the courtyard. It must have been beautiful once.

The centerpiece, a large fountain several thousands of years younger, now lay in need of significant repairs. A half-collapsed side wall with cracked or missing tiles testified that the ancient monuments might stand long after this civilization fell to dust.

Beyond the courtyard, sitting on the bank of the Nile, lay a long two-story building. It could have been a twin to one of the many warehouses along the street. A large bronze sign hung above the main entrance. It read Bulaq Museum of Egyptian Antiquities as if adding a voice to the silent sentries out front that proclaimed this building's difference from the others.

Ben and Louisa had filled the twenty-minute carriage ride from the hotel with small talk and evasiveness. She'd withheld any factual information on the one occasion he'd asked, "How was it growing up on Corfu? I've heard it's beautiful." He got only a "Yes, very" response. He continued to ponder what it would take for Louisa to open up.

With her hand resting in the crook of his elbow, they strolled along a winding path toward the museum entrance. Wide steps led to tall double doors. Water lines rode six feet up the building's walls, evidence of where the last Nile flood had crested and of the culprit behind the fountain's demise.

Ben opened the entry door and followed Louisa into the building. It took a moment for his eyes to adjust to the cavernous room with its two-story ceilings.

The sun streamed into tall, expansive windows set high up on the walls facing the Nile, creating a checkerboard of bright light and shadows. Scattered about were display cases and stands holding six millennia of Egyptian history. From where Ben stood, there seemed to be no recognizable pattern of organization.

To the right of the gate, an older Egyptian man with thick-glassed spectacles smiled and greeted them. Nearby, a young boy sat on a stool. "Welcome to the Bulaq Museum. I can help you with the entrance fee, or, if you prefer, I can arrange a private tour from one of the curators. I highly recommend the private tour. It is worth every shilling to have an expert explain the history of the wonders you will see."

Ben said, "Thank you, but we are here to see Émile Burgsch."

"Oh, splendid. I can help you with that as well," he said, turning to the young boy. "Manu, be a good lad and go fetch Dr. Burgsch."

The boy nodded, hopped from his seat, and trotted through the gate. He angled toward the right side of the building, where the large room seemed to end.

Their greeter turned back to them. "If you will follow me, we'll intercept the assistant curator along the way. Then I can show you part of the exhibits." He invited them through the gate with a sweep of his hand.

Ben followed Louisa through the opening and paused about ten feet inside. They both looked back when the gate clanged shut, and a key turned.

"I'm Haji. I've been with the museum since it opened in 1858." The older man displayed a perfect set of teeth. With Ben and Louisa in tow, he shuffled down the path taken by the young boy. "I was a dentist, but my homeland's history had always fascinated me. When I retired, I wanted to spend my twilight years learning everything I could."

Their guide ignored many smaller cases and stopped before the first significant display. Behind low ropes and resting on a raised platform sat a giant pharaoh made of an unusual dark-green stone with small white ripples. Surrounded by so much history, Ben forgot about the reason for their visit. His imagination ran wild, envisioning the creation of each artifact.

"I was lucky. I assisted the museum's first director, Professor Mariette, when he discovered this masterpiece. We found it buried beneath Khafre's Temple. This is the one intact specimen we found of many such statues. It is the best representation of the glory of the fourth-dynasty Old Kingdom pharaoh. This statue became one of the first artifacts added to the museum's catalog."

"He's majestic." Louisa's voice held a hint of awe. "And so content."

Haji flashed his perfect teeth. "I would hope so. At the time of its creation, Khafre was one of the most powerful men on the planet. So powerful that he had this unusual stone transported seven hundred and fifty miles from its sole source in Nubia. Shall we?"

He continued on a winding path, getting closer to a set of stairs set into the center of the far wall. They passed a display with several mummies lying in their ancient coffins. The wooden lids were as bright as when they were first painted. At every major exhibit, Haji reveled in giving them the highlights. As they left the displays behind, they spotted Émile and the boy descending the stairs.

Haji turned to the pair and made a slight bow. "It has been a pleasure. I will leave you in Dr. Burgsch's capable hands."

They acknowledged their appreciation before Haji marched back the way they had come.

Ben greeted Émile as the boy ran past, chasing his boss. Émile's burned face had changed from an angry red to a light shade of pink and had begun to peel.

"Émile, thank you for meeting with us today. This is Miss Louisa Sophia, the young lady with the unique papyrus that my message mentioned. Louisa, this is Dr. Émile Burgsch."

"Fräulein Sophia, a genuine pleasure." Émile held out his hand, sloughing skin and all.

With anticipation, Ben watched as Louisa took the thin man's hand and gave him a vice-like handshake. Émile's eyes widened at the unexpected pressure.

"Please, Dr. Burgsch. Just Louisa, and it's my pleasure as we need your help with our quest."

Émile's eyes twinkled at the word. "A quest? Aren't we all on the same big cosmic quest?" He chuckled before continuing, "And, Louisa, please call me Émile. I gathered from Ben's message that you are seeking lost Egyptian treasure. Still amazes me how many visitors get the bug, but trust me, I'll aid you as much as my meager knowledge allows. Let's continue this in my office."

Émile guided them up the wooden stairs and down a long hallway into an office that overlooked the Nile. Sailboats and steamships moved up and down the river, their wakes jousting for supremacy.

He motioned them to an oval table with six chairs.

An incredible display of potted daffodils sat at the center of the table. With both order and disorder, the arrangement seemed odd to Ben. A pattern formed in his mind's eye like a puzzle piece falling into place. He wondered if each stalk had been grown to its height and its color picked based on the notes from a song sheet.

As she sat down, Louisa pointed to the arrangement. "The flowers are incredible."

Émile nodded. "Yes, they are. I'll be right back with refreshments and my assistant. They are Ali's handiwork. He has the most incredible green thumb I have ever seen." He strolled out, leaving them alone.

While they waited, Louisa opened her now-repaired messenger bag and pulled out the Antigenes missive. "I certainly hope he can provide us with a clue."

"If anyone can help, it'll be Émile. He's been putting together an exhibit about the Greeks in Egypt. As for a clue, the letter itself says the temple lies to the southeast of Pelusium in a maze of canyons." He tapped his fingers on the table. "That doesn't help us unless we can find the location of Perdiccas's tomb and the map within."

They turned as Émile walked in, carrying a tray with a pitcher of lemonade and glasses. Following him came a dark-haired Egyptian man of about thirty with several days' growth of facial hair and wearing a brown suit.

Émile touched the man's arm. "Let me introduce Professor Ali Mousa. He teaches languages, history, and mathematics at Al-Azhar University. I regard Ali to be the second-smartest person I know, next to my dear Hermine. Ali, meet Miss Louisa Sophia and Dr. Ben McGehee."

Ali stood a few inches taller than Émile and possessed a more solid build than the thin academician. As Ali adjusted his glasses, his bronze pinkie ring with a yellow stone reminded Ben of a freemason's ring. The man's quiet but firm voice snapped Ben out of his reverie.

"A pleasure to meet you both. Let me get this out of our way." Ali lifted the centerpiece of flowers and moved it to the end of the table before sitting next to Émile.

Ben waved toward the flowers. "Émile said you grew the flowers. I couldn't help but think about a sheet of music when I saw them. Am I right?"

Ali laughed. "You have a good eye, Dr. McGehee. It is the beginning of a folk song by a local music group called Hasaballah."

"Remarkable," Louisa said, her eyes going wide with recognition.

Ali smiled. "Yes, well, Émile says you've brought us a mystery to solve."

Émile eyed the papyrus. "Wonderful. Ali and I are eager to see what you have."

Smiling, Louisa lifted the papyrus with care and handed it across the table to Émile. "I was fortunate to acquire several papyri on my trip from Alexandria. This is one of the two written in Greek. I hope you can validate its authenticity and provide us with some idea of whether there are sufficient clues to follow."

Ali leaned until he was shoulder to shoulder with Émile. Both spent several minutes in intense study. After completing his examination, Émile looked up with excitement. "What a remarkable find. From what I can tell at first glance, I believe it to be authentic. We have a few tests we could try to validate the age of the papyrus, though our techniques cannot guarantee authenticity. In some forgeries, people used old papyrus and added the text. What do you say, Ali?"

Ali's eyes had a perplexed, distant look. They came into focus as he looked up, frowning. "I concur. The letter appears to be real, but I'm afraid I will not be much help. My expertise doesn't cover the Greeks."

Émile seemed taken aback by Ali's words, but he gathered himself and turned to Louisa and Ben. "As for the mystery, I assume you want to locate the secret temple with the mythical creature and the gold." He paused and took a drink of his lemonade, his eyes going wide as the anticipation mounted.

Putting his glass down, he grinned. "You're in luck. I remember there being mention of the name Perdiccas in some of our records. If I'm not mistaken, it was in the notes associated with some artifacts we were cataloging from a dig near Pelusium."

Ben sat up straighter. "Émile, that's incredible news!"

Louisa, fidgeting with excitement, said, "Yes, just wonderful!"

Before either could say anything else, Émile held up his hand. "The problem will be finding the information in the archives. Luckily, they were filed after the flood in '78. A good portion of our documents were in the basement. I also want to temper your enthusiasm. Even after the information has been located, there is no guarantee it will lead you to the tomb."

Ali stood and pushed his chair back, startling everyone. "I'm sorry I can't be of more help. Please excuse me." He nodded. "I have a lecture scheduled in an hour." He moved around the table, his hand brushing along the flowers as if playing the notes.

The daffodils seemed to sag a bit, and Ben could have sworn the flowers lost a modicum of color as confused stares followed Ali out of the office.

After the door closed, Louisa turned back to the table, her enthusiasm in no way tempered. "Émile, I'm confident that whatever you can find will be of tremendous help. When we sat down a few minutes ago, we had nothing but a prayer to go on. Now we have *hope*."

Émile chuckled. "Indeed. There's always hope. As for the next step, I'll need some time to dig through the last five years of archives to locate the notes. I recommend you wait at the Shepheard's." More somber now. "If there's anything to find, I'll bring it to you."

Ben stood up. "Émile, we'll take you up on your suggestion. Again, thank you so much for your help." He looked down to see Louisa still seated and focused on Émile.

"Émile, would the museum be interested in purchasing artifacts such as the papyrus? If you recall, I came into possession of a great number of papyri. Other than this document, I would like to sell what I have."

Ben's voice grew stern. "If you can't tell us where these documents were found, then provenance becomes an issue." Resisting the urge to look at her, he felt certain she was shooting daggers at him.

Émile smiled at Louisa. "Unfortunately, the museum wouldn't be able to help. Our money is going to repairs and improvements. There are antiquities dealers in

Cairo, but I recommend you avoid them as many are unscrupulous scoundrels. But again, you're in luck." His eyebrows rose, and his smile grew wider. "Ben and I happen to know someone who loves to collect artifacts such as yours, and he won't be concerned about silly things like provenance."

The two men shared a look. "Charles Edwin Wilbour, formerly of Rhode Island," they burst forth in unison and then laughed.

Elated, Louisa didn't even mind racing up the steps to the Shepheard's entrance as she kept pace with the long-legged and now tipsy doctor. The pair had spent the last four hours on Charles's boat, the *Seven Hathors*. Smitten, as soon as they arrived, the old salty dog had plied Louisa with drinks, compliments, and stories of derring-do.

Several times, Louisa kept Ben from confronting the older man when Charles's lally-gagging crossed Ben's line of moral decency.[1] Playing along while having no serious intentions, she found Ben's chivalry—or was it jealousy?—amusing. Despite these awkward moments, the sometimes-stiff doctor had a marvelous time, judging by his slight swaying gait.

Of course, the true source of her elation came from the two hundred pounds Charles paid for the best twenty papyri. Also, he committed to inquire with an American museum about paying her upward of five hundred pounds for the remaining documents. With that kind of cash, Louisa could live like a queen in

---

1. Lally-gagging is a Victorian term for flirting or behaving in a coquettish manner toward the opposite sex.

Cairo for the next few years. Of course, she'd need to purchase her own place, leaving the Shepheard's and its exorbitant prices.

Only one thing could make for a better day: receiving positive news from Émile. She couldn't wait to start searching for the tomb. As if the gods had heard Louisa's musings, the man himself called out, "Ben, Louisa, over here."

The pair reached the top of the stairs and turned to see Émile waving from a table on the terrace. They made their way through the crowd, with Ben weaving a bit more.

"I'm glad I caught you. I was about to leave a detailed note with the front desk. Hermine's waiting for me." He flashed a sheepish grin.

Louisa replied, "We're sorry to keep you waiting, Émile. We spent a glorious day on Charles's boat. He's even more of a character than you two described." She couldn't hide the excitement in her voice. "I take it you found something?"

With a slight slur, Ben said, "We won't keep you. I'm three drinks past my limit. What do you have?"

Émile beamed with pride. "Look at this." He reached into his jacket pocket, retrieved a small ivory figurine, and then placed it between them.

Louisa peered at the tiny yet ferocious lion. "How does that help?"

Ben reached for the small animal, inspecting it from every angle. Louisa tried to be patient while Émile grinned like a child with a new puppy. Ben propped his glasses on top of his head so he could peer at something on the belly of the lion.

"Perdiccas Companion to Alexander." He looked up to meet Émile's eyes, who nodded, wearing the schoolboy grin. Ben mouthed, "Wow." He put the figure back on the table. "Where was this found? What else do you know?"

Émile pulled a small notebook from his pocket and turned to a page. "I copied these from the notes in the archives. A French team was excavating outside Pelusium when they found the lion near an outcropping known to hold a lot of tombs. I meticulously wrote down the coordinates and accompanying map. Look here."

He poked at the hand-drawn map. "On the south side of the outcropping. They noted all the places they dug, hoping to find the Perdiccas's tomb, and here is where they found the lion." He began talking faster and faster. "They discovered openings to several other tombs, but nothing pointing to the man himself. The archaeologists postulated that the grave robbers found the tomb, stole the lion, and dropped it far from the entrance."

Émile flipped the page. "There are no guarantees the tomb entrance is close to where they dropped the lion, but this should also help. Here's the name of the local manager for their laborers. If you're able to locate him, you should be able to figure out where to start. The French team left after excavating the other tombs, and no one has been digging there since."

Ben glanced over at Louisa. "It looks like we are going to Pelusium."

Louisa turned somber. "We can leave as soon as I take care of that other matter."

"When do you plan to meet with him?" Ben asked.

"Tomorrow morning, but can I ask a favor of you?"

Émile watched the back and forth.

Ben tilted his head. "Of course. Anything for a friend."

"I'd like you to accompany me when I go see him. I don't want to go alone. Can you do that?"

"Sure. Where exactly are we going?"

Louisa set her jaw, determined to see this part of her plan through. "He works at the headquarters for the British government."

Émile said, "Interesting. Who are you visiting?"

Chapter 7

Cairo, Egypt, Abdeen Palace and Shepheard's Hotel, October 1883

As their carriage made its way toward the government offices, Ben contemplated the unknowable enigma of Louisa Sophia. Distracted since breakfast, she'd said maybe five words so far during the carriage ride, if that many. Despite his inquiries, she'd evaded all his questions regarding the identity of her father.

It mattered little to him who the man was. He just wanted to get this chore finished. His only certainty about this meeting was that the man didn't expect his daughter to show up today. Given Louisa's powerful negative feelings toward her sire, sparks were bound to fly when they came together.

In the end, Ben hoped her father would be working today and that any conflicts would be minimal. Without thinking, he stuck his finger under the back of his collar and rubbed around the edge. Anxiousness itched at him, urging him to hurry and start the tomb hunt before his other obligations for Flinders came calling.

As the carriage rolled over the uneven Cairo streets, Louisa stared through the small window without focus. The nervous intensity in her brown eyes showed even in the shaded carriage compartment.

Movement drew Ben's vision down to Louisa's lap. Her hands moved through a series of motions that, at first glance, seemed random. The longer he watched, the more he saw a definite pattern with slight variations on each subsequent pass. Looking at her face, he fell into a sort of trance.

His eyes took in the smooth olive complexion of her neck and the wisp of hair caressing her cheek. He followed the curve of her proud nose to the soft contours of her slightly parted lips. Thankful that Louisa was too distracted to notice his stare, Ben tore his view away as he fought this unexpected yearning.

Why now, and why her?

A dozen years had passed since Nannie and Armistead had left him a broken man. During that time, Ben had resigned himself to the single life. Afraid of experiencing that kind of pain again, he threw all his energy into whatever profession he pursued at that moment.

Today, that entailed digging up and interpreting the past. At any other time, this side trip would be an unwanted diversion. Yet in an odd way, he felt content just to be here in Louisa's presence. What was the lure of this woman, as opposed to the others?

Several times during the last decade, Ben had tried to rekindle that lost part of him. In the end, he only frustrated himself and the women involved.

In London, many well-qualified women had pursued him. Some were as physically appealing as Louisa, and a few of those smart enough to hold his attention on an intellectual level. Whenever he tried to kindle something, it was as if he had put the most delicious-looking dessert in his mouth only to find it lacking sweetness.

At times, Ben had gone carousing alone or with Flinders in the East End, and on occasion, he'd had a quick tryst. To his embarrassment, there were times he'd even paid for a woman's physical company. None of those encounters made him want more like the last thirty seconds he'd spent watching Louisa.

It occurred to him that he might have changed since those days. Taking on a paternal role with Abu had softened his heart a little. Maybe that, combined with this particular woman, had caused his current infatuation. Grateful to postpone further introspection, he put his thoughts aside as they pulled up to the palace.

On previous trips with Louisa, Ben had slowed down to keep to her pace. But today, he lengthened his strides and still found himself a step behind. Because of her haste, he had little time to inspect the palace's exterior. His quick impression: it was less Versailles and more a large, bare-bones, Vienna-style "palace."

He hurried to catch up as Louisa marched past two British soldiers keeping a silent but vigilant guard at the entrance to the building housing most of Egypt's political power.

She stopped at the information desk inside the giant, propped-open double doors. "Can you point me to the Office of the Consul General?"

Louisa's question sparked more of Ben's internal musings about her father's identity. He wondered whether her father worked with Earl Baring as the guard pointed toward the hallway to the right. "The consul general's office is in the east wing. Go to the end, and you'll find the waiting area, miss."

"Thank you." She took off again with the same determined strides.

Five minutes of fast marching down a hallway designed by bureaucrats and decorated for bureaucrats brought them to a large waiting room filled with Europeans and Egyptians in well-tailored suits. Only three men and one woman in the room wore traditional dress.

Ben and Louisa stopped in front of a large desk at a single tall door and waited. On the other side sat a very serious young man, his receding hairline obscuring his actual age. The man ignored them as he wrote with a fastidious hand in a large ledger. After a long minute, Ben expected Louisa to get the young man's attention. Yet content to wait until he deigned to notice them, she stayed motionless.

Another minute later, with a slight raise of his eyes, the young man took his time inspecting Louisa. With a slow blink, he dismissed her and addressed Ben. "May I help you?"

Before Ben could respond, she said in a calm voice, "Can you please tell Earl Baring that his daughter, Louisa, is here to see him?"

The receptionist's eyes went wide with an unspoken question. His questioning look was replaced by a touch of fear. Ben's bemusement at the situation grew.

The man looked at Louisa. "Excuse me, ma'am. Did you say you're Earl Baring's daughter?"

Staring through him until he showed signs of panic, she said, "Yes. Tell him Louisa would like to see him."

"I'll see if he is available. Miss . . . Louisa," he stammered. Attempting to rise, he struck his knee. Rubbing it, the man retreated through the big door.

Ben half-laughed. "This day just became more interesting. And to think I worried this little side trip might delay us."

With consummate imperiousness, she ignored the stares of the two nearest businessmen and turned with a raised eyebrow to regard Ben. His crooked grin grew wider. Dismissing the comment with a big inhalation and a small sigh, she turned her attention back to the door. Her look of pure intensity convinced Ben that the door might explode at any moment.

Several more minutes passed with Ben entertaining himself, observing the waiting room. News of the presence of the earl's daughter spread. Worthy of an academic paper on the speed of gossip, the ripple of whispers, pointing, and sideways glances raced from person to person in the room. The rumor—and who knew the true nature of the rumor at this point?—finally reached the lady in traditional Egyptian clothing. At that point, the door opened, and out stepped the young bureaucrat.

Ben marveled at his change in demeanor as the young man gave Louisa an awkward bow. "Please follow me, Lady Louisa."

Together, they moved around the bureaucrat's desk and stepped into another hall. A red-uniformed soldier evaluated the visitors, judging their risk in a few heartbeats.

The balding young man closed the door and led the way down the hallway past many open doors. Without a doubt, they now trod in the very heart of the British Empire, with its lifeblood, ink and documents in triplicate.

Through each portal, they saw rows of desks where mostly men and a few women sat. Heads down, the bureaucrats scribbled in giant volumes or sometimes clacked away on machines called typewriters. It seemed the new invention had found a willing market in halls such as this.

What drudgery, Ben thought.

After passing hundreds of paper pushers, they reached another, smaller waiting room. An older gentleman sat behind a desk near double doors. Looking up with raised eyebrows, he ignored Ben and focused on Louisa.

"His Lordship is expecting you. Please go in."

The young bureaucrat pulled one door open. They entered a palatial room that could have been the formal study inside a Scottish castle. The heads of a deer, a lion, a cheetah, and a rhino hung from the walls. They stood guard above several large bookshelves filled with gold-gilded books.

Centered on the far wall between two huge windows, an imposing man with a black mustache and temples speckled with gray sat behind an imposing mahogany desk. Louisa approached to stand across from her father as he continued studying the document in front of him.

Once again, Louisa was the model of patience. Her eyes bore a hole through the papers in the man's hands. Ben counted to himself to see how long the earl would play this game of one-upmanship. As Ben neared fifty, the earl lowered the document and looked up.

He spent a six count staring into his daughter's eyes before glancing at Ben for a single count. Attention back on Louisa, he said, "You should have written."

"But that would have ruined the surprise, Father," she said with a flat, emotionless voice. "Aren't you pleased to see me?"

The earl, acting as if he sensed his bad manners for the first time, harrumphed. He stood and walked around the massive desk. She stepped to intercept him at the corner, where they exchanged an awkward hug and cheek kiss.

"Regardless, you're here now, and you look well." The earl gripped Louisa's biceps as he stepped back and held her at arm's length. "Amazing, you're a full-grown woman now. You were so much younger," he trailed off.

She stiffened in her father's grasp. "I was eighteen and about to graduate from the Maison d'éducation de Saint-Denis the last time I saw you. Since you left Corfu, we've had the pleasure just three other times."

He released his grip. "You know I've kept tabs on you. The last I heard, you'd returned to Paris."

She took a step back. "I guess I'm supposed to be grateful that your cronies checked on me every once in a while."

"You know how my life is," came his reply.

She lost her composure, and her words turned icy. "Everyone knows about the life of the great Earl of Cromer, who travels to newly conquered lands to rule benevolently over the indigenous people. All in the name of the Empire." She glared at him. "I'm sure you're doing your best to make the Egyptian people know their place. Will they feel the same as my mother when you left her? When you left me to live the life of a bastard?"

Ben felt uneasy hearing Louisa air her family's dirty laundry and wished for the first time to be somewhere else.

The earl's voice deepened with indignation. "I can't change the past any more than I can change who I am. Why have you come, Louisa? Did you bring a suitor to meet me? It's high time you found a man to take care of you and settle down."

Ben's unease turned into concern for the earl's safety. He knew from experience the man had just made a grave mistake.

Louisa's jaws clenched, and her face flushed, animated with anger. She stepped toward the earl and jabbed a finger toward his chest. "I'll be damned if I ever depend on a man to care for me. My mother showed me all too well that folly."

The two glowered at each other. Ben took that moment to disrupt the argument. "I believe you have the wrong idea, Earl Baring. A pleasure to meet you, by the way. I'm Dr. Benjamin McGehee. I am merely here acting as a friend."

Disengaging from his daughter's death stare, he turned to see Ben's outstretched hand. He looked at Ben as if seeing him for the first time. After that awkward pause, he grasped Ben's hand and shook. He leaned in as if his eyes were trying to pierce into Ben's soul. "If you're not here as a suitor, what kind of relationship do you have with my daughter?"

The earl's hand squeezed harder, and Ben met force with force before unclenching. "About two weeks ago, your daughter and I had a fortuitous meeting at the train station. You could say I saved a few porters from your daughter."

Ben chuckled. "Then, a week later, through serendipity, we met again near the market and spent a carefree afternoon together. Since getting to know her, I've been helping her solve an archaeological mystery that she's stumbled upon. Besides being a medical doctor, I'm also an archaeologist."

The earl frowned, and Ben cleared his throat. "I'm here to prepare for an expedition outside Tanis, taking place next year. With time to kill, I thought I could assist your daughter."

The earl digested this information and turned back to Louisa. "So, is this mystery the reason for your visit?"

In a calm voice, she said, "One of many, Father. I'm here primarily to discuss my finances. I spent the meager inheritance you gave me in Paris, furthering my education."

"That was fast. Not sure it was money well spent. How good of an education could you really get at that so-called women's college? Seems like a waste of money for an attractive young woman."

Her body stiffened. "Good enough that I passed all the Cambridge exams. The same ones the men at Cambridge must pass to matriculate. That's beside the point. If I can rectify my financial situation, I plan on leaving Cairo shortly." The beginning of a sneer formed at the corner of her mouth. "Unfortunately, if I can't, I'll be forced to stay here and seek employment. Maybe I'll drop by your house and finally meet my stepmother. Did you know we've never become acquainted?" Her eyebrows shot up, and her head tilted.

"And you won't," came an emphatic declaration. After a moment, the earl's demeanor changed, his chest puffing up. "It appears I'm being extorted by my own daughter." Sighing, he shook his head. "I have little recourse but to capitulate. How much will it take for you to leave Cairo?"

Louisa paused as if thinking about the matter, but her eyes never broke contact with him. At that moment, Ben was sure he had ceased to exist for the estranged father and daughter.

When the silence became uncomfortable, Louisa said, "Three thousand pounds should allow me to get established. As for the reason that Dr. McGehee accompanied me, we're looking for a lost temple near Pelusium. I'd like you to use your influence to get us the necessary permits and provide us with whatever other help you can. The sooner we're successful in this endeavor, the sooner I leave Egypt."

"You do know we're experiencing a cholera outbreak, and rebels are still harassing foreigners around the country?" The earl scratched his chin. "Well, I won't try to talk you out of this since you seem determined."

Louisa frowned.

"I'll give you four thousand pounds and provide you with a military escort to help with your search, but I have conditions."

Her frown faded, and her chin jutted out.

"First, you will not ask for any more money for at least ten years. You must learn to budget and not squander the money I give you. Second, you'll promise never to approach my wife or to use my name in public, and finally, as soon as you are done with your flights of fancy here, you'll leave Egypt and not return."

She tensed.

The earl puffed out his chest again, expecting a challenge. "If you need more funds after ten years, you can write to me. If I'm back in England by then, seek me out in person. Do we have an understanding?"

Unlike Ben, Louisa seemed unsurprised by the large amount. Ben figured she could live very well for more than a decade with such a sum.

"I knew I could count on you, Father." She flashed a warm smile at him. "I promise to abide by all your conditions. You can send the details to Shepheard's Hotel."

"Good, I expect you to keep your word. The reports I received showed you to be a young woman with a strong sense of integrity. Well, if we're done—" He motioned toward the door. "I'll have Stevens reach out to you with details about the note of guarantee and meeting your escort."

With that, the earl marched forward to open one of the double doors.

As she passed him, she stopped and reached up on her tippy toes to place a kiss on his cheek. "Goodbye, Father. Take care of yourself." She patted his chest with her hand.

With a shocked expression, the earl watched her march away as he mumbled, "Goodbye, Louisa."

He shook Ben's hand, drawing him near. "Dr. McGehee, despite what you just witnessed, I do care for my daughter, and I will hold you personally responsible if anything befalls her on this wild goose chase. Do you understand me?"

Ben leaned even closer. "I'll do my best to do what you can't. Of course, that depends on whether she'll allow it."

Lost in thought, Abu walked back to the hotel room from the second-floor communal privy. He pondered whether he would ever tire of the luxury of indoor plumbing and warm baths. Life in Cairo was as different from his life in Aleppo or at the dig site as gold was to copper.

Drifting back to the big problem at hand, he thought he should talk to Dr. Ben about it. Then he remembered Dr. Ben's awkward discussion with him the previous night. The doctor had attempted to discuss the differences between boys and girls, sex, babies, and romance. During the painful conversation with Dr. Ben, Abu realized that other than biologically and anatomically, Dr. Ben was clueless about girls. He still wasn't sure what had spurred Dr. Ben even to bring up the subject.

Dismissing the idea of getting the doctor involved, Abu went back to trying to find his own solution. Nashwa had been very upset when he'd told her he had to leave.

Is this love?

In his brief life, only the loss he'd felt when his parents died dwarfed his heartache at the sight of Nashwa's tears. He knew he had to go with Dr. Ben and not because the doctor had become his guardian. Abu found himself addicted to learning.

The urge to gain knowledge from Dr. Ben or from every book he got his hands on was as intense as his desire for Nashwa's kisses. A serious relationship would have to wait until he became the man he wanted to be.

Focusing on how to lessen Nashwa's pain, Abu reached for the doorknob and found the door was ajar. He was positive he'd locked it. He looked around. Seeing no sign of the maid or her cart in the hallway, he put his ear to the gap and listened. Drawers opened, and objects were being moved.

What should I do? he wondered.

Abu thanked Allah he had hidden the Antigenes papyrus as Dr. Ben had instructed. He'd stashed the paper in the small opening under the big standing closet. With luck, it would remain hidden.

Not wanting to take that chance, he knew he needed to act, but Dr. Ben kept his extra guns in the same armoire on the other side of the room. A sudden idea formed in Abu's mind. Dr. Ben's long knife, the one with the saber grip, hung from a hat peg behind the door. If he could reach it, he'd have a weapon.

Frightened but buoyed by his plan, he pushed the door, widening the gap a bit more. Heart hammering, he saw the back of a man in a Western-style suit and a turban walking between the beds toward the nightstand. Panic set in as Abu realized he'd left the little ivory lion out in the open.

The man picked up the figurine and brought it close to his otherwise covered face. Abu held his breath, praying for the thief to put it back. He heard the thief whispering to himself and imagined the man reading the inscription.

Abu's breath stuck in his throat as he squeezed through the door. He inched toward the scabbard and watched the thief with his peripheral vision.

Sensing Abu's movement, the man turned his head.

Abu lifted the knife off the peg with his right hand as the man headed toward the door. With heartbeats pounding out a snare drum cadence, he fought the urge to flee. He pulled the knife from the sheath with his left hand, stepped away from the door, and faced the burglar.

With a shaky grip, he pointed the shortened sword at the man. The thief stopped, his eyes darting from the eighteen-inch blade swaying in a circle to Abu's face to the open doorway. The small stack of papyri Abu had left on the desk was now rolled up and sticking out of the man's pocket.

Abu's voice quivered. "Put the carving and the papers on the bed."

The man's eyes grinned under the mask, and he leaped toward the door.

Abu brought the knife up above his shoulder and swung down. The man threw his right arm up in a defensive manner. Abu hadn't had time to aim and, given his awkward left-hand grip on the knife, his strike had limited force.

Time slowed, and Abu's vision constricted. Everything grew dim outside a small tunnel that zeroed in on his target. While the blade moved as if in thick honey, Abu focused on the small amber gem carved into the likeness of Anubis on the man's ring.

Why would I notice that?

Time sped up to a blur. The sharpened edge of Abu's blade had just enough power to slice through the thief's suit, cutting a shallow trench into his arm above his right wrist. The man cried out and barreled into the hallway.

Abu switched the saber handle to his strong hand and raced after the man. "Stop, thief!"

The robber outpaced him by twenty yards.

Not fast enough, al'ahmaq.[1]

---

1. Al'ahmaq is "asshole" in Arabic.

The distance between them narrowed when a hotel room door opened. A woman stepped into the hallway, her back to Abu. She looked over her shoulder, her eyes growing wide as they locked with Abu's. With a blood-curdling scream, she staggered back into the room and slammed the door.

Digging his heels into the corridor carpet, Abu stopped in his tracks. He realized how this must look. Remembering his treatment by the hotel staff, Abu spun and sprinted to his room. As he closed the door, his foot kicked a white object into the hallway. He stared at the little lion through the crack, took several quick breaths, and worked up the courage to retrieve it.

He looked at the knife, a sheen of red oozing along the edge. In a haze, he hung the blade back on its peg and went back to open the door. He poked his head out and looked in both directions.

Go.

With three quick steps, he scooped up the figurine and quick-marched into the room. He locked the door and sat on his bed. He hoped no one came to question him before Dr. Ben arrived. He also hoped the lady down the hall was okay.

His eyes glazed over as he remembered his meeting with Nashwa in an hour. It hurt him to disappoint her again, but he had to wait until Dr. Ben returned. He hoped she'd forgive him enough for the two of them to say a proper goodbye.

Yawning and unsure why he felt so exhausted, he prayed Dr. Ben would get back soon. With that last thought, he lay back on the bed and closed his eyes.

Louisa and Ben walked to the line of carriages outside Abdeen Palace at an unhurried pace. She allowed the silence between them to deepen as she mulled over the conversation with her father.

She couldn't help but congratulate herself. She'd gotten more money than she'd planned, and her decision to bring along Ben had worked double wonders. His presence sowed confusion in her father, distracting him from her ultimate goal. As much as that strategy had worked, Ben had helped in another way. He diffused the tension right before Louisa lost control of her anger.

Not for the first time, the Good Doctor had shown himself to be useful at the most opportune moment. He also seemed more perceptive than most men who would have been babbling nonstop by now. Instead, he showed patience, giving Louisa space.

As they settled side by side into the rear seat of an open-air carriage, Louisa rewarded the man's self-restraint. "Ben, thank you for joining me. I'm sorry you had to see my family's ugly reality, but, as you could tell, I needed someone there to support me."

"No need to thank me. What else are friends for? Besides, it all worked out." He grinned. "Your father's resources will help our expedition. I should thank you for that. Best of all, I now know where you got your fierce nature."

She smiled. "I didn't expect him to provide that much support." She left off that her father had surprised her with both his generosity and not being the callous man she'd expected. Even with her threats, he had no reason to give her the extra money or provide an escort. Of course, none of that exempted him from the resentment he so richly deserved.

Ben nodded. "With your father's help, we'll have our excavation permits expedited, saving us weeks of hassle. Which reminds me, I need to send my friend Flinders a telegram letting him know that his permits are ready, and I'll start the Tanis survey when I get back from this little side adventure." Lucky or astute by her estimation, he ignored the other aspects of the visit as he continued. "I think we should leave the day after we get the information from his assistant. Does that work for you?"

"Perfectly. I need to verify the line of credit with the Bank of England branch here in Cairo, and then we can set off. What clothing should I buy for the expedition?"

Ben thought for a moment and deadpanned, "Well, you already have a nice burqa, so you might bring that along."

Louisa punched Ben hard in his leg, registering a small grunt. "Next time, you'll wear the dress."

He laughed. "Okay, okay, but seriously, you want to make sure you pack for at least a month."

The two continued planning, even after reaching the hotel. Ben followed her up the stairs to her third-floor room. Nearing the door, Louisa grabbed his arm. "Something's wrong."

He inspected the door. "I don't see anything."

Louisa pointed to a tiny thread that hung to the side of the door frame. "Someone's been in the room," she whispered. "When I left, I connected this to the door. The hotel has instructions not to enter the room without my presence, and they've respected that so far."

Ben removed the revolver from his inside pocket. "Can't be too careful," he said in a low voice while reaching for the doorknob.

On finding no resistance, he gestured with his gun for her to step behind him. She moved next to the wall, and he pushed the door open. He rushed into the room with gun raised. She entered as he scanned the entire room. He motioned again for her to stay still. He walked through the room, peering inside the ensuite bath and washroom.

While Ben conducted his inspection, Louisa surveyed the disheveled room. Suitcases were open and drawers pulled out. The contents of her belongings lay on the ground or piled where the intruder had dumped them. Pulled away from the wall, the armoire and the dresser left dusty outlines of their previous locations.

Without waiting for Ben's signal, she located the only items of worth left in her room. Her messenger bag poked out from under several pages of aged papyri that lay on the bed. After a quick inventory, she found all or most of them still there.

"I can't see anything missing, but they were definitely interested in the papyri."

Recognition appeared on Ben's face, followed by a look of fear. "Abu has the papyrus," he said and raced out of the room.

She ran after him, only stopping to close the door behind her. He disappeared into the stairwell. She followed his thudding footsteps downstairs to the floor below. She found Ben knocking on the door to a room down a long hall. As she neared, the door opened. Ben grabbed Abu and brought him into a big bear hug in the corridor.

"Are you okay?" he implored.

Abu's arms hung limp for a moment before they encircled Ben. He mumbled into Ben's chest, "I'm fine, but someone tried to rob us."

Ben released the embrace, and the three of them entered the room. He offered Louisa the desk chair while he and Abu sat on the beds, looking across at each other. As Abu recounted his run-in with the thief, Ben's concern for the boy was obvious.

Abu's voice quavered as he described confronting the robber with Ben's knife. Ben stiffened, his face vacillating between anger and anguish. Abu finished his tale with the lady screaming and him running back to the room to wait for Ben.

As the boy fell silent, Ben heaved a big sigh and smiled his crooked smile. "I'm very proud of you, but next time I would prefer for you to be safe. If the thief had been a trained fighter and wanted to hurt you, you could have done nothing to stop him. It would be better if you hadn't confronted him at all. Do you understand?"

Abu's beleaguered expression grew determined. "Yes, but I don't want to be afraid if something like this happens again. I want to be like you. I'm willing to stand up to evil people, too."

Ben sat in thought for several seconds before saying, "You're right. You've been in dangerous situations before, and it's my responsibility to prepare you. When we get to the dig site, we'll start working on other skills besides academics."

Ben surprised Louisa by how he handled it. Her childhood mentor would have punished her if she'd put herself in so much danger—even over something of great value.

Her uncle had trained her to handle dangerous situations and even how to defend herself, but only as a last resort. His priority always came down to living to steal another day. Not that it worked out that way for him in the end.

Guardian and ward stood up. Ben gave Abu another hug. Louisa could tell from their clumsy embrace that they were unaccustomed to showing affection. The very thought of it made Louisa uneasy herself.

Back in her room, she pondered the significance of Abu's statement to Ben when the two had stepped apart. It reminded her of something Ben had said to her in the alley where she'd killed the robber. His words then eluded her now. She replayed the scene in her head and heard Abu say, "I won't let you down. I know God's able."

Chapter 8

Cairo, Egypt, to Pelusium, Egypt, October 1883

Louisa squeezed past a French-speaking family of four in the narrow passage on her way to Cabin 6. Ben and Abu would join her after securing the luggage in the baggage car. As she reached her cabin and opened the sliding door, she noticed a man walking toward her. He shuffled sideways down the too-small hallway between the train's private cabins. She didn't recognize him until he smiled and waved.

"Miss Sofia, what a surprise! I thought I saw you board the train." He gave a slight bow.

Louisa smiled and shook the man's hand with her customary hard squeeze. "Professor Mousa, what a coincidence. Is Pelusium your final destination as well?" Louisa smiled wider at the grimace on the professor's face.

"Yes, a German excavation near Pelusium requested my assistance. They need help interpreting some tricky hieroglyphics. I should only be there for a few days. And you? Are you traveling alone?" Ali asked, flattening himself into the hallway to let another passenger pass.

Louisa stepped halfway into her cabin. "Ben and his son, Abu, are securing the baggage. They will join me shortly. You're welcome to share our cabin, as there are only the three of us."

"Thank you for the offer, but I must decline. I'm sharing with a couple of colleagues in the other first-class car. Well, I hope Dr. McGehee secures that papyrus. Such a valuable artifact might become a target for thieves. I'll let you get settled. I just wanted to say hello and good luck with your search."

"Thank you. I'm hoping for a drop of luck, but just in case, I've brought along a bucket of brains in the form of Dr. McGehee. And, yes, I'm keeping a close eye on the papyrus." Louisa patted the strap of her messenger bag.

"Ah, I'm not sure Menander meant that quote exactly like that, but he would approve of the added comedy. It's good to see you keeping it close. A pleasure, as always. I hope our paths continue to cross." Ali bowed.

"Ta Leme, Professor," Louisa said as he turned and moved toward the door to the next forward car.

She stepped into the cabin and took in the red velvet–upholstered benches and luggage racks high above each seat. Preferring to watch the way forward, she picked the side closest to the rear of the train and next to the window. She unstrapped the messenger bag and, on tippy toes, pushed it onto the luggage rack above the opposite seat so she could monitor it.

Ben and Abu appeared moments before the conductor made a last tour of the car. He checked tickets and told each cabin that the train would leave in five minutes. Abu had ridden with the carriage driver to the station, so, for the first time, Louisa noticed his bloodshot eyes as if he had been crying.

Giving Ben a questioning look, she pointed her chin toward Abu. Ben grimaced in acknowledgment and placed his cavalry hat on the luggage rack above her. Shielding his movements from Abu, he pointed to his heart with his right hand before bringing his hands together to make a breaking motion. Louisa looked at the teen leafing through *The Republic* by Plato, then glanced at Ben to make a sad face.

For the next few hours, Abu worked on lessons, and Ben read a book. The three of them exchanged only an occasional comment. The longest break in the silence lasted a few minutes as the trio discussed their visit to the pyramids the previous day.

A few minutes before noon, Ben asked whether they were hungry and went to find the dining car. Louisa, patient as always, had been waiting for a chance to find out more about Abu and his relationship with Ben. She also weighed her additional concern for Abu's broken heart. She'd pry into that subject as well, if Ben gave them time.

"I've been meaning to ask you. How did you and Ben meet?"

Abu pulled his eyes away from the Greek-covered pages in his lap and looked her in the eyes. Somehow, his face transformed from sad to grave. As he spoke, his eyes drifted from hers to a distant place. "I have to warn you, it's not as good a story as when you and Dr. Ben first met."

He paused for her reaction. When she gave him none, he continued. "My family owned a restaurant in Aleppo. My mother's father owned it before she and my father took over. It would have been mine afterward." Another pause, but this one seemed to take him off somewhere else. With a head shake, he said, "Dr. Ben was spending several weeks in town before going on to Nineveh, and he came to our restaurant every night. He always ordered the dinner special and would read until closing.

"If we weren't busy, Baaba would talk to Dr. Ben, who appreciated getting to practice his Arabic. By the second week, Dr. Ben began bringing small gifts. Fruit, paper and pencils, stuff like that.

"Twice, I sat with him, and he told me stories about the Babylonian, Persian, and Assyrian empires. For the first time, I began to understand the full breadth of my people's history."

Abu smiled at reliving what Louisa thought must be pleasant moments. Then his face became serious, and his eyes tightened with grief and anger. "I may have only been twelve back then, but I'm not blind. My parents tried to hide it from me. But I knew there were criminals extorting *protection* money from them." Abu almost spit the words out. "Anyway, I guess they wanted too much. I heard my parents arguing about whether they would keep paying."

Abu paused and looked down for a second. A tear left a trail on his cheek when he looked up. His jaw muscles flexed again with anger, and his voice tightened to a whisper. "The night my parents died, Dr. Ben came in an hour before closing to have the special. The special that night was the lamb-stuffed kibbeh. It's funny that I would remember that, but Maama's was the best in Aleppo.

"When the thugs came in, there were no other customers except him. I was in the back doing dishes, so I only heard what happened. They snuck up on Dr. Ben and hit him on the head. Maama and I heard Baaba yelling. Then they hit him." He paused, regaining control.

Louisa's heart felt heavy, but she waited, sensing he would continue when ready.

Abu wiped his eyes with his sleeve. "Maama made me hide under some sacks of potatoes. I watched them drag my father into the kitchen and throw him on the floor. His face was covered in blood. One man had a large curved knife and pointed it at her. He said she'd better give them every ducat we owned, or they would kill my father and sell her to slavers."

The teen's voice became flat and emotionless. "Baaba tried to tell her not to do it, but one of the other men drew his knife and sliced my father across his cheek. I'll never forget Maama's scream."

Abu's eyes took on a glassy look. He chewed on his lower lip before squeezing his eyes tight. His voice trembled. "She gave them the money, and as soon as they had it—"

She saw a terrible wave of fear ripple across his face. Her heart broke watching him relive the worst moments of his young life. Tempted to stop the retelling and put an end to his pain, she held back only because she knew how much courage it had taken him to get this far.

"Those animals killed them both. I tried to be quiet, but I couldn't. I don't even remember them grabbing me." A sob escaped and another, but no more.

"My parents were lying on the floor covered in blood. I didn't know what they were going to do with me, but there was a loud bang, and the man holding me fell. When I looked for the source, I saw Dr. Ben standing a little behind another man who had dropped to his knees."

Abu let out a small, satisfied laugh. "That *al'ahmaq* had a spoon jammed down his throat." Speaking in a hushed tone, he said, "He deserved it. They all did." His voice strengthened. "When I finally noticed Dr. Ben's gun, it looked like the barrel was pointed right at me."

He grimaced. "At that moment, I was glad the nightmare was about to end. I waited for one final explosion, but I never heard it. Maybe I blinked. I don't know, but suddenly I was covered with blood and stuff I don't like to think about."

Abu opened his eyes, sighed, and gave a small smile of relief. "Dr. Ben got the money back and arranged for my father's friend to pay for their funerals. The friend said the thugs' boss would kill me if I stayed, so Dr. Ben took me with him."

He shook his head. "I still regret not being there. For their funerals. At least, Dr. Ben waited so I could say goodbye to them. I remember that." His eyes watered, but before tears could come, he shrugged. "And Dr. Ben and I have been taking care of each other for the last thirteen months."

Louisa made sure he had finished. Then she stood up and crossed over to sit next to him, facing forward. Placing her hand on his, she squeezed. "I'm sorry, Abu. I lost my mother when I was close to your age, and I also had to move away from everything I knew."

She looked at him. "Starting over is never easy, but unlike me, you're not alone. Ben seems to be a good man, and he tells me you're learning faster than he can teach you. If you ever need to talk about that or anything else, or you just want a different perspective than the Good Doctor's, come to me."

Abu smiled down at Louisa, which made her feel a little small. "Thank you, Miss Sophia. I know I don't want to talk about that anymore. If ever. And I'm not sure what else we would talk about."

Louisa let go of his hand and moved back to her seat to face him. She leaned forward. "Well, I'm quite versed in several languages: Greek, English, Italian, Spanish, French, and a little Portuguese. I also have studied the ancients and can read and write in Latin and several dialects of Ancient Greek." Abu's eyebrows shot up, and his eyes went wide. "And I have a bachelor's degree in liberal arts." She leaned closer, and her voice took on a conspiratorial tone. "Besides, I'm a woman. Something Ben can never equal. So, if there are any topics you don't feel comfortable discussing with Ben—say, girls—you can come to me." She smiled, leaning back.

At the mention of girls, Abu broke into a silly grin. Cheeks turning red, he glanced away. A few seconds later, he looked back with eager eyes. "I'm sure you can't be as bad as Dr. Ben. For some reason, he had the *girl* talk with me last week." He snickered. "If anyone else had been there, I would have been embarrassed for him." He laughed along with Louisa for a second before turning semi-serious. "But, really, I don't think I need any advice right now."

"Okay, but if you ever want to talk, just let me know."

With their bellies full, the constant rocking motion of the train took its toll on the traveling companions. Ben leaned against the window, his eyelids heavy from staring at an endless arid landscape that had begun an hour ago when they left the more lush delta region. He sprawled his legs across the aisle over Abu's while the boy slumbered against the other wall. As he drifted off to sleep, Ben's last view was of Louisa curled up on the seat across from him.

A shriek startled Ben. His eyes darted around the small space while his mind reeled, trying to make sense of his surroundings.

"Stop!" Louisa screamed at the top of her lungs.

A comedy of flying arms and legs happened as everyone tried to stand at the same time. As Ben spun around, his arm knocked Louisa backward onto her seat.

"He stole my bag," she yelled, pointing.

Ben's head snapped toward the door. Abu stood in the hallway, gesturing toward the front of the train. "He ran that way!"

Without uttering a word, Ben pushed past Abu and side-stepped down the narrow hallway toward the exit door that had just slammed shut.

Stupid, stupid, stupid.

He admonished himself for not keeping the lion and the papyrus secure. Their expedition would end before they even got off the damn train.

"Excuse me! Coming through!" he yelled at the man who poked his head out of a cabin door. The head disappeared a split second before Ben collided with it.

Through the window in the door, he watched the man clutching the messenger bag pass through the doorway to the next car.

Ben threw open the door and stepped outside. Ignoring the swaying walkway between the two cars, he leaped across the short gap between landings. He grabbed the door handle and yanked back. "Ouch."

He looked at the palm of his hand, expecting to see it turning an angry red from a burn, but saw only a little pink. Using the bottom of his jacket, he touched the metal again. Heat radiated off the brass fixture as he tried to turn the knob.

How the hell?

It wouldn't budge, as if it had been welded in place. Ben banged on the wood. "Damn."

He gritted his teeth and scooted beside the railing at the back of the car. He reached around the corner and found a ladder bolted to the side of the train car. With one good grip on the hot steel, Ben stretched his leg around and planted his foot on an iron rung.

He took a quick peek to confirm there were no oncoming obstacles. The last thing he wanted was to be hanging off the side when another train passed on the track running next to them.

He had a vague awareness of Louisa and Abu approaching as he twisted his body, getting both hands and feet on the ladder.

Did someone yell?

Whatever they said, he lost it in the wind. The loud *thunk, thunk* of the wheels rolling over the rails made him look down. Beneath his feet, railroad ties and reddish brown soil rushed by. His hands tightened on the almost blistering metal.

Tenderfoot mistake. Don't look down.

Facing the cloudless sky, Ben moved with tempered haste up the ladder. At the top, he wiggled onto the roof until he could stand.

Squinting from the wind and dust, he had a moment of doubt.

Ben, you idiot, you're going to get yourself killed.

But just as quick, he imagined Jesse James standing on the roof of a speeding train during one of the James-Younger gang robberies.

If he can do it, then so can I.

Bending to brace against the headwind, he shuffled along the wooden roof. On reaching the end, he watched the man once again close the door to the next car in line. Ben's mind raced as he measured the gap.

It's not that far.

Famous last words.

Ben took a few steps backward.

Don't be a coward.

He sprinted toward the end.

Leaping in the air, he yelled, "Remember the Alamo!"

Despite his jump being true, he stumbled forward and landed on one knee. He shook off the pain shooting through his leg, regained both feet, and quickened his pace.

He knew the thief would need to take his time working through the crowded dining car. And if Ben didn't catch him before he got into the next car, there'd be little chance of retrieving the stolen items.

With a last burst of speed, he jumped over the next gap. He stumbled to a stop, lay down, and scooched backward over the edge. Now his feet dangled over the landing of the second-class car. He kept scooting until he hung by his hands and dropped the last foot to the landing.

Ignoring the pain from his bruised knee, Ben spun around and jumped back to the dining car. He waited next to the door, breathing through his nose and trying to become part of the wall.

Where was his quarry? If the man had reached the second-class car . . . but no, Ben was pretty sure he'd gotten ahead of the robber. Another thirty seconds passed, and the door inched open.

Ben grabbed the wrist holding the doorknob and jerked. Louisa yelped and flew outside. If not for Ben snapping her back toward him, she might have flown over the short guard rail. She ended her recoil and pressed him hard into the wall. His hand still clutched her wrist while his other arm wrapped her body in a desperate, protective hold.

Looking into her startled eyes, he mumbled, "Sorry, I thought I got ahead of him."

Breathy, she replied, "You did. We saw him go in but never saw this door open after we followed him inside."

Somewhere in the back of his mind, he registered the feel of her body pressed against his. Yet he lost most thoughts trying to answer a simple question as he stared into the pools of her deep brown eyes. Was it his imagination, or was she staring back at him with anticipation?

"Uh, Ben, we should, uh, probably . . ."

Louisa tried to disengage from Ben's hold, which brought him out of that moment.

"Oh, yeah," Ben said as he let go of her wrist and unwound his arm. "Sorry."

After moving apart and turning toward the open door, they saw Abu wearing a wide grin. Louisa and Ben made a show of straightening their clothes as Abu stepped outside and closed the door.

"I didn't see him among the diners. He must have switched jackets or have a hiding place inside." The teen nodded back at the dining car. "But I noticed he had the same ring on his right hand as the man who broke into our room. I forgot about the ring until I saw it again. Pretty sure he's not the same guy, though."

"Why do you think that?" Louisa asked.

"The man at the hotel was shorter. More solid."

"What does the ring look like?" Ben asked.

"It has a yellow stone carved into the shape of Anubis."

She looked between the two of them. "Well, I say we go inside and have a drink to calm our nerves. We can look for someone with the ring, but it's no great loss if we don't find him."

Ben and Abu tilted their heads in question.

"I tried to stop you before you climbed the ladder." She shook her head. "That was pretty good, though. After the hotel incident, I decided we needed to keep the papyrus and lion truly safe. I put them where no one can get them without losing a hand." She flashed a sly smirk and patted her chest.

Ben shook his head, realizing she had more there than cleavage.

"Besides, I also asked Abu to make two copies of the original letter. The thief will find nothing but a brief note detailing what I think of his ancestors." With that, she nodded toward the door. "Shall we?"

Abu opened the door for Louisa to pass through. As Ben stepped by the teenager, they shared a look interpreted as, "*Wow.*"

The last two hours of the train ride were uneventful. The ringed culprit continued to elude them, and the incident caused Ben to rethink overall security. Whoever wanted the Perdiccas artifacts had already failed twice. He couldn't imagine them giving up now.

Then there were all the other questions. How many thieves were they up against? So far, the would-be-robbers had abstained from violence.

Would that change?

Ben knew Louisa carried a gun, but Abu had never used one. He'd make sure the boy learned how to.

Standing on the landing, Ben surveyed the Port Said train station. For the second time in as many weeks, he thought about how the train depot and the surrounding land could pass for any train station in West Texas. Well, except for the busy port behind him. A blue-and-white-turbaned Indian cavalryman waited close to the end, holding a sign that read, "Louisa Sophia." Two fellow khaki-clad soldiers stood behind him.

"Follow me," Ben said to his travel companions.

Not waiting for a reply, he hopped down the last step and strode toward the three soldiers. He was sticky from sweat in mere moments as the torrid Egyptian sun beat down on him. While dodging other departing passengers and their greeters, Ben scanned the right hands of each man he passed. He never caught sight of the yellow Anubis ring Abu had described.

The way forward cleared as they neared the man with the sign. Ben could make out three stripes topped by a metal crown on the sergeant's shoulders.

No, not sergeant, but corporal of the horse.

Ben remembered that the British Army used different designations for their cavalrymen. He waved, catching the man's attention. The soldier broke into a wide smile through his well-groomed beard.

Ben slowed. He hadn't noticed Louisa lifting her skirt and jogging to catch up. With a harumph, she stopped next to him, a little out of breath.

The man handed the sign to a soldier behind him and snapped to attention as he addressed Louisa. "Miss Sophia, I'm Duffadar Nahal of the Thirteenth Bengal Lancers.[1] Our orders are to act as your escorts and to help in any way necessary during your stay in Pelusium."

Louisa smiled. "Thank you, Duffadar Nahal. My companions and I are very grateful for your help. May I introduce Dr. Ben McGehee and his son, Abu?"

Ben dipped his head, and Abu raised his hand.

---

1. Duffadar is the British Indian Army equivalent of the "corporal of the horse" or "sergeant" in other military units.

The duffadar wore that same big grin as he nodded at Abu and stuck his hand out toward Ben. "Dr. McGehee, it's a pleasure." Shaking hands, he asked, "I see you're a fellow horse soldier. May I ask your unit and rank?"

Disengaging, Ben couldn't help but smile at the man's infectious nature. "I mustered out as a captain with the Texas Sixth Cavalry." After identifying his old military rank, Ben made a quick mental note to learn the various ranks for the Indian cavalry. For some reason, they used a different system than their British counterparts.

The duffadar raised his eyebrows, looking up at the obvious Union hat.

"Ah, this, it's a long story." He smiled his crooked grin. "I'll share it when we have time. Right now, we need to grab our luggage from the baggage car."

Duffadar Nahal's smile disappeared. Turning to his subordinates, he said in an authoritative voice, "Acting Lance Duffadar, take the sowar to the baggage car.[2] [3] Bring Miss Sophia's and her guests' luggage to the wagon."

Abu chimed in behind him. "I'll show them which bags are ours."

The three of them headed toward the freight car, and the duffadar turned back to Ben. "Would you prefer to be addressed as Captain or Dr. McGehee?"

"Neither. Please, call me Ben. May I address you by your first name?"

"Louisa for me." She gave the duffadar an innocent smile with eyebrows expectant.

The duffadar rubbed his beard in thought for several strokes. Letting go, he broke out into that same wide grin. "Good, good, good. I think we'll have an

---

2. Acting lance duffadar is the British Indian Army equivalent of a lance corporal. The equivalent to the rank of corporal is lance duffadar.

3. Sowar is the British Indian Army calvary's equivalent to private or trooper. It means "horseman" and is different from an Indian Army infantry private known as a sepoy.

amazing time together. My name is Jeevan." In a more serious tone, he said, "If it's okay with you, I will address you as Captain Ben and you as Miss Louisa." He grinned at them. "Anything less formal might give the lads the wrong idea."

He motioned them forward. "We should get going. Our campsite is a little over an hour's ride. Miss Louisa, you may want to change clothes. I brought horses for you and Captain Ben. Unless you prefer to ride in the wagon with Captain Ben's son."

"I'll ride. Just don't leave without me." Her eyes twinkled at her joke. She turned and strode toward the soldiers retrieving the trio's luggage.

Ben nodded at Jeevan. "Thanks for all your help." He paused and rubbed his chin. "One thing. We need to return to town in the morning. I have to find a particular excavation foreman and hire some men."

"I'll come with you, but I suggest you save a few quid. We can put the lads to work. They might think I'm a nice guy if they don't stay busy." Jeevan made a mockery of a stern look.

Ben's face scrunched up. "I'm not sure two men can do the job."

Jeevan chuckled. "Don't worry, Captain Ben. I have twenty men plus myself. Miss Louisa is a very important person."

Ben's eyes moved to Louisa as she walked away. Watching her graceful movements, he thought about the woman's many surprises before he remembered the way she'd felt in his arms. He sighed.

Ben turned back to Jeevan and shook his head. "You don't know the half of it, but that's not my story to tell."

Chapter 9

East of Pelusium, Egypt, October 1883

Ben dusted himself off as he walked back to camp. Ready for lunch, even his grumbling stomach couldn't distract him from his current train of thought. He made a list of what needed to be done, and then he thought about what they'd accomplished so far. Yesterday he'd located and hired Ahmed Gerigar. He was the foreman—or *rais*, as Egyptian supervisors were called—who worked with the French team.

When the rais showed up today, he and his son stowed away their few belongings and got straight to work. He assured Ben that the search for the tomb should begin on the opposite side of the outcropping from where the previous expedition had dug. Gerigar based his reasoning on what he knew of the tombs he had helped excavate during the last twenty years.

The tombs on the side where the French had dug were from a period five hundred to a thousand years earlier than the era for Perdiccas's burial. Ahmed had suggested as much to the French team. He implied, using the kind of anatomically descriptive language that only Arabic can provide, that they were too French to listen.

With this as a starting point, Ben, Abu, Ahmed, and his son spent the day doing an initial survey of the site. They worked on staking off eight rectangles along the base of the outcropping. While they started, Jeevan and the Lancers moved their camp within a few hundred yards of the dig site.

Tomorrow, Rais Ahmed would supervise the Lancers on how to use proper excavating techniques to dig two shallow trenches across the length of each section. All the non-soldiers would follow behind them, doing the meticulous work of going deeper, an inch at a time.

A volley of shots startled Ben out of his planning. The Lancers, doing shooting drills, had created a firing range fifty yards beyond the camp. They were using some small mounds as backstops.

Hope those aren't burial mounds, Ben thought.

True to his word, the duffadar was keeping his soldiers busy. Peering closer, Ben saw that the Lancers had an audience of one. Abu sat on a small boulder, watching the show.

He must have sprinted there from the worksite to be that far ahead of Ben. From a distance, the teenager's posture conveyed enraptured attention. Seeing the boy tickled Ben's memory. He'd promised to teach Abu how to defend himself. As Ben neared the camp, the Lancers broke up and headed back as well.

Picking up his pace, he intercepted the duffadar. "Jeevan, do you have a second?"

"Of course, Captain Ben." He stopped.

"I promised Abu that I'd show him how to defend himself. If it's not too much trouble, I was wondering if you might let him participate in some of your drills."

Jeevan's big smile, always poised to break out, flashed again. "I think that's a splendid idea, Captain Ben." He paused a moment in thought, then nodded to himself. "You should do the drills with him. There's nothing like having your father lead the way."

Ben pursed his lips. *Father?* The word, as well as Jeevan's suggestion, caught Ben flat-footed. Mahdi was Abu's father. He'd been a good man, and Ben doubted Abu thought of him like that.

But he had taken on that role even if this was the first time someone used that term.

It will take some getting used to.

Looking at Jeevan, whose gigglemug never faltered, Ben knew he needed to give the duffadar an answer.[1] He didn't want to relive any part of his life as a soldier. Yet struggling to think of a valid excuse, he couldn't refute Jeevan's logic. Besides, it would help him get back in shape.

He gave the happy-go-lucky soldier a crooked smile. "You're right. It'll be good for us both. Promise you'll take it easy on me, though." Ben raised both hands, palms out. "It's been decades since I wore a uniform."

Jeevan laughed. "Good, good, good. Don't worry, Captain Ben. You and Abu will be amazing when I'm done with you." Without warning, his eyes narrowed, and he turned somber. Looking up a few inches, he stared Ben dead in the eyes. "I'll dedicate myself to making sure that you and Abu can do more than just handle yourselves in a scrap." Grinning with mischief, he slapped Ben on the back. "You'll get a very personal glimpse into why my cavalrymen are the best in the world."

I can't wait, Ben thought.

Walking next to Abu, the two headed back to camp. By that afternoon, they had finished laying out the eight long rectangles.

Ben patted the boy on the shoulder. "I remembered that we're supposed to train."

---

1. A gigglemug is a Victorian term for a person who is always smiling.

Abu's eyes bulged, and a grin split his face, showing all three dimples. "Really? When do we start?" He mimed shooting a rifle. "Are you going to teach me to shoot first?"

Ben raised his hand. "Whoa. Maybe. I asked Duffadar Nahal if we could train with the Lancers."

"That's incredible. I can't wait." He bounced on the balls of his feet. "Will we get to do everything they do?"

Ben shook his head, keeping pace with the elated teenager. "Duffadar Nahal will tell us. I'm not sure when we'll start, so be patient."

As they reached their tent, a Lancer ran up to them. "The duffadar asked me to bring you two."

Not knowing the man's name yet, Ben said, "Where are we going, Sowar?"

The man grinned. "To training."

In almost a whisper, Ben replied, "Oh."

Already?

"Wow. Let's go, Dr. Ben. I can't wait." Abu tugged at his sleeve.

Ben shuffled after the soldier toward the firing range as if marching to the gallows. He had looked forward to getting a little rest before dinner and then reading until sunset. Dragging his feet, he wondered why every Lancer appeared to be heading in the same direction. That's when he saw Louisa among the crowd.

As they neared the field, the Lancers began forming a loose ring, with Jeevan waiting outside the circle.

He sure didn't waste any time.

"Captain Ben, I know how excited you are to get started." Jeevan tried not to laugh.

Sullen, Ben said, "Sure. What do you want us to do?"

"Initiation," Jeevan said. "Every new Lancer starts his time with the Thirteenth by facing one of our veterans in hand-to-hand combat."

Jeevan frowned and added, "Sorry, Abu. You're too young for the initiation."

Abu dropped his head a little, and his shoulders slumped.

Jeevan patted him on the back. "But when you turn eighteen, if we're still around, you'll get your turn."

Abu beamed. "Promise?"

"Promise."

Relieved, Ben stuck out his chest and rolled his shoulders, trying to pump himself up. "So, what do I do?"

Jeevan's smile disappeared. "Lance Duffadar Ram is waiting in the ring." He waved at the circle.

Ben nodded, handed his hat to Abu, and rolled up his sleeves. "Any rules?"

"Nothing you need to worry about," Jeevan said.

Ben scrunched up his face at that but walked forward with purpose. Squeezing between two Lancers, he came to a sudden stop. Across the sun-baked dirt of the practice ring stood a short, skinny, dark-skinned man stripped down to his waist. Ben's first thoughts were that Jeevan had granted his request and was taking it easy on him.

Lance Duffadar Ram stood only a few inches taller than Louisa and may have outweighed her by twenty or thirty pounds. Ben's confidence soared at the sight of his much smaller opponent. Soon, shouts of encouragement rang out in both English and Dogri.

From somewhere, he heard Louisa yell in a bellicose voice, "You've got this, McGehee!"

As Ben took up a classic boxing stance, the wiry man gave him a grin and a wink that made Ben blink.

What does he know that I don't?

Ben shuffled forward and threw a quick jab at the smaller man, trying to find his range. Lance Duffadar Ram's head moved away from Ben's fist as if the two were opposing magnets. The invisible push launched the soldier. He flowed into a dance, a deadly dance with steps Ben didn't know and found impossible to follow.

Between slipping away from punches, the whirling dervish hit Ben with quick jabs. Each blow seemed to find points on his body that, when struck, were more painful than a right hook. Ben countered with jabs and combinations that found nothing but air and left him open to more punishment.

An uppercut caught Ben on the chin. With sunspots dancing in his vision, he fell hard on his butt. Fighting through the pain pulsating in his jaw and his even more wounded pride, he scrambled to his feet.

Shaking his head, Ben tried to relieve the ringing in his ears as the mighty mite warrior closed the distance again. Ben raised unsteady hands, three small men filling his vision. He drew a blank, trying to think of a strategy to save him. He came up with only one.

Aim for the guy in the middle.

The Lancer sent a series of rattler-quick strikes using fists, fingers, and feet. Surrendering all thoughts of going on the offensive, Ben tried to block the blows. He put up a desperate defense against attacks coming from every conceivable direction.

To Ben, the onslaught lasted for several minutes. In reality, it took only twenty or thirty seconds before he couldn't lift his arms. In a last-ditch effort to turn the tide, he rushed in and tried to grab the smallest Bengal Lancer in a bear hug. More slippery than a greased pig, Ram ducked under Ben's feeble attempt.

The shorter man latched onto Ben's arm with both hands and twisted. Using Ben's momentum, the Lancer sent him flying over a shoulder to land on his back. Bruising pain shot through him. Ben's breath burst from his lungs, leaving him gasping for air. Without wasting a motion, the Lance duffadar slithered on top to lock Ben's neck and left arm in a painful hold with his skinny, hard-as-steel legs.

Ben refused to give up despite the pain and his lack of breath. He rocked until he could roll over. Operating on instinct, he wanted to bash the wiry soldier against the hard ground, hoping to dislodge the wild devil of a man. Ben rose on wobbly legs. His eyesight narrowed from a hazy tunnel-view of the man's appendages to a tiny pinprick of light.

Ben's eyelids fluttered and slammed shut. His leaden arm refused to move as he tried to cover his eyes from the blinding light. Shade fell over his face, and he opened his eyes. Three fuzzy blobs loomed over him. He blinked away the spots in his vision until Louisa's, Abu's, and Jeevan's faces came into focus. Jeevan grinned. Louisa's brows furrowed. Abu frowned.

"What. What happened?" Ben stammered.

Abu's face relaxed. Jeevan chuckled.

Louisa shook her head. "You lost." Rolling her eyes, she said, "To the very petite man."

The fight came rushing back. Ben's face became fiery. "How could that little guy—"

Jeevan stood straight and let out a big belly laugh. Ben grimaced as a ray of light fell on his face. The duffadar leaned over, bringing back the merciful shade. "Don't worry, Captain Ben. He does that to everyone."

Abu said in a quiet voice, "I'm glad you're okay." His pace picked up, and he grew excited. "Just before you passed out, the small guy did a backflip off you and landed on his feet. It was one of the craziest things I've ever seen."

Louisa laughed and held out her hand to help Ben up. "Good thing you're better with your gun."

Ben's only consolation for his shattered pride were the many slaps on the back and words of encouragement from the Lancers. Jeevan told Ben he'd lasted longer than most other first-time opponents of the Kalari guru.

The duffadar explained that Kalari was an ancient Indian martial art outlawed by their British overlords. Despite being the smallest soldier in the entire regiment, Ram taught the illegal combat system in secret to all the 13th Bengal Lancers. Minus their British officers, of course.

Ben appreciated that Jeevan never said, "I told you so," during the history lesson. With a single minute of sparring, he'd made his point that Ben needed to sharpen his skills.

Still trying to catch his breath, Ben clasped his hands behind his head.

Jeevan's smile grew sinister. "You look better. Ready to get started?"

Stop smiling, you sadistic bastard. "You like your job too much."

The duffadar double-pumped his eyebrows, and pure elation creased his face.

Shaking his head, Ben thought, *No mas*, but his pride said *sí*, forcing him to nod assent. Hoping never to repeat a thrashing like that again, Ben used Abu for support as they walked back to the ring. Lance Duffadar Ram waited for them with a welcoming smile.

Louisa shifted from a *sarvangasana* pose with her legs suspended straight in the air into a *halasana* pose as part of the Prana Vayu. She lowered her legs over her body until her toes touched the ground, forming a bridge.

She relished the stretching exercises, which were part of the Indian art form known as Vedic Yoga. Guru Ram never let them forget that the practice was older than the pyramids. He insisted they do some poses each day before practicing Kalari.

Impressed by how the small hand-to-hand expert had pummeled the much bigger and stronger Ben, Louisa insisted he teach her as well. To learn as fast as possible, she arranged for private lessons, starting the morning after Ben's fight. For two days, she had the guru to herself. Well, almost. Ben insisted on acting as a chaperone since they trained behind blankets stretched between tents.

A few days into her instruction, the Good Doctor decided that he and Abu should join her in the morning sessions. She'd been a little miffed at first, but at least the exercises kept him too occupied to send any lustful glances her way. Several times in the first couple of days, she'd seen hints of indecent thoughts in his eyes whenever she performed a compromising position like the one she found herself in now.

With the fitting name "the Plow," the current unladylike pose exemplified many other poses. She thanked God she could wear her burglar pants. Loose fitting, they tied at the ankles, never exposing more than a few inches of skin, no matter what contortions the poses called for.

Louisa hated needing to worry about modesty, but as the only woman in a camp full of men, she had to be on guard. Besides, these weren't regular men but soldiers who had an edge to them. Wherever she went and no matter what she did, eyes watched her. Of course, she couldn't blame them. They were the lesser sex, after all.

In her experience, most men were weak-minded and easy-to-manipulate creatures, driven by their immediate wants. If it wasn't sex, it was food, and if it wasn't food, it was the desire to fuel their over-inflated egos with power or money.

Thinking back, Louisa admitted it had all started after the minor incident on the train. Afterward, she'd caught Ben looking her way more and more often.

Knowing how to observe without her subject being aware, she'd caught him staring with brazen intensity several times. Even now, he remained clueless that she'd seen him. Usually, looks of desire like that spelled the end of any man's usefulness. Instead, she found herself somewhat curious about the lanky doctor.

Peeking around her legs, she watched Ben struggle to keep his balance while trying to bring his toes to the ground. She grinned. Since he'd joined her class, she'd started looking forward to his slapstick routine. Suppressing her giggles, she and Abu flowed through the poses while Ben looked ready to topple over at any moment.

As if on cue, Ben collapsed on his side. "Dang it!" He slapped the ground, stirring up the fine Egyptian soil.

"Try again!" yelled Guru Ram.

Louisa and Abu laughed. Ben glared at her before rolling over to struggle back into the pose.

The morning after Ben's drubbing, Louisa began private Kalari lessons with the little guru. For propriety's sake, Ben had insisted that he chaperone these sessions. A short time after her first class, the day's work began with Rais Ahmed supervising the Lancers as they dug two shallow trenches across the length of each staked-out section.

Ben, Louisa, Abu, and Ahmed's fifteen-year-old son, also named Ahmed, followed behind the soldiers-turned-excavators. They did the meticulous work of going deeper, inch by inch, layer by layer with small trowels and brushes. They worked in each trench until they reached a depth of three feet. Louisa surprised Ben with her enthusiasm for the work and her humility. She soaked up advice from each of the other, more experienced excavators. She went so far as to take direction from Abu with aplomb.

When they finished work, Ben and Abu trained with the Lancers until dinner and then went to bed exhausted. This became their daily pattern with one minor alteration. After just two days of watching Louisa's rapid improvement during her private Kalari lessons, he worried he might get dismantled in the ring again—this time by the petite young woman.

The next morning, to Louisa's clear but unspoken irritation, Ben had insisted that he and Abu join her morning sessions. He enjoyed learning the combat system, but the Vedic Yoga used for stretching pushed him beyond his comfort zone.

The evening drills they'd done with the Lancers were more natural for Ben. He knocked off the rust while helping to train Abu in the basics of horsemanship, cavalry movements, shooting, and tactics. Sowar Chib also taught the teenager some riding tricks that Ben didn't even dare try.

The sowar's ability on horseback reminded Ben of some of the Comanches he'd seen back home. The Lancer could ride and shoot from under his horse's neck while hanging on the animal's side with only his legs. At full gallop, he'd shoot, swivel back to sitting, spin to face backward, shoot again, and then face forward again in seconds. Ben marveled at the Lancer's incredible accuracy with a rifle or a revolver.

Demonstrating the moves to Abu, Sowar Chib walked the horse, stepping Abu through the intricacies of each skill. Abu was proving to be a natural. The Lancer said that if he worked at it for several months, he'd be able to master the moves at a trot and be at a gallop within a year.

For shooting drills, Jeevan insisted Ben and Abu learn how to shoot the proper way as part of a dismounted formation. They formed into two ranks, and each line took turns stepping forward and firing. The next group repeated the process while the first reloaded their single-shot, breech-loading carbines. Jeevan showed them how to restrict their field of fire depending on where they were on the line. These skills allowed them to maintain a near constant barrage.

Only when they'd run through the drill using dry-firing techniques, for what seemed the hundredth time, did Jeevan let them do it for real. He had the two lines go through the series four times, shooting at targets at 50 and 100 yards.

During that night's supper, Ben considered the exciting next phase of the dig. For six long days, they had scraped the trenches. Artifacts had been sorted, from ivory combs to pottery shards, based on their rectangle. Today, the team determined the seventh parcel to be the best place to begin moving up the rocky outcropping.

The most exciting finds in section seven were a small limestone carving of the goddess Hera and a Persian coin with the image and inscription of Artaxerxes III, the grandfather of Darius III, whom Alexander had defeated in battle. The coin, in particular, dated the area to Egypt's late Persian or early Greek occupation.

While Ben made new mental checklists, Abu spent the meal raving about the shooting drills to anyone who'd listen. Now, lying on his cot, Ben squirmed and tried to get comfortable as he worried about the impressionable teen.

He sat up and put both hands on the side of his cot, then said, "I know you're excited about everything you're learning, but . . ."

Raising himself on one elbow, Abu locked eyes with Ben. "Are you going to tell me not to become a soldier?"

Ben looked at his hands and pondered the best approach. He gave Abu his best sympathetic face. "Abu, being a soldier can be an honorable profession. There's nothing like the brotherhood that forms when you face danger with your comrades." Ben sighed. "But before you become a soldier, you need to know in your heart that you're fighting for something worth killing for. The second thing I need you to understand is that glory doesn't exist in war. As a soldier, you do whatever it takes to save yourself and your brothers."

Abu's face scrunched in consternation. "Dr. Ben, I know your side lost, but are you saying you regret fighting?"

"I regret it. I regret the lives that were lost, like my brother's, and all the horrible things I witnessed—and sometimes did." He took a moment to gather his thoughts. "But my biggest regret came from what I began to understand later. A big part of what my side fought for wasn't honorable at all. We fought to keep slavery legal, and I didn't understand what that meant."

Nodding, Abu grew solemn. "You know, they still have slaves in Aleppo. I've seen what it does to people. It's pure evil."

Impressed by Abu's wisdom well beyond his age, Ben said, "Right, well, I didn't understand what it meant until later. You remember how the man at the hotel treated you?"

Abu nodded.

"After the war, I saw that kind of treatment everywhere when I was in school. Most of my classmates were much worse than that man. I had to bite my tongue to finish school." Ben, thinking back to that time, clenched his jaws in anger. "After I graduated, I couldn't take it anymore and spoke out." He caught his breath, remembering the backlash that followed his failed attempt to protect a young man from mistreatment.

"What happened?"

"I lost all my fair-weather friends and any hope of starting a business there. Also, the man I tried to help—I just made his life more difficult. That's why I told you to pick your battles."

"I will," he said.

"I hope you get my point."

Abu frowned. "I don't understand the second part of what you said. You don't mean that there are no heroes, do you? You were a hero when you saved me."

Ben sighed in resignation. "I'm no hero. When I killed someone, I wasn't brave. I was desperate. I was trying to save myself or someone else. Understand?"

Abu shrugged. "Sort of."

"Abu, if you have to fight to save yourself or your friends, you'll never have regrets. That's the problem with being a soldier. There were times I had to kill people only because they wore the wrong uniform. My only regrets in life are fighting for the wrong reasons and killing when I wasn't desperate."

Ben pushed aside his nightmarish memories of chasing the retreating Union cavalry composed of ill-trained and ill-equipped former slaves.

Abu hesitated, then asked, "Are there any reasons you would become a soldier again?"

Amazed at the teenager's insightfulness, Ben paused. The question had caught him unprepared. "Yes. There are causes worth fighting for. You need to be careful when making big decisions like that. Does that make sense?"

"Hadn't really thought about it. I'm not ready to become a soldier. I just want to learn everything I can for the next time I'm desperate."

Ben smiled. "And that's what I want as well."

Sweat stung Abu's eyes. He stretched his back after hunching over the rocky soil. With his free arm, he wiped the perspiration off his brow. He grabbed the canteen and took a drink of the lukewarm water, wishing the next half hour would fly.

From where he sat, looking out over the worksite, they were halfway up the outcropping from the desert floor. He counted ten sections staked out, roped off, and dug to a depth of five feet. Ahmed Jr. and Abu were working on Sections 11 and 12. Dr. Ben and Miss Louisa worked higher on the hill, and beyond them, some Lancers were in similar squares, shoveling out the first three feet of dirt.

They'd been at it for a week now, and still nothing. Abu wondered whether he had what it took to be a good archaeologist. Learning new languages and finding artifacts were exhilarating, but this part—digging in the dirt—bored him.

Now, riding, fighting, shooting. Abu loved it all, but not as much as his academics. Thinking about Dr. Ben's discussion a few nights earlier, he appreciated what the doctor had shared. Of course, Abu had never given serious thought to becoming a soldier, but it was nice to have someone looking out for him.

Abu's view of the world, life, and Allah had changed the night he'd lost his parents. He'd promised himself never to be a naïve, innocent victim again.

Next time evil finds me, I'm gonna kick evil's ass.

In the meantime, he prayed for the devil to leave him alone long enough that he could get ready. That's why he threw himself into the training as much as he did his studies, and why he wanted today's work to be done.

Taking another drink, he looked over at his new running buddy. Ahmed Jr.'s head and back bobbed up and down from inside his roped-off section.

Abu yelled over in Arabic, "Ahmed, you ever kiss a girl?"

Ahmed's head popped up as he stopped scratching at the outcropping slope. He grinned. "Of course. I'm not a snot-nosed kid like you." Returning to his work, he scooped more dirt with a big trowel.

"I'm no kid." Abu wrinkled his nose. "And kissing your mother doesn't count."

Ahmed never paused, dumping one spade full of dirt after another into a basket beside him. "Then what was her name?"

Abu smiled, his mind filled with images of her curly hair and brown eyes full of affection. He imagined her soft lips pressed against his.

"That's what I thought." Ahmed snickered.

Abu said in a low voice, "Nashwa." His voice grew stronger but had a forlorn vibrato. "Her name is Nashwa, and she's beautiful." He looked over to see his friend scraping at the ground with ferocity. "Did you hear me?"

Ahmed never stopped moving his trowel, going faster and faster.

Abu jumped to his feet. Even from where he stood, the top of a stone door frame was visible a few inches above the ground. Ahmed moved another spade full of dirt, and the outline of a large flat stone filled the space below the door frame.

That's some pumpkins.

Abu hopped over the short rope and reached Ahmed in a few strides.

His friend paused, his eyes full of fire with a faraway look. "This is so much better."

Abu's head tilted. "Huh?"

"A kiss." He went back to digging, his voice going two octaves higher. "This is so much better than a kiss!"

Abu shook his head, and in his most sarcastic tone, he said, "Okay, *kid*. If you say so. I bet you'll change your mind if you ever find a girl desperate enough to kiss you."

Ahmed Jr.'s smile grew huge. "Shut up and start digging."

Trying to control the giddiness welling up inside her, Louisa focused on the plan. They were here to find a tomb, a map, a lost temple, and, at the end of this long rainbow, riches beyond imagining. She pictured herself with unlimited wealth and the freedom to do anything she wanted. She would no longer need to beg from a father who was ashamed of her existence and never be reliant on any man, for that matter. The thought made her smile as she scrubbed away the sweat and grime from the morning's workout.

More than anything on this trip, she missed the ability to soak in a proper bath. She promised to spend whatever it took of her new largess to purchase a home with indoor water closets and heated water for the tubs.

She rubbed a bar of soap, raised her hands, and sniffed under her arm. Jerking her head back, she sneezed, and her eyes watered. By her estimation, she smelled like one of the goats that the herders brought to the nearby well. Luckily, she had become immune to her body odor after three nauseating days. After putting the soap in its wooden box, she rubbed her armpits.

She wished her deadened nasal protection would extend to the surrounding males. All the men had ripened to a malodorous aroma that she could only describe as a musk ox and a skunk mating in a trash heap. To survive, she had become an expert at suppressing her gag reflex. Her two saving graces were the progress they'd made on the excavation and how incredible she felt from all the physical activity.

Today would be the culmination of their hard work: opening the tomb entrance that the foreman's son had discovered. Ben tried warning her not to get her hopes up. He said there might be one tomb or ten more dug into this section of the mound. The rais concurred, telling her they might have to excavate a lot of tombs before finding Perdiccas.

None of those wet blankets could temper Louisa's fiery enthusiasm. She found digging for lost treasure almost as exhilarating as some of her more dangerous jobs. By the end of today, she hoped to be stepping into a place where no one had trod for more than two thousand years.

Would they find the body of Perdiccas where his assassins had laid him to rest? With such fanciful thoughts, Louisa finished cleaning up, got dressed, and rushed out to the dig site.

By the time she'd hiked up the incline, some Lancers were using bars to pry at the large sandstone block plugging the tomb entrance. It took them an hour to dislodge the stone enough to work ropes under and around it. The men used two pulleys attached to a wooden scaffolding system to lift and move the rock door out of the way.

Louisa shifted from foot to foot as the rectangular slab came to rest on the ground next to the gaping doorway. Ben lit a lantern and walked to the threshold. Looking over his shoulder, he motioned her forward with his chin. She couldn't contain the "Eek!" of excitement that escaped as she skipped to his side.

Holding a lantern at the end of his outstretched arm, he lit a small antechamber. On the closest wall were the painted figures of two women carrying dishes to a man who served up a platter to a humanoid creature with the head of a stork. At least, it looked like a stork to Louisa. Painted next to the stork-man was an oval-shaped design with hieroglyphics inside the border. It looked important.

Ben pointed at the creature and the oval. "That's the god Thoth or Djehuty, the god of writing and scribes." He pointed to other ancient images below the scene, moving his finger back and forth, up and down, his brows furrowed in concentration. "The tomb belonged to Userhat and his family. Hmm." Moving inside, he knelt in front of the wall, his lantern lighting up the Egyptian writing closer to the floor. "He was a mid-level Egyptian bureaucrat, and he managed customs in the city of Sa'inu. The city we now call Pelusium."

Louisa frowned, her voice sullen. "So that's it. We keep looking."

He stood. "Not necessarily. Given how Perdiccas died, they would have had to commandeer a finished tomb. We won't know if this is a dead end." He chuckled. "Pardon the pun. We won't know until we excavate the entire tomb."

She frowned.

He's such a muttonhead sometimes. Good thing he's easy on the eyes.

Hearing about this different type of tomb robbing, Louisa looked at the image of its builder, Userhat. How distraught had he been to find his home in the afterlife taken over by his people's latest conquerors? Would her Greek ancestors have compensated him for his troubles?

Moving his lantern around the small room, Ben stopped at the mound of dirt and small stones flowing out of the only other doorway. "Looks like we have our work cut out for us."

Her mood had risen at Ben's hopeful words, and she volunteered to help clear the chamber. In teams of ten, they rotated an hour on and an hour off. Debris filled the room from floor to ceiling, and they emptied it one excruciating basket at a time. The crews formed a long line and passed the dirt down the outcropping. At the bottom, Abu and Ahmed Jr. sifted through every ounce of soil, looking for concealed artifacts.

Seven hours into the mind-numbing and body-punishing process, Louisa's enthusiasm had whittled down to a tiny nub. Even the Lancers' constant singing outside the tomb did little to lift her spirits. For the first time since the clearing began, Louisa insisted on working inside the closed space.

Yet after a few minutes in the dark, dust-filled space, she regretted her decision. Taking advantage of a quick break, she tightened the scarf over her nose and mouth. She still had to clench her lips not to inhale a mouthful of the millennia-old dust.

To see inside the tomb, they had placed mirrors in strategic places, bouncing diffused sunlight into the chamber. Even in the dimness, the walls showcased incredible artistry. While she worked, Ben stood nearby, brushing dirt away from several vibrant scenes.

The Lancer in front of her passed what felt like the hundredth basket to her. She swiveled at the waist and handed the burden to the next in line before swinging back to do it all again.

From what Louisa could see, the images in front of Ben told the story of a funeral for two of the Userhat family's five children. Moving a foot over, Ben started cleaning a scene showing the family's lamentations. Interesting, but disappointing so far. They'd yet to find anything of Greek origin.

At least, Louisa knew they were near the end of the current room. The last crew had cleared away enough dirt that a foot of the farthest wall near the ceiling was exposed. The end of her labor lay only eight feet beyond her current place in the line.

Sowar Jadav pulled away another shovelful from the bottom of the mound. The dirt shifted at the top and tumbled down several feet, forcing the *sowar* to hop back beside Louisa. Rooted in place, he gaped at the far wall. Following his gaze, Louisa let out a small yelp. What little saliva she had in her mouth turned to mud in an instant.

Despite needing to dislodge the mud pie in her mouth, Louisa stared into the green eyes of a man whose distinctive nose marked him as Greek.

We did it. We found him.

A tall presence settled next to her, but still, she didn't break her silent vigil. She contemplated the incredible life story of Alexander's successor. He had been one of the most powerful men on the planet before his own soldiers betrayed him and buried him here hundreds of years before Christ walked the earth.

The sacred moment ended with a muted yet drawled out, "Well, I'll be. Don't that just cap the climax?"

Louisa's eyebrows furrowed as she turned to Ben. After moving the mud to her cheek, she said through tight lips, "Don't know what you said, cowboy, but we did it." She followed that with a hard, playful punch to his arm.

Rubbing his arm, Ben locked his gaze with hers, his laugh lines visible around his blue eyes. She knew he smiled, even with his face covered by a brown bandana.

"Yes, we did, Miss Sophia. Yes, we did," Ben exclaimed through clenched teeth.

Without warning, he bent down, squeezed her in a bear hug, and raised her off the floor. Louisa's carefully crafted modesty flew out the window as she wrapped her arms around his neck and hugged him back while her feet swung free. She felt him shake with laughter as he spun her around. Slowing, he lowered her to her feet before bending over to cough—choking, she knew, on his own mud pie.

Louisa seated herself on the floor next to Abu, who sat cross-legged next to Ben in the tomb. Two lamps illuminated the half-sculpted fresco. It had been three days since they'd finished emptying the larger chamber. On the first day, the crew had cleared two sunken shafts. Ben said they were the usual location of the deceased's sarcophagus.

The first held the bodies of two toddler children. Twin boys, the walls told, who had drowned in a branch of the Nile that had long ago dried up. They found the second shaft unfinished, dug only half as far as the first. Ben explained that the builders probably intended it to be the location of Userhat and his wives.

Yet the mystery of where the body of Perdiccas lay, much less the temple's location, remained trapped in the past. Frustrated by their lack of progress, Louisa took a deep breath. The three of them spent several hours every morning and each evening when the temperatures were optimal, staring at the scene before them. The remarkable work of art showed two Greek warriors standing on either side of a lion, its head sculpted from the wall.

Drawn by his companions, the painting of Alexander the Great to the left of the lion might very well be the most accurate image of the man in existence. He wore a breastplate and greaves, along with the royal diadem in his hair, and his left hand rested on the lion's flowing mane.

His eyes were his most distinguished feature, one dark brown and one bright blue. They gazed all knowing, mocking the three would-be-sleuths. On the other side of the lion stood Perdiccas in similar armor. His right arm gestured to the lion while his piercing green eyes hinted at the pain of his betrayal.

Louisa thought again about how much guilt Perdiccas's killers carried for murdering their friend. Who else would paint his last picture in such an accusatory manner? Why expose their guilt to the world unless driven by their shame? Of course, none of that helped solve her current roadblock to riches.

Ben assured her this find would make the two of them famous. Thousands of tourists would flock to the tomb for a chance to see this picture of Alexander.

More than once, he lamented not having his friend Dr. Chipiez with him. Chippie, as Ben called him, was the most accomplished illustrator the Good Doctor knew. He told her that the painter could have captured the incredible display before them. Ben, Abu, and Sowar Negi, the best artist among the Lancers, had given it their most diligent attempt, but each drawing was an inadequate imitation.

Putting all that aside, Louisa once again reached for the original papyrus letter from Antigenes. She read out loud the most pertinent section for the hundredth time. "I have left a map inside the tomb of Perdiccas detailing how to find the temple. The Lion of Alexander is the key." She put it down again and glanced over at her companions.

Eyes locked on the drawing, Ben said, "I've been over every inch of the lion on the wall. I can't find any hidden writing or any levers to pull. Nothing."

Abu lifted the small carved lion that rested in front of him and inspected it again. He asked, "How many types of keys are there?" He glanced to the left and the right with raised eyebrows.

Ben shrugged. "Many. Some can decode hidden messages. Maybe the inscription is a cipher for the letter itself?"

"I think we're trying too hard." Abu jumped to his feet and approached the sandstone lion extending from the wall. He held its diminutive cousin in his hand. His fingers disappeared into the big cat's mouth, and his wrist wiggled around.

Ben shook his head. "That's the first thing I tried."

After about thirty seconds of moving his wrist back and forth, Abu said, "It went into some small indentations."

Louisa and Ben hopped up and stepped closer.

The teenager put his free hand on the lion's snout. "The trick was to turn it so its feet were touching the stone. Both sets of feet went into small cutouts. They're an exact match." He twisted his wrist within the feline's maw.

They heard a loud click and the sound of chains moving inside the wall. At a crackling, ripping sound, their heads snapped to the blank wall to the right of Perdiccas. Painted plaster parted, and a thin crack grew into a vertical line.

"I turned it counterclockwise." After removing his hand, he pocketed the ivory animal.

The three of them approached the fissure, but as hard as they pushed, it wouldn't budge. Ben unsheathed his shortened saber. With slow, deliberate movements, he cut away the stucco until he revealed a thick stone door. It had opened inward about a quarter of an inch.

Ben grinned at Abu. "Run, get the rais. Tell him we found a door that needs opening and to bring some men and tools."

Abu dashed out of the tomb.

Louisa, bursting with excitement, bounced on her toes. She watched Ahmed, Ben, and three Lancers push while another pried a steel bar into the crevice.

It took the team fifteen minutes to open the door wide enough for someone to squeeze through. Ben insisted they keep going until two people could enter together. When they finished, the men stepped back.

Taking charge, Louisa moved to the forefront. She led with a shaded lantern, throwing its light forward in a solid beam. From close behind, she heard Ben's labored breathing as she peered into the ominous, still darkness beyond. An ancient musty smell assaulted her nose.

The wall to the left of the door held paintings of Perdiccas's early life story. Louisa lit up the floor in front of her, checking for obstacles or, worse yet, triggers to hidden traps. She inched forward until she stood several feet inside the room. Soon, Ben edged beside her, his lamp casting the room in mellow light.

Louisa felt a tap on her shoulder and heard Abu whisper in an insistent yet reverent manner. "Can you step in so I can see?"

Louisa and Ben took two steps. The room contained a single stone sarcophagus sealed by a slab of limestone. Two of the walls portrayed scenes from later in the general's life. The wall with the door showed three of Perdiccas's comrades impaling him with spears. Her beam of light came to rest on a map drawn on the far wall behind the sarcophagus.

Ben started reading from the stone grave. He translated the Greek inscription carved into the lid. "Polemarchos Perdiccas, companion of Alexander. Leader, warrior, friend." He chuckled. "With friends like these," he pointed to the death scene. "Before we interpret the map, let's look at the man himself. Sowars, please help me move this."

Abu and Louisa went around the coffin to stand with their backs to the map. Ben and three of the Lancers lifted the lid. They strained under its weight and struggled to place it on the floor in front of the murder scene. Louisa lifted her lantern, peering into the open sepulcher.

A bare-skinned grin greeted her from beneath a helmet. Its leather and feathered adornments had rotted away long ago. A tarnished bronze sword rested on an ornate breastplate that showed countless dents and scratches but no signs of spear holes. Either he hadn't worn his armor at the time of his death, or the armor didn't belong to him. Louisa thought the former most likely. Perdiccas would assume he had nothing to fear in the presence of his most trusted friends.

Until the final blows fell. I won't ever make that mistake, she thought.

One bony hand gripped the sword, but the other had fallen to his side and broken apart. Louisa caught sight of a slight gleam of gold lying among the scattered digits. She glanced at Abu, who was concentrating on the crew lowering the heavy lid. Her hand snaked out and grabbed a heavy ring from the coffin.

Louisa shielded it from view below the open coffin's edge and allowed herself a glimpse. The ring was topped with the largest sapphire she had ever seen. The point-cut gem glinted even in the dull light. Ben planned to donate anything found in the tomb to Émile and the Bulaq Museum—a promise she did not agree with.

An uneasy feeling of guilt formed in her gut, but it disappeared faster than a desert dust devil. Before she shoved the ring into her trouser pocket, she made a silent promise that when she sold it, she'd send Ben's cut to the museum.

Within a minute of Louisa's hiding the ring, Ben and a gallery of helpers stood on the opposite side. He spent the next thirty minutes making meticulous notes, cataloging the contents of the sarcophagus before he left Sowar Negi to sketch everything within. With vague awareness of this activity, Louisa analyzed the map.

She spent the first five minutes entranced by the image of a snarling wolf priest painted at almost human size.

Is this the mythical Anubis that Antigenes described?

The creature towered over a smaller but, Louisa hoped, more realistic drawing of an Egyptian temple cut into a cliff.

Abu rambled on and on about the incredible monster and how he would love to meet one someday. She wanted to tell him that Antigenes had merely seen a man wearing a wolf skin and a headdress, but she let him enjoy the fantasy he'd concocted.

The temple drawing reminded her of pictures she had seen of Petra, but the architect's style belied a very Egyptian background. The priest and the temple were on the right side of the map with the tomb drawn on the opposite side of the wall. Between were numerous natural landmarks with vague Greek instructions next to the drawings.

Most of the ancient Greek transcribed on the map consisted of simple numbers and directions, such as east, southwest, northeast, and south. A large box canyon and then a maze of ravines and gullies remained the last landmarks before the temple. The only hints for this last obstacle were the Greek words for *under* and *over*.

She heard Ben give the rais instructions to remove the contents of the coffin and box them for transport.

Brushing her shoulder, Ben stepped next to her. "Between us, Ahmed, and Jeevan's men scouting the area for us, we should be able to locate the temple within a week." He started scribbling in a small notebook.

She grabbed his arm. "I'm no romantic, but this feels so surreal. It's as if we have been gliding along with destiny pushing us straight to the temple."

"Maybe, but I disagree with the gliding part," Ben said. "You almost shot me when we first met. Remember?"

"Are you ever going to let me live that down?" she asked.

Ben's scar twitched. "Counting that time, my life has been in danger no fewer than three times in less than two months. So far, our fate is a mix of danger, mystery, and thrilling discovery."

Louisa bounced from foot to foot. "I've never felt so alive. I love it, don't you?"

"Until now, it's been a piece of pudding." Ben paused and looked past her. "I'd wager that finding the temple won't be easy."

She glanced over her shoulder to follow his gaze. A cold shiver ran down her spine as she looked into the accusing eyes of a dying Perdiccas. Her hand moved unbidden to pat the dead man's ring inside her pocket.

Don't be silly.

She turned back to see Ben's grim smile as he said, "No matter what comes next, I wouldn't change a thing." He gave Louisa one of those looks that left her trying to interpret his unspoken words.

Chapter 10

Southeast of Pelusium, Egypt, November 1883

October ended with the Lancers celebrating a festival called Diwali. Fascinated by his first brush with Indian culture, Ben set out to chronicle the events in his spare time. During the five-day celebration, the soldiers stayed "parade ready." They wore dress-blue tops, keeping their equipment spit-polished and their horses groomed.

The goddess honored would visit the cleanest house first. Thus, the need to take a British soldier's extreme cleanliness to new heights. The Lancers fought a valiant but losing battle against the fine desert dust, making Ben wonder whom the goddess would pick.

Between grooming, both personal and equine, the Lancers—accompanied by Ben and Abu—began long-range patrols. They had a hundred square miles of the Sinai Desert to scour. By the afternoon of the first day, Ben swore he could feel every mile as they searched for the landmarks described on the map. He worried that two thousand years of weathering had changed the landscape. If even a single landmark disappeared, it might be impossible to find their way.

Around scouting missions, the festival continued apace. As part of the traditions, the Lancers lit every lantern in camp. All day and night, they shined. So much so, the Lancers made an extra trip to town to buy more kerosene.

The lights made for a cheerful evening ambiance, even if they didn't contribute to a sound night's sleep—sleep Ben needed more than ever now that he was back in the saddle.

Two days before All Hallows Day, the Lancers stopped work. They fasted from sunup until sunset while paying homage to their ancestors. Sowar Chib informed Ben about a late-night ceremony to celebrate the aforementioned goddess in a rite called Lakshmi Puja.

That night, during the darkest part of the month, they held a prayer ceremony. Around midnight, Ben scribbled notes describing the ritual. It included several miniature statues of gods and goddesses and, as expected, a broom. Afterward, the soldiers lit torches and celebrated under the new moon, eating sweet cakes and rice pudding. Abu had been effusive in his praise of the sweets.

Jeevan said the festivities would continue for several more days, but they would not interrupt the patrols again. The following afternoon, their explorations hit pay dirt. After following several false trails in a maze of gorges and ravines, Ben's squad located a match to the box canyon depicted on the map in the tomb.

Everyone broke camp on the last day of the festival and the first of November. Three groups departed the place they'd called home for most of the previous month. Ahmed and his son headed back to their village while two soldiers drove a wagon filled with the tomb's contents toward Port Said. The rest formed a two-by-two column that included several supply wagons. They traveled southeast toward a mountainous area known as Bir El Malhi.

Riding out from camp, Ben gave thanks that his hindquarters had toughened to the point he could sleep on his back, and his thighs no longer screamed as his horse clopped along. Two hours into the journey, Louisa, who had been chattering like a magpie, fell silent. He suspected she felt new sensations in her thighs, calves, and buttocks. How long, if ever, would it take the prideful woman to admit her discomfort?

At least, Louisa had had the good sense to hold her parasol over her shoulders. Ben envied her extra shelter against the relentless sun on such a windless morning. He had to make do with his wide-brimmed hat and a bandana tied to keep the back of his neck from blistering.

The horizon shimmered in the heat of the desert sun as he wondered what Abu was doing. He turned at the sound of an approaching horse. Jeevan, looking regal in his dress blues, galloped forward on his gray stallion, Chetak. Horse and rider began trotting in step to Ben's light brown mare.

"Captain Ben, what a glorious morning." With a grin, he hurried on. "I've been meaning to ask you about your experiences during the war. Were you at Winchester during Torbert's Charge?" His eyes took on a faraway look. "What I would've paid to see eight thousand cavalrymen charging down the valley."

Ben frowned at Jeevan while thinking he had once again underestimated the duffadar. "I'm impressed. Have you studied very many of our battles?"

Jeevan stared at Ben with palpable intensity. "Oh, yes, Captain. I read up on every major cavalry engagement that I can find."

Ben scratched at the stubble on his chin. "Luckily, I wasn't at Winchester, or I might not be here today. I went to school with two infantrymen who were there, though."

Jeevan sidled Chetak closer and leaned in.

Ben shooed away a horsefly. "They were veterans of other battles, but they said it was the most impressive display and the most frightening moment of the war."

The duffadar used his teeth to wet his lips.

Ben's forehead wrinkled as he retold the story the way he'd heard it. "The line of Union cavalry stretched over a half-mile wide to the front of Fort Collier. Custer's band played right in the center, and countless battle flags flew. They said they were almost blinded looking at the riders, the sun reflecting off thousands of sabers."

Ben adjusted his hat, watching the tension build on Jeevan's face. "When the charge began, they said the sound of thunder drowned out the Union bugles. Got so loud it muffled the sounds of the dueling artillery."

Jeevan gulped, eyes wide.

Ben nodded. "They only survived because they were inside a farmhouse as the tide rolled over the front lines."

Jeevan's eyes lost focus, staring into the distance.

Hoping to take the conversation away from his past, Ben asked, "You were at Tel-el-Kiber, correct? How did the Thirteenth do?"

Shake-wobbling his head in a way Ben had seen only Indians do, Jeevan said, "The lads made me extremely proud." His eyes smiled. "We are veterans of several campaigns. In Afghanistan, we fought for three years but never seemed to win anything."

He slapped his saddle horn. "But at Tel-el-Kiber, the Thirteenth charged the Egyptian fortifications under heavy fire. We overran them and rolled up their line." For a moment, he grew grim. "We lost two of our brothers that day. Two more will never fight again." In his serious duffadar voice, he said, "Trust me, Captain Ben. We can take my lads into Narka itself and emerge victorious."[1]

Ben grinned along with Jeevan, but before he could ask about Narka, Jeevan raised his hand. He bellowed out, "Halt and dismount. Rest for twenty. Water the horses."

Forgetting his question, Ben told himself it would come back to him if it was important enough.

---

1. Narka is the Hindu plain for torture and torment. Unlike Hell, it is not a permanent location for people to live out their innumerable lives.

Chapter 11

Pelusium, Egypt, November 1883

The man squirmed in his tailored brown suit and scratched at his face full of stubble while lying on his stomach at the edge of a small rise. The sun glinted off the yellow stone in his pinky ring as he pushed his glasses up to rest on his head.

He adjusted the binoculars. The fuzzy wagon came into focus as it descended into a slight depression about a hundred yards away. He had arrayed his men around the rim of the same hollow. The one chosen for the ambush.

On the wagon seat, two blue-uniformed soldiers were laughing. Their frivolity reached his ears as he raised his hand high. For a short-lived moment, he regretted what he had to do. These men had done nothing to deserve what was about to befall them, but the stakes were too high. Dr. McGehee and Miss Sophia could not succeed.

I'll make sure they never do.

Even after this unpleasantness, the responsibility would fall on him. The world could never find out about the tomb or the temple. The ambush would be the first step in making sure Perdiccas became nothing but a whisper in the sands of time.

With reluctance, his arm fell back to earth. Ten rifles fired in unison. When the echoes faded, there were no more sounds of laughter.

Chapter 12

Southeast of Pelusium, Egypt, November 1883

With care, Ben rationed the handfuls of water he'd poured into a small tin bowl and washed away the grit and dust on his face and upper body. It had to do until they found a freshwater source in a landscape gone from arid to desolate.

With his face buried in his damp hands, the sounds he heard took several moments to register. A rifle had fired. He looked up, hearing shouts and more gunfire to his right. Ben grabbed the Winchester propped next to his bed and ran out of his tent.

There were a few campfires lit as the sun disappeared behind the orange-and-purple-hued horizon. Horses nickering and squealing at the western edge of camp revealed the source of the commotion. Near them were the muzzle flashes of at least four rifles firing into the desert.

On reaching the picket line, Ben heard Lance Duffadar Ram say in a calm voice, "Hold your fire. They're gone."

Ben noted that none of the horses seemed unsettled but rather excited. He attributed their reactions to being battle-hardened British soldiers, just like their riders.

Ram looked in Ben's direction and saluted. Surprised, Ben made to return the motion before he realized Jeevan had joined them. Then he felt awkward.

Cool as a cucumber, Jeevan said, "Report."

"Duffadar, six riders attacked, attempting to steal the horses. We wounded or killed at least two. Their comrades retrieved them before escaping. We have one wounded: Sowar Negi."

The wounded soldier, wincing, held his right arm where he had tied a bandana. Despite the pain, the sowar stood at attention in line with his comrades. Ben stepped next to the man to examine the wound.

"May I?" Ben asked as he reached for the bandana.

The soldier nodded, pulling his blood-covered hand away.

The bullet had entered the inside of the arm and passed through the triceps. He must have been firing his weapon when it happened for the wound to be below the bone. Ben handed his rifle to the next man in line and removed his belt. He tied it around the makeshift bandage to keep pressure on the wound.

"The bullet went in and out. You'll be fine, but I need to sew you up. Follow me, and I'll take care of it."

The sowar tilted his head at Jeevan.

"Well, go on, Sowar, do as Dr. Captain Ben said."

Ben noted the emphasis on the new honorific as he retrieved his rifle. Sowar Negi nodded, and they began walking back.

For a while, Ben heard Lance Duffadar Ram giving more details. "Two thieves were sneaking up on the guards, using the glare of the setting sun to hide their movements. Sowar Jadav, as he returned from dinner, saw them. He fired the first shots, hitting one. We exchanged shots until riders came out of a small dune about two hundred yards out." The conversation faded away.

Entering the circle of tents, Ben and Sowar Negi found everyone prepared for battle. Louisa and Abu stood next to Ben's tent, revolvers in hand. A weird expression crossed Louisa's face, but Ben chalked it up to concern.

"We're safe. They were after the horses." Ben pointed toward the horseless wagons. "Abu, please get my bag." To Louisa, he asked, "Can you assist me with stitching up Sowar Negi?"

Louisa pocketed her gun. "What do you need me to do?"

"Bring at least two more lanterns. And, if you can find any, bring some whiskey."

Without waiting for questions, Ben guided Sowar Negi to his cot and sat him down. Placing his Winchester back in its nightly spot, Ben helped the sowar take off his blue uniform jacket.

Ben grabbed the one lit lantern from his writing desk and hung it on a small peg above Sowar Negi's head. The belt had done its job and reduced the bleeding to a small trickle. Ben finished inspecting the wound as Abu rushed in.

The teen lugged a small suitcase behind him. In reality, it acted as Ben's doctor's bag. It contained everything he needed to set up an emergency surgery.

"Thanks. Open it over there." He pointed his chin to Abu's cot.

Abu huffed, lifting the heavy luggage. He laid it on his cot, undid the buckles, and spread the specialized case open. Ben took one of his two suture kits from the first panel. Lifting the right flap, he revealed another layer of items in pockets and pouches. Another layer down showed a wide assortment of bandage materials. He returned to the sowar, his hands full.

Abu held out a clean shirt. "You should put this on, Dr. Ben."

With his thoughts focused on the task at hand, Ben gave an absentminded nod. "Grab the writing table and bring it here."

Abu stepped around him, still holding the shirt, and picked up the small folding table. He placed it next to Ben. After putting the items on the table, Ben

147

took the proffered top. He ran one arm through a sleeve as Louisa came in holding two lanterns.

She handed one to Abu, but her eyes never left Ben's body. He wondered if she found his old bullet wounds fascinating. He buttoned the last button, hiding his other scars, and her focus changed.

Ben turned back to the medical chest. He removed a small silver tray and the bottle his brother had sent him. He wished he had better conditions for his first use of the newfangled antiseptic, but this would have to do.

He poured a small amount of carbolic acid into the tray, then submerged the needle and the silver thread he would use to stitch up the sowar.

He looked at Louisa. "Whiskey?"

She smirked, producing a rather large flask. "With Lance Duffadar Judge's compliments."

Ben opened the flask and took a big gulp. Louisa raised an eyebrow.

That's NOT whiskey.

He coughed at the unexpected taste. *Closer to moonshine and beer's spicy baby.*

He'd consumed a lot of the clear liquor back in Tennessee, but this alcohol included flavors of pungent spices.

Sowar Negi laughed and winced in unison. "First time drinking Lance Duffadar's homemade *surāh*?"

Ben blinked several times. Clearing his throat, he said, "Uh—that's some potent stuff—" He tried to catch his breath before pouring a little of the amber liquid over each hand. He rubbed them together for several seconds. "Want some?" He held the flask out to the sowar, who shook his head.

"Do you have a wallet?" Ben asked.

"Yes, sir. Left pocket." He motioned to his coat.

Ben rifled through the sowar's jacket and retrieved a leather bifold wallet. The thought that the small money holder held most of the man's worldly treasures occurred to Ben. Holding the billfold in front of the sowar's face, he said, "You'll want to bite down."

With no more prompting, Negi snatched the wallet with his good hand and bit the leather. Sure the sowar was ready, Ben poured some of the surāh over both entrance and exit wounds. A muffled cry escaped the patient.

"Abu, hand me the stool." Ben sat and took the curved suture needle from the table.

"You two." He jutted his chin at his nurses. "Hold the light up on either side of me."

He started with the exit wound, which was twice the size of the entrance wound. Ben had seen worse exits when a bullet tumbled on impact. He wasted little time contemplating the damage that might have occurred if the bullet had not stayed straight or not missed the bone.

"This is going to hurt, but stay still." Ben locked eyes with his still wincing patient. "I'll go as fast as I can."

Sweat covering his forehead, Sowar Negi clenched his jaws tighter and gave a quick jerk of his head.

Twenty minutes later, Ben worked the bandaged arm into a homemade sling made from the soldier's blue-and-white-checked turban. He gave the sowar orders not to use the arm for two weeks unless they came under fire and to report to Ben each morning for redressing. Afterward, Abu helped the exhausted man to his tent.

On hearing his instructions, Louisa asked whether she could help. She wanted to learn proper bandaging techniques. After some thought, Ben made a note to add Abu to the impromptu training.

Sighing with relief, Ben grabbed the flask. He took another gulp and this time handled the burning alcohol without a problem.

Louisa sat, asking the question Ben had kept from asking himself while he concentrated on the stitches. "Do you really think they were just trying to steal the horses?"

Ben offered the open flask to Louisa. She smiled and took a small sip. He said, "Doubt it. The hotel, the train, and now this? We can't tie this attack to the other two, but there was a thief on the train with us."

Louisa took a bigger swig, her eyes closed. She gave a satisfied sigh and handed it back. He stared at the rim of the flask as she continued.

"Who are they? And what are they trying to do?"

Ben shrugged as he tightened the cap. "I don't have a clue. At first, I thought someone found out about the Perdiccas papyrus and wanted it. None of this makes sense unless they're looking for the temple." He passed it back.

She grew serious. "I think that's the best explanation. They're treasure seekers and want to beat us to the gold. We should let Jeevan know we're up against more than common thieves."

Ben sighed. "I'll speak with him and make sure we double the guard."

Louisa gave the flask a shake. A small amount of liquid sloshed around. "I'll see that Lance Duffadar Judge gets this back with a big thank-you." Her eyes lit up. "I wonder if he can make more of this stuff? It's very good."

They rose for breakfast as the first hints of dawn seeped into the night's darkness. A palpable level of wariness had overtaken the encampment. Despite the air of apprehension, Louisa ate dried dates with a hard biscuit and savored the tea in her tin cup. A tea snob since her years near Cambridge, she needed a warm cup to get going most mornings.

On this trip, she counted herself lucky because the Lancers, to a man, shared her obsession with tea. Whether standard British Army Darjeeling or one of their home region's chai varieties, Lancer tea never failed to amaze her.

Following the attack, Jeevan posted the horses inside the ring of tents and doubled the guard. When he heard the raiders might not be simple horse thieves, Jeevan suggested they request more help from the Pelusium garrison. Louisa and Ben argued against the idea, insisting they hurry to beat their attackers to the temple.

After she and Ben had browbeaten Jeevan into continuing the journey, the duffadar had ordered Lance Duffadar Ram and Sowar Chib to leave before first light. They were to track the previous night's raiders back to their camp and get a full account of the enemy. With everyone fed, the day's journey began. Louisa alternated between watching the two groups of flanking riders and trying to solve the riddle of the map's maze.

How do you go under before going up?

This felt like a better use of her time than worrying about an attack that might never come or thinking about the pain in her lower extremities.

They stopped a little before noon to eat lunch. While chewing on a meal of jerky and crusty bread, Louisa spied some hazy brown lumps on the horizon. Back on her mare, she watched the masses swell and solidify with each passing hour. Soon, a small mountain range came into focus.

At regular intervals, three-man teams rotated between the flanks. On the current rotation, Acting Lance Duffadar Bhagat trotted up to Jeevan and saluted. "Duffadar, we've seen dust clouds for the last two hours and estimate at least ten riders."

Jeevan returned the salute. "Thank you." A frown dragged down the corners of his mouth. "With the other riders' estimate, they have at least sixteen horses and maybe as many men."

A touch of concern crept into Louisa's voice. "Do you think your men can handle the threat?"

A huge smile rolled up Jeevan's face. "Don't worry. Whoever they are, each of my men is worth five of them." He huffed. "Besides, the lads are ready for a little excitement."

Ben's tone became serious. "You know, Jeevan, you're just so gloomy all the time. There must be some way to break that aura of melancholy around you."

Eyes squinting, Jeevan looked puzzled.

Louisa suppressed a snort.

Ben raised an eyebrow, and the corner of his mouth threatened to give him away. He forced his expression back to stone. "Given such a pessimistic view of your men's capabilities, we better hope there are no more than eighty bandits out there."

Louisa doubled over in her saddle, laughing. Her mare's ears spun backward, and she gave her horse a calming pat. She attempted to hide her response to the doctor's sarcasm with her other forearm. She'd heard Ben crack jokes only a few times: the afternoon they'd spent on Charles's boat and each time his life was in danger. Maybe he only found his wit when inebriated or under duress.

A twinkle of understanding dawned on Jeevan's face. His gigglemug widened, something Louisa thought impossible. "I'm the way I am because I believe in the most amazing thing."

Ben's expression vacillated between somber and amused. "What's that?"

"Karma."

Ben tilted his head. "And what's that?"

Jeevan sat straight and pulled his shoulders back. "The universe gives you in return exactly what you put out." He waved his hand in a circle. "For example, you've seen how ugly the world can get. That happens because of all the wankers creating bad karma."

Louisa asked, "What does that have to do with you?"

The duffadar's smile disappeared. "Unfortunately, I have to make up for all the bad things I did in my previous lives."

Louisa wondered where he was going with this.

The grin returned. "If I don't put good karma into the universe, I might be reborn as a dung beetle. Who would want to roll shite around all their days?"

Ben's facade broke. He tittered while Jeevan's ears turned red when he looked at Louisa.

Before he could say anything, she spoke, "You don't need to worry, Jeevan. You're the most positive person I know." She winked. "And I'm not offended by a few curse words."

Jeevan's face relaxed, and he beamed.

Chuckling, Louisa said, "Besides, I've met a lot of *malakas* in my life, and I like the idea of forcing them to spend a lifetime covered in *skatá*."[1] [2]

Ben guffawed and bent over his saddle. He immediately yanked on his horse's bridle as the mare nickered and twisted her head to swipe at him. When she settled down, Ben tried to say something else but started giggling like an adolescent girl. Jeevan belly-laughed, and Louisa chortled at the ridiculousness of it all.

While they were winding down, Ben regained enough composure to say in his most sanctimonious voice, "Why, *Lady Sophia*, I am utterly scandalized." He started cackling again.

Using her best imitation of Queen Victoria, whom Louisa had heard speak at Oxford, she fought sanctimony with self-righteous indignation. Pointing her nose skyward, she said, "*Sir McGehee*, I am a complex woman of many talents. I

---

1. Malakas is Greek for wanker.

2. Skatá is Greek for "Shit/Shite."

do not expect a choirboy such as yourself, who heralds from a backwater colony, and who speaks an abomination of the Queen's English, to grasp the proper etiquette of your betters."

Ben's eyes lit up with mirth and something else while Jeevan bellowed with laughter.

With feigned offense—or was it?—Ben said, "Y'all hold up. Say whatever y'all want about me, but never, ever belittle Texas."

Louisa snickered, but wanting to turn the conversation back to the original topic, she said, "Duly noted. Now, what are we going to do about the men shadowing us?"

"The way I see it, we have two choices," Jeevan said.

Louisa looked at him, expecting a joke, but he continued in the same somber tone.

"We try to find the temple with them harassing us all the way, or we strike first." His brow furrowed. "I prefer to be on the offensive."

"I think that sums it up." Ben nodded.

There must be another way, Louisa thought.

An hour later, Lance Duffadar Ram, riding double with Sowar Chib, caught up to the column. Jeevan pulled on his reins, stopping next to his soldiers who had hopped off the lathered and exhausted horse.

Covered in several layers of grime and sporting a bruised cheek, Lance Duffadar Ram snapped to attention and gave a crisp salute. "Duffadar, we followed the horse thieves' trail to a canyon close to our destination. From their tracks, we estimated there were at least forty riders. As we followed them into a ravine, the bastards opened fire." Ram grimaced, his face twisted with grief. "As we escaped, they hit my horse." With lowered eyes, he choked up. "We made it a mile before she faltered." Then, with a fierce look, anger wiped away his sorrow. "We came back to report as fast as possible."

Jeevan leaned over and patted Ram on the shoulder. "Bhandari, you did well." He straightened and twisted to look at Ben and Louisa. "Do you still wish to proceed?"

Ben nodded. "Yes. Do you have more reservations?"

The duffadar's eyes tightened, and his jaws flexed. "Not anymore."

Louisa chewed on the news and pondered how to overcome this even more dangerous problem as they made steady progress toward the mountains. An idea formed, and she waved an excited hand at the two men. "I have another option." They turned to face her. "We set up camp away from the actual entrance and pretend to be searching for the canyon. Then we sneak off to find the temple."

Ben scratched his stubbled chin. "That could work, but they're watching us. They'll become suspicious if they don't see you and me."

Louisa reached up to remove the pins holding her hat to her hair. She held the hat out to Ben. "Sir McGehee, can I borrow yours?"

Ben chuckled as he took off his pork pie and exchanged it for Louisa's postillion.

Plopping it on her head, she wrinkled her nose as she felt and smelled Ben's sweat. "Do you think Abu will mind wearing women's clothes?"

Ben led the caravan to the best place to fake a search. By two in the afternoon, they'd stopped on a mound littered with large boulders. It sat about a mile from a maze of gullies and ravines leading to a wide canyon, which Ben knew wasn't the correct one. The actual starting point lay several miles away.

With enough space to house the horses, the wagons, and the tents, the rise made the perfect place to camp. It also provided ample cover if they were attacked and

360 degrees of visibility over the surrounding flat ground. If their competitors attempted another raid, the desert floor would become a killing field for the sharp-shooting Lancers.

That night, Louisa, Jeevan, Ben, and two Lancers would sneak into the desert, putting Louisa's plan into action. Ben had to assume their enemy had been to the tomb and copied the map after they left. The scavengers did not need to spend a week scouring for landmarks, either. They planned to follow Ben and Louisa's group to the actual entrance. Of course, they would find nothing if they followed the wrong Ben and Louisa.

Won't matter if I can't recruit some decoys, he thought.

"I'm not doing it. I'll be a laughingstock." Stomping his foot, Abu crossed his arms across his chest. Glaring at Ben, the teenager appeared to dare him to say something.

The boy's resistance angered Ben but also confounded him. Why did he feel so much pride in the boy right now? "You'll get over it, and they'll forget after a while." Ben's face grew hot watching the boy's eyes tighten. "I'm tired of arguing with you. I'm your guardian, and you'll do what I say."

Through clenched teeth, Abu said, "I won't."

"You damn sure will. Besides, this will hopefully keep us from having to fight the thieves."

Abu's eyes drifted to the ground, his jaws unwinding.

Hoping to reassure the boy further, Ben switched to a soothing voice. "It's embarrassing, but it may save someone's life."

Abu sighed. "Fine." The word sounded anything but.

Louisa said, "I'll give you five pounds for helping us out, Abu."

Ben hadn't noticed her at the tent opening until she spoke. His stomach tightened as Abu looked at her, his eyes widening.

She smiled back. "That's right. Five pounds, now, and I'll buy you a brand-new suit when we get back to Cairo."

"Really?" Abu asked.

Louisa nodded. "You'll be so handsome. The girls won't be able to resist you."

Abu grinned, and his face turned brownish pink. "That sounds great."

"Here." Louisa held out the note.

The teenager grabbed it.

"Come to my tent. We'll pick out the right clothes." Louisa motioned for him to follow.

With a sour face, Abu shot darts dripping with resentment at Ben and marched out.

After spending so much time working with the teenager, the Lancers had adopted Abu as their unofficial mascot. Some men had taken on a big brother role with him and were teaching him Dogri.

Abu had found a friend in Sowar Singh, the youngest Lancer at nineteen. Ben had been grateful to see Abu act like a teenager these last few weeks with Umrao and Ahmed Jr. as buddies. For the first time that Ben could remember, the boy's eyes did not have a constant edge of sorrow.

Umrao Singh was also the tallest of the Lancers and volunteered to be Ben's double. The two friends would get to pull off the ruse together. Ben hoped Abu would see it as a consolation, but when he saw the friends in costume, Ben had to bite his lower lip not to laugh.

Inside Louisa's tent, a miserable Abu wore her linen work blouse, linen skirt, and white hat with the blue ribbon. The sleeves of the dress and the skirt were a hand too short but, from a distance, should pass muster. Next to him stood a grinning Umrao, wearing Ben's trousers, suit jacket, and cavalry hat.

After some intense scrutiny, Louisa suggested Abu use her parasol to better hide his face. In the end, everyone but Abu thought the plan a grand idea.

To pull off the charade, a group of eight Lancers, Abu, and Sowar Singh would leave camp each day to search the dead-end maze and false canyon. Ben figured the bandits were waiting until they found the actual entrance to strike, but to be on the safe side, he set a three-day deadline to find the temple. If the search team failed, they'd go with Jeevan's plan and eliminate the threat.

For the rest of the day, Ben worked with Abu and Louisa on bandaging. Abu would redress Sowar Negi's wound while the real search team looked for the temple. Despite Abu's irritation with Ben, the teen mastered the concepts with ease.

Who knows? Ben thought. *Maybe he'll become a doctor someday.*

Chapter 13

Bir El Malhi, Sinai Desert, Egypt, November 1883

Close to midnight, Ben led the group of five back the way they'd come. Each of their horses wore hoof coverings to further muffle their escape. Rolling his neck, Ben tried to get used to the cape of his replacement cap he'd borrowed from Jeevan.

He whispered to the duffadar, "Where'd you get the Legionnaire cap?"

At the same decibel level, Jeevan told him, "Port Said. Great story. I traded my turban to a French Foreign Legionnaire from Portugal. He said he had joined because he'd murdered someone back home. Please don't lose it."

"I'll treat it like my own."

Well away from camp, Ben led them in a semi-circle toward the starting point for their search. They would begin near what he believed to be the actual box canyon, based on the tomb map. Locating what he suspected was a tunnel, using ancient cryptic messages and landmarks, would be the challenge.

The clues spoke to a particular sign or natural feature marking the entrance. Paranoid from the news that the thieves had last been seen nearby and might notice Ben's group, he decided they couldn't waltz across the half-mile of open ground in the canyon. Instead, he would take them along the rim of the cliffs to keep them hidden. He also hoped the elevation would provide the vantage point they needed to locate the mysterious landmark. Worst case, they'd use ropes to scale down to the canyon floor to search at ground level.

At first light, the group made its way up a small animal path to a clearing at the top of the cliffs. Sowar Jadav stayed with the horses while the team of four played leapfrog across the rocky, broken landscape. Sowar Lama took point. He set up a lookout position while Louisa, Jeevan, and Ben pushed ahead to the next good hiding spot. They reversed roles before starting over.

With an exaggerated hand wave, Ben let Louisa know the best way to navigate the current stretch of rock.

"*Dr. McGehee*, what *ti diáolo* is your problem?" Louisa hissed.

As if you don't know, he thought.

Fighting his fear of heights, Ben turned and crouched down. He used his left hand to balance on the nearest rock, a mere five feet from the thirty-foot drop. His eyes darted from the edge to Louisa's icy stare. "What do you mean?" he shot back in a hushed tone. He tried to stay calm, but his ire rose, commensurate with the drop in temperature of her look.

Jeevan stopped short. In a voice loud enough for both of them to hear, he said, "Is there a problem?"

Louisa looked over her shoulder. "The doctor and I are having a *friendly* conversation."

As Louisa turned back, Jeevan leaned around her with his eyebrows arched in the universal "What'd you do?" look.

Louisa's glare bored into Ben. "You were a jackass to me during the first aid lesson, but I bit my tongue. Now you're giving me the silent treatment. Why?"

Ben shot her a stern look. "Let me ask you something. Do you always have to do it your way?"

"My way is almost always the best way."

Ben clenched his jaws, sucked in a big breath, and blew it out his nose as he counted to five. "Have you considered that your way might be the wrong way when it comes to raising a teenager?"

Louisa leaned her head back, and her brow furrowed. "So this is about Abu?"

Ben said in a low growl, "You're damn right it is. It was not your place to bribe him."

"Well, it wasn't like your bullying was working," Louisa snarled back. "My approach was the most expedient."

Ben pointed to his chest and raised his voice enough that his reply echoed back. "Oh, yeah, great job. You just taught him he can blackmail me the next time I need him to do something."

Louisa opened her mouth to fire back, when Jeevan whispered in his drill sergeant voice and not his good karma Jeevan voice, "Shut up."

Louisa twisted to look at the duffadar, who glared at both of them with narrow eyes and a curled lip.

"You are like the new parents of a toddler. This ends now. I won't allow you to jeopardize the lives of my men with your foolishness." He took a breath, and the lecture continued. "You will apologize and shake hands. We will hear no more of this until we get back to camp." An angry Jeevan pointed. "Miss Louisa, you will apologize for not consulting Abu's guardian on a parental decision. Captain Ben, you will apologize for being a pansy and not speaking your mind earlier."

Both of them averted their gaze at the "take no guff" body language coming from a man used to commanding dangerous warriors. They locked eyes, spitting fire at each other.

Ben muttered, "I wasn't the one who brought it up." He drew a death stare from the duffadar. Looking back to Louisa, Ben said, "You first."

Through gritted teeth, Louisa whispered, "Fine. I'm sorry I didn't speak with you first."

Ben thought she bit off the rest of the sentence because of the double barrels shooting her in the back. The boiling pools of brown trying to melt him into his boots were anything but sorry. Scowling, he replied, "I accept your apology. I'm sorry for not telling you how upset I was earlier." His tenor deepened to a bass. "Next time, *you'll know.*"

Jeevan cut him off. "Now shake hands, and let this be the end of it."

The two continued their staring contest as Ben stuck out his hand. This time Louisa grabbed his hand with all her might. Ben bore down, meeting her force with more of his own. The two of them leaned into the shake, trying to get leverage.

Louisa never flinched.

At that moment, with their dirty hands clasped and angry eyes locked, Ben had a sudden, potent desire to kiss this aggravating, stubborn, gorgeous woman. He fought the urge to yank her to him and mash his lips to hers.

Shocked by his own animalistic hunger, Ben blinked first. With a gulp, he forced his way out of the vice-like handshake. He could have sworn that he saw disappointment on Louisa's face when he broke contact.

"Now, let's get back to business," said Mr. Good Karma.

Ben returned to picking the safest path forward, but that moment kept sticking in his mind. In the six weeks he'd known Louisa, she had never admitted fault. Until ordered to, anyhow.

Anyone would get irritated with that woman, Ben thought.

That said, she wasn't as unreasonable as some women. She had some redeeming qualities. For example, she didn't waste his time on frivolous things like the woman he wanted to forget. Also, her fierceness and sense of adventure pushed him to do crazy things like this wild goose chase.

She's not all bad, but damn it.

It took the team several more hours to work along the ridge to the back side of the canyon. As the rest of the group ate lunch in the shade of a small overhang, Ben lay at the edge of the drop, scanning for the landmark from his map.

Unable to find it, he peered again at his hand-drawn map, triple-checking what looked like a paw print. Drawn next to the Greek phrase "travel under the paw of Anubis" was the word σπέρα, which he had translated as "hope."

He assumed the paw would be a series of rocks or a natural formation like all the other map landmarks. Lost in the puzzle, Ben didn't hear Louisa approach until her shoulder brushed his as she lay next to him. He jerked at the touch and bit back a small yelp.

"For a tough guy, you scare easier than a *mikró korítsi*."[1] Louisa grabbed his wrist and brought the map closer to her.

"Well, you shouldn't sneak up on people like that," said Ben, fighting the urge to yank the map away and wanting to scoot closer to her at the same time.

"May I?" she asked. He had to choke down a growl when Louisa lifted the map out of his grasp. She rotated it around at different angles. Every few seconds, she'd poke her head from behind the map long enough to reevaluate the landscape below. As Ben's agitation boiled over, she exclaimed, "Ah hah! *Je comprends*."

"What?"

Louisa pointed below. The sun had passed its zenith and begun its descent behind them, causing the outcroppings atop the canyon walls to cast a shadow on the box canyon's floor.

He still didn't see it.

"Keep looking."

---

1. Greek for a "little girl."

It hit him like a thunderclap. "Duh. They drew it from the other direction, and *spera* didn't mean 'hope.' It's short for *kalispéra*."[2] Ben looked behind them to find the source. The outcropping they'd chosen for their lunch shelter had four toe-like rocks on top of the larger pad.

He turned to find Louisa evaluating him with a smug Cheshire Cat grin planted on her face. His elation at solving the problem and the moment of gratitude he felt evaporated, replaced by intense displeasure. This time, he felt zero desire to kiss her.

An edge of indignation entered his voice. "You don't have to be so proud. I would have figured it out, eventually. Anyway . . ." He let his irritation go. "Good job. Let's get going."

After using binoculars to surveil the surrounding area for any sign of their pursuers, the group secured a rope to a boulder about ten feet from the ledge. Ben put on leather gloves, gripped the rope, and backed toward the edge. "Jeevan and Lama can lower you when I get to the bottom."

Louisa twisted her face and mouthed an exaggerated "Okay." She slow-rolled her eyes. "See you at the bottom."

Inching his way down the side of the cliff, Ben leaned back with his boots anchored to the stone and the rope twisted around his belt on one side. Still confused by her reaction, he made it ten feet from the top when he quit trying to figure it out.

I'll never understand that woman.

A few small rocks fell to his right. Seeking the source of the tiny avalanche, he saw Louisa hanging onto the side of the cliff. His mind racing to the worst conclusion, he thought she'd slipped off the ledge. Yet instead of falling, she

---

2. Kalispéra is Greek for "Good evening" or "Good afternoon."

floated down the wall. His moment of fear turned to relief before changing to agitation.

With quick, sure, practiced movements, she went from one hand or toe hold to the next, finding purchase in the tiniest cracks and ledges. He stopped, stunned at the ease and speed with which she descended.

Without pausing, she gave him a wink as she moved below him, stirring him back to action. He made his way down the last fifteen feet to the ground, still thinking about how her eyes had shone while she spidered down the rock.

When he reached the bottom, she slapped him on the back and snickered. "*Good job.*"

I deserved that, he thought.

In a few minutes' time, she'd bested him twice. He pushed down his pettiness and went magnanimous. "Very impressive. Where did you learn to climb like that?"

She bit back whatever witty reply he imagined she'd armed herself with and said, "Home. Corfu has a lot of cliffs, and I've climbed them all."

"You must have had a lot of fun growing up there." He almost missed her slight frown that formed at his words. Filing that away, he signaled up to Jeevan to come down.

They found the entrance along the escarpment in a straight line from the paw-shaped shadow. Cut directly into the cliff, a notch five feet deep hid an arched opening that started to the left. Even from above, it would be almost impossible to tell that the small cutout led to a tunnel.

Ben doubted the builders had used the shadows to line up their tunnel. He found it miraculous that Antigenes and his men had stumbled upon the entrance at all.

Could have followed someone.

Without thinking, he looked over his shoulder for a second. The canyon remained as empty as a church on Mardi Gras.

The Greeks probably put the rocks there.

He refocused on the tunnel, peering into the darkness beyond the arch. Preparing to enter the tunnel, Ben and Louisa lit small lanterns they'd brought for this very purpose. Ben led the way, with Louisa bringing up the rear, providing light for the Lancers sandwiched in the middle.

The first things Ben noticed were the slight slope downward, the tall ceilings, and the smooth walls. At over eight feet tall, he wondered why they'd wasted so much labor on unnecessary headroom. Running his hand along the wall, he found no traces left by rock-working tools.

Ben soon lost any concept of the distance they'd traveled in the tunnel's oppressive gloom. To compensate, he used his pocket watch to keep track of the time they spent underground. After they had walked for ten minutes, he spotted a small gleam on the dust-covered floor ahead.

Ben picked up a *khopesh* and brushed it off. Holding the question mark–shaped sword in the light of his lantern, he examined the blade and its handle made of smoothed bone. The group crowded close. Given what Ben knew about the missing army of Perdiccas, its pursuit of an Egyptian army, and that a temple might lie ahead, it wasn't unexpected to find an ancient relic. The surprise, for Ben, was that this khopesh wasn't ancient enough.[3]

Holding out the sword, Ben said, "We're on the right track, but this is strange." The group had formed a small circle with the weapon in the middle. "Most swords like this khopesh are from 1,000 B.C. or older. Instead of bronze, this blade is made of Damascus steel." He pointed to the colored striations in the met-

---

3. A khopesh is a curved, scythe-shaped sword used by the Ancient Egyptians, as well as many of the Semitic peoples of the time.

al. "Look at the amazing bluing technique and the etchings. A master swordsmith created this."

The blade showed no signs of rust. Designs he'd never seen on any ancient weapon covered the polished steel. Why the owner had abandoned such a valuable weapon, he couldn't say. Ben finished up his teaching moment. "This is less than nine hundred years old, which adds another mystery. The weapon's date of creation shows the temple being in use a thousand years after most Egyptian religions disappeared." He spun the weapon and held it out, handle first. "Take a look, and when y'all are done, Sowar Lama, please secure it for me."

Handing the khopesh to Jeevan, he continued forward into the dark. Soon, the others' footsteps echoed on his heels. Focusing on the grade leveling off and starting upward, Ben missed the alcoves. He'd taken two steps past the openings when he heard, "Captain Ben, shine your light over here."

Ben stepped next to Jeevan, who pointed his revolver into a void on the left. "I could swear I saw eyes."

Pulling his revolver, Ben thrust his lamp into the void. Dark outlines came into focus. They looked at a statue of Anubis, or so he assumed, based on the shape of the head. What made him pause were the eerie golden eyes glittering back at him from the darkness.

Jeevan shuddered. "Gives me the creepers!"

Stepping forward, Ben illuminated a much bigger space than he'd first imagined. In the middle of a square room, the statue solidified into the visage of a giant black Anubis.

Is that really Anubis?

A wolf-headed, humanoid creature sat on a chair, wearing priest's clothes. It held the common Was scepter in its right hand.[4] In its left, it held a symbol Ben

---

4. The Was scepter is an Ancient Egyptian symbol of power and dominion.

had never seen in Egyptian iconography. The object was the size of a grapefruit and shaped like an eight-sided diamond.

The priest's small, rounded ears made the creature look more like a common wolf. The absence of tall, pointed jackal ears made Ben question whether the creature represented the Egyptian god at all.

The eyes glinted back at Ben from two orbs painted a distinct color of amber above a smiling snout. If wolves could do such a thing. Something else was off. It took a moment for it to come to him. The hands and feet were not human. With four fingers and what appeared to be a thumb, the digits of each hand ended in long claws, but the feet had even more of a wolf's paw shape. Ben had to pinch himself. Here was a statue that might pre-date Anubis himself. Such an incredible find might herald even greater discoveries to come.

Flinders, eat your heart out.

Jeevan's voice trembled. "Who is that supposed to be?"

"At first, I thought it was Anubis, the Egyptian god of death, but the features are all wrong, so your guess is as good as mine."

Ben moved around the statue, inspecting the entire space. The alcove was a crypt with three rows of holes carved into each of its three walls. Most of the shafts held a wooden sarcophagus, inserted head first.

He found it strange that no drawings or carvings adorned the walls. With the others in tow, Ben crossed the tunnel to the room's twin. He found fewer coffins but also one big difference. A female wolf presided over this crypt. The statue had four human-shaped breasts, stacked two by two, under her full-length gown, punctuating the creature's nonhuman features.

"Jeevan and Lama, please help me remove a coffin." Everyone stepped close to one of the filled holes in the middle row, and Ben put his lantern on the ground. With the coffin at waist height, he grabbed one foot, and Jeevan held the other.

"On three. One, two, three." The two men pulled. The coffin scraped forward about six inches, allowing the sowar to grab the end. "Okay, again." They pulled in unison, and the coffin slid several inches out of the hole. Louisa stepped up, and together the four of them pulled until only the head rested on the stone.

"Have you ever seen a coffin this big?" Jeevan nodded toward the extra-large sarcophagus.

Ben shook his head. "Let's lower one end to the floor."

They grounded the feet, picked up their lanterns, and inspected the wooden lid. Adding to Ben's consternation, there were no hieroglyphics and zero paint on the coffin top, carved to resemble a female wolf priestess.

Could it be predynastic?

Ben unsheathed his long knife, stuck it in the crack of the lid, and pried. Jeevan and the sowar followed suit until the group heard a sucking sound as the lid came loose.

God only knows when this was sealed.

"Let's put it over there." Ben directed them to place the lid against the wall.

Louisa pointed her lantern at the head and gasped. "So morbs." She shivered and said, "That can't be a dog, can it?"

Adding his light, Ben found tattered clothes and bones. Ancient Egyptians mummified animals by the thousands, so to find the remains in this state added to the deepening mystery of its age.

He shrugged. "No, but maybe there's a wolf species that large." He peered at each of the glowing faces around the ancient casket. "The skull could belong to an ancient species that died out like the mammoths. The temple followers might've found a graveyard of giant wolves and venerated them. That could explain the lack of mummification because they were already bones."

"If you say so." Louisa lifted her shoulders.

"Why did they put clothes on it?" The sowar's eyes were enormous.

Ben scratched his chin. "Good question. They probably bestowed the title of priest or priestess on each skeleton they found. Hopefully, we'll find some hieroglyphics to tell us what happened." He walked back into the tunnel. "Let's go. I don't want to run out of kerosene down here."

It took another ten minutes of steady walking before Ben sat his lamp down and interlaced his hands on top of his cap. "Well, this is disappointing."

The others leaned around him to find a jumbled pile of rocks blocking the way forward. Louisa squeezed by and climbed the rubble as high as she could without sliding down. Stooped over, while perched several feet off the floor, she became a statue.

Ben scrunched up his face. "What're you doing?"

Louisa held up her finger and shushed him. They watched as she closed her eyes, moving her ear toward the corner, and tilted her head one way, then the other. She moved to the left side of the cave-in talus and went silent again.

In a brief pause, she grabbed a few rocks from the top corner of the pile. She tossed them to Ben and Jeevan. They passed them back to the sowar, who began a small pile. After each rock or two, she held her hand up to the corner. Then she backed down the heap of stones.

Louisa pointed at the small hole. "If we dig there, we might be able to get out. I felt and then heard a very light breeze. After I removed those rocks, it's now a decent current."

Ben scampered up the ramp of medium-size rocks using careful, measured steps and held his hand to the corner. Sure enough, he felt a slight current, which meant they must be close to the exit. During the entire journey, they'd encountered nothing but still, stale air.

"Good job." He grinned at Louisa. "We've come this far. I reckon we should give it our all." Moving back down, he said, "Form a line. Louisa, take the lead since you're the lightest."

She scooted around him, took her place at the top, and began passing back stones. It took an hour of assembly-line work for them to dig a man-size hole four feet deep. With only her boots visible on their side, Louisa called over her shoulder, "We're through. I can even see some light ahead."

The team members redoubled their efforts, and ten minutes later, they shook off the dust on the exit side of the blockage. Ben sighed in relief. They had more than enough kerosene for a return trip. Emerging into daylight a short walk later, Ben squinted and held his hand up to shade his eyes.

Shaking the sunspots from his vision, he kept blinking while assessing their surroundings. They'd come out near the top of a large hill. He hadn't noticed the incline being enough for them to have climbed so high. One more unanswered question for the pile.

In front of and beneath them lay a small valley with a taller hill on the other side. Ben wanted to see if he could tell where they were in relation to the tunnel's entrance, so he scrambled up the twenty feet to the peak and looked in the direction they'd come.

A brilliant blue sky with scattered white striations hung above an impossible maze of ravines and gullies. From where he stood, it was about a mile to the box canyon. He shook his head. They'd never have gotten this far without finding the tunnel and digging through the blockage.

Louisa joined him. "One step closer."

"Thanks to you. There's no way we would have crossed that before we ran out of time." Ben turned around to inspect the hill on the far side. "The map said we're supposed to go up, so let's see what's on the other side."

Maybe the tension they'd felt since leaving the main group had gotten to him, but Ben thought they should celebrate by lightening the mood. He grinned. "Race you to the bottom." Without waiting, he began taking loping strides toward the valley below.

"Hey, cheater!"

Still grinning, he raced past Jeevan, who gaped at the two of them. Tapping the duffadar on his arm, Ben said, "You're it."

"Oh, no, you don't."

Soon, several sets of pounding feet echoed off the hill. Nearing the bottom, Ben felt the steps getting closer and heard heavy breathing. On the valley floor, he ran to one of the few feeble bushes surviving on the barren land and grabbed a branch. "Base!"

Louisa sprinted past him. "Race you to the top."

Jeevan had his hands on his knees when a laughing Sowar Lama ran by, pursuing Louisa.

"We'll see who gets to the top first," Ben mumbled under his breath, jogging after her.

Ben found the climb much more strenuous than the descent. Halfway up, he thought he might start walking, but he'd begun to make up ground on the petite young woman. Hope sprang, if not eternal, just enough to give him the spark he needed to increase his tempo.

Even huffing up the hill, he marveled at how gracefully the light-footed Louisa glided over the rugged terrain. Distracted, he almost missed Sowar Lama dropping to his stomach near the summit. With emphatic arm waving, the sowar signaled for them to stop.

Louisa slowed and slunk into a crouch after Ben passed her. He stooped down to her level and fell back to match her pace. At the top, they lowered themselves to their hands and knees and crawled toward the sowar.

Before they could see over the peak, she said, "We'll call this one a draw."

Ben chuckled until he peered over the edge, then went speechless.

Impossible.

On the far side, a fifty-foot-high cliff anchored a natural crescent-shaped valley. Carved into the stone at the center of the moon-shaped bluff was a colossal temple facade. Giant columns ran along the front, sculpted from the rock. They created an impressive lead-up to a large triangle-shaped entrance.

The artists in the tomb had done a remarkable job rendering the temple layout. From Ben's current vantage point, he saw a large hole in the ridge beyond, running in a straight line from the entrance.

Must be the open-air sanctuary holding the temple's altar.

The next sight left Ben dumbfounded. A small village spread across the valley floor, full of people going about their lives. Even with the naked eye, he could see that half of the villagers wore the tunic-and sandaled-uniform of most of today's Egypt. The other half wore Ancient Egyptian dress and hairstyles.

Ben lifted his glasses and rubbed his eyes.

Unreal.

Tomb paintings had come to life. These ancient ghosts were very much flesh and blood. To emphasize the absurdity of what he saw, Egyptian warriors flanked the temple entrance. One had a khopesh and a shield, while the other stood ramrod straight with a rifle on his shoulder.

"How?" Louisa asked.

"Uh." Try as he might, Ben had no words for Louisa.

Stirring up dust, Jeevan crawled next to him. "Who are they?"

Ben sneezed into his sleeve. "I think they're the ones who tried to rob us."

Louisa tore her gaze from the scene below to look at Ben. "Really?"

He dug a pair of binoculars out of his kit. "It makes the most sense. They haven't been trying to beat us to the treasure."

"They've been guarding it," Louisa whispered.

"Exactly."

Jeevan frowned. "What now?"

The presence of an active village had changed Ben's thoughts on many topics. Somehow, this secret society had survived in the Sinai for thousands of years. Some might chalk it up to the site's remoteness, but to Ben, the primary reason had to be the importance its inhabitants placed on keeping this place a secret.

Someone from the village had learned about the Perdiccas papyrus and had set out to stop them from reaching the temple. The fact that the inhabitants below had escalated to shooting at the Lancers meant they would have no problem killing to stay hidden.

Even with the increased risk, Ben couldn't pass up this opportunity. He caught Jeevan's eye and then Louisa's. "I have to get a closer look."

The four of them spent the rest of the day watching the village and the temple while discussing options. The safest plan was to find a way across the cliffs to the open-air atrium.

Determined to get a first-hand look at a society that until today Ben had thought extinct, he suggested he and Jeevan make their way down to the village and steal some clothes. At night and in disguise, they would attempt to enter the temple because the guards never appeared to challenge anyone.

Louisa argued against Ben's plan as dangerous. She championed going across the cliff to the atrium. When Jeevan sided with Ben, she relented without a fuss, which Ben found out of character for her.

The duffadar's reasons were sound. Crossing the cliff would expose them for too long and involve crossing dangerous ground in the dark. When Louisa refrained from demanding to join them on their mission, a seed of suspicion took root in Ben's mind. Yet as he prepared for the night's reconnoiter mission, his concern became lost in the details.

When darkness overtook the valley, Ben and Jeevan worked their way down the slope, approaching the village. The duo had left all their supplies and most of their identifying clothing with Louisa and Sowar Lama.

Carrying only their revolvers, extra ammo, and an empty bag, they headed for a small adobe-style home on the edge of the town—the one with a laundry line full of hanging clothes. Reaching the dwelling's backyard, they stopped behind a small garden shed. That spot gave them access to the clothes and an excellent visual of the house.

Ben peered around the corner, guarding the back door, his revolver ready. Jeevan shuffled out of the shadows to abscond with two light-brown tunics and several long pieces of cloth. From behind a bed sheet, his hands snaked out to unpin first one and then the other dress-length shirt. Jeevan ran back in a crouch. He handed the clothes to Ben and moved with stealth toward the back door.

"What are you doing?" Ben hissed.

Near the threshold, Jeevan grabbed something and raced back with a huge grin. He held up two pairs of sandals. Ben gave him a thumbs-up while shaking his head. Taking turns, they changed behind the shed, putting their clothes in the bags they'd brought.

They were both dressed like villagers. Ben whispered to Jeevan, "Ready?"

The duffadar's eyes lit up, and his bright white smile glowed in the moonlight. "Always."

Ben nodded and led them through the darkness, skirting behind several homes. They stepped out of the shadows onto the torch-lit, sun-hardened avenue as if they belonged. Ben's plan required them to be bold while avoiding the residents.

With only a few villagers on the road, Ben felt confident they would reach the temple until a constant flow of people began streaming into the street.

So much for the plan. Keep calm. Don't panic.

Ben walked on the outside of the road, trying to hide behind Jeevan. Within a few minutes, hundreds of men, women, and even children joined the throng heading toward the temple.

Must be the entire village.

The crowd shuffled forward in silence with what he could only describe as a sense of reverence. Like fish clinging to the edge of the school, the duo moved up the temple steps. Ben edged beside Jeevan, putting him between Ben and the upcoming soldiers. The guards greeted the villagers with a silent salutation. The first would touch his mouth and then his heart. The second started at the heart and moved to his mouth.

As Ben neared two huge blazing braziers on the nearest side of the entrance, his jaws tightened. The closest guard looked right at them and touched his mouth and then his heart. Ben nodded to hide his eyes before touching his hand to his heart and then moved it to his mouth. Out of the corner of his eye, he saw Jeevan touch his mouth and then his heart.

Oh, shit.

Ben clenched the handle of his revolver, but the man just smiled and waved them through the opening. Ben floated between the giant columns, inching to the outside again as they walked through the tall triangular portal into a torch-lit hallway. A profound surrealness washed over him. No longer attempting to scry into the past through the eyes of the dead, he was experiencing history in real life.

Funneled closer together, people in the crowd bunched up and slowed. Ben grabbed Jeevan's sleeve to stay connected as he brushed along the side of the tunnel. For five minutes, the group shambled forward to the echoes of hundreds of sandals slapping stone. From above the villagers' heads, Ben saw the parade spilling into the temple's natural atrium through another triangular portal.

A hallway branched off in both directions as Ben moved closer to the exit. Beyond the portal, villagers continued to encircle a raised altar.

At the intersection, Ben pulled Jeevan out of the stream. He went to one knee and fiddled with his sandal, hoping the villagers would ignore them. Keeping up his ruse, he glanced down the hallway.

Instead of two solid walls, the side facing the sanctuary consisted of a series of intricate railings and columns. They formed a cloister looking into the small canyon. It reminded Ben of a monastery in Italy he'd once visited, looking for medieval-era documents about Nineveh.

As the last of the stragglers went by, Ben hopped to his feet and pointed with a nod away from the exit. They moved three columns farther into the corridor and stepped up to the railing to hide in the column's shadow. Anyone glancing down the hallway would find it empty.

Jeevan leaned in and whispered, "What are we doing?"

Tilting his head toward Jeevan, Ben lowered his voice. "I want to watch. Not be a participant."

Hundreds of villagers formed a circle around the altar. Hidden, Ben and Jeevan observed as the people greeted one another with the silent salutation.

Out of the relative silence came low chanting that refocused Ben on the torch-lit scene. The crowd soon picked up the slow rhythm, growing louder with each pass. After several verses, Ben realized it was the dead language of Ancient Egyptian being sung by native speakers.

The linguists had gotten a lot wrong but a lot right. Able to discern every third or fourth word, Ben recognized a few phrases: Fiery One, Great of Valor, Dweller within the Cavern of Her Lord. They were all names of deities mentioned in the Book of Gates who guarded the way to Egyptian paradise in the afterlife.

Hearing footsteps in the main tunnel, he and Jeevan squeezed farther into the shadows. The people closest to the entrance moved aside, allowing a group of ten men to enter the ring and walk up the steps leading to the altar. The gap filled in behind them.

The first eight men wore a mixture of clothing like the villagers. As Ben viewed the procession from behind, the last two captured most of his attention because of their contrasting apparel.

Of Nubian descent, the much darker man on the right wore the white linen half-tunic of Ancient Egypt. Shirtless, he had a shaved head, except for a long braid formed at the back of his skull. Around his neck hung the most dramatic piece of jewelry, a broad-collared necklace made of glass beads, lapis, and gold. Next to him walked a stocky man in a modern brown suit.

The new group stopped short as the crowd on the far side of the altar parted. When the circle closed again, a beautiful melody rose from the assembled, and they swayed back and forth. Ben wished he'd brought his binoculars because, from thirty yards away, he couldn't make out the details. Looking over to Jeevan, he blinked to see the soldier holding a small pair of binoculars.

"Can I borrow those?" Ben whispered.

Giving a slight shake no, Jeevan held up a finger as he brought the binoculars to his eyes. Silence fell over the crowd, and Ben turned back in time to see the impossible. Two giant wolf heads bobbed into view, attached to long hairy bodies as they moved up the far steps.

The brown canine humanoid was a little larger than the gray one, but both wore linen half-tunics and broad-collared necklaces like the Nubian's. Several grapefruit-size objects were on a tray carried by Gray while Brown held a Was scepter and a melon-size diamond-shaped object.

"*Mainū badanāma kītā jāvēgā*," escaped from Jeevan, much louder than a whisper.[5]

Mouth agape, he shook the binoculars at Ben. Ben grabbed them and squinted through the lenses to get a closer look at the costumes. At the current distance, their movements were very realistic.

---

5. Mainū badanāma kītā jāvēgā is Punjabi for "I'll be damned." I have chosen to use Punjabi, instead of actual Dogri, because of the lack of an online translation tool for Dogri.

By the time he had the correct focus, the two creatures had moved around the altar and now had their backs to him. He tried to use his will to magnify the scene more than the binoculars did.

This is NOT possible.

Leaning toward the fantastical scene, Ben had half of his body over the railing when he began to topple. Jeevan grabbed a fistful of Ben's tunic and pulled him back. Ben never looked away from the creatures, enthralled by Brown and Gray moving like living creatures. He couldn't find a single inconsistency to dissuade him that they weren't.

When the earlier incantations resumed, the creatures faced each other. Brown took the items off the tray, one at a time, and held each up. As Ben watched the wolf's profile, the creature spoke.

The same human language flowed from the giant canine, and Ben knew in that instant that what he saw was not a human dressed in a costume. There was no way to match up that voice with the movements unless the creature was real.

During the soliloquy, Ben recognized only one word, *seba*.

Star, door, or gate. More references to the Book of Gates.

Brown first held up each of the four balls, spoke several sentences, and sat it down on a corner of the altar before moving to the next. Finally, the wolfman picked up the diamond object and said some similar words before handing it to the gray wolf.

Brown produced a scroll from which he appeared to read. As he did, Gray, holding the diamond, rotated it in his hand/paws and pressed on different sides with a finger.

Just when Ben thought he would never see anything as remarkable as these creatures, the gray wolf turned to the altar, leaned over the center, and tossed the diamond into the air with the same care someone might toss an egg to a friend.

Instead of slamming against the stone top, the eight-sided object bounced in the air before floating higher.

Holy shit!

It lit up and spun in midair. Seconds later, the four balls glowed and rose of their own volition from each corner of the altar. Then they revolved as if tied by an invisible string to the diamond. Ben turned his magnified gaze to the sky, looking for strings that had to lead to a hot-air balloon. Finding nothing but a sky full of bright stars, he shook his head, trying to dislodge the impossible, as the objects spun faster.

Four beams of intense white light shot out from the diamond, touching each ball. Ben jerked the binoculars away. More beams shot out from the balls, connecting them together. The five objects floated higher until they hovered about twenty feet over the altar. The center diamond rose a little above the rest until everyone stood in awe of the rotating, glowing pyramid of light.

The villagers dropped to their knees, raised their hands to the sky, and bowed to the incredible display. As one, they chanted a single muffled word: "Seba. Seba. Seba."

While people were lying prostrate, the solid ropes of light blinked out, causing Ben to see streaks in his vision. The objects descended until they rested on the altar.

Ben kept trying to blink away the literal stars in his eyes as people in the crowd came to their feet. The wolfmen turned toward Ben and Jeevan. They ducked behind the carved stone railing, eyes a few inches above the top.

Two by two, the ten men who had walked in earlier received a blessing from the wolf priests. Last in line, the odd couple of Nubian and Suit stepped forward to stand in front of the creatures at the top of the altar. They lowered their heads while receiving the creatures' blessing.

The brown wolf priest handed the scroll to the Suit. He opened it and turned, along with the Nubian, to face Ben and Jeevan. Ben banged his hand on the railing while bringing the binoculars up to his eyes. He bit back an exclamation. He had wanted to get a good look at the man, but he didn't need binoculars.

Ben had met the suited man a few weeks earlier.

Professor Ali Mousa read from the scroll. Flabbergasted, Ben didn't listen, his mind racing with the implications. It all made sense now. The hotel, the train, the attack in the desert.

Mousa was part of the village cult and was behind all their troubles.

When he stopped reading, the villagers cheered. As he handed the scroll to the Nubian, Ben found it curious that the professor no longer wore glasses. Mousa's partner read another section. When he finished, a second cheer rose from the crowd.

Together, they turned back to the canine priests, gave Gray the scroll, and bowed before facing the tunnel entrance. As they exited, the crowd parted, and the other eight men fell in line, soon joined by the villagers who bunched up to leave the temple.

Ben and Jeevan stayed scrunched next to the column as the villagers filed out. They watched the wolves go around the altar and disappear down the steps. The objects still lay on the altar.

Why?

Communicating with hand signals, they waited ten minutes to confirm everyone had left the sanctum.

As they stood to leave, Jeevan grabbed Ben's arm and pulled him down. His arm jerked out, an emphatic finger pointing up the cliff wall to the right of the altar.

What?

Slight movement drew his attention. A shadow drifted down the face of the cliff, slithering across the rock face until it passed out of sight below the rail.

Ben clenched his jaws because even in the dark, he knew the apparition could belong to only one person. He hissed, "Damn it, Louisa!"

Until that afternoon, he'd never seen a climber with such skill. When he got a chance, he would read her the riot act.

When he thought it couldn't get any worse, the petite figure, clad all in black, danced up the steps of the altar. She began grabbing the objects and placing them into a black bag. Finally, she held up the scroll and peered at it for a second before bagging it as well.

Planning to intercept her, Ben stood to climb over the rail. Jeevan held him back and pointed down the covered walkway. Footsteps were approaching. The last thing Ben saw before he and Jeevan jogged toward the tunnel to the exit was an inky ghost gliding up the cliff wall.

It took Louisa an hour to make her way over the uneven ground on top of the cliff back to the location of her ascent. At every new obstacle, she fought the urge to stop and examine the contents of the bag slung over her back. Every language that Louisa spoke had some saying about curiosity followed by death, so she restrained herself.

Thinking about the amazing scene she'd witnessed at the temple brought a smile to her lips. She felt confident Ben and Jeevan hadn't been able to get into the temple with that many people around. She also hadn't seen or heard any disturbances, so she doubted the villagers had caught them, either. She'd bet anything that the boys were back at the camp, frantic at losing her. No helping it.

Better to ask forgiveness and all.

The disappointment of finding the temple occupied and not filled with gold, while unfortunate, did nothing to tamp down her excitement. These magical objects were incredible. When she learned how to use them the way the wolf men did, she would become the wealthiest woman in Europe.

Well, not the wealthiest. She'd share the bounty with her partner, of course. By her estimation, she'd done more than 50 percent of the heavy lifting the last couple of days. Putting all thoughts on the back burner, she climbed down the dark rock face with nothing but her sense of touch and memory.

She moved with stealth across the valley floor and back up the large hill, trying to decide how to tell the men what she'd seen. Should she start with the professor being behind the attacks? Or tell them about the shocking real-life wolf creatures and the incredible magic objects?

She'd leave out the creatures because Ben would never believe her without seeing them himself. Especially the magic part.

Maybe they'll just be happy I'm alive.

Crossing the summit, she felt something amiss. The team's kits were still piled up in the same location as when she'd told Sowar Lama she was going to relieve herself.

Instead of looking for her in a panic, Jeevan and Ben sat, cool as cucumbers, on two rocks they had pulled up near the bags. Despite the darkness, they stared right at her. Like a stern father, Ben had his arms crossed and his back stiff. As always, she would let them speak first to get the lay of the land.

In a strong yet quiet voice, Ben asked, "Are you proud of yourself?"

Louisa pulled the thin black mask she wore over her head and stood regarding the two men. "Well, yes, I am. I had the most incredible night of my life."

"Oh, we know. We were there," he growled through tight lips.

Louisa's mind raced. She fired back, seeking more information. "Really? Then you know everything."

"Yes. We know you lied to us and scaled the cliff walls in the dark without a rope. We know you saw the ceremony, and we know you took the mag—" He paused a heartbeat and snarled, "We know you stole the artifacts." He stood and took two long strides to be right in front of her. He towered, looking down, his glasses having slid halfway down his nose. Her gaze inched up as she looked him in the face.

Do your best, Dr. Livid.

I've been lectured by Mère de la Nativité.[6]

He kept going. "I also know you're not just some well-educated woman born to a powerful man. I've been trying to decide how many lies you've told and whether you simply used me." He shoved his fist under her nose and opened his hand. "I looked through your bag, Miss Sophia. Did you win the papyri in a card game or were they stolen from the same place you stole these?"

O skatá!

She looked down to see Perdiccas's ring, as well as the jewelry she'd stolen from the Louvre. The thought flashed through her mind that she should've kept everything on her person. Then she looked into Ben's eyes. "I would never steal from my partner, but I may have taken a few liberties with how I obtained the papyri."

---

6. Mère de la Nativité (Mother of the Nativity) was the strictest teacher/nun at St. Denis, a Parisian boarding school. It is one of the all-girls boarding schools created by Napoleon for girls whose fathers won the Légion d'honneur. Louisa attended the school from the age of twelve until graduating at age eighteen. To learn more about the prequel, Louisa Sophia and The Last Chance Tour, set during Louisa's time at St. Denis, go to www.HistoryIsMagic.com and subscribe.

Ben's face contorted with rage, but she never got to hear his coming tirade because Jeevan stepped up and grabbed their arms.

She squirmed as the duffadar tightened his grip. "As entertaining as this has been, and as excited as I am to see how this conversation ends, it has to wait. The villagers are going wild. There is a large group with torches and lanterns headed this way. It won't take them forever to find us."

In the valley below, several dogs yowled as if to punctuate his words.

Ben broke free from his grip and pushed a finger toward Louisa's chest. "You'd better hope we live to finish this." He turned to the pile of kit bags, shoved the jewelry into his own, and grabbed his rifle. "Keep up."

Little talking took place as they rushed through the tunnel and jogged through the box canyon. Halfway across, Ben pushed them to go faster. The sun began peeking over the horizon when Sowar Jadav, who had stayed with the horses, met them where the cliffs narrowed to the entrance.

Louisa looked back toward the tunnel and saw several lights pop out from the hidden entrance. Shots echoed around the empty canyon. Fear driving her now, she raced to catch up to Ben. He never looked back at the sound of gunfire as he rushed to his horse. He and the Lancers mounted and galloped away without waiting for Louisa.

She mounted a few seconds behind them and kicked the sides of her horse. In a few moments, she exited the canyon and left behind the villagers' gun sights as the crack of rifles chased after her.

Already well ahead, Ben urged his horse to greater speeds, and the Legionnaire hat on his head flew free.

Jeevan slumped over Chetak as he watched his treasure fall to the desert floor. Within a few heartbeats, the duffadar straightened his shoulders and yelled, "Yah!" His war horse leaped to the challenge, closing the gap to Ben's mare.

Racing to catch up, Louisa didn't understand Jeevan's and Ben's urgency. Their pursuers didn't have any horses. Still breathing hard, she stood in her stirrups, leaned over her saddle, and urged her horse into action. Eschewing the circular route, they headed straight across the desert.

As she bounced along, at last it dawned on her. They weren't afraid of getting caught from behind. The villagers were watching their base and would go there to recapture the objects. An icy fear took hold of Louisa's heart. She prayed they would reach the camp before Abu and his friend headed to the canyon as part of the ruse.

She glanced over her shoulder, and a dust cloud rose out of the desert a mile back.

How?

As she shook her head, the camp's rocky rise came into view. Ben and Jeevan exchanged words she couldn't hear. Jeevan kicked the sides of Chetak, and the impressive stallion leaped to the challenge as if chased by fire. The gray warhorse and his rider disappeared inside the ring of boulders a full quarter-mile ahead of her. Seeing a large group of horses on the opposite side of the encampment, she gulped, her worry soaring.

As she reined in her horse inside the ring of tents, organized chaos greeted her. Men raced to take up firing positions behind boulders or wagons placed in gaps between the giant rocks. When Louisa's feet touched the ground, a Lancer grabbed her mare's reins. He didn't say anything but led all their horses toward the picket line.

Abu stepped in front of her and startled her with a big hug. After a second, she returned it. "Allah 'Akbar. You're back." He pushed back a step, plucked her white felt hat off his head, and plopped it down on top of her droopy one. "There's no way I'm going to meet my maker wearing women's clothes. I need to change."

Louisa tugged at his sleeve as he turned. "Hold on. When you get done, meet me at my tent. I need your help with something." With a warm smile, she added, "And it's great to see you, too."

Abu raised an eyebrow. "Sure thing. Dr. Ben told me to come, uh, protect you, anyway."

Louisa's eyebrows shot up. "He said he wanted you to protect me, did he?"

Guilt painted his face, and he shrugged while averting his eyes. "Well, those weren't his exact words. Something about keeping you out of trouble. But I'm sure he's also concerned about your safety."

She slow-rolled the first word and smirked. "Right." She jerked her chin toward the tents. "Well, don't just stand there. Go get manly. You can't protect me like that."

Abu grinned and sprinted toward his tent.

Louisa strode after him, but the mouth-watering smells of breakfast and tea made her sniff the wind. Even though it was mid-morning, the cooks always made extra for anyone who might have been pulling guard duty. Grateful at the chance for a hot meal, she followed her nose to the source.

She wolfed down fresh-baked lentils and a hard biscuit before she carried a second cup of tea back to her tent. With caffeine coursing through her veins, she shook off her physical exhaustion and lack of sleep. A mercurial energy seemed to emanate from the strange artifacts that pressed into her back, giving her an extra jolt of vitality.

She went straight to her suitcase and retrieved an extra box of ammunition, then placed it near her pillow. As she sat on the cot, she pulled the Bulldog revolver from a hidden pocket and flipped out the cylinder. After counting to five, she closed it and put the gun next to the box of bullets.

One by one, she removed the objects to get her first close look. The first sphere's unnatural lack of weight astounded her because it looked like carved stone. On close inspection, she determined its composition to be a metal she'd never seen.

Each ball had a similar makeup. A pencil-width line etched the globes at what she would consider the equator and prime meridian, while each one had a distinguishing symbol carved into its north or south pole. When she inspected the diamond, it looked like two pyramids stuck together at their bases. An etched line formed the seam where the pyramids became one.

Written into each of the eight sides was a large symbol under a line of four smaller characters, surrounded by a frame. The marks didn't look like any text she'd ever seen. She hoped Abu, who had been studying the various Egyptian writing systems, could shed some light. The answer might be in the scroll.

She plucked it from her bag and opened it. Stunned, Louisa stared at the *paper* that wasn't. Thick and malleable as vellum, the *paper* had an unnatural sheen to it. Text in an unknown language glowed on the strange material. When she rolled it up, the words disappeared from the surface as if they'd never been there. She unwound it again, and the symbols popped back into existence as exposure to light brought them to life.

"Incredible. How?" Louisa's gaze intensified, trying to will an answer into existence like the text. "Doesn't look Egyptian," she mumbled.

"You're right. It's not."

She jumped off her cot an inch.

Abu looked as mannish as a thirteen-year-old boy could. He wore wool pants held up by suspenders over a linen shirt. In his hands, he rotated the diamond, studying every side, his eyes darting across its dull gray surface with unbroken focus.

Louisa waved to capture his attention. "I'm not sure you'll believe me, but tonight was incredible." He gave her a quizzical look as she continued, "Short story: We found the temple occupied by a cult. The friendly folks surrounding our camp are from a village near the temple. They are plotting our deaths because of those." She pointed to the object in his hands.

"Ben *meant* trouble." Abu gave a nervous chuckle. "Go on, tell me what you did."

"Why do you think I did anything?" False indignation crept into her voice.

"Because he is Dr. Responsible, and you are you." He chuckled to himself.

"Okay, maybe we watched a strange ceremony at the temple. And maybe the wolf monsters from the tomb drawings are real."

Abu's mouth went to one side, and his eyebrows rose.

"And maybe a professor we met at the Cairo museum is part of the cult and behind all our problems. Oh, and these artifacts are magical." She lowered her volume. "And maybe I stole them."

He whistled.

Her voice grew more robust, and she sped up. "But let's not focus on that. I was hoping you could help me figure out how they work. Worst case, we can destroy them or at least threaten to destroy them to keep the mob from killing us." Louisa stopped to catch her breath.

"*Sure*, the wolf-priests are real." Abu's eyes narrowed. "You mean you saw live wolves walking like men? Next, you'll tell me you heard them talking."

Abu laughed and grabbed his stomach. She held up a hand and cut him off with a shake of her head. "Everything I'm telling you is the truth. Ben and Jeevan were there. They saw everything. You can ask them." She gave him an "I dare you" look. "I was too far away to hear them, but the two wolves were giants. At least seven feet tall. I saw their snouts or whatever moving as if they were talking. You can ask Jeevan if they heard them, but they were very real, and they used these," she indicated the items before them, "to perform some type of religious ceremony."

Abu rolled his eyes.

Louisa took a deep breath. "You'll see. Now to the more important stuff. The priests did something to these objects. They started glowing and floated into the air before shooting out beams of light. It was more incredible than seeing monsters come to life."

Abu scoffed.

Louisa held up the scroll and turned the reading surface toward him. She unfurled it, a half-inch at a time.

His eyes bulged. "Al'ama, did you see that? The words just appeared as if by magic."[7]

She knew she had him.

A rifle roared from the edge of the camp, and they turned as one.

"Here they come!" a Lancer bellowed.

She and Abu squatted behind her suitcases with their guns pointed toward the tent opening. Peering over the buckles of the luggage, she hoped the extra books she carried might offer them a modicum of protection.

More rifles fired from the direction where Louisa had entered the camp, with return shots heard in the distance. Abu licked his lips, and Louisa felt perspiration form on her forehead as the gunfire and the sounds of galloping horses grew closer. From the small gap, she glimpsed low-riding villagers race by wagons and boulders, spurts of fire coming from weapons resting on the necks of their horses.

No bullets landed near them, and the sound of hooves soon grew distant. When no other shots came, they sat on the cot. With his breath coming fast, Abu gulped as he holstered his Schofield.

He picked up the scroll, and the two of them shared a nervous look. Together, they peered at the text. All the symbols on the scroll were the same ones she'd seen

---

7. Al'ama is Arabic for "blindness" but is used like "damn."

on the objects. No, that wasn't right. There were different repeating symbols. The scroll contained only six lines of text and nothing more.

"I've never seen this language, but it might not matter." Abu slapped his knee. "Because these are instructions."

Ben put down the binoculars and contemplated their predicament. He yelled over to Jeevan, who was lying behind a large rock about twenty feet away. "I hope you're wrong."

"Wrong about what?" Jeevan twisted to look back. "You know I'm never wrong."

Ben yelled back, "You better pray you're wrong this time. You said every Lancer is worth five of those guys, but if my count is correct, we're outnumbered seven to one."

Jeevan grunted at Ben's gallows humor and fired back. "What an amazing opportunity, wouldn't you say, Captain Ben? Of course, a Bengal Lancer can handle seven of this rabble, but because I'm so generous, we'll save the extra two for you and your fancy Winchester. If you're not up to the challenge, let me know."

It was Ben's turn to grunt, but he lobbed another volley Jeevan's way. "I told you, I'm a little rusty. How about you guys take six each? I'll handle the rest with Agnes."

A giant grin split Jeevan's face. "Deal. While we wait, why don't you tell me why you named your rifle 'Agnes'?"

Ben chuckled. "Might as well. My father, God rest his soul, was a very learned man. A doctor as well. He taught all his children to read Greek and Latin, but some said he didn't have a lick of frontier sense." Ben paused to remember the countless hours he'd spent in study sessions with his father.

Jeevan cleared his throat.

Ben nodded and felt his mouth tug at his scar as he grinned. "My mom, Agnes, was the opposite. She stopped her schooling in third grade to work on the family ranch. Her family were rough and tumble Scottish immigrants. The McCubbins were the very definition of frontiersmen. She taught all her kids, including my sisters, how to shoot, hunt, skin and dress a deer, set a trap, and fish. She even taught me how to ride."

He pushed his hat up and wiped his forehead with his sleeve. "To this day, my mother's the best marksman I've ever known. She could hit a nickel from two hundred yards." His voice grew sad. "She passed when I was fighting. Since then, I've named every rifle I've owned after her. Mom never let me down, and to this day, my rifles haven't failed me, either. Knock on wood." Ben readjusted his porkpie and rapped twice on his rifle's stock.

Jeevan gave him a rueful smile. "That's a beautiful story, Ben. It sounds like you had wonderful parents."

"I did. What about you? Tell me about your family."

Jeevan's eyes drooped. "My mother died giving birth when I was two, and my father went crazy. The baby was stillborn as well, and I didn't have any other siblings." He sighed. "My family was one of the biggest landowners in our village, but we lost most of that as my father fell apart."

With a melancholic look, Jeevan said, "A family of servants raised me. They made sure I didn't grow up unloved. My adopted mother's karma was like a fresh breeze on a spring day." His smile grew bright. "She saw the magic in everything and the good in everyone, if they had any. When I was fifteen, my father killed himself, and I gave my adopted family all the remaining land. I used the last of my family's money to buy a posting with the Lancers."

Ben frowned at his friend, wishing he could console Jeevan. "I'm sorry, but I bet both your mothers are very proud of the man you've become."

"Someday, I'll find out." Jeevan's sad smile touched Ben's heart.

Ben nodded and peered toward the distant sandy berm, hiding the villagers.

But hopefully not tonight.

The military men expected the temple followers to attack during the night. Ben didn't see a reason to negotiate. Professor Mousa wouldn't allow them to live with what they knew.

This was all that damn woman's fault. She had been trying to get him killed since he met her, and she may still get them all killed because she stole the artifacts. If they had gotten away unnoticed and made a show of giving up the search, Ali's people might have let them go. Later, Ben and the Lancers could have returned with the entire Pelusium garrison.

As much as Ben tried to put it out of his mind, he couldn't help but feel guilty for putting Abu in danger. Before the attack, he would ensure Abu and Louisa barricaded themselves at the center of camp.

While he ran through ways to set up their defense, he heard a shot followed by a warning cry behind them. The familiar sound of charging horses reached his ears as several Lancer carbines drowned out the approaching hooves.

Before he could look to their rear, a hundred rifles fired in unison to their front.

Dust and rock spit up in front of their defenses. Impressed with the discipline of the Lancers, Ben heard a single nearby rifle reply. The shot came from the best sharpshooter in the squadron, Acting Lance Duffadar Bhagat. A thousand yards away, a man who had been shooting while kneeling toppled to the ground. He rolled down the little rise the villagers used for cover. The shot sent the rest of the men scrambling behind the mound.

"Six more!" came Jeevan's jovial yell.

The sounds of mixed rifles and pistols closed around them. The villagers who had been behind them raced by their fortified mound. A bullet hit about a foot above Ben's head, and sandstone shards rained down, forcing him to turn away.

He looked for a shot, but the riders were well past his location. They were so low on their horses that he had no choice. With the horsemen halfway to the mound where the other villagers waited, he pulled the trigger.

One of the galloping horses missed a step. With a shriek, it tumbled into the hard-packed Egyptian earth. The rider flew from his mount before careening over the ground to a lifeless stop.

"Bully!" Jeevan laughed. "Five more."

Ben's reply caught in his throat. He looked skyward at the presence of a blue veil, forming a hazy screen between him and the scalding afternoon sun. He watched in horror as the spinning pyramid of light he'd seen the previous night rose above Louisa's tattered tent.

Standing in the ruins, Abu and Louisa stared at the display as if hypnotized. As the object spun faster, Ben also watched, mesmerized. His gut told him it was an unfolding disaster. A disaster he couldn't stop. A dome of semi-transparent blue light radiated outward from the pyramid's apex. The translucent bowl touched down somewhere beyond the villagers' rise.

A high-pitched humming sound threatened to burst his eardrums, and goose-bumps prickled his skin. In terrified silence, he watched a giant beam of light shoot into the sky and slam into the dome of blue. Ben's vision turned an impossible white, and he felt himself falling.

Chapter 14

Fields of Eisodos, Alexandria, Baru, An 5660, Day 1

Louisa no longer wondered what it would be like to fall from a mile-high cliff. She fought through the queasy feeling still roiling her stomach. Awareness of her other senses came one at a time. First came touch. Wheat stalks pushed at her back. Second came the strong smell of grass and the soft sweet aroma of flowers.

For a moment, Louisa lay there soaking in the pleasant sensations, trying to dissipate the worst hangover of her life. An idea stirred. How could she be hungover? She pulled up her last vivid memory. Abu stood at the table in her tent, touching the symbols on the diamond object while she described each strange letter on the scroll to him. As he tapped on every glyph, it glowed, accelerating their excitement.

The first line of instructions had been the most difficult because it referred to the four round objects. Nothing happened until she remembered the wolf creatures arranging them into a square. It took several tries for her to place them in the correct locations.

Once aligned, the balls pulsed with light. As she directed Abu to the last symbol, the spheres floated into the air and melted the cloth of her tent, which fell like streamers. The heavens exposed, the sky transformed into a diffused blue.

The diamond flew out of Abu's hands to join the spinning spheres. Together, they formed the pyramid of light she had seen the previous night. It danced to a different routine this time, spinning faster than the eye could follow. A blinding beam exploded out of the top of the pyramid, and she began to fall.

"Where the hell is Louisa?"

The angry words shook her out of her reverie. She blinked away the darkness and stared up at a cloudless sky. Etching the almost translucent blue, two thin streaks of silver stretched across the heavens. She followed the threads until her eyes locked onto a moon. Not the moon but a moon. She knew this was not her moon, as certain as she knew the face of her mother. She turned her head, following the streaks until her eyes lost focus. Something blocked her line of sight.

Adjusting her eyes, she saw wheat-like stalks of a plant about two feet tall, topped with small flowers in every shade of yellow and purple. The flowers could not hold her attention because the stalks shimmered in a chaos of changing colors. Zeroing in on a single plant, she realized it adhered to a pattern of blue, red, pink, and then repeated. Each new color rose from its roots up to the flower above, followed by the next.

"Abu. Abu. Where are you?" Ben's voice sounded closer, with panic replacing anger.

Louisa pulled her gaze away from the plants and sat up on her elbows, looking toward the sound of his voice. Her breath caught in her throat as she looked at another moon, also not her moon. Flicking straight up to the moon she had seen moments earlier, her eyes bounced back and forth until she convinced herself this was no hallucination. She moved her head to the other side of the horizon and finished the painting with the most beautiful of sunsets.

The sun caressed the tips of a distant range of snow-capped mountains—each peak, a rival to the mighty Matterhorn. Shutting her eyes and holding her breath for several counts, she tried to quell the tightening in her chest.

Oh, Lord, what happened? What have I done?

She forced herself to fall into the breathing techniques she'd learned from her uncle to become a shadow. She replayed the calming words Lance Duffadar Ram used to guide his pupils through the poses of the Prana Vayu.

Breathing stabilized, she opened her eyes. Abu struggled to stand only five feet away. She pushed herself up as Ben enveloped him in a hug. Their embrace broke apart as she reached her feet. She wobbled a little, her legs uncertain of their purchase as if she had stepped off a boat on the high seas back onto dry land.

Finding her equilibrium, she tore her focus away from the now scowling Ben to look around the immediate vicinity. The remnants of her shredded tent lay in tatters; the objects, now dull gray, lay among the cloth and the grass. The frame formed a rectangle around them as they stood in an endless sea of flowers. Tents, wagons, horses, and boulders of various sizes all seemed alien to this place.

She turned away as Ben stepped in her direction, then she bent to retrieve the magic artifacts that had caused their current predicament. She placed them in her black bag. Jeevan's voice barked orders in the distance as she reached for the last sphere.

When she finished, she straightened and stared at Ben's heaving chest. She closed her eyes and winced, expecting a tirade that didn't come. After a few moments, she looked up with a sheepish expression. Lightning shot from his eyes, his scowl transforming into a red face full of anger.

She whispered like a regretful child, "Sorry."

His red face turned purple and contorted through a series of emotions, from rage to exasperation. He stammered, trying to unleash in words the fury in his eyes. All the while, his hands clenched and unclenched in rapid succession at his sides.

Whoa, Dr. Livid's about to blow.

Louisa flinched to avoid the uncorked spittle raining down as Ben bellowed, "Sorry? Sorry? You're sorry? What the hell did you do?"

The sinking feeling in the pit of Louisa's stomach came as a shock to her. She'd prepared herself for the coming dressing down the same way she'd faced so many verbal assaults from Mère de la Nativité at St. Denis. She'd keep a contrite face while emptying herself of any emotion and, in particular, pride. That way, she could take the most egregious blows to her ego without response or lasting effect. Her current emotional state reminded her of how'd she felt when she disappointed her mother. Why would what Ben thought make her feel this way?

Snap out of it.

"Well, it wasn't just—" She stopped, seeing Abu shake his head as he stood a little behind Ben. His hands, held low, shook in small frantic waves. *Don't do it.* Swallowing hard, she gave a quick nod. "I was trying to see if I could figure out how to make the objects do what they did at the ceremony. We thought the scroll could be a list of instructions. I followed them and then . . ." Louisa's eyes dropped, and her voice trailed off.

Ben took three big breaths and held each for a few seconds. Seething, he replied at last, "Louisa Sophia, your chicanery has plumb fucked us all. Wasn't it bad enough that you were going to get us killed with your thieving ways?"

What the hell did he just say? Tricky Fruit Fucking?

I messed up. But who does he think he is?

Her head snapped up, her eyes full of rage. They reflected the emotions in Ben's blue mirrors.

Ben stammered on, "But now you just—Well, I don't know what you just did. I don't know if we're dead and this is heaven, purgatory, or . . ."

Louisa's blood boiled at the Not So Good Doctor's first use of vulgar language directed her way. Her growing irritation shoved aside her concern over that other uncomfortable feeling. Preparing to unleash a verbal lashing of her own, she paused. The sight of the scintillating grass reminded her of what she had wrought. She bit her lip, choking back her unspent storm.

Stay calm.

To redirect the conversation, she latched on to the last part of his tirade, which had sparked the adventurer inside her.

"We're on a different planet." Her speech became more rapid as she spoke, matching her growing excitement. "Just like from Verne's *Earth to the Moon*. Have you read it?"

Ben grabbed his hat and threw it on the ground. "Damn it, Louisa!"

"Do you know what this means?" She stared into his pools of blue flame.

His voice became icy calm. "Yes. I read the book. They never found out what happened to the travelers they sent to the moon." The sneer on his face threw kerosene on her sparking anger. He extinguished all the fires with his next words. "I'm a cussed fool for trusting you after last night. Did you know that your little magic act brought the villagers with us?" His chin poked over her head. "We're probably going to die the same way we would have back on, uh." He closed his eyes and shook his head. Popping them open, he said, "Back in Egypt."

At the mention of the villagers, Louisa spun away from his accusing glare and the backdrop of the mountains. She faced an ocean of grassy flowers. About a mile across the undulating, shimmering field, she saw a gathering of men. A smaller group broke away from the larger and approached their location.

She squinted until she was sure. "Well, it looks like they want to talk. They're carrying a white flag."

Ben looked over Louisa's shoulder and saw three men walking toward them with what looked like a white shirt tied to a rifle. The man in the middle wore a suit, marking his identity even from a distance. Glancing down to give Louisa one more look of disgust, he said to Abu, "Run. Get Jeevan. Tell him the villagers are coming to parlay. You stay with the Lancers."

Abu seemed to give Louisa a sympathetic look. "Yes, sir." He took off running to the sounds of the duffadar's orders to corral the startled horses.

While Ben waited for Jeevan, he compared Louisa's incredulous, preposterous words to his own plausible scenarios. No other explanation made sense. Two moons above and a field of strange light-pulsing plants assured him they were no place on Earth.

If not Earth, then where?

Her theory explained the wolfmen at the temple, making the current reality even more probable. The creatures weren't some macabre folktale come to life but aliens from another planet. The objects had to be some sort of transportation device.

If that's the case, he thought, *these aliens may look at us like we would an Aztec.*

Before he could mull over the ramifications of the technology gap, Jeevan tapped him on the shoulder. The always jovial and steadfast Jeevan had genuine concern in his eyes. "Captain Ben, *ki khārāpa abasthā*." Jeevan stopped and gave an exasperated sigh. "What the hell is going on? Some of my men are about to lose their minds."

Ben attempted a weak smile. "I wish we had time to work it out on our own, but we have to deal with our visitors. I want you with me when I speak to them, but let me do the talking. These guys may have some answers." Ben paused and patted his friend on the shoulder. "Your responsibility is to keep your men from panicking. There's no telling what each of them is thinking. Before our meeting, run back and tell your men to stay calm. We'll share everything we find out. Rely on their discipline. If you think it'll help, order them to prepare for a fight if the negotiations go bad."

Jeevan's face relaxed a bit, as if his mind had settled on having something else to focus on. "Sounds good. I'll be back in a few minutes."

Ben estimated the approaching trio would be about two hundred yards out by the time Jeevan returned. Louisa, he saw, had absorbed every word. With an edge, he said to her, "Since you got us into this mess, keep quiet. Do you think you can do that?" He would brook no excuses from her, and he backed it up with his sternest look. For a moment, he pictured his father's face in the middle of a lecture.

"Yes, sir, Captain Ben." Louisa used her best Jeevan impersonation. She followed this with her normal soprano voice. "I promise not to cause any more trouble."

She tilted her head and gave him puppy dog eyes. Louisa being contrite and trying to manipulate him were both new experiences for Ben. He felt righteous indignation welling up, but before he could react, Jeevan returned. Professor Mousa and his men had closed to about 150 yards.

Raising his hand, he yelled, "Stop!" After looking to his left and right, he waded through the grass.

With his hand on the grip of his revolver, he eyeballed the negotiating party. As he loosened the pocket army in its holster, the revolver felt lighter than usual. He had to resist the urge to pull the gun free and see whether it was loaded. He had double-checked all his weapons while they were waiting for the villagers to attack, so he had to trust that the bullets were there. The weight issue could wait.

When they were fifty yards apart, he yelled toward the three men, "Put the rifle on the ground, and drop any other weapons!"

Ben paused while Mousa and the Nubian man conferred. Ben checked on the third man, looking for any signs of danger. Ali untied the white shirt from the rifle, and the flag bearer laid the rifle on the ground. Ben started forward again.

The Nubian removed a short sword and a dagger and held them up for inspection before placing them on the ground. The professor pulled a small revolver from his pocket, held it above his head, stooped, and came up with empty hands.

When the two parties were fifteen feet apart, the three of them stopped, and the six of them sized one another up. Ben spoke first, "Professor Moussa? Is that what I should call you? I assume you know what the hell is going on."

The professor sighed. "Unfortunately, I do. I know we are all in a big mess because of the two of you." He poked his finger at Ben and then at Louisa. "I tried to stop you before things got out of hand, but here we are, living in a nightmare."

The Nubian spoke in the same language they had heard at the ceremony. Hearing the language used in conversation and not as ceremonial jargon, Ben assumed it was Ancient Egyptian with hints of Coptic. That made sense, but the language also contained notes of dialects he had only heard from North African tribesmen. The man continued for about twenty seconds, addressing them and Ali.

The man's tone did not hide his anger. When he stopped, Mousa nodded, then translated. "This is Hem-netjer Panehesy of the Keepers of the Seba.[1] He demands that you immediately return the Seba, surrender your weapons, and come back to Memphis to meet with the high priest."

Ben listened to the demands, trying to keep his best poker face. He waited for a ten count before replying, "Ali, I'll just call you that. I don't know what is going on, but I don't trust you, and I don't trust the padre here." He stared into each man's eyes before focusing on Ali. "We damn sure won't lay down our guns. If

---

1. The Seba is made up of the five artifacts used to create a portal from one planet to another. A Seba can take everything not attached to the planet's surface and transport it to the designated location on the other planet. The radius of the area affected by a Seba can be quite large. The word seba in ancient Egyptian means "star, gate, or door."

you want to continue this discussion, you need to explain where we are, how we got here, and how we get back."

Ali shook his head and gave his mouth a resigned twist before he translated what Ben had said to the Nubian. The dark-skinned man leaned away and spat, never breaking eye contact with Ben. Straightening, he said three words in reply.

Ali nodded. A scowl settled on the priest's face as Ali spoke. "You are on the planet Aaru, and your own foolishness brought you here when you stole and activated the Seba."[2]

Ben interjected, "Aaru? Like the Ancient Egyptian heaven, Aaru?"

Ali smiled, his voice growing ominous. "I can assure you this is not heaven, but yes, that Aaru. In fact, because of the two of you, I have failed my life's mission, and you may have just doomed everyone on this planet."

Taken aback at the fatalistic words and matching tone, Ben asked, "What do you mean?"

Ali stared at the ground. He looked up with sadness. "I spent my life preparing. My ancestors spent generations guarding the temple, waiting for the return." He paused, and the sadness became anger. "It takes five hundred years for the Seba to soak up enough power to make two trips. One from Aaru to Earth and then back to Aaru. You two fools wasted the return trip. My mission was to return with help for the coming Lamentations."

This shit keeps getting better and better.

Damn it, Louisa.

---

2. Aaru is the name of the planet that Ben, Louisa, and Abu find themselves marooned on. The Ancient Egyptians believed that Aaru was the heavenly field of reeds presided over by Osiris.

Ali pursed his lips and blew out through puffed cheeks. "You need to come with us. We may not have much time to figure out how to stop the coming slaughter."

Louisa broke her promise and blurted out, "What are the Lamentations? How do you power the Seba?"

While she spoke, the priest growled and looked at Louisa with loathing.

Ali answered, "I don't know everything about Aaru, but the story goes that every five hundred and fifty-one Earth years, an army of demons—they call them reapers—comes to Aaru and kills everyone. These times are the Lamentations. The only way to power the Seba is for it to be exposed to the sun, the moon, and the stars for five hundred years. That's all I know."

Ben glared at Louisa with almost as much anger as the priest before saying to Ali, "And what was your mission?"

Ali's eyes narrowed in thought. "I guess it doesn't matter now. We were going to use the Seba to bring the entire Pelusium garrison to Aaru."

Jeevan gasped and stepped back. Ben glanced at the duffadar, who had a look of horror on his face.

Ben knew he needed to wrap up the discussion and buy them time to come up with some options. He addressed Ali, "This is a lot to digest. We need to discuss among ourselves before we agree to do anything with you." Ben looked over his shoulder at the purple, red, and orange sunset. "We're also running out of daylight. Let's agree to speak again in the morning. We'll give you our answer, then."

Ali translated to the priest, who nodded.

The professor's eyes narrowed as he looked at them, and his voice grew serious. "Choose wisely. We're your only hope of surviving."

He, the villager, and the priest picked up their weapons and made their way back to their camp. Ben watched them leave as he scrambled to devise a solution to this impossible mess.

Chapter 15

Axclatca Pass, between Remus and Alexandria, Baru, An 5660

As the golden hour approached, Emperor Caesar Octavius Remus II, Chosen of Ahura Jupiter, King of the Remulan Empire, took slow sips of a chilled white wine from the Gelan region. From his shaded perch on a small hill, he dissected every detail of the 6th Legion and their auxiliary cohorts' drills. All ten units of the green-clad 6th flowed through both legion-wide and individual unit formations. Their auxiliary archers, skirmishers, and attached light cavalry worked on complementary maneuvers.

At present, the center of the formation coordinated with a cavalry unit of Aswārān, which had formed a wedge and was galloping hard toward the rear of the 6th's 1st Cohort.[1] At the right moment, the legionaries performed a perfect parting. The Aswārān soldiers lowered their lances and pulverized the center of an imaginary enemy line. With as much urgency as when they'd separated, the 1st

---

1. Aswārān are the heavy cavalry of the Sassanid Empire, which were later called "cataphracts" by the Europeans who adopted their weapons, armor, and tactics.

closed the gap, moved into wedge formation, and followed the cavalry into the now gaping imaginary hole.

Octavius made a mental note to tell Faustulus to purchase the vineyard for this particular vintage and inform the 6th's Legate, Marius, that 4th Cohort, 3rd Century, needed extra drills as they were sloppy and slow. Slow enough to endanger the entire legion.

Octavius had once made it a point to know every officer under his command. He regretted no longer being able to do the same since assuming the throne. Otherwise, he would have berated the centurion himself about the unit's deficiency.

"Emperor Remus, sorry to interrupt, but I have received news from the hysakas capitol," Aquila said in that irritating yet soothing voice.

Octavius put his drink on the table and waved his hand, dismissing the large contingent of slaves who were on constant call to serve his every whim. He also looked at the leader of his personal guard, giving him an over-the-shoulder nod. The guards moved with haste to step out of earshot.

At the same time, Bennu, his ever-present *babiakhom* wind singer, placed a special set of earmuffs over the small openings that served as her ears. She raised her winged arms wide, and Octavius felt a slight breeze that signaled the conversation would be safe from other wind singers.

The stage set, he turned his head to regard Aquila the Turd. The man made Octavius's skin crawl, but next to the emperor himself, the first counselor was indispensable. Besides advising, he acted as the empire's head of intelligence.

There were moments when Octavius considered getting rid of his father's old right-hand man. As much as he would love to do so, he also knew that without Aquila's aid, he would have never assumed the throne. He wondered whether he could keep it without the man's continued help. Instead of taking that risk, he kept Aquila close and well-rewarded.

"Yes, Aquila. What do you have?"

The first counselor replied in his same calm yet sickening manner, "Hem-net-jer-tepi Anhurmose has activated the Seba and sent a team back to Earth. As we discussed, this has the potential to upset your plans.[2] Every new group of Earthlings has brought new weapons or other military advances that might tip the balance."

Octavius straightened in his leather folding chair and placed his elbow on the armrest. He took time to consider the new information. Aquila became a statue, willing to wait for eternity for his emperor's reply.

After a long pause, Octavius added his thoughts. "A waste of time and so dangerous. The *hysakas* have learned nothing from the Phantom Lamentations. All we got from that folly were those damned Nipponese. It's obvious to all but the traditionalists that the Reapers are no longer a threat." He sighed, picked up his drink, and took a sip. "No use rehashing this for the hundredth time. Those fools have opened Pandora's box once again. What do you suggest we do about it?"

The statue became animated. Octavius saw the slight uptick at the corner of the man's mouth as he said, "It's imperative that we find the Earthlings as soon as they arrive. Recruit them to our side if possible. If not, we should study them until we can determine their weaknesses and eliminate the threat."

Octavius counted to five to add some weight to his reply. "A sound plan. I find it convenient that our goal of absorbing Alexandria into the empire will give us the Fields of Eisodos."[3]

---

2. Hem-netjer-tepi is the high priest of the hysakas. It means "First Servant of God."

3. The Fields of Eisodos are a grassy plains area where all creatures using the Aaruan Seba device have appeared. In Greek, eisodos means the entrance.

Aquila nodded, though Octavius sensed the man had factored in the use of the Seba long ago. A frightening thought dawned on him. The fields were the primary reason Aquila had been pushing Octavius to turn toward Alexandria instead of continuing to conquer the weaker nations to their south and east.

Aquila coveted the fields, not Alexandria. He wanted to intercept the Earthlings when they first arrived.

Now it made perfect sense, and it scared him. How long ago had the snake laid his plans? Octavius chided himself for underestimating the manipulative power of his first counsel.

He put that aside and continued his instructions, even knowing they were redundant. "Do whatever it takes to have our people in place to intercept the Earthlings. Promise them kingdoms of their own if necessary."

Aquila smiled, which made Octavius shudder. "I've taken the liberty of calling for Iskur. He'll arrive soon. His group should be able to get to the fields ahead of us to make contact. At the very least, they should be able to monitor the Earthlings to assess their abilities."

"Very well. Now, back to our more immediate issues." Octavius took a sip of wine, which had warmed beyond his liking. He puckered his lips and put the glass down, desiring to wrap this conversation up so he could have Bennu chill the glass again. Still, he had a few more topics for Aquila. "The Alexandrians have dug into the pass. It will take everything we have to dislodge them. Do you have news about their capabilities or the size of their forces?" Octavius held up his hand, pausing Aquila. "The last of our forces should arrive today. I would like to give them a full day's rest, but we don't have that luxury. We can't allow the Alexandrians more time to strengthen their defenses."

Aquila smiled, but his eyes didn't. "Yes, that's unfortunate, but I have no doubt the men will perform well for their emperor. As for news, our scouts have obtained information that we are facing the Alexandrian's Fourth Stratia, led by Polemarchos Alexandria ben Zev i Hurasu.[4][5] We know she is the most experienced leader in the Alexandrian military.

"We believe several reserve *stratia* have been dispatched from Neos Hierosolyma to help shore up the Fourth Stratia that we are facing and the Third Stratia guarding the narrows on the coast.[6] We don't have a timetable on these reserves' arrival, but we must assume that they are within two *khonsu* of reaching the pass, given the timing of my information."[7]

The emperor nodded. "This increases the urgency. Have you readied the Yasana Ceremony for tonight?[8] I will do the offering to the waters myself. It's important that our soldiers see me call upon Ahura Jupiter to overcome the

---

4. Stratia is Greek for "army".

5. Polemarchos is Greek for "the general in charge of an entire army." The polemarchos will command several strategos. These underling generals oversee a taxi, which is the equivalent of a regiment-size unit of troops, under their command.

6. Greek name for "New Jerusalem," the capital city of the nation Alexandria.

7. A khonsu is the two-day period it takes the Aaruan moons to do a complete cycle. Thus, the entire planet thinks about time in khonsus more than in singular days. In Ancient Egypt, Khonsu was the god that represented the moon and is literally translated as "traveler."

8. Yasana Ceremony is the primary Zoroastrian ceremony that appeals to Ahura Jupiter. A Roman/Sassanid hybrid version of Zoroastrianism is the state religion of Remus.

followers of Angra Mainyu Orcus.[9] [10] Make sure the ceremony starts two hours after Triplets."[11]

"Of course, Emperor, I will personally ensure the ceremony happens as planned."

"Thank you, Aquila. Ahura Jupiter willing, our legions will crush them tomorrow and secure the pass. Please send Faustulus to me. I have several items I wish for him to address."

---

9. Ahura Jupiter is the Remulan Zoroastrian monotheistic God of good. Ahura Mazda is the name of the God on Earth, but on Aaru, the deity was renamed to include the head Roman god.

10. Angra Mainyu Orcus is the Remulan Zoroastrian force of evil. Remulans see all of life in a struggle of good versus evil. Orcus, the Roman god of the underworld, was appended to the end of the original name.

11. Triplets is the name for sunset on the first day of a khonsu. Aaru has two moons, Shu (Son) and Mata (Mother), that complete their rotations every two days. The planet's sun is called An (Father). Shu orbits along the prime meridian of the planet, while Mata orbits along the equator of the planet. Sunrise, noon, sunset, and midnight for each of the two days have unique names.

    Primary Hours of the Khonsu

    - Valley — Sunrise of the first day of khonsu.
    - Son — Noon of the first day.
    - Triplets — Sunset of the first day.
    - Twins — Midnight of the first day.
    - Peak — Sunrise of the second day.
    - Father — Noon on the second day.
    - Seeking — Sunset of the second day.
    - Mother — Midnight of the second day.

Chapter 16

Fields of Eisodos, Alexandria, Baru, An 5660, Day 1

As the last few rays of twilight faded away, Louisa heeded nature's call behind the biggest boulder on the edge of camp. Grateful that a few large rocks had traveled the universe with them, she used the light of the central campfire to guide her way back. With every stride, the thigh-high stalks threatened to trip her. In the end, she resorted to high-stepping her way through the stubborn grass.

She entered the glow of the fire as Ben stood to address the assembled group. She moved to the side of him and the duffadar. Everyone but the four Lancers on guard waited to hear what Ben and Jeevan had to say. With the fire casting an orange glow, Louisa looked into the face of each man, trying to gain a measure of the Lancers' level of anxiety.

Ben began by relaying everything Ali had shared with them about their current predicament. Louisa held her breath when he brought up the Seba. She inhaled again only after he left out her role in triggering their "journey."

Well, what else do you call it when you travel across the universe to another planet?

When he reached the part about them being stranded on this new world, there were exclamations in Dogri and English as the Lancers unleashed their fear, anguish, and anger.

Jeevan raised his hand and ordered them to speak one at a time. One of the Lancers expressed his agony at never being able to see his family again, and a third of the soldiers nodded their agreement.

After letting them vent, Ben got to the actual goal of the meeting. "Now that you know what we're up against, we need to discuss our options."

Jeevan jumped in before Ben got rolling. "Lads, I need you to understand that we're sharing this information because you deserve to know." Jeevan's tone changed to his commanding voice. "*But* we should be happy that we're the ones who got sent here." Many of the men shared a look of confusion. "We prevented those men out there—" He pointed toward the villager's camp. "From shanghaiing the entire garrison. For that alone, you are all heroes." He gave a proud father's smile to his men.

"I have one last thing to say before I let Captain Ben finish. You are still in the British Army, and I am still in charge." Jeevan glared at the crowd, challenging anyone to dispute his words. When no one dared, he continued, "We will discuss our options and get your input. Afterward, I, and only I, will decide for the Thirteenth Lancers."

He let them absorb his words before commanding, "No matter what I decide, you will act like the professional soldiers you are. Do you understand?"

"Yes, Duffadar!" came the resounding shout.

Based on their body language, many of the men relaxed and became more at ease after Jeevan disabused them of the notion they had a say in the decision making.

With a satisfied look, he turned to Ben. "Please continue."

"Thank you. As I was saying, the people over there—" Ben jerked his thumb over his shoulder toward the villagers. "They want us to surrender and put our fate in their hands." He held up three fingers. "Here are our options."

He switched to a single finger. "We surrender. Stuck on an alien world with no understanding of the dangers, this might make the most sense." He shook his head. "Of course, those people were trying to kill us a few hours ago." He added another digit. "We fight." He shook his head again. "But we're very outnumbered."

Louisa kept reading the Lancers' body language as they listened. Their slight nods, hand movements, and shoulders relaxing made it clear they respected Ben.

Now back to three. "Finally, I want to give you a little hope." Some men sat up straighter at the word. "I believe the objects that transported us here are an advanced form of technology. There must be another way to power them besides sitting them outside for five hundred years." Ben gave the audience his crooked grin. "Our best option is to escape. Then we find out more about this planet and the objects." His smile faded. "I won't lie. It's a long shot, but the artifacts are our only real chance to find a way back home."

Not bad, Doctor Do Good. How do we get away?

The gathered soldiers began speaking with their neighbors, and Louisa strolled around the fire, picking up bits of conversation.

After coming full circle, she settled into her previous spot when Ben held up his hand. "Questions? Or maybe someone has another option?"

Lance Duffadar Ram stood up. "If there was another way to power these objects, wouldn't the people who made them know how to do that? Also, what do we do about these demons they talked about?" He sat down.

Ben nodded. "I've been thinking about your first question, and the only thing that makes sense is the people out there are not the ones who created the artifacts. No one creates something that takes five hundred years before it can work. There's a lot more to the story than they shared. As for the Lamentations, all the more reason to run. They don't have the right to kidnap anyone and force them to fight."

Acting Lance Duffadar Ghadge stood. "What about the creatures that Jeevan saw at the temple? What if this is their home? Isn't it better to surrender now?"

As Ghadge sat down, Ben answered, "I do believe the creatures live here, but humans do as well. One of the men we met with is a native. They said that they capture soldiers from Earth every five hundred years to fight the demons. It stands to reason that there are a lot more humans here. Maybe we can find someone to help us." He sighed before finishing with a firm voice. "To me, it's worth the risk, and for what it's worth, I will never give up trying to get us home."

Louisa wanted to keep the ball rolling in option three's direction. She stepped forward and raised her voice. "If we run, how are we going to get away? We can't just outrun them."

Jeevan's smile exploded. "We cheat."

For the next few hours, the camp came to life. Working with haste, everyone went about their responsibilities in near silence, but at some point, the noise of their activities needed to stay hidden. To cover their work, the Lancers sang many of the songs they had during their time excavating.

As Louisa buckled her last suitcase, Ben and Abu arrived to check on her. They began picking up her belongings during a break between songs. Out of the silence, Sowar Jadav's beautiful tenor filled the void with a haunting melody. Louisa stepped between Ben and Abu, who had stopped in their tracks. Javdav's words lifted her soul.

Louisa didn't take her eyes off the singing sowar while Abu whispered to the two of them. "He sang this song one other time. It's a poem called 'Journey Home' by a famous Bengal writer, Rabindranath Tagore. Namdeo translated it to Dogri before putting it to music. The words have a different meaning to me now." He translated the song with a whisper.

"The time that my journey takes is
long and the way of it is long.
I came out on the chariot of the first gleam of light and pursued my voyage
through the wildernesses of worlds, leaving my track on many a star and planet.
It is the most distant course that comes nearest to thyself,
and that training is the most intricate, which leads to the utter simplicity of a tune.
The traveler has to knock at every alien door to come to his own,
and one has to wander through all the outer worlds
to reach the innermost shrine at the end.
My eyes strayed far and wide before I shut them and said, 'Here art thou!'
The question, and the cry, 'Oh, where?' melt into tears of a thousand streams and deluge the world with the flood of the assurance 'I am!'"

Chapter 17

Fields of Eisodos, Alexandria, Baru, An 5660, Day 2

Roused from a fitful sleep moments ago, Ali took off on an angry march across the thousand yards of shimmering grass and flowers to the camp of the Seba thieves. The sun—or An, as the natives called it—cast a small shadow in front of him as it dawned over the western horizon behind him.

Just one more thing to get used to about my new home.

As he neared the campsite, what appeared to be men in the predawn light came into focus. Around several tents and a single wagon stood a number of scarecrows wearing British army jackets, along with one sporting a dress. Ali's gaze followed the trail of trampled grass left by the thieves as they'd fled. The path ran straight toward the mountains.

He turned to the villager who had awoken him. "You said they were singing for much of the night. When did it stop?"

The man scrunched up his face. "Around midnight."

Lost in thought, Ali did the quick math. His hands waved over the tops of the flowers near his thighs. Everywhere his hands passed, the plants grew taller, and their flowers morphed from yellows and purples to icy white. The cavalrymen had a full six-hour lead on them, and many of his men were riding double. If they all tried to pursue the thieves, he doubted the entire party could catch them. They would need to send a group of single riders.

They needed to track the thieves' movements. The professional soldiers would outmatch a smaller group, but they couldn't afford to lose sight of the Seba. If they did, Ali's failure would be total.

All the white flowers around Ali faded to black.

Chapter 18

Axclatca Pass, Border between Remus, Alexandria, Baru, An 5660, Day 2

Atop the earthen ramparts, Alexandria Ben Zev i Hurasu, Polemarchos of the Alexandrian 4th Stratia, waited for the Remulans to begin their attack. Two-thirds of her 20,000-soldier army stood in battle formation. Their lines stretched across the two hundred yards that made up the mouth of the Axclatca Pass.

Behind her soldiers, a 20-foot wide and 20-foot-deep trench dissected the pass, where it narrowed to 50 yards. Small bridges spanned the divide, leaving a path up and over the earthen ramparts where she stood.

On the cliffs above, four trebuchets and four catapults commanded the prairie to her front. A hundred *chevaux de frise* littered the field, their long wooden spikes a silent testimony to the violence to come.

Eight Remulan legions and their auxiliary cohorts stood at the edge of the 4th Stratia trebuchets' range. The Alexandrians were outnumbered four to one. The chances of holding the pass depended on her preparations and the arrival of the 2nd Stratia. The bravery, execution, and sacrifice of her soldiers would decide not only whether they held the pass but if Alexandria continued to exist as a nation.

If the Remulans gained control of the canyon, her country could not stop them from taking Neos Hierosolyma.

Arrayed in a three-deep checkerboard pattern, the Remulan formations doubled the width of the Alexandrian front. Horses moved behind the enemy legionaries as Alexandria checked the position of An. The star had risen a third of the way toward its zenith. In unison, several banners were held high at the rear of the various enemy units.

Remulan light cavalry poured through the gaps in the gameboard, forming groups of twenty in front of the legionaries. Following them came hundreds of light infantry. Minutes passed as these new troops organized themselves. At last, the blare of a dozen *cornu* filled the air.

With a yell, the cavalry and the infantry trotted forward. They remained at a jog until the first stones flew from the 4th Stratia's trebuchets perched on the cliffs. The Remulans' advance became a full-out sprint. They raced across two hundred yards of open ground to the closest of the giant spikes.

Most of the smaller rocks flung from the Alexandrian trebuchets failed to reach the charging Remulans, but the commander of the last engine timed his shot better. As one, a wall of three-pound, sharpened rocks pulverized an entire group of horsemen. Alexandria cringed at the screams of the dying horses.

A trumpet sounded to her immediate front—large lanes formed in the middle of her waiting taxis of phalangites. Out of tunnels of giant spears ran a thousand archers. They sprinted to the first row of *chevaux de frise*. Reaching the mark, they rained arrows down on the enemy's light horse cavalry and infantry.

Some enemy horsemen dismounted at the first of the wooden spikes, then tied ropes to the trunks that made up the axles of the giant caltrops. More than a few horses and their cavalry turned infantry dropped, pierced by arrows. The remaining riders urged their straining horses to dislodge the massive spikes. In fits and starts, they dragged them back toward the Remulan lines.

Small groups of enemy foot soldiers raced past the first row of obstructions, heading for the next line of giant caltrops. They ran as a group, holding their shields up to protect against the falling arrows. Still, some fell. Reaching their targeted chevaux de frise, they tied ropes to the wood.

The Remulan cavalry played leapfrog, dragging away the tethered spikes. After an hour, the game had cost the Remulans hundreds of lives, way too few for Alexandria's liking.

A few hours before Father, the enemy sounded their large curved horns again. Bloodied horsemen and infantrymen retreated to the safety of their lines, having removed more than half of the giant spikes.[1] The game pieces making up the first row of the checkerboard stepped off.

Alexandria gave a silent prayer to Adonai for the souls of all the men and the women she would lose today. She prayed they did not give their lives in vain, and if she were to fall, that He would take her into His embrace.

She again brushed aside her frustration at Basileus Philip's refusal to bring the nation's entire militia to hold the two chokepoints between the countries. If they could hold the pass and the straits, while bloodying the Remulans, the empire might turn toward easier prey.

With the battle beginning in earnest, Alexandria refocused on the action. Her troops knew their roles and the contingency plans. She had little to do but provide moral support.

For herself, even more than her soldiers, she needed to be here to watch the beginning of the struggle for her nation's survival. Alexandria had prepared for this moment her entire life. Zev i Hurasu were warriors, soldiers since arriving

---

1. Father is the name of noon on the second day of the khonsu or two-day lunar cycle. During Father, An is the only visible heavenly body.

from Earth. Instead of adding weight to her shoulders, she felt buoyed, feeling her ancestors' spirits beside her now.

The individual cohorts of Remulan legionaries shifted into their famous testudo formations. Shields moved to form a turtle-like shell over all the men. This stopped most of the smaller rocks until the Alexandrian trebuchet commanders switched to two hundred–pounders, capable of hitting and rolling.

A grin crossed her lips as a round boulder struck a turtle, leaving a wake of mangled Remulan soldiers. Her smile faded. With so many enemy cohorts coming forward, the Alexandrian siege engines couldn't keep up. She couldn't help but admire the enemy legion's fanatical discipline, marching toward death.

One of her trumpets called out, and the archers retreated behind her phalangites standing eight deep. As the first Remulan turtle reached one of the remaining giant spikes, its formation became malleable, enveloping the giant wooden quills. An invisible force lifted the device, turning it perpendicular to the turtle's march. Pre-sighted by the cliff-side artillery, the devices served their purpose. Two catapult balls struck the Remulan cohort, killing and maiming an untold number of troops.

More precise shots pulverized another slow-moving tortoise. Closer now, Alexandria could hear the enemy's orders relayed between units. Each shelled formation began double-timing around obstacles in its path.

She grew grim as a dark cloud appeared in the distance. The darkness flowed forward in a herky-jerky movement, moving like a school of fish. When it reached the original Remulan line, the school broke in two. Smaller clouds raced toward the cliffs at either end of her line. She'd prepared for the Remulans' wind singers, but looking at the two giant flocks of *bata*, she knew her estimations had been low.[2] [3]

The swarms of two-foot-long flying mammals dove toward the Alexandrian siege engines and their crews. The creatures' masters, four wind singers, glided far above, well out of arrow range. Bata tumbled out of the air as Alexandrian archers and slingers on the cliffs fired into the wall of furry flesh.

The creatures continued to fall, but as time passed, fewer dropped until the cliffs were as still as death. Her elevated artillery now silent, Alexandria commended hundreds of souls to Adonai. She clenched her jaw, and a single tear left a trail over her scarred cheek. She swallowed the anguish.

Tomorrow, I will cry for you.

Moving like a single organism, the much smaller flocks stuttered and twisted away from the graveyard. Alexandrian archers on the flanks launched waves of vengeful arrows at the creatures. In the end, a paltry number of the flying carnivores would return to their masters. She hoped the Remulans didn't have more, or her strategy for the rest of the day would be for naught.

The rest of the Remulan checkerboard lurched forward, and she refocused her gaze on the battlefield. Small horns trumpeted from the closest turtles, a hundred paces from her troops, and each turtle shell split apart. Out raced hundreds of light infantry, each soldier carrying a small shield and two pilum.

---

2. Wind singers are babiakhom or humans who can understand, translate, and manipulate almost any language, as well as the air, in a great-enough degree for the gliding babiakhom to generate lift to fly. Human wind singers must wear special wings to achieve flight.

3. Bata are a species of flying mammals similar to a bat, but they do not use radar or live in caves. The giant flying mammals are as big as hawks and act as the dominant avian predator species on Aaru.

Alexandria had anticipated the Remulans' use of the javelin-like spears. Tipped with soft metal, the spearheads bent when they embedded in wood, rendering a shield unusable. Her counter, soldiers in each of the first six rows, had extra shields and had practiced replacing any impaled ones. More surprises awaited the attacking Remulans. She prayed they would be enough.

Her archers killed many of the lightly armored infantry before they could throw their javelins. Still, hundreds of the enemy's lethal rods arched up in a jagged wave. Some found wood, a few found flesh. The cries of the Alexandrian injured announced the outcome. A second but smaller wave of javelins flew toward her lines. By the time the Remulan spearmen retreated, less than half of the pilum-throwing light infantry remained.

With the Remulans closing to seventy paces, the enemy horns heralded another shift. Turtles morphed into wedges. With a great shout, they launched themselves at the wall of Alexandrian phalangites, who had yet to lower their long spears.

The enemy legionaries crossed an invisible line, and the first three ranks of Alexandrian troops fell to the earth. They exposed ten raised earthen works, each protecting a ballista. Thunking sounds filled the air as eight-foot-long missiles sought the Remulan wedges.

Not all found flesh, but where they did, holes formed. Impaled by the giant bolts, sometimes two, three, and four Remulan soldiers flew into the ranks behind. Cries of the dying became preeminent as Alexandrian ballista crews scrambled to launch a second salvo, and archers aimed at gaps created in the enemy's shield walls.

On the right flank, three Remulan wedges struggled to reform when a second salvo hit the helpless legionaries. A whistle blew, and Alexandria's rightmost taxi parted. Three triangles of her cataphracts emerged, each aiming for a different broken formation.

Mesmerized, Alexandria watched her horse-powered block of lances roll through and over the now panicking enemy foot soldiers. Having cleared the tangle of Remulans, they wheeled around and charged again, crushing the survivors. Three cohorts destroyed, the Alexandrian heavy cavalry raced back through the gap, which filled in behind them.

Across the Alexandrian front, smaller tunnels opened, freeing her elite Lochem. Four man-powered wedges charged the closest Remulan legionary units. Twenty yards from the enemy, the last two rows of Lochem launched their own javelins toward the Remulans, sowing chaos. Alexandria enjoyed using her enemies' tactics against them.

The hostile soldiers came together with a dissonant crash. Without solid shield walls, the point of each Lochem wedge penetrated two to three ranks deep into the Remulan formation. Once her elite unit was engaged, their unique training and weapons came into play.

Each Lochem in the first row carried an oval-shaped shield and wielded a curved khopesh. They hooked and pulled down the enemy's shields to their immediate front. Behind them, their yoke thrust eight-foot spears over their shoulders into the exposed torsos of the enemy legionaries. Dozens fell as the Lochem wedge pulled and stabbed in an orchestrated dance.

Within a minute, each of the assaulted enemy cohorts turned and fled toward the fast-approaching second wave of Remulans. Disciplined, the Lochem reversed direction and raced toward their tunnels. Despite devastating losses, the remaining enemy units maneuvered into the holes created by their dead comrades.

To keep her ballista in the fight, she needed them to keep coming. She wouldn't waste troops by using the same failed tactics if she were in command on the opposing side. The Remulan commander must have had similar thoughts. Horns blew, and the enemy legionaries began moving out of ballista range.

She issued orders to the waiting Lochagos. "Sound the withdrawal. Hold out until you get word from the second wall. When it's time to go, go. Hagne's taxi has rearguard duty, so don't hesitate. HaShem willing, I'll see you there."

He saluted. "Yes, Polemarchos. I won't let you down." He yelled, "Withdraw." Several horns blared at the bottom of the wall.

Remulan catapults pulled by oxen moved foot by foot into range of her front lines. Her troops withdrew with practiced precision, racing to get over the wall before the catapult crews deployed their weapons. Turning toward the stairs on the embankment, she looked down the pass as far as she could see. She vowed to make the Remulans pay for every inch.

Adonai, may the Remulans run out of blood before we run out of canyon.

Chapter 19

Axclatca Pass, Baru, An 5660, Day 2

"Duffadar, we have signs of pursuit," called Sowar Betigeri.

As one, all heads twisted to the rear to see a small dust cloud rising behind their trail. Ben realigned himself, placing the mountains on his left as they had been for the last four hours of daylight. The dust cloud put their pursuers about five hours behind.

After setting up the fake camp, complete with decoy soldiers, the castaways had fled to the west. It had taken their column most of the night to reach the end of the sea of grass. At that point, they turned north, using the mountain range as a guide.

If north is really the direction we're going.

The mountains now gave the illusion of being big enough that Ben felt like he could reach out and touch them. The Earthlings continued moving over ground that would be considered lush by Egyptian standards. To him, the current landscape, with its short grass and occasional bare patches, seemed almost bereft of life after he'd experienced the fields of glowing grass.

Ben felt Louisa's stare and glanced over to see her looking his way. Holding on to his irritation, he ignored her and spoke to Jeevan, "Either our ruse didn't work as long as we hoped, or they split their group to ride solo. What do you think?"

Rubbing his hand in loving strokes along Chetak's neck, Jeevan replied, "Should we send a few men back to slow them down?"

Ben read between the lines and shook his head. "If we kill more of them, Ali may decide that capturing us is off the table."

Jeevan gave him a disappointed frown. "Then we won't kill anyone." He waved over Lance Duffadar Ram.

The wiry soldier clucked his horse forward and galloped to Jeevan. "Yes, sir."

"Do we still have those two boxes of caltrops?" Jeevan asked.

The lance duffadar nodded. "Yes, sir."

"Good. Take three men and lay them out for our new friends. Do not engage. Just verify they work and double-time it back." Jeevan gave a half-salute.

Ram saluted and pulled on his reins. His horse spun, and he called out in Dogri. Several horse soldiers peeled away from the column and joined the lance duffadar at the last wagon. After a few minutes, Ram and three lancers moved in the opposite direction, retracing their morning tracks.

Jeevan patted Chetak's neck. "We'll pick up the pace. We can head into the mountains if that doesn't slow them down enough. Either lose them or, in the worst case, find the ideal location for an ambush." Jeevan twisted in his saddle and yelled down the column, "To the trot!"

Ben dug his heels into his horse's side to match the new pace set by Chetak, the undeniable stallion in charge. Working on syncing his own bouncing body to his horse's new cadence, he pondered the situation. Ben wanted to end the threat, but he hoped to avoid more bloodshed. If they could keep their lead, maybe other choices would appear. They had a limited window because the wagons could not move at this speed for long.

For several hours, they alternated trotting for thirty minutes, walking the horses for thirty, and then the entire column dismounted to lead their horses on every fourth walk. Without the wagons, the handpicked and well-trained war horses could keep this pace until sundown, but they had at most an hour left before horses pulling the wagons could do no more than walk the rest of the way. Even then, they risked laming the wagon teams at this pace.

An hour later, Lance Duffadar Ram and his squad caught up to the column. He galloped up to Jeevan, and his horse, lathered and winded, fell into step. "They have around forty men. The trap hobbled about half of the horses, so they're riding double."

Jeevan sighed and said, "That'll have to do. Good job. We will walk the rest of the day. Pass the word."

Ram saluted and dropped back, giving orders.

Louisa asked, "How long do we have before they catch up?"

Ben peered over his shoulder. Based on the dust cloud, the villagers had made up little ground, but even with them riding double, that would soon change, given the column's current speed.

Jeevan dismissed the threat with a wave. "This group doesn't have enough men to attack us head-on. We will continue moving to keep some distance between us and their main force, but sooner or later, we will have to face them."

Ben ran over their limited options again when another Lancer raced their way from the north.

Jeevan grunted, launching Chetak toward the rider as if shot from a cannon. Ben urged his mount into a gallop, racing to catch up to the gray warhorse. Sensing another presence, he peered over his shoulder to see Louisa leaning over her speeding mare with a look of pure exhilaration.

He rolled his eyes. Knowing that her misplaced passion might well be the death of them, he gritted his teeth, his anger sparking. His horse pulled at the reins, forcing him to check his own direction. The gap to his destination was shrinking fast and his anger dwindling as well.

"Whoa!" Ben called out, pulling on his mare's reins to slow their approach to where Jeevan and the sowar exchanged salutes.

By the time his horse stopped, Ben heard the sowar say, "Two miles ahead, Negi and I were intercepted by twenty horse archers. They surrounded us before we could get away but didn't harm us. They're all human, but we couldn't understand them." He smiled. "We used hand signals to communicate that I would come back and deliver a message."

"Could you tell what language they spoke?"

"I'm not sure, Duffadar, but they tried speaking several. One sounded similar to the language that Miss Louisa likes to use when she sings." The sowar blushed.

Louisa had pulled up on the other side of Jeevan and smiled.

Jeevan asked, "Anything else?"

The sowar nodded. "They kept using the word *Kuru* and pointing to us, so finally, I nodded yes. They seemed to relax, and that's when they let me go."

Jeevan chuckled. Leaning over, he slapped the cavalryman on the back. "Good, good, good. That's how you think on your feet. Get back to the wagons and grab a bite to eat. I think we'll go speak with these archers and retrieve Sowar Negi."

Louisa's furrowed face showed the same puzzlement Ben felt.

As the sowar's horse trotted away, Jeevan maneuvered Chetak to regard them. "I'm not sure, but I think they believe we are Kuru warriors."

"What are Kuru warriors?" Louisa beat Ben to the question.

The jovial side of Jeevan always made Ben feel a little brighter.

With a wide grin, Jeevan said, "The Kingdom of Kuru was one of the first great Indian empires. It existed about three thousand years ago. One of our great epics records a civil war that took place at the time. Some soldiers who fought in these Lamentations must've been from Kuru."

Ben grinned. "You should promote the sowar. Maybe we can play along with this."

Louisa gave an impish smile. "Why, Dr. McGehee, I do believe you want us to be confidence men. I would've never suspected you could be so devious."

Ben looked Louisa in the eye until her grin faded. In a flat tone, he said, "I have a long way to go before I'm a master of deception like you."

The column had gone no more than a half-mile when a small group of riders appeared in the distance. They stayed too far away for Louisa to guess any more than they were shadowing the column.

She assumed the horse archers had sent some men to follow the sowar. The group stayed several hundred yards off their left flank for the next half-hour. She lost sight of them as the column entered an area of rolling hills, but she sensed they were still there.

During this time, Louisa continued mulling over the mess she had made. She should have felt remorse at stranding them all on this alien planet, but she couldn't find it within herself. She felt destiny drawing her forward. The things she'd hoped to accomplish back on Earth seemed small compared to what awaited her here on Aaru.

Of course, the unknown factors required her to adapt. She'd prided herself on always being truthful about her motivations and methods. Her uncle's words flashed to mind. "The only sure plans are those that change as quickly as the circumstances. If you don't adapt, you die. Never let pride, or what you think you know, stop you from accepting what is."

In the past, Louisa knew, as if by instinct, when to leave her stubborn streak behind. Many times, this sixth sense had allowed her to survive. Today, that meant she could no longer afford to be a lone wolf. To survive and thrive, she needed a pack.

No, I need a tribe. But how?

It had been almost a decade since she'd attended St. Denis and she could rely on someone other than herself. She'd only joined that friend group out of necessity to fight a common enemy: the Rule Book and the sisters who enforced it.

That's it. Enemy of my enemy. Be a lot easier if he'd get over being upset at me. Doesn't he see the opportunity before us?

Getting back to "trusted friend status" with Ben had to be the first order of business. Jeevan might be in command of the Lancers, but the duffadar looked to the captain for guidance, making him the unspoken leader of their expedition. Ben's icy demeanor revealed how far she had to go to make things right, but she vowed to keep trying. If that meant restraining her wild side to help the others get home, then she would do that.

Once he trusted her again, maybe she would explore her burgeoning curiosity about Ben becoming something more than a business partner—something she'd never consider back home. Yet being marooned could make a girl rethink her life's goals.

She looked at the rangy man riding ramrod straight as he bounced along. Brown, wavy hair curled out from under the brim of his hat, brushing the scar that stood out against his tanned cheek.

Emotions filled her at the sight. Some she understood, like the mild agitation aimed his way. The mix of desire and fondness was an unusual sensation for Louisa. She took a deep breath through her nose, letting herself feel what she would suppress otherwise.

Strange. But maybe it makes sense.

Ben wasn't like other men. How he took care of Abu and looked out for her had shown her his true heart. Together, they made a good team.

She wasn't looking to get married or, God forbid, have children, but this adventure had taught her that the two of them were stronger together. If allowing these feelings to grow meant solidifying their dynamic duo on an emotional level, ensuring her the tribe she needed, then that would be her plan.

There might be other options than Ben as they explored this new world. But even in the best scenario she could imagine, marrying some prince to become a queen, she found severe drawbacks. She had slim chances of finding a male on this planet she could trust like Ben, much less connect with on an intellectual level.

Besides, being a queen didn't appeal to Louisa as much as being the hero of her own swashbuckling adventure.

Every hero can use a trusty sidekick.

Ben represented the best option available, and it didn't hurt that she found the man attractive. Never a seductress, Louisa pondered just how she might win his heart.

Topping a slight rise, she spotted a wisp of smoke. After following it to its source, Louisa found a group of about twenty horses in the valley below. Their riders lounged around the fire. A few pointed and yelled, urging the group to action. They hurried to mount, spinning their horses to face Louisa's group before growing still.

A diverse crew, the horse archers, comprised of men and women in equal proportions, expanded Louisa's vision of a woman's possible roles on this planet. The Aaruan cavalry, wearing matching uniforms of blue trousers and red, long-sleeved tunics under leather armor, looked to have stepped out of an adventure book.

Headwear appeared to be an individual choice. It ranged from leather caps and metal helmets to free-flowing locks. Fifty yards out, Jeevan called a halt. Even at such a distance, Louisa sensed the deadliness of the storybook warriors, which dampened her growing excitement.

With his duffadar face on, Jeevan said, "Let's go." He walked Chetak forward.

Louisa and Ben followed while the rest of the column waited.

"Remember your roles. Jeevan, you're in charge. You're an envoy from the Kingdom of Kuru." Ben grimaced. "I hope that name holds up. Louisa and I are translators."

She and Jeevan agreed.

Ben removed his revolver and rested it across his saddle horn. His eyes never left the horse warriors, putting Louisa on high alert.

Twenty yards away, four horses stepped to meet them. Each archer held a medium-size, curved bow in one hand and a single arrow in the other. A man with black hair and a woman with blond, both faces tanned, were the outside riders. The middle pair were Sowar Negi and a short, wiry man wearing a plumed, conical helmet. The groups stopped, a yard separating the horses, who nickered their own greetings.

Speaking first, the wiry man sounded like he was using Hebrew.

Replying in Hebrew as well, Ben pointed to Jeevan. The man answered with a few more words, some familiar.

Ben translated, excitement in his voice, "This is Decadarchos Seth Heron ben Leshem of the First Mounted Archers of the Fourth Stratia. I believe it means he's a sergeant and part of the Fourth Army. He also speaks Greek. I told him that Jeevan's a special military envoy, and we're his interpreters."

Addressing the soldier in Greek, Ben said, "Thank you. The envoy would very much like to meet with the commander of the Fourth Stratia."

In between the two, Louisa leaned toward Jeevan, translating the conversation into English.

The weathered *decadarchos* shifted in his saddle, appraising them with stern eyes. "You must understand, these are trying times. For all I know, you're Remulans, sent to be a Trojan horse. Before I do anything, I have a few questions. What's the message you wish to deliver? Also, why does your envoy not have a babiakhom to translate?" Pointing at Ben, he asked, "Why do you wear small windows over your eyes?"

Touching his glasses, Ben turned up one side of his mouth in puzzlement. "The envoy is on a special mission and can only speak with the commander." He shrugged. "I don't know the details. He says that it can help in the fight with the Remulans."

Stop making assumptions, Ben, Louisa thought.

"We're translating because of trust. We've worked with the envoy for a long time. Finally, these—" Ben pushed his glasses up his nose. "Allow me to see better."

Louisa kept relaying the conversation to Jeevan.

With a furrowed brow, the decadarchos leaned forward. "I'll take you, but I can't guarantee you'll meet with the polemarchos." A wry smile creased his sun-leathered face. "She's kind of busy." With his tone growing grim, the smile disappeared. "At the first sign of a threat from any of you, we'll kill you all."

"What do you think?" Ben directed his question at Jeevan.

"Remulans? Do we want to get caught up in that?" Jeevan licked his lips.

"I'm not sure it matters," Louisa answered. "We need allies, and the group behind us will catch us if we don't go. Besides, it will look awfully suspicious to say no, now."

Ben nodded. "She's right. We have to gamble. What do you say, Envoy?"

Jeevan smirked. "Lowly interpreter, please tell the decadarchos to lead on."

With a crooked smile, Ben said in Greek, "The envoy is pleased. He asks that you show the way."

Sergeant Leshem nodded and spoke to the woman next to him. "Take the first stichos and keep watch for the Second's vanguard."[1]

---

1. A stichos is a Greek military unit that represents 8 to 16 men.

"Yes, Decadarchos." She kicked her horse and galloped off to the east.

The leader gave a command in Hebrew. The cavalry pivoted and led them north. Jeevan waved an arm, signaling the Lancers to march.

Rolling over the hill, on the far side of the valley, fifty more mounted archers surrounded the column. Though they were armed only with simple bows and arrows, Louisa didn't doubt the warriors could make good on the decadarchos's threat. With the die cast, she knew their lives depended on a favorable roll.

Clanging alarm bells rang loud and clear in Ben's head as soon as they were surrounded. The archers' heightened alertness couldn't be due to Ben's group, given the disparity in numbers. He weighed the idea of engaging the decadarchos in conversation again but thought better of it. That route opened him up to saying something that might expose their lies.

Since he couldn't figure out what lay ahead, Ben took a survey of the closest archers. For the most part, they rode in silence. On occasion, they bantered back and forth in the raunchy way soldiers do. Speaking in Greek and Hebrew, they sometimes used both languages in the same sentence. The combined culture fascinated him.

One rider wore a necklace with the Star of David, and another had the Shin symbol carved on her saddle. This spoke to a religiosity grounded in Judaism, while their uniforms said otherwise. They reminded Ben of illustrations he'd seen of Scythian horse archers. Hours of observation and theorizing left him no closer to understanding the warriors' true origins.

Maybe we're about to get some answers.

The mouth of a large canyon beckoned them northward. The surrounding cliffs stretched to the east and the west as far as he could see. Atop the bluff strolled several sentries carrying bows. A squad of spear-wielding Greek infantrymen in full armor stood guard at ground level. They could've been models for the painting of Alexander and Perdiccas in the tomb.

The decadarchos exchanged words with the soldier in charge, who waved them through. As they rode past, the guards' eyes bored lethal holes into Ben and his friends. The stone walls, a type of bluish limestone, were an unusual contrast to the sandstone canyons of Egypt.

As they stayed in the middle of the vast gorge, their horses' clopping echoed between the towering stone walls. Tents set up to either side of the broad avenue came into view. All but the last few were empty. From within, loud moans carried over the reverberating sounds of hooves.

Two men ran toward the largest tent, carrying a soldier writhing on a stretcher. With all the sides tied up, the big pavilion revealed the activity within. At the sight of two large wolf creatures treating the wounded, he gripped his reins tighter, causing his mare to miss a step. Behind him, several Lancers exclaimed out loud.

Jeevan glared at his troopers. "Shut it. Don't act surprised, no matter what you see."

The message flowed with military efficiency and reached the end of the column before most of the soldiers saw the aliens. The current bloody patient stopped yelling and thrashing in an instant. Before Ben rode out of earshot, he heard her speaking to the—*What are they? Medics?*—in a normal voice. His eyebrows rose.

How?

Past the tents, the passage curved to the left. As the riders rounded the bend, a line of medieval siege engines came into view. Lined up fifty yards in front of two trebuchets were four catapults.

Louisa's mouth gaped open. "Wow." A trebuchet's enormous arm rotated around, flinging what had to be a two-hundred-pound boulder.

In quick succession, several catapults followed suit. Large stones flew over the top of the canyon at unseen targets. Human crews rushed into action, their backs straining to turn large cranks. The great machine's arm retracted in steady jerks while other men stood by to load more missiles.

Abu pulled up next to Ben, forming a foursome. "I saw the wolf people. They're so tall. Did you notice they don't have tails? Look at that!" Abu exclaimed and pointed.

Mixed within the teams of human soldiers were two new types of aliens. In the middle of the massive machines stood a five-foot-tall, greenish creature wearing cropped pants. The fuzzy tail poking out of a pre-made hole was the only part of its body with fur. It looked like a baboon, and its colored snout gave it the appearance of a hairless mandrill, an animal Ben had seen at the London Zoo. In place of a red-and-blue snout, this creature sported one of light yellow and pink.

The aforementioned babiakhom? Babi means "baboon" in Egyptian. Coincidence?

The field behind the siege engines held rows of spherical boulders in front of more rows of large blocks of stone. Moving amid the rock garden were three diminutive creatures. Fox-like, they stood on hind legs, reaching a height of three to four feet. Each wore a blue shirt and pants, their bushy tails swishing. With bodies and hindquarters of reddish brown hair, the aliens had black eyes, wrists, and hands like a raccoon's.

Jeevan's eyes bulged. "What's that?"

He pointed toward the closest fox, which was placing its hands on one of the large unshaped blocks of stone. Clouds of dust shot from the rock, joined by the sound of grinding as if a saw worked across the stone surface.

What the hell?

The corner smoothed out, taking the form of the already-carved boulders. Nearby, a human crew of four men backed a small wagon up to one of the pre-carved stones. They lowered a ramp-like gate. Another fox walked to the stone sphere and held its hand over the rock without touching it. Ben blinked, and his jaw dropped.

The rock rolled toward the ramp with no one's physical touch, gaining speed until it ran most of the way up the incline. Humans helped move it the rest of the way into the bed of the cart. After closing the gate, they pulled the wagon toward a trebuchet.

Not possible. But more impossible than the walking, talking wolves and whatever that baboon-like creature was?

Ben couldn't deny he'd just seen some sort of alien raccoons defy the very laws of nature.

Yes. It's way more impossible. There must be a scientific explanation.

Louisa hissed, "Magic. These creatures can use magic." She sat up, arrow straight, and tilted her chin skyward. "How else do you explain it? This is more fantastic than I could ever imagine." She finished her quiet exhortation with a giggle.

Ben smiled but thought, *Damned fool. She's why we're in this mess.*

Abu fidgeted in his saddle. "Did you see the green creature's wings? When it lifted its arms, you could see a giant flap going from under its arm to the thing's body."

As they plodded between the war machines, both trebuchets sent boulders arching into the blue. Ben's feelings of dread overtook any talk of magic and aliens. "No one should get excited. We're riding toward an active battle, and we don't know which side is winning." He rubbed his temple, trying to reach the ache behind his eyes.

Louisa's face became more solemn, and Abu ran his hand through his hair.

"If we end up on the losing side, the victors may treat us like an enemy," Ben declared, his voice grave.

"Then let's make sure they don't lose." Jeevan's beard split into a wide smile. "You can finally show me what Agnes can do."

Ben scoffed.

Abu's voice rose an octave. "If there's fighting, can I use a carbine?"

Ben felt the blood drain from his face, and his stomach went queasy. He locked eyes with his son. "No. If anything happens, you and Louisa will take cover and stay behind the Lancers. If things get desperate, you can use the Schofield."

"Captain's right." Jeevan's grin disappeared.

Abu slapped his saddle horn.

"You can keep me safe and out of trouble." Louisa winked at the teen.

He returned a sheepish smile. "With us as a team, what could go wrong?"

Louisa giggled with Abu. Something nagged at Ben. When she saw him watching, she put her hand in front of her mouth, choking back the laughter.

Puzzled by the inside joke, Ben worried about dealing with this two-headed monster.

Team Abusa is nothing but trouble.

Ben's chuckle stuck in his throat. Running past, a stretcher crew carried an infantryman with a stab wound. The next porters hauled a female soldier. A green-fletched arrow protruded from the collar of her breastplate. The faint sounds of yelling and the clanging of metal drifted toward them.

As they stepped into another straightaway, the din of a battle grew. Less than a hundred yards ahead sat something Ben wished never to see again. Though sweat was beading on his forehead, he shivered.

A twenty-five-foot-high wall of dirt stretched across the canyon from cliff to cliff. In place of the cannon from his memories stood six ballistas. Instead of riflemen in gray or blue, the top crawled with what looked like Greek archers in blue tunics and Jewish infantrymen. Wearing white under shiny, scale armor, each Hebrew soldier held a Shin-decorated shield in one hand and a khopesh or a spear in the other. Ben's eyes flicked from the wall to a set of boulders flying overhead. They arched high over the fortification and seconds later crashed unseen in the distance.

In the middle of the wall, a stream of Greek *hoplites*—the only word that came to Ben's mind—streamed over the rampart. Carrying round shields and long spears, the soldiers descended two sets of stairs to the base of the wall. They joined entire units of men who had collapsed from exhaustion. Ben's column halted well behind the battle-weary warriors.

The decadarchos pointed to the left side of the wall and said in Greek, "The polemarchos is over there. The three of you, come with me."

Louisa translated to Jeevan.

Turning grim, Jeevan yelled back down the column. "Look lively, lads. There's a chance we'll get some action. Use the wagons for cover and distribute one hundred rounds per man. Ram, you're in charge." The Lancers leaped into action and moved with determined haste. A prideful look flashed in the duffadar's eyes before he nodded to their guide.

Ben leaned toward Abu. "Get two hundred rounds from the luggage, and help the Lancers distribute theirs."

Abu nodded, but his eyes shifted with uncertainty.

Ben patted his arm. "It's going to be fine. Just focus on one task at a time."

Ben nudged his horse forward, and they moved toward stairs on the wall's far left.

Ben dismounted and left his mare with an archer. The leader and three of his soldiers escorted them up the stairs. After reaching the dirt landing, Ben looked over the top of the five-foot wall that shielded them and the defenders.

The earthen rampart, dropping at a sharp angle, ended at the edge of a rectangular ditch. A wooden drawbridge lay across the expanse, with hundreds of hoplites waiting on the far side. They crossed in groups of twos and threes. Several hundred yards of empty canyon floor led from the ditch until the road made a sharp left.

The sounds coming from around the turn were alien yet familiar to Ben. The cries of the wounded and dying stayed unchanged, no matter the weapons of war or what language they spoke.

Scanning the landing, he discovered a small group of Greek soldiers and one of the babiakhom. They stood behind a solitary figure who leaned on the wall, staring outward. From behind, Ben couldn't guess the general's height. Along with a breastplate of polished silver, he wore a plumed helmet with tall white feathers.

The babiakhom looked Ben and his friends over, tilting its head toward them. Its goat-like pupils caught Ben by surprise. One of the waiting soldiers whispered into the baboon creature's fleshless ear before stepping back.

The general turned and invalidated Ben's assumption. An athletic, middle-aged woman dissected them with her piercing green eyes. She had been beautiful at one point, but the missing tip of her nose and the burn scars covering most of one cheek marred her face.

The general considered their threesome as she spoke.

Ben touched his ear. He heard the general's speech in English with her actual Greek words playing in the background.

"So, you're Kuruan and have a message for me?" Her green eyes, heavy with responsibility, grew sad. "I'm afraid you're too late. The Remulans will take the pass, and the Fourth Stratia will be no more, by Mother."[2] Her emerald irises grew fierce. "I'd give you an escort to the capital, but I need every soldier."

---

2. Mother is midnight on the second day of the khonsu and represents the end of the current khonsu and the beginning of a new khonsu. The moon Mata is the only visible heavenly body at that time.

Jeevan's eyes bulged. The *envoy* gulped, got control of himself, and raised an eyebrow at Ben, who shrugged.

The general looked over her shoulder toward the rising cacophony. Punctuating what she'd said, several thousand hoplites backed around the corner. Their long spears pointed the way they'd come. In rhythm, they stepped backward and thrust with a grunt before repeating. By the tenth step, a mass of helmeted men with large, rectangular, dark-green shields pushed against the points of the hoplites' spears.

"Tell the artillery to aim for the turn," the general spoke to the babiakohm.

The lips on the alien's snout moved as he appeared to whisper to himself. The polemarchos turned away from the travelers to regard the battle again. A minute later, screams punctuated the impact of stones slamming into the mass of green.

She turned with a tight-lipped grin. "How many soldiers do you have with you?"

Jeevan nodded, giving Ben permission to speak.

"We have eighteen cavalrymen, the envoy, and three others." Ben fell silent, hoping she wouldn't ask for assistance. He didn't want to get caught in another losing cause, and he saw no reason to put their lives in danger in an unknown war. Besides, not being certain of the *envoy's* response made him nervous.

The polemarchos frowned. "I recommend you leave as fast as possible and head for Neos Hierosolyma. The decadarchos will lead you to the entrance of the pass. You'll be on your own from there." She gave him a rueful smile. "If you meet the Second Stratia, tell them the polemarchos of the Fourth gave you a message for the polemarchos of the Second." Her eyes took on a distant look. "Tell Judah we'll fight to the last. Implore him to send as many soldiers as their horses can carry to the pass." She chewed on her lower lip. "Also, tell him I said for him to offer you an escort to the capital." She stopped, her eyes asking for a reply.

"Polemarchos, thank you. We'll do as you ask, and we'll pray for you and your men." A discordance rippled through the din, focusing everyone's attention on the battle. "Oh, shit." Ben's eyes bulged. Horrified, he saw the right flank of the Greek line crumble. Hundreds submerged under a wave of lance-wielding medieval knights astride stout warhorses.

Pierced and trampled, the hoplites shrieked in terror. A throaty victory shout rose from their tormentors. Panicked, the Greeks closest to the breach broke formation and sprinted for the drawbridge. In moments, the entire line disintegrated. Without mercy, infantry that Ben now recognized as Roman legionaries butchered the fleeing men.

His mind flashed to a snowy February day in Mississippi. Union cavalrymen made up of former slaves had engaged the Texas 6th. Ill-equipped and inexperienced, the Union soldiers panicked. His memories were as he lived it. In a dreamlike state, he floated outside his body as he and the rest of the regiment ran down the fleeing men.

Goosebumps prickled Ben's arms. He spun to his companions. "Time to go."

He saw horror etched across Louisa's face, the slaughter on the field mirrored in her eyes. She stood frozen, like a statue, with tears running down her cheeks. Ben grabbed her wrist and dragged her toward the stairs. Jeevan was halfway down when Ben reached the first step.

He glanced back at the rout. His trepidation reached a level he hadn't experienced for two decades. Petrified, he froze. Thousands of legionaries charged across the field, a mere fifty yards from the trench. Hundreds of these wannabe-Romans carried long ladders.

Remulans. They're Remulans. Irrelevant, stupid.

On the rampart, Greek soldiers strained against ropes, raising the drawbridge. Grim-faced, stranded troops formed a futile defensive jetty against the coming tide of green. Arrows and ballista bolts flew from the wall, engulfed by the crushing green surf. Dozens fell, but Ben knew the defenders couldn't stop the inevitable. It would take minutes—not hours—for the wall to fall.

We won't make it.

Louisa pulled at his grip. "What are we waiting for?"

Ben moved, following her down the steps. "Get to the wagons and stay with Abu. Help with ammo or injuries."

"Why? Aren't we running?"

Ben yelled to be heard over the roar of war. "Too late. They'll breach the wall."

She glanced over her shoulder, her eyes wide.

Twenty yards ahead, Jeevan looked back, too.

"Form a firing line," Ben screamed.

Jeevan held up a thumb and disappeared into the row of wagons.

Lancers climbed up to stand in the wagon beds or took up firing positions in the front. Other Lancers pulled unhitched horse teams away from the wagons. Ben and Louisa sprinted through the nearest gap and heard a frantic, "Dr. Ben, over here."

They ran toward Abu's voice to find him on top of the leftmost wagon and reaching into a large travel trunk. He came up with a box of bullets in one hand and Agnes in the other. Ben climbed into the wagon and took the rifle by the forestock from Abu.

Ben looked at Louisa and pointed at the ground. "Stay under the wagon, and don't shoot anyone unless they're wearing green and you can see their eyes."

She gave him a long, grim stare, then ducked out of sight.

Ben handed the teenager his pocket army. "Replace the barrels with the long ones on both revolvers, like I showed you."

Abu bent over the trunk and began rummaging around.

Cocking the rifle, Ben continued his instructions. "Then make sure they're loaded. Hand me one when I ask for it. Stay behind the trunk and reload. Okay?"

Abu rose with two metal cylinders. His voice trembled. "Yes, sir." His eyes hardened into steel. "Is this one of those desperate times?"

Ben put a hand on his shoulder. "If I tell you to shoot, you shoot." He squeezed. "Stay low. When you aim, aim for the chest. Focus and breath the way Jeevan taught you. Understand?" Praying he could keep them safe, Ben faked his best cocky smile, trying to reassure Abu. The teenager nodded and crouched.

Heart pounding, Ben turned his attention to the wall. The rush of war slammed against him, its euphoric venom racing through his veins. His addiction, chained and hidden for decades, broke free. Soaring at the thrill of walking death's edge, he went to the one place he hated to love.

God. Give me strength.

He'd seen good men trade their humanity for the power and invincibility of battle lust. Most died, ceding control to a beast that feasted on fear and violence, always needing more. But for the grace of God and an angel in a nurse's form, he would've never survived.

A mighty internal struggle ensued. Wrestling his addiction to an unstable stalemate, Ben harnessed the battle's energy. A fearless hyper-awareness settled over him.

The green-plumed helmet of a legionary popped over the top of the rampart. As fast as he'd come, a defender stabbed him with a sword. Another green torso pushed over the wall to be skewered by a Greek spear. Threatened by nearby Remulans, the ballista crews picked up weapons, leaving the giant crossbows still. Without help, the legionaries would soon be too many for the Greeks to handle.

Jeevan bellowed his orders. "Lancers, don't let any of them get over the wall. If it's wearing green, kill it. Fire at will!"

Two Remulan soldiers had secured a spot on the landing and fought back to back. Ben heard the crack of one Martini-Henry carbine and then another. The pair crumpled before rolling over the ledge on the near side of the wall.

Shaking himself, Ben looked toward the location of where he'd met the polemarchos. Several giant boulders flew into his vision, then dropped out of sight beyond the wall. Eyes darting left and right, Ben sought the white-plumed helmet and found it at last. The polemarchos used her khopesh to hook the top of a rectangular green shield and jerked the attached legionary over the edge. The falling soldier's scream ended the instant he slammed into the ground.

Near the polemarchos, one Remulan became two. Taking aim, Ben squeezed the trigger as a legionary drew back to stab the polemarchos's unprotected side. The shot took the soldier through the chest. Lifeless, he slumped half over the wall. The polemarchos's khopesh lanced over the other soldier's shield in a slashing motion and struck the man's head. A spray of red arched high as the man disappeared beyond the wall.

Several of the polemarchos's aids jumped in front of her, engaging the next invaders. Ben took aim and hit a Remulan standing on top of the wall, swinging down with his short sword. The man twirled around and fell out of sight. The polemarchos turned, head swiveling until she found Ben. They locked eyes. Ben touched the brim of his hat, and she gave a single nod before turning back to the fray.

Shirt drenched in sweat, Ben did not know how long the battle raged. Like an automaton, he held his breath, took aim, blew out, and pulled the trigger. He levered another round into the chamber, seeking his next target. Gunned down before gaining purchase on the wall, Remulans died by the score. A hazy cloud grew around the wagons from the black powder smoke of twenty rifles. Using bullets to estimate how long he'd been at it, Ben knew he'd emptied Agnes and both pistols more than twice.

He traded the empty rifle for a revolver from Abu when a stream of Greek hoplites sprinted past the wagons and up the stairs. Their white tunics lacked luster under gleaming silver breastplates. The fresh troops soon began to stem the flow of green.

Ben scanned for targets but could find none. Ballista crews returned to work, slinging missiles at hapless Remulans on the other side. Keeping a wary eye on the situation, Ben and the Lancers stayed at the ready until the defenders raised a cry of victory.

Jeevan yelled, "Stand down. Reload. Get water."

Ben sought out the polemarchos. Another Greek officer rushed up the stairs. He drew her into an embrace, which Ben thought carried more emotion than one officer's for another.

Abu stood, and Ben put his arm around the teen's shoulders. "You did great."

Louisa climbed up to stand next to Abu. Reaching across the boy, she passed a canteen to Ben. "What's going on? I couldn't see much."

Ben leaned Agnes on the trunk, grabbed the canteen, and then took several big gulps. After he wiped his mouth with his sleeve, he handed the water to Abu.

"We pushed them back." Ben pulled off his hat and wiped away the sweat with his other forearm. "At least, for today. Let's get some rest."

By the time the trio reached the canyon floor, the polemarchos and her retinue were jogging toward them. Her once-pristine white uniform and filigreed armor were now disfigured by blood and more.

Damn. She's scary.

As the polemarchos of the 4th Stratia stopped in front of Ben, Jeevan ran up with his gigglemug on full display. Ben bit back a chuckle, staying stoic in front of the Greek warrior.

The polemarchos cocked her head. "As I suspected. You've traveled much farther than Kuru." She put her hands on her hips and grinned. "Earthling."

The jig's up.

Ben sighed, the rush of battle seeping away.

Her eyes narrowed. "We will have much to discuss tonight over dinner." She started to leave but turned back to him with a wry grin. "If no one has said it yet, welcome to the Kingdom of Alexandria and the planet Aaru."

Chapter 20

Axclatca Pass, Baru, An5660, Day 2

It had been three hours since the battle had ended. Three hours since Ben's inner demon had once again challenged him for primacy. He caught his hands shaking and willed them to be still while he waited.

Soon after the fight, the Earthlings took over tents near the camp they had passed earlier. To everyone's relief, based on several wrinkled Alexandrian noses, the newcomers received fresh water. After washing his clothes and bathing for the first time in a week, Ben lost his goat stench.

To Ben's consternation, Abu insisted on coming to the dinner. Using a persuasive argument, the teen said their group would seem less threatening. About to acquiesce, Ben had to think it over again when Abu's new partner in crime threw her weight behind the young man.

"Abu, that's a great idea. Don't you think so, Ben?" Louisa's raised eyebrows challenged him to say otherwise.

Ben closed his eyes in frustration. He knew Abu, as he often was, might be percipient in ways the adults were not. But should he let *her* get her way?

Keep your powder dry. Save that Abusa veto for when it counts.

Smiling through gritted teeth, he said, "Fine. But look your best." He stopped short of saying something about manners, as his dad would have.

As for the goals of the meeting, the group agreed to probe for as much information as their hosts would share. They needed to know about Aaru and the Seba as soon as possible. As the agreed-upon spokesperson, Ben had prepared for different scenarios. The polemarchos deciding they represented a potential threat was his greatest fear. No matter what, they were at her mercy.

Rubbing at his sore shoulder, Ben tapped his toe with mild irritation outside the polemarchos's tent. Having donned his suit jacket for the first time since the train, he felt a little confined. Jeevan soon joined him, looking resplendent in his dress blues. The duffadar's waxed mustache formed two curled points, and his groomed beard looked like a soft, black chin-blanket. With a confident and mature air, Abu sauntered up a short time later, wearing his Friday best.

Where is Louisa? That woman—

The thought ended as his eyes widened. Gliding between two tents, Louisa looked stunning. Her midnight hair flowed down her back in the middle of her blue silk dress.

Gorgeous.

And untrustworthy.

He tried to ignore her beauty, and his eyes narrowed as he attempted to rekindle his anger. That worked until she got close enough for the scents of lemon and lavender to wash away his animosity. She tilted her head to her male audience and gave them a shy smile.

"Thanks for joining us." He heard the half-hearted irritation in his voice and switched to sincerity. "After you." He motioned to the tent entrance.

Ben followed Louisa, Jeevan, and Abu. As his eyes adjusted, the others shuffled farther inside, a nervous tension in their steps. By the time Ben stepped next to the boy, he tensed up as well. The babiakhom, who had been with the polemarchos, stood before the group.

The green alien spoke, and Ben knew the words coming out of its mouth were Greek, but somehow he heard them in English. His ears picked up the original speech like another conversation he could hear from the next table in a restaurant.

Seeing the baboon-like creature speaking up close, Ben noted a small incongruity. The babiakhom's malleable lips approximated a human's as it spoke, but the creature's longer snout-like jaw worked closer to a puppet's, snapping open and closed with each new syllable.

"Polemarchos ben Zev i Hurasu bids you welcome. I'm Lochagos Qeb of the Alexandrian Wind Singer Taxi. As non-Aaruans, you're probably unaware of the purpose of a wind singer." Skin unfurled as it raised its hands wide, flaps running from the underside of the arm to the waist.

Flying-Baboon-Squirrel.

"That's some pumpkins." Abu grinned, his face full of awe.

The babiakhom chuckled and lowered its arms. "We can sing many songs, but for this meeting, I will sing two. First, I'll translate everything said. Wind singers can understand, speak, and project any language. That's why each of you hears these words in your native tongue." The wind singer blinked. Translucent membranes retracted over horizontal pupils before the lids closed. "In addition, I'm singing another song, making it impossible for anyone outside to eavesdrop on our conversation." Qeb waved toward the six-person table in the center of the tent. "Please wait to introduce yourselves until the polemarchos arrives. Make yourselves comfortable."

They made their way to seats on both sides of the table. Ben scanned the spartan interior, filled with folding tables and chairs. He surmised this to be the Polemarchos's headquarters. Ben sat next to Abu, across from Louisa, and Jeevan took the other seat. Getting comfortable in the foldable leather chair, Ben perused the map on the table.

When each person had settled, Qeb moved to the end seat between Abu and Jeevan. He pointed to the map, showing more of the loose skin. "While we're waiting, the polemarchos asked that I acquaint you with the geography of Alexandria." Qeb poked a section of the map with mountains on one side and a large body of water on another.

Between them were symbols unknown to Ben. A blue line ran below Qeb's finger, and the strange symbols stretched between the mountains and then to the water.

"We're here in Axclatca Pass." Qeb's finger moved to the open area below the strange symbols. "South of the pass is the nation of Remus, Which, as you have seen, is attempting to invade Alexandria." His finger made a circle around the area above the strange symbols. "North of the pass, up to the end of the mountains, is Alexandria. Our first ancestors founded our nation two thousand seven hundred and fifty An ago. You need to understand, An is the name of our sun and what we call a year. Our first ancestors were the remnants of Alexander the Great's army who survived the Lamentations." Qeb looked around the table. "Do you understand what the Lamentations are?"

Rubbing his chin, Ben worked out the math. He knew the year Perdiccas's army went missing, and it didn't add up. He made a mental note to ask about the differences in time. Also, some of Qeb's explanations about the map were confusing.

Abu spoke before Ben could ask a question. "Qeb, my name is Abu. I don't want to offend you, but you're the first nonhuman we've, er, uh, spoken with. I have a question. Are you male or female?"

Qeb's baboon lips curled up at the corners. "You didn't offend me, young one. I should have considered that seeing a talking, uh, monkey, is quite different for you. I'm a male babiakhom. My species—the hysakas, the big wolves—and the stirithy, you call them *foxes*, came to Aaru as slaves of the Ancients." He held up his hand. "I'll explain. The Ancients, a race of immortals, enslaved our peoples long ago. We're not sure exactly how long." He raised his arms, and a cool breeze flowed over the table.

Ben's glasses fogged, and Jeevan shivered.

The babiakhom gave them a double-lidded wink. "They endowed us with our innate singing abilities to better serve them. We don't know why, but well over ten thousand An ago, the Ancients simply disappeared, leaving us alone."

With flushed cheeks, Abu said, "Thank you, but I have one other question. You said that your language interpretation magic was a song. I don't hear you singing."

Qeb nodded. "You're correct. You might call a singer a wizard or mage and a song a spell. I don't have to vocalize the song. I can sing in my mind. The more I practice, the easier it gets."

Abu nodded, and Jeevan asked, "Why is Remus attacking your country?"

Qeb's forehead scrunched up, giving him a solemn look. "The emperor of Remus doesn't believe the *ripvor*—laymen call them "reapers"—will return. Because of this, he decided he's free to conquer all of Aaru." His upper lip twitched into a slight snarl. "The Remulans follow a religion that sees all outsiders as servants of their devil. His subjects are religious fanatics. It makes an ambitious man like the emperor even more dangerous."

Ben had questions, too. He stepped into the conversation to get back to the earlier part of the discussion. "Qeb, I have a lot of questions. First, you stated Alexandria is to the north of the pass. As we made our way here from the fields where we, uh, arrived, I was certain we were going north. But according to the map, north is in the other direction."

Qeb shook his head. "Ah, yes, I once read that An and what you call the Sun work opposite. Each morning An rises in the west and sets in the east."

Louisa interjected, "That'll take quite a while to get used to."

Ben and his party nodded in agreement. "Thanks for the explanation. Just so I get the timeline correct, we know the year when the Greek soldiers disappeared from Earth. The number of An you gave us is about four hundred and eighty more than the number of years on Earth. How many days are there in an An? Also, I've noticed feeling stronger than normal. Is Aaru smaller than Earth?"

Qeb nodded along with the questions. "Each An is three hundred and twenty-six days. We divide our calendar into ten months of sixteen khonsu each. There is a three-khonsu period at the end of each year, which is a holiday called Anu. As for the size of Aaru, the planet's circumference is about twenty-two thousand and five hundred miles."

Before Ben finished doing the math in his head, Louisa leaned toward the babiakhom. "So, Aaru is ninety percent as big as Earth, which is why we feel stronger. We are used to Earth's greater gravity. That doesn't account for all the discrepancy in the length of a year."

It took a few more moments for Ben to finish. "If both planets spin at similar speeds, then combined, you have the difference. Aaru's An is roughly eighty percent of a year."

Louisa beat him to the question that sat on the tip of his tongue when she asked, "What's a kahnzu?"

"I don't know when you arrived, but I'm sure you noticed that we have two moons. Every two days, the moons go through a cycle we refer to as a khonsu. You'll learn the specific times associated with a khonsu quick enough." Qeb tapped his hand on the table twice and nodded.

Another ode to Ancient Egypt. Khonsu was one of their moon gods.

"Last question regarding time. How many hours are in a day?" asked Louisa.

Qeb tilted his head. "Twenty-four."

Jeevan produced a pocket watch from his jacket. "Then, can you tell me what time it is?"

Qeb looked at the watch with curiosity. "Does that device tell time? How fascinating. I'd estimate it's three hours past Seeking. I don't know what that maps to on your device."

Jeevan handed Qeb the watch. "This is a pocket watch or a clock. The number twelve represents both the middle of the day and the middle of the night. Each number around the circle is an hour. So one o'clock is one hour after what we call noon or midday. Does this make sense?"

Qeb turned the watch around in his hands before bringing the face close to his snout. His eyes moved with each tick of the second hand. "Amazing. We call midday by two names, depending on whether it's the first day of the khonsu or the second. Today, it's called Father, but on the first day, it's called Son. Seeking would be the number six."[1] He handed the watch back.

Jeevan looked at his watch. "We have twenty-four hours in a day, sixty minutes in an hour, and sixty seconds in a minute. Is your system the same?"

Qeb scrunched up his snout, which bared his teeth. The babiakhom's molars proved to be more human than a baboon's. "Yes, we use the same system. You can test it out tomorrow with an hourglass to see if there is any difference."

Jeevan looked hopeful. "Yes, I will. Thank you." He began winding his watch.

---

1. The Aaruan year has 10 months of 32 days, which comes to 326 days in an An. There is a 6-day or 3-khonsu holiday period at the end of the year. The Aaruan week is 8 days long, consisting of 4 khonsu. They work 6 days and rest 2 days. The khonsu is based on the 2-day cycle that the two moons travel. Thus, time is thought of in periods of two days. Special names are given to the various times during the day, based on where the moons are. For example, when the two moons and An are lined up, it's "Triplets." An alone is called "Father."

   Months/Yarns

   1. Aru (Birth) — Spring

   2. Poru (Plant) — Spring

   3. Baru (Bloom) — Spring/summer

   4. Choru (Tend) — Summer

   5. Taru (Flourish) — Summer

   6. Zoru (Prepare) — Fall

   7. Naru (Harvest) — Fall

   8. Foru (Fallow) — Fall/winter

   9. Yaru (Endure) — Winter

   10. Ru (Rest) — Winter

   11. Anu (Blessed Father, a 3-khonsu celebration) — End of winter

Qeb added, "If it's not the same, a metal singer can build you a new one or fix the one you have. Just show them how it works, and they should be able to duplicate it."

Ben found the conversation interesting and added metal singer to his list of questions. Yet he wanted to get back to more important topics because time moved regardless of how many man-made time frames humans created to mark its passage. His next question would hopefully bring more insights. "You mentioned that there are three intelligent nonhuman races on Aaru. Is that correct?"

Ben was unsure, but he thought Qeb smiled. "Technically, there are four and sometimes five nonhuman races. There are also three human derivatives."

Ben's jaw went slack.

"The native species of Aaru is an insect race. They're like an ant colony. Intelligent, but their way of thinking and communicating is very different. They stay to themselves in what we call the hives." He pointed back to the strange symbols on the map. "These represent hives. They are very territorial. Veer from agreed-upon paths, and an entire army could disappear without a trace."

"And the derivatives?" an excited Louisa prompted him.

The polemarchos swept into the room, looking very different from the blood-covered soldier of a few hours earlier. Curly red locks fell to her shoulders, contrasting with the mid-thigh-length, silk chiton of pure white. She had it pinned over one shoulder, and the belt at her waist held a simple sheathed dagger.

Moving with the grace and power of a leopard, she reminded Ben of the living embodiment of Diana, the goddess of the hunt. Qeb stood, and the rest of the table followed.

She came to stand behind the end seat on Ben's side of the table. "Thank you for joining me. I hope Qeb has been informative while you were waiting. Let me introduce myself again since you've brought an extra guest." She flashed a warm smile at Abu. "I'm Alexandria ben Zev i Hurasu, Polemarchos of the Alexandrian Fourth Stratia, or what's left of her." The smile went flat. "And you are?"

Ben started. "Polemarchos, thank you for your hospitality. I'm Dr. Ben McGehee, and this is my son, Abu." He touched Abu's shoulder. The teenager nodded and smiled.

Louisa followed with a slight lean of her head. "Louisa Sophia. It's a pleasure to meet you."

"Polemarchos, I am Duffadar Nahal of the Thirteenth Bengal Lancers." He gave a formal bow.

The polemarchos smiled and opened both hands toward the chairs before sitting down. As they took their places, a man and a woman moved into the tent wearing simple tunics. One carried a platter filled with roasted and sliced meats. The second held a tray with steaming vegetables on one side and pita bread on the other. Qeb rolled up the map on the table, making room for the dishes.

Ben's stomach rumbled as the mouthwatering aromas reached his nose. Several more servants arrived. One laid out beautiful wooden plates with matching chalices. Another filled the cups with what looked like wine. The group followed the polemarchos's lead, staying silent as the servants worked. Last, a large bowl of what looked like hummus settled into the center of the table, and the servants disappeared.

Alexandria gestured toward the food. "Please enjoy. We can speak as we eat. I believe I interrupted your conversation." She looked at Qeb.

"Yes, Polemarchos. I was about to explain the different types of human races."

"Make sure to cover how they came to be."

"Yes, ma'am." He turned his attention to the Earthlings, who used the pause to fill their plates. "Where to start? Hmm." He used a long index finger to scratch his neck. "The beginning is best. Five thousand six hundred and seventy An ago, a group of hysakas priests discovered the Seba and released the song within."

Louisa and Abu exchanged a strange look, causing Ben to drop the meat he had piled on a piece of pita bread. It plopped back to his plate, and heat rose in his cheeks.

What did that mean?

"When they did, they traveled to Earth. To their dismay, they couldn't figure out how to make the Seba bring them back. The story goes, they met some primitive humans. Many of these humans worshiped them as gods." Qeb's horizontal pupils twisted on their axis, becoming vertical slits of black on a bed of amber and drifted up toward the top of the tent.

So strange.

Jeevan's eyes went wide, and he whispered, "Creepers."

Qeb's pupils flipped again. "They helped bring civilization to the ones you call Egyptians. Aaru's Kermans are their descendants."

That explains a lot.

Qeb pursed his lips and took a sip from his cup in a very human fashion. "The priests experimented for ten An before getting the Seba to sing the song to bring them home. When they did, they were living in a large human city. To their surprise, the entire city, its inhabitants, its seeds, and its livestock came with them. The number of humans counted in the tens of thousands. This event is the start of our calendar. Humans arriving is An zero."

Several of Ben's puzzle pieces fell into place. The babiakhom had just solved the mystery of the Sumerian city of Mari for him.

Can't wait to tell Chippee.

Abu stopped Qeb. "Sorry to interrupt, but is this meat pork? It doesn't look like it, but it smells like it. My religion doesn't allow me to eat pork."

The polemarchos's laugh rumbled from deep down. She gave him a reassuring look. "No, Abu, we don't eat pork either. Everything we eat is kosher. Are you Jewish?"

260

Abu shook his head. "No, ma'am, I'm Muslim."

Tilting her head, the polemarchos replied, "I'm not sure what that is, but don't worry. The meat is from an animal said to be from the hysakas's home planet. It's called a zehorg. It's a large, furry, flightless bird, but, yes, it tastes like pork. All the flavor without the sin. Qeb, please continue."

"These humans, being insatiably and foolishly curious creatures, explored many Ancient sites. They found magic artifacts like the Seba but different."

Ben, picturing a black-clad thief taking the Seba objects from the temple altar, glared at Louisa over his cup. She grinned back and winked. Closing his eyes, he worked to keep from spewing the delicious wine across the table. She chuckled.

"The artifacts bestowed some new abilities on a portion of the humans. They kept experimenting, which resulted in two different races. The elves and the welves. Both have the gift or curse—depending upon your viewpoint—of immortality."

How?

Jeevan's cough stopped the conversation. A jolly laugh bubbled up from deep inside him. The polemarchos's brow furrowed, and Ben tapped the table to get Jeevan's attention. The Lancer held up his hand with a finger raised. When he regained control, he cleared his throat. "Sorry, but are you serious? There are actual elves on Aaru."

Qeb seemed taken aback. A tone of indignation filled his voice. "I can assure you there is nothing funny about it. Both races are pompous and arrogant and look down on all mortals. Good thing they hate each other with a passion." He calmed. "Luckily, the hysakas captured the devices before the humans caused more damage. Thank Hashem, both races breed infrequently, and neither can sing."

Ben leaned toward Qeb. "Do these people really call themselves elves and welves? If they were Sumerian, they wouldn't know what an elf was."

The wind singer chortled, bobbing his head in time to the sounds. "Ah, yes. They originally called themselves the *ašte* and *hum*."

"So, *point* and *white* in Sumerian." Ben tilted his head.

Why would they be called that?

Qeb nodded as he took a quick sip. "Correct. Their new names, elves and welves, might be the only positive contribution to come from the dwarves."

Jeevan and Abu started laughing, bringing a stern look from Louisa. Ben added his own glare at the two.

Still snickering, Abu asked, "You mean short, stocky, super-strong men with long beards?"

Qeb looked at the polemarchos with questioning eyes when Ben said, "I'm sorry for my son and my colleague. We've seen and done so many impossible things in the last week that nothing should surprise us at this point." He finished by elbowing Abu and kicking Jeevan under the table. The two sat up straight and stifled themselves.

Qeb began again. "They are short, stout men, but some have beards and some don't." His lips twisted. "Two Lamentations ago, in forty-four twenty-two, seafaring warriors known as Norsemen were brought to fight the ripvor. During the fighting, they discovered another device. It gave them greater strength and somewhat longer lifespans."

Eyes wide, Abu leaned toward the babiakhom.

"Subsequent generations became shorter and more stout until they reached their current stature. It's hypothesized this supported the bigger bones needed for so much strength. The hysakas captured this device as well, but not before these dwarves split into three nations." A clearing sound came from the back of his throat, and he puckered his lips, looking like he wanted to spit. He swallowed and said, "No one wants more dwarves. Most of the current ones are simply barbaric and have become a scourge."

Ben was about to ask about the Seba when the polemarchos held up her hand. "Thank you, Qeb. But before you field more questions, I have a few for our visitors." Her commanding voice drew everyone's attention. "Dr. McGehee, please tell us how you came to Aaru. If you're willing, tell me where the rest of your group is."

Ben had prepared for this question. Going back and forth, he struggled with how much to share about the temple, the theft, and the villagers. In the end, he decided he'd tell most of the truth. They had to gamble with the cards they were dealt. "Miss Sofia discovered an ancient letter that discussed a missing Greek army. Probably your ancestors. She and I set out to discover what we could about the mystery." Straightening his shoulders, Ben continued, "She asked for my help because, besides being a medical doctor, I'm a scholar who studies ancient cultures. Jeevan and his soldiers came with us to protect Miss Sophia."

"Are you a noble?" The polemarchos's eyebrows rose, and her green eyes flicked to Louisa.

Louisa's jaws flexed, and her eyes tightened. "Only my father."

"Ah." The polemarchos turned to Ben.

"We eventually found a strange temple and saw our first aliens. Two, uh, hysakas priests did a ceremony with the Seba. We didn't know what it was, but we took it and accidentally caused it to sing, bringing us to Aaru."

Ben stopped there, waiting for questions. The polemarchos tapped the fingers of her right hand on the table. Ben didn't dare interrupt her.

Her hand stilled. "So you don't have more soldiers? There's no bigger camp?"

Where is she going with this?

"That's sort of correct. When we triggered the Seba, we were under attack by people from the temple. Around two hundred in total. They came with us, and one of them was Aaruan, a human priest." Ben smiled. "We had a parlay. They explained that the Seba only works every five hundred Earth years, and we had put the entire planet in danger. Finally, they demanded we surrender." Ben raised both hands off the table, palms out. "After discussing the matter, we took the device and ran. We decided we would look for a way to power the Seba. That was last night."

The polemarchos leaned in, resting her elbows on the table, and interlaced her fingers. "The demise of the entire world's population is a possibility. If the ripvor return, which is in doubt, we must defeat them or die. That is the curse of the Lamentations."

She separated her hands and leaned back in her chair. "On the bright side, it was never the number of Earthlings that defeated the ripvor. It was their advances in military weapons and tactics. Some recruited soldiers were better than others in providing an advantage. For instance, the dwarves helped very little until they received their added strength."

Ben pursed his lips and blew. "That's good to know. I'd hate for our carelessness to cause a disaster. Polemarchos, may I ask you a question about the ripvor and the Seba?"

The polemarchos smiled. "Call me Alexandria, please. I would be happy to answer your questions, but indulge me a little longer. At the wall today, you and your soldiers used a new weapon, killing hundreds of Remulans. What are these fire sticks, and how do they work?"

Ben moved his hand to his holster. "Alexandria, likewise, call me Ben. I'd like to show you one of these weapons. It's called a gun. May I?" She nodded. He removed the revolver and placed it on the table, pointing it away from everyone. "What we used at the wall are rifles. They're a type of gun that's more accurate at longer distances. This smaller gun is a revolver because the bullets spin in the cylinder like this."

He picked up the gun and spun the cylinder. When it came to a stop, he pulled the barrel forward and twisted to expose the bullets in the pocket army. He removed one and handed it to the Polemarchos. She examined the brass casing as he said, "That's a bullet. The gray part, at the top, is like an arrowhead. The brass portion holds gun powder. When you pull this trigger," he put his finger on the trigger, "the powder ignites, and the explosion sends the tip flying so fast you can't see it. That's what killed the Remulans."

Turning the bullet around, she scrutinized it from every angle with a little smile. "Amazing. It's so small. How many of these guns and bullets do you have?"

Instinct told Ben to be cautious. "I think we have about fifty guns. I'm sure the villagers each had one, but we don't know where they are. The problem is the bullets. We used ten to twenty percent of the ones we have, and we can't make more."

Rubbing her chin, Alexandria leaned forward. "We'll ask one of the metal singers to make bullets. Is your gun powder the same as what we call black powder? The Nipponese brought it with them during the Phantom Lamentations. We only use it to blow up fortifications or lay traps for the enemy." She smiled wide, and small wrinkles formed on her scarred cheek. "We used most of the stratia's supply at the second wall, but I'm sure we have a little somewhere. Tomorrow we'll try to make more of these bullets."

Ben smiled. "We will. Thank you. Alexandria, can you help us with the problem of how to power the Seba?"

Narrowing her eyes, she tilted her head. "I'm not sure how."

Ben waved one hand in a circle. "Based on what the priest told us and what Qeb shared, the Ancients created the Seba. I think it uses something we call electricity to power its, uh, song. It's a new technology on Earth. We generate electricity to power artificial lights and other machines."

She scrunched her face. "Interesting." The word dripped with equal parts doubt and curiosity.

"Much has changed on Earth in the last five hundred years." He shrugged. "Anyway, the Ancients must have had a way to power the device other than leaving it in the sun for five hundred years. Is there anywhere we can learn more about the Ancients?"

Alexandria looked to Qeb, who answered, "In the mountains, there's a site built by the Ancients. It's a three- to five-day journey from here." He shook his head. "I doubt it will help you. No one can read Ancient. Not even us wind singers." He pulled his lower lip over his upper before pursing both. "The Ancients guarded the knowledge of their magic. They gave our ancestors a form of writing very different from theirs."

"On Earth, it's part of my job to decipher the meaning of ancient languages." Ben turned to the other end of the table. "Alexandria, would you allow us to travel there?" Ben felt his companions tense, holding their collective breath. Their fate rested in the polemarchos's answer.

"Create more bullets and show my metal singers how to make your guns. Afterward, you may go to this place." Alexandria gave them all a rueful smile. "Without your help today, our people would be slaves, and my soldiers would be dead." She struggled to get the words out as a single tear fell onto her unscarred cheek. "I owe you much, and my country owes you even more."

Her smile turned warm. "Ben, why do you wear those things over your eyes? The only people I've ever seen wear something like that are welves."

He took his glasses off and held them up. "They help me see. My eyes have an issue called nearsightedness. Without glasses, everything far away is blurry."

Alexandria frowned. "And you've had this malady your entire life?"

"Since I was thirteen," Ben answered.

"That's unfortunate. We will cure you of this illness now. Qeb, call for Khepri."

The babiakhom stood and walked outside the tent for a short while before returning. "She'll be here in a few minutes."

Alexandria said, "Good. Do you have questions while we wait?"

Louisa jumped at the chance. "Polemarchos, uh, Alexandria. Please, call me Louisa. I wondered if you could provide us with a guide to the Ancient site?"

There she goes again.

After curling the pita bread slathered with dip and piled with zehorg into a miniature bowl, Ben took a big bite. Abu refilled his cup and lifted it when Ben shook his head and gave him the look.

That's enough, big guy.

"Khepri's alpha—you'd say her 'lead spouse'—Ssherrss, may be able to guide you. I'll assign both of them, along with a stichos of Lochem, to accompany you. The site is deep in the Nefru mountains, which is part of the welven kingdom of Kutha." She frowned. "Hopefully, they'll leave you alone. If not, it always helps to have a few extra men. Ben, Ssherrss is the metal singer who will help you make bullets."

Louisa gave a slight bow of her head. "Thank you. I have a question about the ripvor. They're the same thing as reapers, correct? What are they, and where do they come from?"

Ben dipped another piece of bread into the hummus, glad to let others direct the conversation. His stomach kept reminding him how little he'd eaten the last few days. The dip contained a strange seasoning, but it worked to satisfy his hunger pangs.

"They're a race of reptiles from another planet. It must have been another slave planet of the Ancients." Alexandria took a sip of wine. "Some of them are singers with the same magic as our singers. They even have stout lizards comparable to dwarves. When they come, they bring an immense army and kill everything in their path." She put her cup on the table. "A lot of knowledge about them gets lost since they only come every 688 An. The last cycle didn't happen. It's now been 1,300 An since anyone has seen a living ripvor."

Abu raised his hand. "Excuse me, but if they have the same magic, can't you communicate with them? Has anyone ever asked them what they want?"

Alexandria flashed a mother's smile at the teenager. "That's a good question. You remind me of my son. He's close to your age and smart like you. As to your question, yes. Several times, they captured ripvor and asked that very question." She shook her head. "Most refused to speak, but when my ancestors fought in their Lamentations, they captured the ripvor leader. Its only words were, *Only the smartest and the strongest*. Not another word, even after days of torture from a life singer."

Conversation screeched to a halt. Ben's eyes bulged at the sight of a giant wolf stepping through the tent flap.

Whoa.

His and Abu's reactions caused Louisa and Jeevan to look over their shoulders. The wolf wore a light-blue toga-like dress, similar to the polemarchos's chiton.

It said, "You asked for me, Polemarchos?"

Alexandria waved to Ben. "Yes. This man has an affliction with his eyes. Please help him."

"Yes, ma'am." Khepri's gaze settled on Ben. "Do you have a name?"

Gulping, Ben lost his ability to speak until Abu gave him a nudge. "Uh, I'm Ben."

Amusement filled the canine's eyes, which made Ben even more discomforted. He'd seen happy dogs but never an amused one.

"Good. Come here." The tall whiskers of an eyebrow lifted. "Please."

Looking at his companions, Ben sought support. Louisa reached across the table to give his hand a reassuring pat. As he pushed up from his seat, she mouthed, "Be brave."

He took several faltering steps around the table to stand in front of the towering wolf. Feeling small, he straightened to his full height.

She. Yes, Qeb called the hysakas her.

That, along with the dress, woke up the manners Ben's mother had drilled into him from birth.

"It's a pleasure to meet you, Miss Khepri," he stammered, holding out his hand.

The she-wolf looked down at him, baring her teeth in a smile. Or so Ben prayed. She ignored his hand, her snout moving close to Ben's left ear. With a long sniff, she took in his scent before moving to look him in the eye. The smell of unknown flowers lingered after she pulled away.

"It's nice to meet you, Ben, but I have an alpha. The formal title would be Mrs. Khepri. Instead, just call me Khepri." Her sharp-toothed smile returned. "There's no reason to be afraid. I'm here to help you." She pointed a long finger at his face. "Can you take that contraption off?"

The Greek to English translation he heard in the foreground did not do her voice justice. Ben liked the strong, soothing alto voice echoing in the background. It should have calmed him but not today. Besides his discomfort, he found following the gigantic wolf's speech pattern disconcerting.

Khepri's race lacked the flexible lips of Qeb's people. He heard the translation while watching her mouth move like a hand puppet, but with the matching words echoing in the background.

He removed his glasses, folded them in his hand, and held them at his side. Everything became fuzzy except for the enormous wolf's head grinning at him.

She placed her hands on both sides of his face. Black, dog pad–like skin covered her palms and the bottoms of her fingers. Ben expected roughness similar to the pads of his childhood dog, Rufus, so her supple skin was a surprise. Yet her touch couldn't keep his attention for long because the sight of her trimmed, pointy nails contributed to the sweat beading up on his forehead. He swallowed and took a deep breath.

Keep it together.

Warmth radiated from her hand-paws. The heat seeped into his skin, moving over and through his entire body. A slight burning filled his eyes with tears, while a soothing sensation washed over the rest of him.

She removed her hands, and Ben blinked away the tears. He took his eyes off the smiling wolf's snout and looked around the tent with caution. It took a moment, but the results were undeniable. The faces of his companions, who watched with apprehension, became sharp.

Holy shit. Praise God.

"Everything's so clear. It's a miracle." He turned back to Khepri and clasped her bigger hand in both of his, then shook it while grinning ear to ear. "Thank you, Khepri. Thank you."

He looked at Alexandria, but she raised a hand. "No need to thank me. No one on Aaru lives with such limitations." She reached up and touched her fire-scarred face, her eyes going to a faraway place. "Unless they must." Her vision returned to the present, and she smiled. "Life singers, like Khepri, heal them. It's not a miracle. It's magic."

Ben nodded, and the big wolf woman bowed to the polemarchos. "I'll take my leave now."

Alexandria said, "Thank you, Khepri. Inform Ssherrss that both of you will work with the Earthlings starting tomorrow. Report to Qeb. He'll give you the details of your new assignment."

"Yes, ma'am." Khepri placed her fist over her heart and left the tent.

Ben took his seat and put his now-unneeded glasses into his pocket.

Alexandria looked to Qeb. "We should finish the night with a song. Send for the singers."

The babiakhom left the tent and returned a few moments later. Three men and two women followed him. A man and a woman stepped in front of the remaining trio. The three in back started playing instruments that appeared to Ben to be a kithara, a lyre, and an aurolos.

The singers sang a duet, bouncing between Hebrew and Greek. Qeb's translations made the story easy to follow. This time, the singers' voices were at the forefront, with the translation further away. The song, called "Birth of a Nation," reminded Ben of an ancient Greek poem. It told the tale of Alexander's troops and their eventual victory over the ripvor horde.

"Reapers come to harvest, Lamentations renewed

The Keepers did summon Alexander's Greatest

Lochem yoked two by two, Zev's Wolves to war flying

Salvation on the edge, Hurasu's bow sang true

Arch Demon, arrow pierced, Sorrow to Rejoicing

A war won, Aaru saved, Alexandria born."

When the song finished, everyone clapped, and the music group, after bowing, exited the tent.

Louisa stood and turned to Alexandria. "Polemarchos, would you mind if I sang a song to show our appreciation of your friendship?"

"By all means."

Louisa's beautiful voice filled the tent. It took several verses for Ben to realize she sang a new American song, "I'll Take You Home Again, Kathleen." Louisa had translated it to Greek from English, which Qeb translated back to him in English. The translation echoing in the background allowed everyone to appreciate the beauty of Louisa's voice. Ben prayed for the poignant words to be prophetic.

"Across the ocean, wild and wide, to where your heart has ever been

since first you were my Bonnie bride.

The roses all have left your cheek.

I've watched them fade away and die.

Your voice is sad when e'er you speak and tears bend your loving eyes.
Oh! I will take you back, Kathleen, to where your heart will feel no pain and
when the fields are fresh and green. I'll take you to your home again!
I know you love me, Kathleen dear, your heart was ever fond and true.
I always feel when you are near that life holds nothing dear but you.
The smiles that once you gave to me, I scarcely ever see them now
Though many, many times I see a dark'ning shadow on your brow.
Oh! I will take you back, Kathleen, to where your heart will feel no pain
and when the fields are fresh and green, I'll take you to your home again!
To that dear home beyond the sea, my Kathleen shall again return.
And when thy old friends welcome thee, thy loving heart will cease to yearn.
Where laughs the little silver stream beside your mother's humble cot
and brightest rays of sunshine gleam there, all your grief will be forgot.
Oh! I will take you back, Kathleen, to where your heart will feel no pain
and when the fields are fresh and green, I'll take you to your home again!"

Chapter 21

Axclatca Pass, Baru, An 5660, Day 3

Continuing to pace, Octavius tried to tire out his growing irritation. Never once did he lose focus on Aquila's questioning of the second of the two legionaries. The two had been involved in the attack on the third Alexandrian wall and survived. Each told the same story. They reached the top of the assault ladders, following their comrades. The soldiers in front of them fell the instant they climbed over the wall, without being struck by a sword or an arrow. These men, more cautious, peeked over, looking for the source.

They found dark-skinned men standing fifty yards to the rear. The soldiers in strange uniforms held long wooden sticks, like a staff, with two hands, pointing them in the wall's direction. As he watched, fire and smoke came out of the poles. Where the staff pointed, another comrade fell. Dead, despite there being no one near him.

One of the empire's life singers entered the tent as soon as the last legionary left. Octavius stopped his pacing and returned the man's salute and salutation. "Praise Ahura Jupiter, may His Light shine upon you, Emperor."

"May you be an instrument of His Light, Life Singer," came the ritual reply from Octavius.

Aquila added a quote from the Avesta Aaru. "Acting as the light of justice, may we return the followers of Angra Mainyu Orcus to the hells whence they were spawned."

Despite misgivings about the man, Octavius had come to appreciate the first counselor's ability to harness the faith. He bent its followers' fervor to achieve the empire's goals, and thus Octavius's. A believer in Ahura Jupiter himself, he doubted that everyone not of the faith served the Evil One, but he had no problems leveraging this tenet of Remus's state religion.

From the fire in his eyes, the man standing before him would offer up his life with a simple word from Octavius. The life singer believed Ahura Jupiter had anointed his emperor. When he was first crowned, the sheer power of such fanaticism almost overwhelmed Octavius. Now it gave him confidence. No nation could stand against such an invincible force for long.

Octavius returned from an intoxicating vision of his destiny when Aquila ordered, "Life Singer Ardashir, report your findings to the emperor."

Standing at rigid attention, the man replied, "Yes, First Counselor. While treating wounded men from the last assault, I encountered strange wounds. I detected something lodged inside them, like an arrowhead, but there was no shaft. By hand, I retrieved what appeared to be metal projectiles. They looked like shot from a sling." The life singer opened his hand, showing three dull gray objects in his palm. "Given the compression of two of the projectiles, no sling could have fired them."

Octavius walked over and inspected them. Similar in size to the tip of his pinkie, one object held close to its original shape of a tapered cylinder. The other two were flatter and misshapen. Octavius picked up the most irregular one.

The life singer's eyes darted to see which one Octavius held. "Emperor, that wounded man said whatever struck him penetrated his shield and breastplate."

Octavius raised his eyebrows. "Thank you, Life Singer Ardashir, you did very well. The first counselor will see that you receive a commendation and a promotion. Dismissed."

The man's stone facade broke with a smile. "Thank you, Emperor. Hail, Octavius!" He saluted and marched out of the tent.

Octavius waited for the man to leave before he turned to Aquila. "Before I forget, have the first two men flogged for cowardice."

A sneer formed at the corner of Aquila's mouth. "Of course."

Putting the man's sadistic nature aside, Octavius said, "It is as you feared. The Earthlings are already here. They must be helping Alexandria. There is no other way to explain our defeat."

Aquila's voice dripped with a conciliatory tone. "It's the only plausible explanation, my lord. I'll send a bird to warn Iskur. His band is making its way toward the Alexandrian camp." He smiled, a sinister look in his eyes, sending goosebumps up Octavius's arms. "I'll instruct him to capture one or more Earthlings, along with the new fire sticks. He has orders not to harm the Earthlings, in case we can turn them to our cause."

Octavius nodded. "Order Primipilus Titus Vorenus of the Praetorian Guard to take two squads of men and the welven scout through the mountains to rendezvous with Iskur."

Aquila gave a slight nod.

Octavius's mind refocused on the strategic situation. "Good. We must reevaluate our overall goals. With the enemy's reinforcements and these Earth weapons, we must adapt. Trying the straits is not an option. Our navy has improved, but they're still no match for the Alexandrians. No, we must abandon hopes of taking Alexandria for the moment. Kerma is our next target."

The first counselor pursed his lips. "You are most wise. How do you wish to proceed?"

Octavius frowned, trying to read Aquila, but the man remained inscrutable. The emperor sighed. "We'll fortify the pass and the strait. The Second, Fifth, Sixth, and Ninth Legions took the brunt of casualties. They will garrison the fortifications. Get replacements sent from Remus." He began pacing once again. "Have the Seventh camp between the pass and the strait to act as reserves for both. We'll take the rest of our legions and join Naresh's eastern army. Send him word to carry out the Kerman invasion plans. Ahura Jupiter willing, he'll take Kerma before we reach him."

"As you command, Your Majesty. May you be an instrument of His Light."

Chapter 22

Axclatca Pass, Baru, An 5660, Day 3

Louisa's hair fell over her shoulder as she attempted to gain a better view of her new attire in the full-length mirror that came with her borrowed tent. A masterpiece, the dark wood frame melded with the reflective glass, creating an intricate, organic design. She marveled at the beauty of the piece, as well as the Greek maiden reflected within.

Before leaving dinner, Louisa had asked their host how to obtain some Alexandrian clothes. Seeing the polemarchos, and later Khepri, the giant hysakas, made Louisa envious. She admired the beauty, simplicity, and utilitarian nature of their classical Greek dress.

The next morning, Louisa awakened to the sounds of a bustling military camp and discovered a serious young female soldier waiting outside. Louisa opened her tent flap. "Can I help you?"

Holding a bundle of garments, the girl, no older than seventeen, identified herself. "I'm Dimaerites Esther of the Lochem. I have some clothes for you." The muscular warrior stood an inch taller than Louisa and wore scale armor with her curly red hair tied up in an unflattering bun shaped like the conical helmet hanging from her belt. She stretched out both arms, pushing the clothes toward Louisa.

As she turned to leave, Louisa asked, "Esther, would you mind helping me? I'm Greek, but we no longer wear these kinds of dresses."

The serious soldier scrunched up her face. Waiting for several moments, Louisa expected her to say no, but the young woman shrugged. "I have a little time."

As Louisa changed, her helper laughed and pointed. "What are those?"

Looking down at her undergarments, Louisa tugged at her top. "My knickers?"

The young woman nodded, a trace of laughter still on her lips.

There's a pretty girl buried under that hard exterior.

Louisa pulled her top over her head. Esther's face twisted in confusion as the garment fell to the ground. "Where I'm from, people are very modest," Louisa said. "It's stupid, I agree."

Louisa dropped her bottoms and took up a piece of silk. She tried to bring it over and around her body. Esther rolled her eyes and tsked. Louisa took comfort in knowing some things were innate to all teenage humans.

A patient Esther demonstrated how to pin the dresses to use single or double shoulder straps. After Louisa mastered the basics, Esther showed her how to tie the long chiton to be most alluring. Admiring her exposed thigh in the mirror, Louisa thought how such a look would have caused a scandal only a few days earlier back home on Earth. She grinned at the thought. At last, she settled on a pale-yellow, knee-length chiton, using the double-shoulder-strap technique Esther had taught her. Spinning in front of the mirror, she felt more than unencumbered; she felt unchained.

Long had she desired to be free of the claustrophobic European dress codes. And the judgments that came with them. At least in the desert of Egypt, she'd worn linen pants and blouses without ramifications. Even then, Western mores kept her from wearing her preferred "workout" outfit, except in the Kalari class.

Too bad that men's inability to control themselves made freedom of dress impossible. At least, on Earth. For a moment, she reconsidered the reactions she might get to her attire from the men in her tribe. That's how she thought of everyone on this odyssey. Just as quickly as the thought knocked, she slammed and bolted the door, chiding herself.

New world. New rules.

Any man who tries to put restrictions on me will regret it.

Louisa reached for Esther's arm as she moved to leave. "Esther. Thank you so much for your help and the gifts. I assume these are your clothes. How can I repay you?"

Esther bowed her head. "You're most welcome, Louisa. My mother was correct. You're gorgeous, and the clothes have never looked so beautiful. As for payment, she said your beauty is only surpassed by your exquisite voice. Would you repay me with a song?"

"Gladly." Basking for a moment in the compliments, Louisa gave the teenager her most radiant smile. "Esther, you're very young to be a soldier. Who are your parents?"

Esther beamed. "I'm Ester ben Zev i Hurasu i Enoch. You met my mother, the polemarchos of the Fourth Stratia. My father is Judah ben Enoch, polemarchos of the Second Stratia." She paused at Louisa's raised eyebrows before saying, "As for being young, it's my destiny. When I was born, my parents placed a sword in my crib." Her voice grew serious. "Each morning I pray to Adonai, *Should I die today, let me die with a sword in my hand.*" Esther turned toward the exit.

"Let me know when you want your reward."

Grinning, the Dimaerites looked back. "Oh, I should have mentioned. My mother gave me command of the troops accompanying you to the Ancients' site. We should have many opportunities for a song. I'll check on you later. Until then."

Esther threw open the tent flap, stepped outside, and smacked into Abu.

Abu had no choice but to step back and catch himself as the short, solid soldier bumped into him. Gathering himself, he said in half-broken Greek, "*Parakaló synchoréste* me." Only then did he get a look into the jade-green eyes searing him with a fierce intellect. His eyes bulged. An aura of confidence and physical power radiated from the young woman. He stood rooted in place as the soldier's eyes narrowed, and her face grew stern.

The movement of her full lips broke the hypnotic spell of her eyes, only to capture his imagination anew. She said something in a language that his mind refused to translate. Grateful to have uttered anything before becoming awestruck, he struggled to respond.

The spell broke when the young woman stepped to the side and brushed past him with a huff. He heard himself mumble something incoherent. Twisting his head, he watched the soldier march away. Drawn to the muscular legs propelling her, he stared until she disappeared.

Amazing.

Abu shook his head as if to shake off a stunning blow. Remembering why he'd come, he shifted to look forward, only to feel his jaw drop. His almost fourteen-year-old brain reeled from a different type of feminine blow. A Greek goddess stood inside the tent. Hopeless, his mind tried to reconcile what he saw with his expected image of Miss Louisa. The goddess doubled over in laughter, her soprano giggles providing the final missing pieces to the puzzle his brain sought to solve. Abu blinked.

Get it together.

Miss Louisa stifled her laughter enough to say, "Cat got your tongue?"

Finding his mouth dry, he coughed, trying to gather enough saliva to speak. "Miss Louisa. You look . . . , uh," he trailed off and started again, "you look, well, you look beautiful. Different but beautiful."

The woman straightened up at the mention of her formal name and gave him a calming smile. "Thank you, Abu. Is there something you need?"

Sheepish, he replied, "Yes, ma'am. Dr. Ben asked me to see if you're ready to join him and Duffadar Nahal. The metal singer just arrived." Abu's voice grew worried. "Also, I wanted to speak with you alone about Dr. Ben." He paused a beat. "I don't know who else to ask."

Miss Louisa's face mirrored his concern. "Come in." She shifted over to a small table, motioning for him to sit as she did the same.

Abu took a moment to gather his thoughts before saying, "I'm worried about Dr. Ben. Last night was the worst I've seen."

Louisa leaned forward. "Try starting at the beginning."

Abu nodded. "Dr. Ben gets these nightmares. Sometimes he mumbles and is restless. Other times, he thrashes around like he is fighting for his life or screams out. That's enough to worry anyone. It's the times he wakes up suddenly." Abu swallowed. "Well, he cries out and sits up. I swear it looks like he has seen the face of the devil himself." He whispered, "Allah yahmini."[1]

Frowning with concern, Louisa paused and nibbled on her lower lip. "Does this happen all the time?"

He could hear the worry in her voice. "No, this is the third time. The first time lasted for about six weeks. It started the night my parents died but became less and less until it went away. Dr. Chipiez said it's because of what happened to Dr. Ben in the war. The second time was in Cairo. It only lasted a couple of nights. It started the night he said he saw you at the suq—market, I mean—and you went to eat." He tilted his head, and she fidgeted but said nothing. "But last night was the worst. What can I do, Miss Louisa?"

"Hmm."

---

1. Allah yahmini is Arabic for "God protect me."

Abu watched her expressions change as she turned the problem over.

She looked at the floor. "I won't get into any details, but I dealt with a traumatic event several years ago. Afterward, I had bad dreams for a while. Thank God, I've put that behind me." She looked him in the eye with unwavering confidence. "You might have dealt with something similar after your parents died. The difference is that Ben has lived through a lot more of these horrible moments. He should talk to someone about what happened during the war and these recent events." She patted Abu's hand. "The only thing we can do is support him the best we can. Other than sleeping, does it seem to affect him in other ways?"

Abu tilted his head. "Not too much. The first time, he also lost a little weight. You'll see today. He looks tired." He scratched a spot on top of his head. "The first time he got an hour or two of sleep each night for a week. After I talked to Dr. Chipiez, and before it started going away, I thought he might be sick in the head."

Louisa squeezed his hand. "It'll be okay. We'll help him. Yesterday was the most horrific thing I have ever seen. I pray to God, I see nothing like it again." She gave him a warm smile. "We're all alone here on an alien planet. We. You, me, Ben, Jeevan, and the rest of the Lancers are the only ones we can rely on, so we have to take care of one another. I care about each of you, and I'm glad you came to me for help."

Abu gave her a grim smile. "I know I can count on you. I know Dr. Ben listens to you. He may not show it, but he—" Abu stopped himself and lowered his eyes.

Louisa smiled back at him. "I care for Ben, too."

Abu thought about her sincere yet noncommittal statement. As much as he wanted Dr. Ben to be happy, he had to accept reality. Dr. Ben's and Miss Louisa's feelings for each other might never grow in the way he hoped. Changing the subject, he said, "We should get going, Miss Louisa."

"You're right." She stood and put her hand in the crook of his arm. "Lead the way."

Nearing the tent he shared with Dr. Ben, Abu had waited as long as his patience could muster. "Miss Louisa, who was the soldier leaving your tent when I got there?"

Louisa lowered her eyes, and her chest moved as she suppressed a chuckle. She looked up with a solemn face. "Oh, her name is Esther. She is the polemarchos's daughter and gave me these new clothes."

Crestfallen, Abu whispered, "Oh."

Louisa smiled a knowing smile. "Did I forget to mention? She's leading the troops going with us to the site in the mountains."

A desperate Abu tried to hide his rebounding mood but to no avail. "Oh, that's good." He blushed.

Louisa's body shook with good-natured laughter.

Sweeping past Abu, who held the tent flap open, Louisa took in the scene. A six-person table dominated the center of the space, with the cots pushed to the edge of the tent. Seeing its occupants tied her thoughts into a wild jumble of knots. She shook her head. Even after last night, the sight of walking, talking *aliens* took her breath away.

That the ones she'd met appeared as more evolved cousins to animals from Earth did little to help. Ben's back was to the entrance, while to his left, at the end of the table, sat Khepri, towering above everyone. Her presence almost made Louisa miss the much smaller fox bandit seated on the other end. Intense amber eyes evaluated Louisa from within a bed of black. She scrambled to untwist the knotted memory of this race of creatures.

They're called stirithy, damn it.

Jeevan, who sat facing the entrance, said, "Miss Louisa." He stood up.

Abu stepped next to her as the rest of the table stood. Remembering her recent conversation, Louisa inspected Ben as he turned. He appeared about to speak when his tired, bloodshot eyes opened a little wider than usual. They flashed down to her ankle-high, laced sandals. Drifting upward in a languorous fashion, he inched his way to her face.

Unlike his previous furtive glances, the brazen heat behind his eyes smoldered. A flush rose from her breasts to her neck before she reined it in. Instead, she raised a single questioning eyebrow and narrowed her eyes.

By transference, Ben's cheeks reddened as he said in Greek, "Ssherrss, may I introduce Miss Louisa Sophia?"

With an angled bow of his head and in a voice resembling a growly cat's purr, the stirithy spoke in her native tongue. "Mmissss Louissa Ssophia, a pleassurre to mmeet you. Mmy namme iss Ssherrss."

It may have been the sharp teeth or the look of steel in the stirithy's eyes, but either way, Louisa sensed someone with a gruff, serious personality. She stood ramrod straight, emulating the way she used to respond to Mère de la Nativité. "It's a pleasure, ahh." A furrow of lines formed on her forehead. "Ssherrss. So good to see you again as well, Khepri. Please don't let me interrupt."

Before they sat, Khepri said, "Nice to see you as well. Please excuse me. There are several other errands I must perform before we leave."

Khepri moved around the table to Ssherrss. Louisa stared in fascination as the hysakas bent down to the stirithy's level and licked his foxlike snout before nuzzling into his neck. If a fox could blush, Louisa felt sure Ssherrss brownish-red fur would have turned bright red. Without returning her signs of affection, Ssherrss said, "Be back before Triplets."

"I promise, mmmurrramms," came Khepri's reply as she disengaged to tower a full two and a half feet over her alpha.

Translating the last purr to *agápi mou*, Louisa waved bye to the giant.

How strange. Aliens forming romantic relationships across species.

With the group seated, Ben leaned over the table to place three bullets in front of Ssherrss. As he straightened, he gave Louisa a chastened lopsided grin.

Despite Ben's bloodshot eyes, Louisa couldn't help but notice how much bluer his eyes were without his spectacles.

Damn, he's handsome. He looks much less a bookman.

Ben waved at the bullets. "I'm sure the Polemarchos spoke to you about our guns. We have several types, but the important thing is our guns use these like arrows. Unlike arrows, once used, they won't work again unless we rebuild them. The polemarchos said you might be able to help us make more."

Ssherrss leaned forward and reached for the largest cartridge, the one used by the Lancers in their rifles. Louisa expected to see a paw like a raccoon. Instead, the black hairless hands had what appeared to be four long fingers. Bigger than a raccoon's, they were splayed out at equidistant angles from his palm. As soon as he took the bullet, Louisa covered her mouth and gasped.

All thumbs.

Unlike the Earth saying, Ssherrss had no problem with dexterity. He held the bullet up and spun it in his hand. Louisa, like the rest of the Earthlings, let out louder exclamations. The lead bullet twisted off the brass casing and floated into Ssherrss's other hand. He turned the case over and shook out the black powder within.

The stirithy met the eyes of his audience. "Mmosst of it iss very sssimmple. Therre are only thrrree typess of mmetalsss mmaking up the sstrructure. I cannot make the exploding powderr or the mmaterrial hidden inssside thiss." The metal of the casing began to dissolve, then formed small droplets suspended in the air as if gravity didn't exist. A small metal percussion cap fell into Ssherrss's left hand. The droplets of brass solidified and clattered to the table. He placed the lead projectile next to the deconstructed casing.

Jeevan's body tensed as he waved a hand. "Please be careful with that. It is a small explosive."

Louisa translated his English to the stirithy.

Ssherrss nodded. "I will. I ssensse mmorre mmmetalss ussed to mmake this."

Ben looked surprised. "Yes. That's the primer. When struck, the compound inside ignites the black powder and expels the bullet. It uses mercury, copper, and some other non-metal ingredients to make it. The brass part is called the casing and requires lead, copper, and zinc. If we gave you the compound for the primer?" He pointed at Ssherrss's hand. "Can you make bullets?"

A low rumble rising in his throat, Ssherrss stood and reached down to pick up a bag from the dirt floor. The table shook under its weight as he plopped it to the side of him. His many thumbs made quick work of the two buckled fasteners.

He placed three different-colored metal bars on the wooden surface and waved his hand over each one. The metal melted and slid off each block, creating three liquid rivulets stretching upward. Two streams merged to become a levitating blob. The third reshaped itself into a jelly-like copy of the lead projectile from the original bullet. After hardening, it drifted down to settle on the wood next to its twin.

A thin tentacle grew from the blob and transformed into a thin layer of brass. The process paused for a moment as the tentacle detached from the rounded metal. The primer levitated from Ssherrss's hand and settled with soft precision onto the newly formed brass platform still hanging in midair.

A soft purr came from Ssherrss as he flexed his fingers in a pulsing in-and-out motion. The brass tentacle reattached and continued building on that original layer. During the next few seconds, a brass cartridge case grew from the bottom up until complete. Hardened, it drifted down to rest upright on the table. The magical display ended with the lead bullet floating up and over before sinking into place to form a cartridge.

Snout lifted, Ssherrss had an expression of smugness. "If you have black powderr and the exploding commpound, I can make forrty to fifty of thesse an hourr."

"Amazing," came Jeevan's drawn-out exclamation.

Abu's awestruck countenance and Ben's slack-jawed expression joined the duffadar's. Louisa wondered why this display affected them more than Qeb's incredible abilities. No matter how impossible, she found it undeniable. On Aaru, magic was real.

Abu brought her out of her thoughts when he exclaimed in broken Greek, "Incredible. Ssherrss, can humans sing like you?"

Ssherrss focused on Abu. He replied in a flat tone, as if suggesting they should already understand these things. "Of courrsse, hummanss of the Ssinging Guildss can ssing."

Abu's voice went up an octave. "How do you join one of these guilds?"

"Mmosst humman ssingerrss are born frrom two parrentss who ssing the ssamme ssongss. Once a yearr, two normmal hummanss arre gifted with the ability to ssing."

Ben's eyes widened in understanding. "So there are devices like the Seba or the ones that made the elves that can give humans these powers?"

Ssherrss nodded in affirmation.

Abu's voice went back to normal. "How do you get chosen for the gift?"

"The guild holds trrialss forrr orrphanss and childrren put forward by theirr parrentss at twelve," came the stirithy's reply.

"Damn," escaped Abu's mouth before he realized he'd said the curse word out loud.

Ben frowned and cuffed the young man, using much less force than one of the mothers at St. Denis would have. Abu rubbed the back of his head. "Sorry." Cheeks flushing, he sank into his seat.

During the demonstration, Ben's eyes had lost their tiredness. Excited, he addressed Ssherrss, "Do you have the metal called mercury? We'll need it to make the primers. Also, we'll need to create several devices before we can transform the mercury and create a primer. If I give you drawings of these devices to be made from metal and glass, would you be able to create them for me?"

The stirithy paused a beat, and a thumb rubbed behind one pointed ear. "Verry little mmerrcurry. You'll need to usse Alexandrrian ssscaless forr the dessignss. I'll give you a rrulerr. How long will it take you if you have the deviccess and mmerrcurry?"

Ben scratched his chin for a second. "If I have all the devices and the supplies, it'll take two days to make a very small amount. We'll need to conduct a lot of tests." He twisted his mouth toward his scar. "We need to get the black powder power levels correct and the primer mixture just right. If everything's readily available, it'd probably take two to three weeks." Tapping the table twice, he said, "I think the polemarchos intends to make a lot of guns for Alexandria. But without the supplies needed, it would make more sense to wait until we get back from the Ancients' site. Give me a few hours to diagram the devices, and then you can create them before we leave. Can you make glass?"

"Mmmm, hmmmm." Ssherrss bridged his fingers in front of him. "Yess, mmetal ssingerss mmake glassss. I'll assk the Polemmarchoss perrmmissssion to leave afterr you give mme the planss." He placed the remaining metal bars into his bag, then retrieved a long, thin board with marks etched along the length. After handing the board to Ben, he stood and gave a curt nod. He strolled out of the tent with purpose.

Ben held up his hand. As soon as the stirithy was out of earshot, his hand dropped. Louisa asked the question that had her nagged since she'd seen Ben's mood change. "I assume you have a plan."

He flashed them a weary smile. "Yes, I do. Ever since we spoke with the polemarchos, I've worried how guns will change this planet."

Putting both hands on the table, Jeevan spoke in a conspiratorial tone. "What do you mean?"

"We saw yesterday." Ben's mouth flattened. "I can't believe that was just yesterday." He crossed his arms and frowned. "It seems like it happened ages ago. Anyway, they may have something that mimics magic, but they fight like they're in the Middle Ages. If any single country learns how to make guns and bullets, they could conquer the world. We can't let that happen."

Surprised by his dire projections, Louisa asked, "Could it get that bad? How do you stop it?"

"The primers, right?" A sinister sneer deformed Jeevan's face, shocking Louisa. Never did she think Mr. Optimism could be so conniving.

Ben's head bobbed. "That's right. Until the demonstration, I was concerned whether they could create mercury fulminate. As incredible as their magic is, they haven't discovered a way to sing complex chemistry." His brows shot up. "Sorry to go on a tangent, but I suspect that using magic has kept them from innovating in the sciences. That's why they still use bows and arrows. We can control the process if they can't do the chemistry. The devices Ssherrss is making will help me in the distillation process. We'll be able to make the ethanol, copper nitrate, and nitric acid needed to form mercury fulminate." He locked eyes with each of them. "We must keep the process a secret. They can create the guns and casings, but we will do the rest."

Turning over the idea, Louisa found a hole in Ben's plan. "What about Professor Moussa and the villagers? Don't you think one of them can duplicate your work?"

Ben sat back, pondering the new obstacle she'd thrown at him. "Maybe. All we can do is stay in control of the process on our end. If we can't power the Seba,

I'll teach each of you the process when we get back. We'll be power brokers. If someone abuses the guns we dole out, we'll stop making primers."

Louisa frowned. "I really hope you're right."

Louisa's frustration finally reached a boiling point. For the previous three hours, she and Abu had worked on deciphering the language on the Seba and the scroll. Their progress started and ended with him copying each symbol into a couple of notebooks. In the end, they found twenty unique symbols but zero understanding.

Referencing books on hieroglyphics and cuneiform, they concluded the Ancients' language had no relation. Abu gave up and sat reading the Alexandrian scrolls Qeb had provided to them.

With a loud sigh, Louisa stood and went to the suitcase on top of her cot. She checked to make sure Abu remained occupied and propped the top up a few inches. She used one hand and snuck out a small silver flask before dropping the lid. After turning her back to the teenager, she unscrewed the top and took a sip. A small amount of the herbal-flavored homemade surāh lingered on her tongue before she swallowed. She took a longer swig. The warm liquor coated her throat, and her tension eased. The flask went back to its home.

As the liquor warmed her insides, she thought about the internal war that had raged in her since their arrival. Her adventure loving-side had joined in a ferocious battle against her guilt at marooning them. A self-truce had broken out once she committed to help find a way home for the others. In the meantime, she'd enjoy her experiences to the fullest.

Unable to make headway on the language problem that nagged at her, she let it go for the moment. Louisa spun toward Abu with a new purpose and saw a visitor standing outside through the open tent flap.

Esther asked in Greek, "May I come in?"

"Of course. What can we do for you?"

Abu shot to his feet at the exchange and gave a slight cough.

Glancing at a very nervous Abu, Louisa had to suppress her merriment. "Oh, Esther, this is Abu. I don't believe we have formally introduced you."

Not waiting for Esther's acknowledgment, Abu stepped forward with a grin. He held out his hand and said in practiced Greek, "It's a pleasure to meet you."

A frown creased Esther's face for a fraction of a second. She regarded Abu and his outstretched hand for a long moment. "We've met."

Reaching across, she grasped his forearm and caught Abu off guard. He took a second to mirror her grip. Louisa grinned at the twitching Abu as electricity shot through his arm.

In a stern voice, Esther said, "I am Dimaerites Esther ben Zev i Hurasu i Enoch. You may address me as Dimaerites Esther."

Abu swallowed at the formal introduction and show of dominance. "Uh, well, nice to meet you, Dimaerites Esther. Call me Abu."

With a curt nod, Esther disengaged, dismissing him as she addressed Louisa. "I spoke with Ssherrss. He said that whatever he's working on with your friend will not delay our departure. Something about only being able to finish the work in Neos Hierosolyma. The polemarchos asked that we start our journey as soon as possible." In a less formal tone, she said, "We'll be leaving at first light. I brought warmer clothing for your group. The mountains are cold at night. If there's anything else I can get you for the journey, now is the time to ask."

Louisa considered this, but nothing specific came to mind. She looked to Abu. "Anything we need?"

Abu's face lit up. "I can't think of anything, but Dimaerites Esther, can I ask you a few questions? About the history of Aaru and Alexandria?"

She weighed him and her answer. "My men are taking care of most of the preparations. What questions do you have?"

Abu smiled. "Thank you. Why don't you and Miss Sophia sit? I don't mind standing."

Louisa moved to the table, and Esther, more hesitant, followed. To avoid towering over the women, Abu knelt. "Miss Sophia and I are trying to understand more about the Ancients and their writing. Can you tell us anything about the languages used on Aaru?"

Esther removed her helmet from her belt and placed it on the table next to the two books. Tied in a curled bun, Esther's auburn locks looked stunning, an exotic pairing with her dark olive complexion. "May I?" She picked up one book and leafed through it before grabbing the second.

Louisa watched Abu watching Esther. The Dimaertes's face went from inquisitive to confused to understanding. Abu's went from excited to awe filled to smitten. Louisa thought about how fond of the young man she'd become when Esther's words recaptured her attention.

"I never thought much about it. It just was, but each group of humans brought their languages and system of writing with them. The elves, welves, and the first human nations speak a language called Eblan. They use this form of writing." She held up the book on cuneiform. "The hysakas, stirithy, babiakhom, and the human nation of Kerma all use these forms of writing. They speak the same language, which we call Aaruan since it is the oldest." This time, she gestured to the book on hieroglyphics. She set the books down and looked at Louisa and Abu with a tilted head and raised brows.

Abu rushed to ask a follow-up question. "Did the Ancients speak the same language as the other nonhuman races? We call that language Egyptian."

"It's been a long time since I learned the oral legends of Aaru's earliest history. However, as I remember it, the hysakas's, stirithy's, and babiakohms' first ancestors spoke different languages. They had many traditions as well. The Ancients forced them to forget everything. Within a single generation, they spoke and wrote only in Aaruan." Without thinking, she twirled a loose auburn curl around her finger. "The Ancients used a completely distinct language. One legend says that even the babiakhom couldn't translate. It kept the slave races from learning the secrets of their singing."

Louisa twisted her lips to the side of her mouth. "That's why no one understands magic objects like the Seba. It's all guesswork."

Esther nodded. "Yes. Some Ancient artifacts and even some of their buildings still sing after ten thousand An. In some structures, light appears when you enter and disappears when you leave. Other Ancient facilities sing all day and night. No one knows why. I've never seen it myself." Her stoic face broke into a tight-lipped smile. "That's why this journey is so exciting."

"What else do you know about the site we're going to?" Louisa asked.

"Ssherrss said the welves and stirithy refer to the site as the Tomb of Mortals. Supposedly, many explorers have died there." The soldier's smile disappeared. "The few who returned spoke of being attacked by Ghosts of the Ancients." Esther's voice never wavered, and her face remained unconcerned about the dangers ahead.

Although the young soldier didn't show it, Louisa's alarm bells were going off. "Are there other dangers we'll face on this trip?"

Esther's grin returned, turning sly, along with her eyes. "If we were a a bigger group, the welves might see us as invaders, and if we were a smaller group they'd see us as easy prey.. We'll take every precaution to deter them."

Louisa dug deeper. "Is Alexandria at war with the welves as well?"

"No, but the mountains are theirs." She shrugged. "They're assholes to everyone—except the stirithy, of course. They are eternally at war with the elves and will attack them on sight. Luckily, we don't have any pointies going with us, or we'd be in for a fight for sure." Esther smiled.

Abu's face scrunched with puzzlement. "Why are the stirithy safe?"

Esther glanced over her shoulder, peering outside. "Hidden deep inside the mountains is the stirithy's nation, Grrommerrk. The two are allies. The pale faces protect the furballs. In return, the furballs build the pale faces' underground cities."

One of Louisa's eyebrows went up at Esther's nicknames for the other races. Pushing aside her first encounter with Aaruan racism, she asked, "I have one last question. Is there a common language that everyone speaks?"

Esther placed her helmet back on her belt. "Most educated people and merchants speak Aaruan. It's the most common language. Most of that same group also speak the languages of their neighboring countries." She pushed away from the table and stood. "I speak Eblan, Latin, Aaruan, Greek, and Hebrew. Most of my soldiers will only speak the two Alexandrian languages, though." She stopped to tuck that unruly curl behind her ear. "It's time I go and see that the preparations are happening as they should. I'll see you in the morning. Please make sure the warm clothes get distributed to the rest of your group."

Louisa smiled, coming to her feet. "Of course. Abu and I will take care of it. This has been very helpful."

Abu concurred, "Yes, thank you, Esther."

Her shoulders stiffened and came forward in a slight bow. Straightening, she marched out. Abu's eyes followed the soldier until she disappeared from view.

Not wanting to embarrass him, Louisa waited until he focused back on her. "Please find Jeevan and ask for some of his men to help with the clothing distribution. Before you bring the Lancers back, tell Ben and Jeevan we'll meet them at Ben's tent in half an hour. We need to hold regular meetings to share all the information we're learning. I'm sure they've picked up a few interesting tidbits themselves."

"Yes, ma'am. I'll also ask Duffadar Nahal to have the cooks bring dinner. I'm famished. See you soon." Books in hand, he hurried out of the tent.

Her hopes of gaining easy access to the Ancients' knowledge were now dashed. She pushed aside her guilt and any self-pity, as memories of her mother's wisdom flooded forward. As she did from time to time, Louisa recited all of Mama's mantras.

Always remember, my little Louisa, life's not fair, and nothing worthwhile comes easy.

The only way forward is to work and, when necessary, to fight.

If you stop trying, you're choosing to die. You can still be alive but dead inside.

Work, fight, live, but most of all, my little Louisa, love. Love with all your heart.

The first three were all she'd ever known—watching Mama die from a broken heart as much as the consumption always made Louisa question the last mantra. She wondered whether this time was different. Would she dare to love like that?

Memories of Ben hugging Abu after the hotel break-in and that moment she'd shared with the Good Doctor on the train popped into her head. Pushing aside the unfamiliar feelings that came with the memories, she began packing.

Chapter 23

Axclatca Pass, Baru, An 5660, Day 3

"Enter," Alexandria said as she finished signing off on the daily reports.

The soldier swept through the tent flap, exposing a darkening sky. She strode with purpose before coming to a stop. "Reporting as requested, Polemarchos." She saluted by bringing her fist to her heart.

Alexandria put down her metal quill and focused on the soldier standing at rigid attention in front of her desk. "At ease, Dimaerites."

The young woman's body relaxed, and her eyes drifted down to look her commanding officer in the eye.

Alexandria raised her eyebrows. "What have you learned?"

The young woman's face stayed stoic. "They are serious about learning the secrets of the Ancients. We discussed the different languages and writing systems of Aaru, but I don't think it helped." She paused a beat, then said, "May I speak freely?"

The polemarchos's eyes narrowed, but her chin jutted her permission.

"Why don't you take them back to Neos Hierosolyma and force them to reveal their secrets?"

Alexandria sighed and stood. She went around the desk and put a hand on her daughter's shoulder. "Sometimes, I forget how young you are." She dropped her hand, and, with a mother's teaching voice, she said, "Honor, family, and motivation."

Esther tilted her head, and her brow furrowed.

"We owe these Earthlings a debt of honor. Without their intervention, our nation would soon be enslaved." She shook her head. "Learning how to make these guns and bullets might well determine whether we are able to stay free. Were that my only consideration, honor would not win over practicality."

Esther nodded and looked to speak, but Alexandria held up her hand as she said, "More important than what the Earthlings know is who will lead Alexandria during this crisis. If our leaders were not so incompetent, we would not have needed a miracle to save us yesterday."

She took Esther's hands in hers. "Your father and I have decided that our nation needs a strong hand to survive."

Esther's eyes widened.

Alexandria confirmed all that they risked with a squeeze of her daughter's hands. "If we were to return to the capitol with the Earthlings, our family would lose control of them and their guns." She leaned toward Esther. "Your father left an hour ago with samples of guns and some bullets the Earthlings gave us. He also has the diagrams of the devices that Dr. McGehee said he needed to make the final component of these bullets, along with all the information he shared. We will gather the best scholars at the estate and decode what we need, with or without the Earthlings' help."

Esther nodded as she looked up. "And motivation?"

Alexandria's lips twitched. "Allies are much more productive than slaves."

One of Esther's hands pulled away, and her finger twirled a loose strand of red locks while she bit her lip. Alexandria waited, her mind drifting back to her daughter as a toddler contemplating some critical information with the same face and unconscious twisting of hair.

Esther let go of the red curl. She gripped her mother's hands with steel in her eyes. "What do you need me to do?"

The corners of Alexandria's mouth turned down. "Get close to them and learn everything you can. But I hope you never have to carry out your most important task."

Esther nodded.

Alexandria closed her eyes for a second. She opened them, her voice grave. "Dr. McGehee must never fall into the hands of our enemies. Do you understand?"

With a gulp, Esther said, "Understood."

Alexandria hugged her daughter and whispered into her ear, "Bring us honor."

Esther hugged her back. "In life and death."

Chapter 24

Nefru Mountains, Choru, An 5660, Day 4

Bleary-eyed, Ben squinted as the first light of An peeked over the western cliff of the Axclatca Pass. Thousands of tiny crystals in the blue stone reflected the sunlight. Mounted and now moving, the column wound its way back toward the entrance to the canyon road.

Sleep deprivation had given Ben the gift of zero patience. As a result, he resented all the positive energy flowing from his travel companions. Most of all, he resented himself for not being able to join in their excitement. All the Earthlings exuded nervous anticipation about visiting the Ancients' site and exploring more of this new world. Even the Alexandrians coming along were eager to visit the fabled location.

His goal today: avoid all conversations if possible.

As he plodded along, Ben's muddled mind tried to focus enough to calculate the size of their expanded party. Four mounted archers led the column toward the mountain path to the Tomb of Mortals.

What an unfortunate name.

Louisa and Abu shared the details they had learned from Esther at last night's dinner. Ben had little to add because Ssherrss had been less forthcoming about today's journey. The all-too-serious stirithy didn't do idle chit-chat and simply wanted to work on conjuring the diagrammed distilling apparatuses into existence.

The only other interesting bit of information came from Jeevan. Using an Alexandrian hourglass, he determined an Aaruan hour to be fifty-five Earth minutes—just one more of the countless differences in this new world.

Remembering his initial math problem, Ben started over. The four escorts were to set up a camp near the path and take care of the group's horses until their return. There had been no sighting of the temple villagers, and Qeb assured them of a safe journey to the path.

Damn it.

Beginning once more, Ben used his fingers to count. The escorts made four. Behind that group rode the odd couple of Khepri and Ssherrss. Even seeing their affection firsthand, Ben struggled to comprehend the mismatched lovers. Glancing at the pair farther up the column, he noted how Ssherrss looked like a costumed child riding a pony as he sat on his small horse. Then, to the stirithy's right, came the damndest sight.

Khepri, the six-and-half-foot-tall wolf-like hysakas, appeared childlike as well, but on a different scale from her mate. She swayed on a saddled *kabuah*. With the height, length, and girth of a rhino, the Frankenstein creature retained a large scary horn but not in the right place. Instead of a rhino snout, a long elephant-like trunk hung below an ivory horn that thrust skyward from the creature's forehead. Several inches from the end, the long nose split into translucent, octopus-like tentacles that were as capable as any hand.

When Khepri first joined the column, the Earth-born horses bucked with fear of the strange beast. It took ten minutes of soothing talk and copious apples for the Lancers and Ben to regain control.

Behind the couple came ten Lochem, led by Dimaerites Esther. They were along to provide added security. Most of the infantry appeared uncomfortable on their horses, but the young woman leading them was born to the saddle. Then came Ben, Louisa, and Jeevan, followed by the rest of the Lancers and the wagons. Abu rode toward the rear with his friend Sowar Singh and his riding instructor, Sowar Chib.

The trio used the slow pace to practice the riding skills Chib had taught Abu back in Egypt. For a moment, Ben almost forgot to account for the four Lancers riding ahead and on the flanks. In total, thirty-six travelers had left the Alexandrian camp.

When the breeze blew just right, the scent of lemon and lavender made it through the pungent smells of horses and men. Each time, Ben's train of thought careened off track, going places it shouldn't. With considerable effort, he refused to look at the source of the perfume. Since yesterday, impolite thoughts came unbidden at the mere sight of Louisa.

His anger at her role in their predicament had all but faded. A very forgiving person, Ben could count fewer than a handful of long-term grudges he continued to nurse. That amount of effort he saved for only the worst kinds of low-down, dirty, backstabbing, hateful people.

Louisa had been none of those, no matter how reckless and irresponsible she'd been. He had bigger things to deal with than figuring out his growing feelings for her. He needed to focus on getting a decent night's sleep and finding a way home.

But she won't let me.

Her adoption of Alexandrian dress made it all but impossible for him to stay zeroed in on his priorities. Ben couldn't deny being attracted to Louisa back on Earth, but he'd always been a gentleman. He felt confident he'd been successful in hiding his desires. Now, though, his lust was giving him away. Thoughts hazy, he chewed on how her simple change in dress was destroying the walls he'd erected to protect their partnership.

For example, today Louisa showed up wearing her new style. In place of a modest blouse, she wore a white, long-sleeved silk tunic with a loose neckline over blue pants. Her ebony hair shone all the brighter while the neckline drew his eye to her long, olive-skinned neck. As the least daring new outfit she'd worn, the tunic should not have stirred his blood the way it did.

The more he thought about it, he realized she had changed more than her clothes. It made sense that exotic clothing, in place of Victorian dress, could change one's thinking. The Earth clothing's associated moral dictates were now out of sight and thus out of mind. Still, none of that could account for the increased intensity of his feelings.

What really changed?

At his 50 percent brain capacity, he took a long time before it dawned on him. Since he'd met her, Louisa had exuded confidence, competence, grace, and elegance. Along with new clothes and a new planet, she had swapped her default standoffishness for a sense of freedom.

It reminded Ben of how horses in a herd of mustangs moved versus their domesticated peers. She now moved with the same unbridled passion.

It's seductive as hell.

And that's why he stared at the canyon walls instead of looking her way and kept every discussion she started with him short and to the point. He felt pleased with his new insights.

Louisa caught him off guard as she made a loud clucking sound and kicked her mare. She trotted around the Lochem toward the odd couple. Despite more self-recriminations, Ben couldn't take his eyes off her as she sidled next to Khepri.

Louisa's frustration with Ben had caught up and surpassed her concern for him. Since breakfast, he'd been surly and gone out of his way to avoid conversation. Abu's worries were easy to understand when she first saw Ben's blood-shot eyes and dour expression. Yet she couldn't help him if he refused to even communicate. Needing a distraction, she decided to visit Khepri, hoping to find out more about the mismatched lovers.

Louisa pulled up next to the giant wolf and twisted her neck at an uncomfortable angle to look Khepri in the eyes. The hysakas, swaying with the lumbering gait of her mount, looked down from her perch atop the strange quasi-elephant-rhino and said in Greek, "Miss Sophia, how are you?"

"Good morning, Khepri. I'm well. Trying my best to enjoy our journey." Flashing a rueful smile, Louisa said, "Unfortunately, my traveling companion is being antisocial. I thought I'd say hello to you and Ssherrss. Afraid I can't see him, but good morning to you, too, Ssherrss."

From the far side of the blue-gray creature, the gruff stirithy purred, "Good Mmorrning, Mmissss Ssophia."

The taciturn stirithy met her expectations by offering no more words. Louisa chuckled. "Khepri, may I ask you a personal question? I'm curious. How did you two become a couple?"

Khepri laughed deep in her throat, and a derisive snort came across the wall of kabuah flesh. Hoping she hadn't struck a nerve, Louisa waited for the hysakas to respond.

Without turning, Khepri used her left arm to send some signal to her mate. "Don't worry about Mister Grumpy. He's just tired of the same old question. But I don't mind sharing our story." She tilted her head, focusing on a point in the distance. "It's all because of the dwarves."

Louisa knew her expression must have shown the puzzlement Khepri expected. The giant wolf chuckled. "Some say our story's sad. It started that way, but I don't think of it like that. When I was five and Ssherrss was eight, dwarves raided our town. We lived in a city on the coast."

Her eyes lit up. "My father provided healing services, and his mom was the best metal singer in the city. We never knew the other existed, but then the dwarves came in their longships." Her eyes drooped with sadness. "They snuck over the walls one night, opened the gates, and slaughtered thousands or made them slaves. When the barbarian devils left, the survivors found hundreds of orphans in the city. Ssherrss and I were two of the ten nonhuman orphans."

Eyes misting, Louisa remembered Abu's story.

Khepri kept going. "For a month, they housed us in a small camp while they looked for extended family. As sad as losing our families was, the real challenges had just begun. With so many grief-stricken, angry children, some bullied us. A few even blamed us for what happened just because we were different." The hysakas stared at the ground.

Louisa, remembering her own harsh childhood, didn't hide her anger as she said, "I know what it's like to be an outsider. To have no one on your side. Children can be cruel."

Nodding, Khepri took a deep breath. "The caregivers had placed all of us non-humans together. That week, three older and much bigger human boys came to our tent to bully us. The first one pushed me to the ground and called me horrible names, but Ssherrss came to my rescue. Thinking about it always makes me smile." She grinned, open-mouthed, her tongue hanging down a little as she panted. "I was lying on the ground when a red blur of teeth and claws rammed into the bully. It was like they had kicked a sleeping *taluk*.[1] In the end, the bullies ran off, but not before they got in a few hard licks against Ssherrss."

---

1. A taluk is a mammalian snake-like creature on Aaru. It grows four to five feet long and is covered with spines like a porcupine, except on its belly. It is very fast and has a nasty disposition.

She glanced over at her mate before turning back to Louisa. "I was still very young, but I remember trying to heal him. It was the first time I tried to use my abilities. I'm pretty sure I didn't help much." She shrugged her shoulders. "Maybe I healed a few scratches, but from that moment forward, we looked out for each other. Eventually, we were the only non-humans left. I'm positive a stirithy family would have taken him in, but he refused to leave my side."

Enthralled, Louisa asked, "Why couldn't you get adopted? What happened next?"

Khepri's ears twitched and rotated. "Stirithy families are like human families. There's a father, a mother, and their children. Extended family is the same. For them, adoption is acceptable."

Khepri furrowed her brow and widened her eyes, making her look sad. "Hysakas families are not like that. The alpha can be a male or a female and can have multiple mates. Unfortunately, they never accept an outsider's children. Only new mates. None of my kind would ever adopt me."

Louisa's jaws clenched, her anger rising.

Khepri shook her head. "It's instinctual. It's difficult for humans to understand, but even the Ancients couldn't change it."

"Interesting."

Khepri scrutinized Louisa for a moment and sniffed. "When no families came forward, we and about a hundred human children went to an orphanage in the capital. Because of our talents, we started studying with the human guilds at age twelve." The she-wolf shook her head, her voice filling with remorse. "Being raised and trained by humans made us pariahs among our kind. Because Ssherrss was older, he had to leave the orphanage when he turned twenty."

Her long tongue came out, licking her nose and chops before she smiled that half-open smile. "Luckily, he found an older stirithy living by himself near these mountains, providing metal singing services to a nearby village. The elder, desperate for help, apprenticed Ssherrss and taught him everything. Lucky for you, they visited the stirithy capital twice and passed by the Tomb of Mortals both times."

She placed her hand over her chest. "Ssherrss always promised to return for me, but I worried anyway. The day I turned twenty, I stepped out of the gate, full of fear, only to find my Ssherrss waiting. He didn't know it then, but we were already much more than friends. Males of all species seem to be a little slow-witted when it comes to romance."

"Harrummph," came a growl from over the mountain of kabuah.

"You know it's true," Khepri snapped over her shoulder.

"Men aren't the only ones. Romance is a mystery to me, too." Louisa's cheeks grew warm.

"I can help with that." Amusement flashed in the huge wolf's eyes. "Anyway, that stubborn grump captured my heart the moment he rescued me. He's been my alpha ever since. It took a while, but he finally accepted me in that way, too. When we couldn't find a place to call home, we joined the Alexandrian army. Here, we've found respect and acceptance."

"What a beautiful love story." Lowering her voice, Louisa whispered, "I know I'm being nosy, but I'm pretty sure you can't have children. Do you want to?"

"We try." Khepri snorted as she snickered. "But you're right; I'll never bear children. I'm hoping we can add another submissive female to our family."

Louisa's eyebrows shot up.

Khepri shrugged. "I don't have a problem sharing my alpha. Finding a stirithy female with an open mind will be difficult, but this is my most ardent wish for us. I'd be so happy helping raise his offspring. And, even though he'll never admit it, he wants the same."

Ssherrss rattled off something in Aaruan. Another arm wave and hand signal from Khepri flew his way. Her eyes laughed even if she didn't vocalize her response to what must have been a reprimand from her lover. Her expression slid into the mischievous. "What about a mate for you? Dr. McGehee seems to be a good catch as far as humans go. I know you both like each other. Why do you hesitate?"

Louisa blushed.

Turnabout is fair play, I guess.

"How are you so sure he likes me or that I even care about him in the slightest?"

"Oh, that's easy. Emotions take on distinct odors. I smell them like you see different colors. The stronger the emotion, the brighter the scent. You mask it better than him, but the nose doesn't lie." She tapped her snout.

Startled that her confused feelings for the Good Doctor had olfactory confirmation, a demure Louisa smiled. "I'll have to remember your nose when I'm around you." She tapped her shorter sniffer twice and said, "I've sensed some interest from him, but before we came here, I wasn't looking for anyone. But now? I'd be lying if I said I haven't thought about it."

"And?" Canine brows twitched.

"It's complicated. My experiences with men are nothing but tragic."

Khepri leaned over, patting Louisa's head, and consoled her with drooping eyes.

Louisa bottled her laughter at the hilarious irony, saying, "I don't know how to connect emotionally with a man. Ben seems reluctant as well. Besides, he's dealing with some demons right now. I hope they don't become a bigger problem."

Why are you blabbing so much? she wondered.

Head angled, Khepri murmured, "Hmmm." She rubbed up and down the bottom of her snout during the long pause. "This morning, I smelled worry and tiredness on Ben. As for his reluctance, he'll be ready when you are. He's an alpha, like you." She nodded. "It's difficult in such circumstances, but two alpha relationships can work for humans. The polemarchos and her mate are such a match. So don't give up."

Louisa grinned and reached over to pat Khepri's thigh. "Thanks for the advice. If you don't mind, may I confide in you again?"

"That would be nice." Khepri winked at her. "We girls have to stick together."

At the mouth of the pass, they angled across miles of semi-arid land toward the intersection of the two closest mountains. By midmorning, the column entered a series of rolling foothills covered in short grass and low bushes. Large herds of gazelle and zehorg grazed. The animals looked upon the intruders with curious apprehension.

It took hundreds of startled, fur-covered, flightless birds stampeding away from Ben to rouse him from his sleepless stupor atop his mare. As soon as the last of the fast, yet short and rotund, avians topped the nearest hill, Ben's chin again touched his chest, eyes turning to slits.

Around noon, they reached the point where the twin stone behemoths converged. A small path cut its way up the right side of the leftmost giant. In the closest flat area to the trail, they helped the four horse archers set up a base camp.

As Ben nibbled on a lunch of dried meat and sweetbreads, he gazed at the sky with a numbed mind. The lone celestial body, An, looked natural, painted against an almost cloudless canvas of light blue. He imagined being home for the briefest of moments, and his weariness disappeared. Then, as his eye registered the unnatural threads of silver dissecting the horizon, the date-flavored muffin in his mouth turned sour.

Feeling shitty once again, Ben tossed the bread to the ground and stood to sort through his luggage. After lunch, the Earthlings converted half of their mounts into packhorses. They loaded only the essentials, which included borrowed two-person tents, food, clothes, medicine, books, and bullets. To Ben's further irritation, Louisa and Abu insisted on double-checking his work.

Reorganized, they started up the path, leaving behind wagons, half of their horses, and one large kabuah. Impatient and grumpy, Ssherrss hurried them along the trail with a gruff Greek shout, "Keep up!"

Single file, Ben followed Louisa, who walked behind Khepri as they ascended the mountain. Bone weary, he put one heavy boot in front of the other. With his reins over one shoulder, he pulled his horse along. Or did he use the reins to hold himself upright as he leaned into the slope? Even simple thoughts became unsolvable equations in his current state.

They crossed the tree line, causing Ben to look around. Some flora looked familiar, such as pines, maples, and elder trees. At higher elevations, the predominant trees appeared to be clusters of white aspens. Many alien plants and trees were close by, mixed among the Earth species. Like analyzing a landscape painting created by several artists using different styles, he had to rely on his gut to tell him which were native and which were transplants to a new biosphere.

Many of the smaller native plants had an iridescent element, like the flowering grass. Others, speaking to their non-Aaruan origin, had elements of evergreens, succulents, and ferns in equal parts. Ben's biggest puzzlement came from large trees with gnarled branches covered in long red moss. He'd seen moss-covered trees in parts of the Deep South and Louisiana, but he'd never encountered red moss. He stopped at one such tree growing a few feet off the path. What had looked like moss instead fluttered in the light breeze like shaggy hair.

Ben reached to touch it when Louisa grabbed his wrist. He twisted in slow motion to see her smiling. "Khepri said to leave those alone. They're called *melabu*.[2] Part animal and part plant. When threatened, they swing their limbs around and scream loud enough to make your ears bleed." She moved her face closer. "There shouldn't be any other dangerous plants. She'll keep an eye out just in case. I'll stay here and warn everyone else."

"Thanks," he mumbled, unmoving.

Louisa gave him a pat on the back and a small shove. "Go on. I'll catch up."

Her push brought Ben out of his daze. He climbed, forcing each foot up through what felt like a pool of molasses.

---

2. A melabu is a tree/animal hybrid found on Aaru that is covered in a coat of red shaggy hair. The creature has both a blood stream and a root system. It can move its limbs to defend itself and elicits an incredibly loud scream when threatened. To mate, the roots of two trees grow toward each other until they meet. Melabu find the opposite-sex tree using their voices, making various whale-like, high-pitched sounds. Melabu offspring grow inside the mother until they form a hard seed-like shell. After reaching maturity, they are spewed into the air, like spores.

Chapter 25

Outside Alexandrian Camp in Axclatca Pass, Choru, An 5660, Day 4

Djoser leaned closer to the boulder, following the shrinking shade. He'd spent the last six hours hidden among the rocks along the rim of the pass, listening. Anyone else might have succumbed to the tedium, but not him.

This rare ability made him the best.

Sorting through hundreds of simultaneous conversations took skill and patience. With his singing, he searched for the needle in the haystack.

The babiakhom cycled with rapid precision through the stream of babble he'd caught on the wind. Like untangling a giant ball of yarn, Djoser pulled a single string and amplified the words. Pushing the rest aside, he sought the unusual. Most times, he heard orders, complaining, joking, or discussions about the recent battle. Without curiosity, he tossed these strands away, then pulled another until he found an anomaly.

"I'm telling you, Griffin, the Earth woman had the most beautiful voice I've ever heard."

"Is it true she's as beautiful as the others say?"

"She's too short and skinny for my tastes. You know I like 'em curvy with a big round bottom."

"I wish I could've heard her sing before they left."

"I got lucky for sure. Guess they headed for the capital."

"I'm not so sure. Orin bitched about his Lochos having to give their tents to the Earthers, even though they had their own."

"Not our problem. Hope we get sent back home soon. I could use the rest."

"Doubt it. The pig-fucking Remulans probably want to finish what they started."

With a simple thought, Djoser dropped the ball of yarn. He called Horus, his martial eagle, and gave her new instructions. Stationed several hundred yards overhead looking for patrols, two- or six-legged, she made one last circle and sped away toward the north.

Iskur would demand an immediate update, but his elven leader and the rest of the gang were out of range. Djoser calculated the need against the danger of not waiting for nightfall. In the end, he justified the risk because Horus reported no one nearby.

Decision made, Djoser popped his head above the boulder and scanned for threats. The broken landscape stretched from the lip of the canyon to the mountains. He harvested every sound, seeking the slightest hint of movement.

Nothing.

Alone, he stepped out of the shade. He had to be careful. Touching the ground a quarter mile from the edge could be a death sentence, and he wasn't foolish enough to disturb the Hive.

After picking out his path with care, he jogged over the flattest of the rocky ground. The song of flight chimed in his mind, and Djoser spread his arms. A swirling gust of air filled the patagium stretched tight from his arms to his torso.[1] An inch at a time, Djoser's feet left the ground. His speed growing, he flew a few feet above the plateau to avoid any eyes from below. With the danger zone growing close, he gained altitude and soared to the northeast.

Thirty minutes later, Djoser tucked his arms and angled into a dive. As the details on the ground rushed toward him, he sang to his partners in the small clearing below. He alerted them of his approach as he stretched out his arms a little and pulled out of the dive. Wings fully extended, he brought his feet underneath him and put the brakes on his descent. An inch above the grassy field, he transitioned his glide to a walk, lowering his arms. An elf and a hysakas marched his way.

When they came to a stop, Iskur didn't say a word. He also never broke eye contact. Djoser sang the interpretation song so his boss would hear his words in the elf's native Eblan. "The Earthlings left yesterday or today going north. I sent Horus to find them."

Iskur smiled. "Good work. All we can do is wait. Did you find out anything else?"

"Not much. There's a pretty woman with them. They said she has a beautiful singing voice. That's all I heard. I came as soon as I knew they'd left."

Iskur nodded. "Interesting. We'll leave when Horus comes back. With any luck, they only have a day's lead and no more."

---

1. Patagium are the folds of skin under a babiakhom's arms. This skin is connected to its body and allows it to fly. It is the same as a flying squirrel. It is assumed that babiakhom could only glide until the Ancients gave them their singing gifts.

Chapter 26

Hurra Pass, Nefru Mountains, Choru, An 5660, Day 4

From behind a tree on the slope of the mountain pass, Shanesha watched. He and his men observed this band of humans from the shadows for a second night. As the group of about two hundred made camp, he tracked the location of the guards. Their leader was speaking with a dark-skinned Kerman who looked like a priest. The previous night, at about the same time, some brigands had misjudged this same group of seemingly unarmed villagers and attacked. They didn't live to regret it.

Surprise enabled the raiders to kill a few, but the tide turned as soon as the men below began using strange new weapons. Fire erupted from short poles that the peasants cradled like a crossbow or metal tools they held in one hand. When the flames came out, brigands fell as if struck by the hand of a god. The next morning, Shanesha inspected several of the corpses. Each body showed evidence of puncture wounds similar to being stabbed by a short metal rod.

Intuition told Shanesha that Kutha needed to understand and possess these new weapons, but wariness gave him pause. The leader of the not-so-innocuous humans wore strange clothes. The stocky man with his face full of stubble wore brown pants and a matching jacket. He stuck out like an elf's ears. This and the strange weapons made Shanesha suspect he shadowed a group of Earthlings.

He hesitated to make a definitive call because most of the men below could have come from one of several Aaruan nations. Regardless, tonight his soldiers would use his race's advantage to overwhelm them. They would capture the weapons, along with the leader.

If all goes well, Innana will reward me handsomely.

Chapter 27

Nefru Mountains, Choru, An 5660, Day 5

As the edge of An touched the peak looming before them, the travelers reached a small flat grass field off to the side. Ssherrss called a halt.

With little more than muscle memory, Ben helped Abu unpack and unsaddle the horses before setting up both tents. Abu, giving him a concerned look, insisted on watering and grooming the horses himself. He led them toward a stream on the far side of the small plateau.

Bleary-eyed, Ben somehow registered the Lochem building several large fires in the clearing, along with a ring of smaller fires farther out from the camp. The lesser pits' flames flickered through the trees as the sky darkened.

Strange.

A mere automaton, he forced himself to eat a piece of lamb jerky and an apple, washing them down with half of his canteen. He hung his hat on one of the taller stakes holding up the near end of the tent, then undid his holster and crawled inside. Sleep came as soon as his head touched the bedroll he'd laid on the grass.

Then, with a start, Ben woke. He pulled himself up on his elbows in the pitch blackness, his body a spring under tension. Blinking several times, he tried to dispel the visages of his latest nightmare. Cold sweat covered his body, and he shivered. The crisp mountain air filled his lungs, and he smelled the rich aroma of lavender and lemon.

A soft hand touched his, and he heard a soothing voice singing what could only be a child's lullaby. Unable to translate the Greek with his confused mind, Ben felt his body relax. He lay back and rolled to his side to seek the source of the song and the scents.

He couldn't see Louisa's face, but he felt the warmth of her soft breath as she sang. Disappointment surged through him when the tender touch disappeared, the echo of her warmth lingering on his hand. He focused on the enchanting voice as a blanket was pulled over his body. With a sense of peace, Ben felt his eyes grow heavy.

Chapter 28

The edge of the Nefru Mountains, Choru, An 5660, Day 5

Bastet and Kheket, Djoser's two *caracals*, lynx-sized cats with tall pointed ears, slunk through the shadows, stalking the lone Alexandrian guard.[1] The soldier walked in a wide circle around a sputtering fire in the center of the Earthlings' camp while Iskur's gang hid in the shadows outside the reach of the flames.

Without a sound, the cats sprang from the side and the back. Eight sets of claws and two sets of sharp teeth tore into the man. His startled cry set off a flurry of activity. Arms flailing, he attempted to reach the source of his pain and stumbled. Kheket dove for the man's unprotected neck, teeth flashing.

By the time Djoser reached the fallen man, the soldier's legs twitched a few more times and lay still. Djoser sang to his pets. He praised them and sent them away from the body. Even the beast trainer could lose control of his familiars if an animal came to think of men as meals.

On the far side of the fire, Djoser saw two more Alexandrian soldiers shoved to their knees in front of Iskur. The leader's two elven henchmen, Cruel and

---

1. Caracals are lynx-size cats with tall, pointed ears that are native to Africa and the Middle East.

Sadistic, as Djoser thought of them, pushed down on the men's shoulders. As Djoser made his way around the fire, he found a fourth man lying in a crumpled heap with flame-propelled shadows dancing over his face. His neck twisted at an impossible angle, and the man's eyes stared, unseeing, at the stars. His killer, Shemush, strode a few yards ahead of him toward the prisoners.

Djoser found torture distasteful but acknowledged its necessity and effectiveness in certain circumstances. This was one of those circumstances. The interpretation song humming in his head, Djoser came to stand between Iskur and the prisoners.

In an almost soothing voice, Iskur said, "If you tell us where the Earthlings went, I will show you mercy. The choice is yours."

The man on Iskur's right answered by spitting at the gang leader's face. A chill ran through Djoser as Iskur showed the slightest hint of a smile. Nonplussed, the elf relaxed his palms on the jeweled pommels of his twin short swords and shifted his chin toward Shemush.

A life-singing, torture specialist, the seven-foot-tall hysakas made a growling sound. He stepped forward and back-handed the soldier's helmet off before enveloping the top of the soldier's head in a massive hand-claw. Sadistic, the elf holding the man's shoulders, jerked his hands up and away.

Seconds later, the Alexandrian's defiant visage became a mask of pain. His mouth opened, but only a gurgling sound came forth as blood seeped from his ears, eyes, and nose. The soldier tried to move his hands up to grab his head when every muscle in his body clenched at the same time. His jaw snapped shut with a loud crack.

As fast as they'd started, the spasms ceased. The man's body tried to collapse, but Shemush held a fist full of hair, keeping him upright on his knees. Sobs racked the Alexandrian's body while tears watered down the blood on his face.

A sinister chuckle rumbled deep in the giant's throat.

To the second man, Iskur said in his icy, calm way, "My friend can keep you both alive for days. He will bring you to the edge of death, eliciting new, unbearable pain each time. When you sip the sweet release of death, he will bring you back from the brink only to begin again.

"You should know." He flashed his eyes at the hysakas. "He loves his work. Most days, I'd let him have his fun, but I'm in a hurry. You have one last chance. Where did they go?"

The soldier's bulging eyes darted from Iskur to the hysakas to his comrade weeping next to him. On the second eye circuit, he bowed his head, his voice quivering. "They left after Father yesterday. Going to a place called the Tomb of the Mortals."

For a single breath, Iskur's brow furrowed. "Why?"

"They didn't tell us anything. We're supposed to wait here. I overheard the stirithy speaking to an Earthling. That's the only reason I know anything. I swear."

"Who else is with them? How many are in the group?" Iskur tapped his fingers against the grip of his swords.

The man's voice trembled as tears flowed down his face. "The stirithy, a hysakas, ten Lochem, and about twenty Earthlings. Most of them are soldiers. The soldiers all looked like they were from Kuru." He gulped and snorted a snot bubble. "They have another man, a boy, and a woman who aren't soldiers and not from Kuru. That's all I know."

Iskur brushed a long strand of hair behind a pointed ear. "Hmm. How did the Earthlings and the stirithy understand one another?"

The man's words tumbled out in a rush. "Some of them spoke Greek."

"What of their weapons?"

The prisoner's face twisted in bafflement. "The cavalrymen carried swords and lances. None of them wore armor."

"You did not see or hear about them using their fire sticks?"

The Alexandrian's face still appeared puzzled while his eyes darted around like a trapped animal. Stuttering between sobs, he said, "I . . . I, don't, kn . . . know what you're talking about."

Looking at each member of his gang, Iskur stopped when he locked eyes with Djoser. The babiakhom wind singer shrugged his answer to the unspoken query. None of the gang had a question.

Iskur looked at the two elves standing behind the kneeling men and gave his henchmen a deliberate, long-lasting blink. Djoser kept his face placid as Cruel and Sadistic, sporting wicked, sneering smiles, drew their daggers across the throats of the now-useless prisoners.

Chapter 29

Nefru Mountains, Choru, An 5660, Day 6

Abu's familiar low-level snoring welcomed Ben back to the land of the living. The only memories of his dreams were pleasant. As he lay there, he thought it strange to have dreamed of Louisa singing him a lullaby until he sniffed the faintest hint of lemon and lavender.

It wasn't . . . a dream.

Unsure how to react or even feel about what she'd done, Ben realized how clear his thoughts were. He felt like his old self for the first time in days. A sense of gratitude for Louisa's kindness washed over him. He'd have to thank her. It sure beat walking around like the undead. Working his way out of the tent, he did his best not to wake Abu.

A few others were up and moving in the glow of early dawn, but most of the camp remained still. This didn't mean silence, as several soldiers sawed away loud enough to wake a hibernating bear. Before grabbing his hat, Ben buckled on his holster and checked that he had a loaded revolver. Then he dug into his saddlebags and retrieved his grooming kit and a few sheets of paper, wondering what the Alexandrians used for perforated paper.

At the edge of camp, he tipped his cap to the Lancer and the Lochem soldiers standing guard. He stayed downwind of the camp, moving another fifty yards through the trees until he found a large bush where he put his tin of supplies on a shelf of branches.

Ben had unbuttoned his britches and started to pee when the bushes rustled behind him. The hairs on his neck stood up as he eased the pocket army free. He spun, looking for the source of the disturbance, and almost shot the wiggling metal-gray lump.

His finger eased off the trigger, and his jaw dropped at the giant bug that had taken no notice of him. Three feet long and two feet tall, the largest roly poly he could have ever imagined chomped away on leaves about ten feet away.

"Whew." As he moved the gun back to his hip, Ben felt wetness on his hand. Realizing he'd peed on himself, he cursed.

He pushed his arm straight out and shook away drops of urine. Then, out of the corner of his eye, he saw a blur fly by. A creature the size of a mountain lion landed on the roly poly and pierced its hard shell with a pincer-like mouth.

Loud crunching sounds accompanied the bite as bug goo gushed from the insect's back. A strange shrill cry followed, and the giant bug's six legs thrashed about under its shell. Ben thought that if a cougar had the head of a giant gopher, along with mottled green-and-brown fur, it would be this creature.

Heart pounding in his chest, Ben took two hesitant steps to the left and tried to edge around the bush behind him. His eyes and revolver never wavered from the brutal scene. He grimaced, feeling the twig break before he heard the loud snap from under his left boot. The gopher-cat's head swung in his direction. Ben aimed between the creature's blood lust–filled eyes as bits of shell and greenish goo dripped from its two giant teeth.

In his most soothing voice, he said, "Good kitty. Keep eating."

Muscles along the beast's shoulders tightened. Its roar matched that of the pocket army as it sprang from the bug's back. The brute leaped a half second before the shot, but the bullet tracked true, striking the lion's chest. Ears ringing,

Ben had no time to think. He yanked the gun back in line from the recoil and pulled the trigger again with the creature mere feet away. The second bullet went through the savage gopher's wide maw and exited the back of its skull.

Undeterred in death, the muscled monster struck Ben's chest, driving him backward into the bush. His breath fled, and his arms windmilled as he fell. Branches broke under him and, sandwiched, he sucked in quick, short, desperate breaths.

Urine-drenched, broken branches poked at his back while two hundred pounds of sinewy carnivore covered him like a blanket. Its lifeblood pulsed onto Ben's stomach as the creature's heart sputtered to a stop. As oxygen reached his lungs, Ben took several deep breaths. He lifted his head and stared at the giant razor-sharp teeth inches from his neck. Shouts came from the direction of the camp, and he panicked.

His panic was almost as intense as when he'd first seen the bug get attacked. He pushed and tugged, struggling to get the dead gopher off him.

Damn it. Not with my pants down.

With every movement he made, sharp sticks jabbed and scratched at his back. Giving up on getting free, he laid aside his revolver on one of the giant paws stretched out beside him. He winced with disgust as he wormed his hands through the thick, fresh blood, reaching under the fur-and-muscle blanket.

Almost. There. Got it.

With things back in the right place, Ben worked on the buttons of his pants. He got the first one reattached when the two guards he'd passed ran up to loom over him. Sowar Chib's and the female Lochem soldier's expressions showed genuine concern. The pair pulled the creature's body to one side, their eyes going wide. Ben glanced down to see himself covered in blood.

A sheepish smile creased his face, and he felt his scar tug at his mouth. "It's not mine." He repeated the phrase in Greek when the woman's expression did not change.

The soldier nodded before pinching her nose. The smell hit Ben, and he laughed with relief. In death, the gopher lion had vacated its bowels. He shook his head.

And I was worried they'd know I'm lying in my own pee?

Happy to be alive, he kept laughing at the absurdity of it all. Soon, the small crowd that had gathered laughed along.

While helping him to his feet, the soldier said in Greek, "Tyche the trickster's bad luck almost got you killed. Ninkilim usually leave people alone, but if they sink their teeth into you, they don't let go unless they tear off a piece of you. HaShem has blessed you."[1]

Ha. I killed the Sumerian Lord of Rodents. Is a gopher a rodent?

"I count myself extremely blessed," Ben said in Greek, dripping sarcasm as he gestured toward the mess. He grew serious and said, "But you're right, I got lucky, and I thank God for my good fortune." With both hands, he swiped some of the blood off his shirt before he picked up the grooming kit, which had fallen to the side. "I should clean up. Thanks for the help." To Sowar Chib, he repeated it in English.

Leaving the carcass behind, Ben angled through the trees toward the small stream running parallel to the campsite. Somehow, his hat had stayed on his head, but he could tell from its off-kilter angle that it had taken a beating. When his hands were clean, he needed to set that right.

---

1. On Earth, Ninkilim is known as the Lord of Rodents, a Sumerian god. On Aaru, it is a cougar-size mammalian predator with giant pincer-like teeth that are used to pierce and latch onto its prey.

At the gurgling brook, Ben stripped down to his knee-length drawers. He tossed the rest of his clothes into the bushes because they weren't worth salvaging. Only his boots and hat remained. As he squatted next to the creek, he felt the familiar fatigue that came as the adrenaline drained away.

The tiredness didn't last. An icy chill ran through his body when he plunged his hands into the freezing water and washed the gore away. With clean hands, he splashed his face and opened the kit. He took out the shaving cup, brush, and his last piece of Colgate shaving soap. He frowned, wondering how to find an Aaruan alternative.

Ben whipped the soap and spring water into a lather before brushing the sudsy cream around his face. He made sure to avoid the scar tissue, which would never grow hair again. He took out a compact mirror and the straight razor and made slow strokes with the blade, moving with the grain of his stubble.

With a smooth face, he put away the shaving supplies and retrieved a small piece of charcoal and a twig with a frayed end from the kit. He rubbed the blackened wood over the surface of his teeth, making sure to avoid tasting any of the substance. He followed the rough scrub by brushing the black away with the stick's bristles. He finished by washing out his mouth and packing the tin.

Now for the hard part.

He took off his hat and tossed it on the mossy ground next to his holster before pulling off his boots and socks. With a glance around, he peeled off his underpants. Pausing, he held up the blood-covered cotton and shook his head. He dunked them in the brook and rubbed as much coagulating liquid away as possible before laying them on a rock next to the stream. Without a stitch on, he stared at the slow-rushing water, trying to work up the courage to wash the rest of his body.

Stop being a lily-livered yellow belly.

With a deep breath, Ben stepped into the deepest spot in the middle of the stream and plopped down.

"Sake's alive! Holy shit, that's cold." Ben's teeth rattled in his head as he rushed to scrub away the creature's lifeblood.

Motivated by the cold, he cleansed his body as fast as possible. His clean skin turned an angry red from the freezing water. If the day's indignities had not already been enough, he heard girlish laughter behind him. He swiveled to find Khepri with her head thrown back in hysterics. She loomed over Louisa, who had bent over howling at the hilarity.

"When did you get here?" Ben chattered through clenched teeth.

Khepri said in Greek, "Just now, but we heard you before we saw you." She chuckled again.

Ben, unwilling to get out of the water, glared at the two of them. After a long time, when he thought he'd lost the feeling in his feet, Louisa straightened. A hand covered her mouth, a feeble effort to stifle her giggles.

"The guards told us what happened, and we came to make sure you're not hurt. I can help you with all the scratches when you finish bathing." Khepri winked at him.

Too distracted by the cold to think about a dog winking at him, Ben clattered out a stern "Louisa. Turn around."

Still holding her hand over her mouth, she shook her head no. She jerked her eyebrows and chin up twice, challenging him to stand up in all his glory.

Chilled to the bone but as clean as he could get, Ben was desperate. "Damn it, Louisa, please turn around."

Her hand dropped, and with a mischievous grin, she shrugged in mock disappointment before executing an about-face.

Ben hopped up and worked his way to the side of the stream, tip-toeing as fast as he could. On dry grass, he grabbed his underpants. As he put them on, he heard Khepri speak in an indignant but, he hoped, sarcastic tone, "And what of my modesty, human? Do you think I'm not attracted to your hairless body?"

More red from embarrassment than from the freezing water, Ben stammered, "Ah, I'm sorry, I, uh, didn't."

Khepri cut him off. "Well, you'd be right. You hairless apes are very unappealing." She placed her giant hand on Louisa's shoulder, and they snickered.

Water streamed off his body, and the morning air felt like little pin pricks as his outer layer began to wake. Teeth chattering, he hopped around on one foot, pulling on the right boot and then the left. He swept up his hat and plopped the still-disheveled pork pie on his head. At last, he scooped up his holster, pulled himself up straight, drew back his shoulders, and stormed away with a loud huff.

Out of the corner of his eye, he saw the two of them turn and redouble their laughter.

His ire rose to new heights while immature giggling followed each of his embarrassed steps. He pushed his chin higher and double-timed it to the trees.

Having awakened a few minutes earlier, Abu wondered where Dr. Ben had gone. He began breaking down the tent they shared. A commotion drew his attention to his almost-naked guardian marching across the bustling campsite.

How does that man find so much trouble?

For modesty, Dr. Ben wore only a pair of bloodstained underpants between his hat and boots. The Alexandrians in camp, for their part, held back, trying to help the tatterdemalion save face.[2] Yet the Lancers couldn't resist twisting the knife. Whistles and catcalls followed Dr. Ben until Duffadar Nahal yelled above the noise, "Hello, handsome. Tiger got your tongue?" Hearty laughter spilled out of the jolly soldier and his men.

---

2. A tatterdemalion is a raggedy fellow whose clothes hang all in tatters

Dr. Ben stopped and turned to the smiling faces of the Bengal Lancers. He kept spinning until he found the duffadar. "Almost. That darn rat-lion thing almost ate me for breakfast." Breaking out a crooked smirk, Dr. Ben bowed to his audience. "Don't be jealous, boys. It's not the first, nor will it be the last pussycat I have to tame." He chuckled along with the Lancers at his double entendre.

Out of the crowd came a shout, "Keep dreaming, Captain! Five pounds says you'll never catch the cat you want!"

Another yelled back, "I'll take that bet! My money's on the Capt'n!"

Dr. Ben frowned as the Lancers formed a huddle, debating and betting on his chances. He marched off. The huddle broke up only after Duffadar Nahal admonished them to get to work.

When Ben reached their tent, Abu asked, "Are you okay?"

Dr. Ben gave him a tight-lipped grin. "Nothing but hurt pride. Just need some clean clothes."

Abu jumped to his feet. "I'll get you some, but you should take care of those cuts first. Your back's bleeding. Want me to get your doctor's bag?"

"Don't do that. I'll take care of his wounds."

Abu and Ben turned at the sound of Khepri's Greek words. While Abu worked out the translation, Dr. Ben's red face and neck turned splotchy. He appeared to want to say something but clamped his mouth shut. After staring at the hysakas for a long moment, he gave her his back. "Fine."

Fascinated, Abu cataloged Dr. Ben's wounds. At least four bleeders oozed red, while many more angry trails marred his back, shoulders, and neck. The big she-wolf placed her hand on Dr. Ben's arm, and he stiffened. Within moments, reddened skin mutated through a series of healing states until nothing remained but pinkish, healthy flesh. Abu stepped closer. A few of the deeper scratches had left tiny scars. Two weeks of healing had taken place in under a minute.

When she removed her hand, Dr. Ben turned, but she said, "Hold still." Khepri pulled a piece of cloth from a bag hanging at her waist. With several broad strokes, she wiped away all the blood. "Okay, you're good to go."

A mollified Dr. Ben faced the hysakas. "Thank you, Khepri."

"Anytime, Ben."

She seemed to stop herself from saying something more as she walked away.

Abu grabbed one of Dr. Ben's favorite outfits from their shared suitcase: a pair of brown pants and a linen shirt. He found the question he'd lost because of the morning's strange happenings. "How did you sleep, Dr. Ben?"

Dr. Ben's eyebrows shot up at the question. "Much, much better, Abu. Thank you."

"No need to thank me, but there is someone you should thank." He raised his eyebrows.

Dr. Ben gave a curt nod and crawled into the tent to get dressed.

Relieved, Abu recalled his conversation with Miss Louisa the previous night. She'd suggested Abu get her at the first sign of Dr. Ben's nightmares. Just after midnight, he'd whispered her awake.

Abu's eyes went wide when the petite woman crawled into the doctor's tent in the middle of the night. When she sang, Abu forgot about any impropriety as he curled under a blanket outside. He fell asleep to the soothing sounds and didn't know how long he'd slept. At some point, she must have gotten him up and back into his bedroll.

Abu hoped Dr. Ben would soon get back to normal. While they finished packing the tent, he worried that this new incident with the lion-thing might make things worse. Ssherrss said they had two more days before reaching the Ancients' site.

Two more chances for the nightmares to return.

Abu reminded himself to speak with Miss Louisa during the hike today. He needed to thank her for the help and make sure she could do it again if needed. Of course, he hoped to run into Esther along the trail.

If he could work up the courage, he'd have a proper conversation with the young woman who had captured his imagination. Because he became tongue-tied every time he was near Esther, he planned on taking Umrao along. His friend would provide the moral support Abu needed to strike up a conversation.

Abu thought, *What the hell?* as he and his best friend stepped to the side of the path after speaking with Miss Louisa and Esther.

His mind raced from confusion to fear before landing on a state of seething anger. His wrath pointed an accusing finger at himself before turning toward his friend. Sure, Abu was to blame for not telling the Lancer how much he liked Esther, but *damn it.*

How could Umrao stab me in the back like this?

The morning had started well enough as the group recommenced its march up the trail. Buoyed by Dr. Ben's improvement and his anticipation of speaking with Esther again, Abu's confidence soared. Even the increasing angle of the climb didn't discourage him.

When he spoke to Miss Louisa, she assured him she would continue to help Dr. Ben as much as possible. About that time, the very person he most wanted to see joined them. Esther stepped back from the Lochem and began marching alongside Louisa. Thinking it providential, Abu introduced Umrao to her.

Then everything went to shit.

Sure, his friend was five years older than him, tall, and handsome. But damn it, why did she have to look at him like that, and why did he have to smile at her like that?

Trapped in his morass of thoughts, he snapped his head to look up the hill when Esther yelled, "Attack!"

It took Abu a few precious seconds to realize that his crush had drawn her sword. She faced a man running out of the tree line from the uphill side of the path. As the young woman parried a vicious slash from the attacker's short sword, the ring of steel on steel brought Abu out of his trance. Umrao, acting quicker, ran five yards ahead with his saber in hand.

Legs pumping hard, Abu leaned into the steep path. Time seemed to speed up and slow down at the same time. The dueling swords were going faster than he could follow, but he felt as if he were running in quicksand. Desperate to help Esther and Miss Louisa, he pulled his Schofield revolver from its holster and cocked the hammer. His pounding heart thumped in his head, almost drowning out the fighting.

The attacker pushed aside Esther's khopesh, which she'd aimed at his midsection. In a smooth, lightning-quick motion, he sidestepped and lunged. With his longer reach, his sword stretched past her curved blade. A last-second hop kept her from getting skewered in the side.

Even Abu could tell the attacker outmatched her in size, skill, and speed. He wished Esther could use the shield strapped to her back as it might even out the contest. Fearing he'd never reach them in time, Abu put everything into scrambling uphill.

As the green-and-brown-clad man slipped past her guard and stabbed Esther's exposed thigh, a shot rang out. The attacker jerked a step backward. A wounded Esther dipped to one knee as Louisa fired her small revolver. Red spouted a second time from the man's chest.

Undeterred, the wounded man regained his footing and stepped toward Louisa. She put another bullet into his right shoulder before he grabbed her wrist and twisted. The small gun clattered to the ground.

Esther used the distraction to hook her khopesh around the attacker's ankle and pull. The man stumbled as his leg jerked from under him. Another man, who could have been the first's twin, rushed from the trees toward the kneeling soldier's back. Mere feet from Esther, Umrao slammed into him, taking the two of them to the ground.

Five yards from the action, Abu brought the Schofield into the firing position. With a two-handed grip, he tried to get a shot at either of the prone attackers. Even with three bullets in him, the first man pulled himself up, and Abu swung the barrel toward the man's chest.

As Louisa bent to retrieve her revolver, the bullet-riddled man, from his knees, grabbed her arm. Before Abu could fire, Umrao rolled downhill to his left, a big gash across his chest. In shock, Abu moved the gun away from his first target and aimed at Umrao's attacker, climbing to his feet behind Esther.

The moment unfolded in glacial time as Abu squeezed the trigger. Somehow, he noticed the man's pointy ear right before the bullet tore through the man's skull. Blood and brains exploded out the back.

Abu fought the revolver's recoil as Louisa screamed. A giant wolfman had come out of nowhere and placed his hand on Louisa's back. At the hysakas's touch, she collapsed into the creature's arms. Abu tried to line up a shot, but the hysakas threw Louisa over his shoulder, blocking any chance he had.

In a surreal state of shock, Abu gaped at the giant, hairy wolfman wearing a shirt and pants and loping downhill on the path toward the woods. Panicked, Abu ran after them when he heard steel on steel behind him. From over his shoulder, he watched as the bullet-riddled man reached his feet again. Sword overhead, the man swung down at a sluggish Esther, who moved her khopesh as if through mud to block it.

Three Bullet Man's sword fell from his hand when another shot rang out. The elf—what else could he be with those ears?—fell backward. Abu looked for the source. Dr. Ben stood below with his Winchester pointed toward the fallen man.

Abu looked back to where the hysakas had taken Louisa and saw nothing but trees. His arm went slack, and his pistol dropped to his side. He'd failed in every way possible. Stunned, he turned in a circle. Esther crawled toward the downed elf and pulled herself to a kneeling position. Somehow finding the strength, she raised her khopesh and slammed it down across the dead elf's neck.

Unable not to look, Abu watched the elf's head slow-roll down the hill, gaining momentum with each wobbling spin. He followed it until the severed head hopped and bounced high, then careened off the path into the brush.

Ben put his hand on Abu's shoulder. "Where's Louisa?"

As if hearing Ben's voice from far away, Abu raised his empty hand and pointed. Ben took off and disappeared into the thick trees. As Abu watched him go, he remembered his best friend. Time twisted and settled back to normal as he saw Umrao writhing in pain on the ground.

Eyes shut and grimacing, Umrao held both hands over his bleeding wound. Abu willed himself to get to his friend. Later, he couldn't remember whether he ran or walked, but before he reached Umrao, Khepri appeared. She put her hand on the young Lancer's bleeding chest. His pain eased away, and in a few seconds, the bleeding stopped.

Without doing more than stem the bleeding, Khepri jumped to her feet. She raced to Esther, who had collapsed next to the headless body. Khepri cupped her hand over Esther's wounded thigh. Abu marveled as the bleeding ceased, and the four-inch gash sealed itself. The hysakas snapped her long, clawed fingers twice, catching his eyes with hers. "They'll be okay."

Shame overcame Abu, and he hung his head. "It's all my fault." Choking out a sob, he fell to his knees. "I lost her."

Chapter 30

Nefru Mountains, Choru, An 5660, Day 7

The trail Ben followed disappeared from one step to the next. He backed up to the last clear signs of passage and spiraled outward, conducting a slow, methodical search. He pushed down his rising sense of panic.

How could you lose the trail?

He looked for a broken branch or a trace of a footstep under the dim forest canopy. Louisa's face flashed into his thoughts.

Tempted to bargain with God, he stopped himself. God would do as he pleased, regardless of what promises Ben might make. Instead, he refocused on finding the trail. How could a creature the size of a wendigo, carrying a—albeit petite—woman, just disappear?

On his fourth large spiral, his frustration bubbled over. The imprisoned demon inside him raged at those who had taken her, demanding a pound of flesh. He let out a loud, "Arrrgh!"

From behind, he heard a disapproving Greek voice. "That won't help uss find Mmissss Ssophia."

Ben spun to see Jeevan, Ssherrss, and a mix of Lochem and Lancers behind them. Agitated, he growled, "I lost the trail. I don't know how. It was plain as day. Then poof. Nothing, as if they flew away."

A very serious Ssherrss said, "You'rre not too farr off. The kidnapperrss have a babiakhomm with themm. It'ss wiping away the trrail and sscatterring the ssccentss." The chest-high stirithy bent toward the ground and sniffed. Back and forth he paced, sniffing here and there. Ssherrss turned his masked face to Ben. "It will take mmuch longerr, but I can trrack themm. I jusst have to find the placcess they have not been."

Ben bit his inner lip, the pain helping him push the fiend under the rock where it slept. He promised to let the monster feast when he caught up to the bastards that took her. A little calmer and with a spark of hope, he said, "Lead the way." To Jeevan, he said, "Let's form a cone with Ssherrss at the point. Pair everyone up. Stay in sight of the pair to the left and right. Move slow and adjust to Ssherrss as he follows their scent."

Giving a few terse orders and hand signs, Jeevan had the Lancers and the Lochem organized and moving. Ben pushed down his rising panic at the rescue group's snail-like pace. To take his mind off Louisa, he thought about his son. He felt terrible about leaving Abu back on the main trail. The teenager would need assurances he'd done the right thing. Ben, who saw only the last few seconds of the fight, was so proud of Abu for saving Esther's life.

All that needed to wait until they found Louisa. Ben hoped her kidnappers had targeted her as an Earthling and not because of her beauty. Either way, he prayed they would catch up with the assailants before anything bad happened. More thoughts of Louisa being hurt or worse flooded his mind. Comparable to the fear that overcame him the day he lost Savage, he felt that if he lost the fierce, spirited Louisa, he would lose a piece of himself.

He took a deep breath and reminded himself that *God's able* to save her, Ben just needed the faith to do what he could. With renewed determination, he pushed his doubts and worries aside as useless emotions. Only focus and action would make a difference on his part. The rest he left to God.

For four hours, they moved through the thick forest, angling down the side of the mountain. On a quick water break, Ben huddled with Ssherrss and Jeevan in the lee of a copse of giant redwoods, as the forest's shadows deepened. "It'll be dark soon, but we have to keep going. Our only hope is when they stop for the night. Ssherrss, what do you think?"

Whiskers twitched at the end of a reddish-brown snout. "It will be verry difficult, esspeccially with sso mmany. Ssomme will get losst. Ssend everryone back, exccept forr two of the Lochemm and you two. Therre cannot be mmorre than thrree to five kidnapperrss. With yourr gunss, we can mmatch themm."

Before Ben could answer the stirithy, Ssherrss held up a black hand. The fox-like creature raised his snout high and sniffed the air. He whispered, "Remmulanss."

Good. We're close.

"How?" Jeevan hissed.

Ssherrss tapped his nose. "Sstink of garlic and onion."

Ben asked, "How far? How many?"

"Not ssurre how mmany. On the otherr sside of the clearring." He pointed toward a small flat treeless section of forest, about thirty yards wide next to the redwoods.

In Ben's estimation, the trees and the underbrush on the far side could have concealed an elephant.

Hand signals flew from Jeevan to the four Lochem and three Lancers with them. The men hustled to put the big trunks between them and the ambush.

Ssherrss walked to the shaded area of the nearest tree and said, "I will flussh themm out."

He went to all fours in a bed of lush moss. Ben knew his eyes were as wide as Jeevan's as the ground around the stirithy began to move. A layer of earth, topped with the mossy padding, inched up Ssherrss's arms and legs and slithered over his clothes until only his eyes showed from two holes in a mound of fuzzy grass.

He padded to the edge of their fort of trees and dropped to his belly. Sticking to the darkest shadows around the clearing, Ssherrss crawled without making a sound to the trees on the other side. If Ben hadn't known what to look for in the gloom, he would have lost track of the moss-encased stirithy.

With his free hand, Ben touched the top of his pistol grip before tapping the D-shaped hilt of the long knife hanging from the other side of his holster. His leg shook as he tried to free the extra energy that shot through his body from anticipating the coming violence. Inside, Ben's monster stirred.

As the small berm of moss slid into the underbrush, the sky above the clearing filled with long dark shadows. Thunk. Thunk. Javelins collided with trees or sank into the soft mountain soil with a whisper. A spear slammed into the wood six inches from Ben's head, and he put his back to the tree.

The shadow of another spear streaked past and struck a Greek soldier just above the knee. The man screamed in anguish and collapsed to the ground, the tip of the javelin protruding from the back of his thigh.

Several guns roared as the Lancers fired into the undergrowth where the spears had originated.

Ben peeked around the tree, the barrel of his Winchester leading the way. He couldn't see anything. The sky continued to darken as An disappeared.

Come on, damn it.

"Hold your fire!" Jeevan yelled.

For several minutes, there were only the whimpers of the wounded man and the exhortations of his comrade who tried to stem the flow of blood.

Ben kept his eyes trained on the opposite woods while searching his mind for anything that might help. They didn't even have a lantern or anything flammable to help light up the narrow field. The Remulans appeared smart enough to neutralize some advantages of the Earthlings' guns by waiting to attack until they were in complete darkness.

A booming crack sounded from across the clearing. Part of the forest canopy began to shake, and there were several yells of alarm in Latin, followed by a thunderous crash. About ten yards behind the first line of trees, something sparked and streaked from one trunk to the next, in and out of sight.

Wherever the spark had been, flames grew, flickering brighter and brighter. Within a minute, a huge blaze about sixty feet long lit up their ambushers' hiding place. The moment of clarity became muddled as smoke created a haze around the bonfire.

Ssherrss, you crafty racoon. I could kiss you.

Ben saw movement near one tree at the edge of the glade and fired. Jeevan's carbine spouted flames next to him, and a legionary tumbled into the open.

"Impetum!" screamed someone out of the woods. Too many shadows for Ben to count solidified into legionaries, their capes flapping as they raced across the small field.

A rage of anguish and hatred coursed through his veins, and he roared, "Mori fututorum!" as he pulled the trigger. Without pause, Ben levered in a fresh round, found another dark shape, and fired again.

All around him, Jeevan and the Lancers fired. The dark outlines of Remulan soldiers closed to ten yards when the remaining three Lochem stepped through the gaps in the trees to meet the charge.

Ben pulled the trigger one more time, and the head of a legionary snapped back. He dropped Agnes and grabbed his pocket army. The first Remulans slammed their shields into those of the Lochem, pushing the Greeks backward.

Jeevan ran to the right side of the three-Lochem wall, shooting his revolver from his hip. A Remulan cried out for a second before the Lochem's sword took him in the throat.

Ben released the chains, and the beast inside shook off its shackles. His senses became hypersensitive as his thoughts became death.

Stripped of his humanity, Ben stepped from the tree to the left of the mini-wall. A legionary raced toward him, his rectangular shield leading the way. Ben aimed just above the round metal boss protruding from the shield and squeezed off two shots. The man took several faltering steps and fell at Ben's feet. The pop of revolvers came from all around.

The Greek soldier anchoring the wall stumbled into Ben, his head whipping sideways as a Remulan gladius caved in his helmet.

Ben stepped onto and over the downed Remulan to free himself from the falling Lochem. The enemy soldier reared back with his short sword, seeking a second kill. On instinct, Ben fired from the hip.

The corner of the man's shield chipped away as the bullet hit the Remulan's shoulder with a meaty whack. The sword fell from his fingers, which had lost all their strength in an instant. His face full of rage, the legionary bull-rushed Ben.

The enemy soldier stumbled over his downed comrade, or he would have knocked Ben to the ground. Instead, he pinned Ben's revolver to his gut and kept pushing him backward.

Ben dug the heels of his boots into the soft dirt and grabbed the barrel of his gun with his left hand. The burns from the hot barrel didn't register with the monster's mind bent on tasting more death. Ben swung the end of his pistol grip toward the Roman-style helmet with a strength his offhand shouldn't have had.

The bird's head skull crusher punched through the helmet's softer metal and sent the man's head whipping in the opposite direction. The legionary tumbled backward. The monster followed him to the ground, swinging until the man's face turned to bloody pulp. Eyes wild with the ecstasy of the kill, the beast jumped up, seeking another victim.

"Ben!" Jeevan shouted.

The human part of Ben spun to the sound of his name while the monster inside switched the gun back to his right hand. Jeevan was on the ground, a legionary straddling him. The duffadar had his hands on the man's wrists, keeping the Remulan's gladius suspended above Jeevan's heart.

The pocket army roared twice in quick succession and sent the Remulan's brains flying into the clearing.

Jeevan grinned, then his eyes widened.

Ben sensed the blow coming and twisted to the side. Pain like hot lava shot through him as a javelin sliced through his belly. The head of the spear came out of his side at an angle, and Ben screamed. Ben dropped his gun, his monster of death fleeing from the pain.

A Remulan with a hardened, emotionless face and wearing a centurion helmet held onto the shaft. He pushed forward, injecting Ben with more molten suffering.

Louisa's frightened face swam in his mind, and the thought of failing her filled him with fury. He willed his hand to find the hilt of his knife and yank it free. He raised the blade and sliced at his tormentor's hand just as the centurion began to pull back.

The eyes of the stoic killer in front of him widened as three of his fingers separated from his hand. The Remulan stumbled backward, dropping the javelin. The weight of the spear pulled at Ben's body and brought him to his knees.

The legionary looked with wild eyes past Ben and ran into the redwood copse. A bullet pounded the tree he'd just passed before he disappeared.

Ben's eyes drifted back to the metal sticking out of his body, and he wondered how he was still alive. Only the wooden shaft, its end stuck in the dirt, kept him from collapsing. Tears of frustration streamed down his face.

God, I can't fail her now.

Like the echoes of a symphony's crescendo, cries of the wounded replaced the thunder of violence that had shattered the peace of the mountain forest.

Jeevan knelt beside him and began inspecting his wound.

"Get it out," Ben demanded.

"Can't. Not without killing you."

"Let mme look," said the walking moss creature that appeared behind the duffadar.

Jeevan stood and stepped aside as Ssherrss shook his body the way a wet dog might. Blood-covered dirt and moss flew away as if propelled by a cleansing wind.

With a worried tone, Jeevan said, "I think it missed anything vital, but if we pull it out, you might bleed to death."

"Then we won't pull it out." Ssherrss produced a nasty-looking dagger and bent down to grasp the golden cape of a dead Remulan. He cut away two long strips.

He looked Ben in the eyes. "This mmight hurrt a little."

The stirithy went to his knees on Ben's side and grabbed the metal shaft on either end of the wound. The metal near his black paws turned red.

The slight burning sensation made Ben wince, but the metal parted so that the point, along with the shaft, fell free. The metal still inside Ben stayed in place. The nubs at the ends of the giant metal splinter flattened and created metal plugs that covered the puncture points.

Ssherrss began wrapping the strips of cloak around Ben's waist. "Had to limmit burrnss. Khepri can't curre burns."

An image of the polemarchos's burned face flashed into his mind before morphing into Louisa's.

"We have to keep going. How bad?"

"We lost all the Lochem. My lads all have wounds but none as bad as yours." Jeevan shook his head. "We need to get you to Khepri."

"No. We keep going." Ben held out a hand to Jeevan, who pulled him to a standing position.

Dark lumps lay all around the clearing where Remulans had met their demise. The blaze on the opposite side had died down, but smoke filled much of the woods and part of the clearing.

Ben asked, "Can you pick up the trail?"

The stirithy hurmphed and nodded. "Sstay closse." He headed toward the least smoky section of the woods.

With clenched jaws, Ben took a step. The pain stabbed him as if he had been shot. His breath came in short, shallow gulps, but he put one boot in front of the other.

I'm coming.

Louisa's eyes popped open. She let out a cry as the feeling of getting pricked by a thousand stick pins radiated across her body. Overwhelmed, her brain, which had just a moment ago been unconscious, seized up. Agony blurred her vision, but she heard a chuckle through her cries of pain.

"Stop, Shemush. I want to speak with her first. How can she and I become friends if you are playing silly games?"

Louisa heard a disappointed huff. The suffering stopped faster than her brain could register. A slight warm, soothing feeling replaced the pain, and Louisa's latest cry died in her throat. She struggled to take control of her situation, staring at a strange sky filled with unknown constellations.

Still not home.

Memories flooded back. The attack and trying to save Esther from the man who'd stabbed her. Then nothing. Still dazed, she brought her head level and realized she sat on a boulder with her hands tied behind her back. She could hear the gurgling of a small stream nearby as she looked around. She ignored the others with her, trying to gauge where her captors had taken her. They were in the bottom of a small ravine, its walls sloping up and away from the stream that bubbled along about ten feet away.

One by one, she regarded her kidnappers. A babiakhom stood the farthest from her. The flickering light from the small fire outlined the creature in eerie shadows. Using all of her senses, she heard the distinctive purrs of at least two cats, which drew her eyes down. The tails of the strange knee-high beasts curled around the baboon-like creature's thighs. A giant hysakas stood one long clawed arm's length away, canine teeth bared.

As she shifted her eyes, she locked onto two deep lakes of brown. In front of her, bending down to eye level, was the most handsome man she'd ever seen. *Correction*, *elf*, she thought. She tore her gaze from his hypnotic brown eyes to his high cheekbones, prominent nose, and full lips positioned between two very pointed ears.

A knowing smile appeared on the perfect face in front of her. This elf knew the effect he had on women. His show of arrogance brought Louisa back to her spitfire self. She gauged the distance to be too far to give this *kólos* a good headbutt, so she settled for kicking straight up, aiming toward the cleft chin on the smug elf's square jaw.

Without taking his eyes off hers, he moved with lightning speed. He bobbed his head just out of range of Louisa's boot. His hands came down on top of her knees, pinning them in place. Despite her increased strength on the smaller planet, he held her secure. Also to her disappointment, his beautiful face stayed just out of reach as his smile broadened with swagger.

He took a moment to recapture her eyes. "I like you. When you tell me what I need to know, I will enjoy taming you." To illustrate, he shoved her knees apart and stepped forward. He grabbed the back of her head and brought his mouth to hers. Louisa whipped her head back and forth in revulsion but soon thought of a better strategy. She leaned into his forced kiss, opening her mouth a little, and bit his lip with everything she had.

The elf's head jerked away. He laughed, disregarding his bleeding lower lip. An evil-looking sneer crossed his handsome face before being replaced by an amused yet pompous smile. "Yes, I can't wait to play with you, my pretty songbird."

Once again, Louisa watched with fascination as the movement of the elf's mouth did not match the Greek she heard. The language in the background sounded a little like a harsh version of Hebrew, Arabic, and Egyptian, all mashed together as he continued. "My name is Iskur. Soon you will call me master. I have it on good authority that you have a lovely singing voice, Earth woman. I look forward to hearing you sing after I break you. Of course, if you cooperate, you will avoid any real unpleasantness. Let us start over with something simple. You now know my name, what is yours?"

Louisa glared at the bastard and shook her head no. A hint of disappointment flashed in the elf's eyes, which Louisa tried to ignore. Out of her peripheral vision, the hysakas reached out with a soft touch on her shoulder. She felt a searing pain, as if her feet were being branded by a hot poker. A startled cry flew from her mouth, and tears welled up as the pain disappeared.

The handsome face frowned. "Little songbird, I have no wish to hurt you, but you *will* tell me anything I want to know. So, again, what's your name?"

Stunned at the shock of pain she had just felt, Louisa tried to figure out her options. Not one to pray, except in times like these, she said a quick one to the Almighty that Ben and the Lancers would reach her in time. She turned her head and stared into the darkness, seeking salvation. She drew on her training to control her breathing.

The elf grabbed her chin and centered her vision on his face again with a strong jerk. Her eyes narrowed with determination as she set out to make him work for each piece of information.

"Louisa Sophia." Her mouth clamped shut.

With a smirk on his bloody mouth, the elf said, "That wasn't so bad, was it?" He stood and waved his hand around the ravine. "Were you expecting to find your friends out there?"

He chuckled. "They won't be coming. I left them a little gift."

Her mind became a tangle of emotions.

He has to be okay. They all have to be okay.

Iskur stooped down to her eye level. "Now, songbird Louisa, I need to know about your weapons. Tell me how they work."

Louisa had hoped this question would come last. This *kópanos* knew a lot about her and the rest of her party's capabilities.[1] With a firm grip on the reins of her thoughts, she focused on one of her other exemplary skills, lying. "They're magic wands and staves, built by the Ancients. We discovered them along with a device that brought us here."

Always include a little truth.

The elf named Iskur glanced at the hysakas, whose hand still rested on Louisa's shoulder. The giant wolf shook his head, and the elf did a slow blink. The terrible sensation started at Louisa's toes and worked its way up her legs at stampede speed as if a thousand spiders were crawling up her body.

She shivered and shook her head, fighting against the most morbid feeling ever. As if one living creature, ten thousand spiders struck. Louisa clenched her eyes shut. She screamed as thousands of pincers stabbed her, followed by the searing pain of venom burning her from the inside out.

---

1. Kópanos is Greek for "jerk."

When the pain stopped again, Louisa panted, unable to catch her breath. When she peeked out of a slit in her eyelids, Iskur ensnared her vision again. "I'm sorry for the pain, pretty Louisa, but your song was full of lies."

Iskur raised his eyebrows. "But I'm impressed. I was born on Earth over forty-six hundred and sixty years ago. You should be proud. You are the first person to tell me a lie that I could not detect in at least a thousand An. It's a skill you pick up when you're as old as I am." He pursed his lips and clucked his tongue three times. "Unfortunately, for you, my pretty lying songbird, my friend Shemush, like all life singers, can detect even the best lie with a simple touch."

Iskur's face went placid as if what came next would bore him. "For every small lie you tell, the pain will increase. What you have experienced so far is just a small sample of what Shemush can do. So, once again, how do your weapons work?"

Louisa shuddered, and fear gripped her like nothing she had ever known. Eyes closed, she ran through her breathing exercises until she held her terror at bay. She didn't have a choice. She would tell him anything he wanted.

I'm sorry, Ben.

The weight on her legs disappeared, and she opened her eyes. Iskur had turned to face the darkness, holding a short sword in each hand. His head tilted this way and that. He appeared to be straining to listen. Next to her, the hysakas pulled a giant two-headed ax over his shoulders and took several steps toward the now-hissing caracals.

What the hell's happening?

From the edge of the firelight, a cat screamed out in pain. It hopped several feet straight into the air before falling limp to the ground. A white shaft protruded from its side. Louisa's hysakas torturer growled and ducked as a streak of white flew by his snarling head. The wolfman charged toward the unseen archer and disappeared into the darkness.

Merde.

Louisa fell backward, rolling over the boulder, to land on her feet in a crouch behind the waist-high rock. She arched her back, pushed her bound hands low, and fell to her butt. With a little more wiggling and stretching, she worked her tied hands around her feet until she had them in front of her.

She peeked over the boulder. The elf seemed to be flowing through a hypnotic death dance. In rhythm to an unknown song, he quick-stepped and twisted his body as two shadowy arrows streaked through the space he had just occupied. Lunging, he engaged two figures that leaped at him from the darkness. Sparks flew as the elf parried blows from both swordsmen.

Out of the corner of Louisa's eye, something ran toward her, and she ducked down again. The babiakhom's membraned wings glowed in the firelight as he sprang one-legged off her rock seat. He flew into the darkness above the lip of the ravine without a whisper or a breeze.

Without knowing the nature of these new attackers, Louisa delayed acting on the idea of escaping into the night. Although she was grateful to God, they were *not* the literal cavalry for which she had prayed. Resigned to seeing how it played out, Louisa began chewing at the knotted rope around her wrists. The sounds of fighting continued just a few yards away as she pushed everything into the background except the task at hand.

It had been more than a decade since she had practiced the ability, but at least once a week for several years, her uncle had restrained her, locked her up, or put her in an impossible situation, requiring her to escape. His rough smoker voice kept time in her head while she manipulated the knot.

As the ropes fell away, she heard his words again: "The best thieves avoid getting caught, but the greatest thieves never remain caught."

The cry of pain from the melee on the other side of the rock brought her back to the present. Instead of looking, she felt around on the ground, grasping for any weapon she could find. She grabbed two jagged stones, each about the size of an apricot, but the oversized pebbles were a pitiful defense. Armed with little more than courage, she dared to look over the small boulder as the dance playing out around her reached a new crescendo. Four men with albino skin surrounded Iskur, the arrogant elf.

As if powered by an unseen force, he turned aside each blow, thrust, and slice from the albinos. The elf, a mere shadow silhouetted by the campfire, dodged three attacks simply by twisting and flowing within the current of steel. Like the fluidity of a mongoose's strike, a sword streaked away from the elf's body with the flick of his wrist. The albino closest to Louisa dropped to his knees. Seconds later, the man's head lolled backward before plopping to the ground behind the headless body, which remained kneeling.

Louisa's instinct told her that the three remaining albinos had no chance against the ancient elf. For a heartbeat, her terror returned, to be replaced by an anger she had never known.

That evil bastard has to die.

She stepped around her torture throne and moved deeper into the shadows but closer to the sword fight. Her arm cocked, she channeled every bit of fear the evil bastard brought forth and knitted it into the righteous wrath of God himself. A fury-fueled trance settled upon her, mind and senses becoming preternatural. She visualized the elf's dance.

The imprint of his next three steps in her brain, she let her missile fly.

Die gamiménos, die.

The stone arched over an albino's shoulder, following the downswing of the man's sword arm. Iskur spun into the man's attack and deflected the sword away without even needing to see the path of his own sword.

The rock replaced the space where the albino's sword had been, the clang of steel masking the briefest hint of whistling. With a satisfying thunk, the jagged stone smacked into the elf's high cheekbone as he continued his spin.

Yes.

To Louisa's glee, the dancer lost count with the silent music and stumbled a half-step. The other dancers never lost the beat, piercing Iskur in the leg and the side. The third albino slashed across the back of the elf's knees, severing both hamstrings. Without a sound, Iskur fell flat on his face.

Triumph mixed with anger fed her satisfaction, shocking Louisa at how she could relish someone's death so much. She backed farther into the dark with silent footsteps, watching the three men with apprehension. They continued stabbing and slashing the downed man several times each.

Two of them used ropes to tie the pointy-eared demon's hands and feet. Louisa thought it very odd to tie up a dead person, but she needed to worry more about facilitating her escape than the fate of that bastard.

Moving into the gloom toward the embankment, she concentrated on scaling to the forest above. As she crept forward, she smacked into something solid. She scrambled not to stumble backward and grabbed the leather-armored chest of a lean but solid man. She looked up, and her mouth dropped open. Two golden orbs peered at her from a face the color of the moon.

The agony kept Ben from sensing Jeevan's unexpected stop, and he dragged his foot through a pile of fallen leaves until the tip kicked the back of Jeevan's boot. The searing pain in his side made him bend and tighten his grip on the duffadar's shoulder, but he stopped.

Ssherrss, standing in front of their ragged line, sniffed the air. Without facing Jeevan or Ben, he said in Greek, "Don't mmove. We'rre ssurrrrounded. We have no chance againsst themm in the darrk."

Ben's head swiveled, as he sought the threat with both eyes and ears. He raised his revolver and looked for a target in the pitch-black forest. Straight in front of him, he heard a disembodied voice with a strong accent speaking in Greek. "You are trespassing, stirithy. Why do you bring Alexandrians and strangers into our home?"

Ssherrss answered in some sort of Semitic language Ben had never heard. The hidden voice replied in the same language.

Unable to see his hand in front of his face, Ben felt Ssherrss shift. "The welvess want uss to go with themm to a nearrby ccity. Theirr goverrnessss will want to sspeak with you. They also have someone with them who says he can heal our wounds."

Ben shook his head while aiming toward the source of the voice. In Greek he spoke into the darkness, "Someone kidnapped one of our people, and we won't go until we find them."

Again, the voice came out of the blackness from a different location, replying in Greek, "You are not the only trespassers we have come across this night. Your friend has been liberated. She will join you soon."

It took several heartbeats for Ben to process what the disembodied voice had said. With slow movements, he holstered his gun. Jeevan lowered Ben's Winchester, which he was carrying for Ben.

A familiar voice in the darkness said in English, "I'm coming out."

From the shadows, the outline of a man moved forward with his arms held high. When he was only a few feet away, Ssherrss pulled out his dagger. The blade grew pink before turning a hot, blacksmith-fired red.

In the glow, Ben made out the face of Professor Ali Mousa, and all of his plans to get them home crumbled. "Is Louisa safe? What are you going to do with us?"

Ali frowned. "I haven't seen her, and I'm just as much a prisoner of these animals as you are."

"What?"

The professor shook his head. "The welves killed Panehesy, along with many of our men. They spared me because they assumed I was an Earthling. We can discuss our situation later."

Ali pointed at Ben's bandaged midsection. "We will move faster if I take care of that. May I?" He grabbed the knot, untied it, and unwound the strips of cloak.

Ben winced as the dressing came free. He said through gritted teeth, "What can you do?"

With his strange piercing exposed, Ali placed a hand on Ben's stomach and another on his back. He turned to Ssherrss. "Take it out."

A familiar heat flowed from the professor's hands into Ben's body. The metal-singing stirithy hovered his hand near the metal. The plugs thinned and became straight again. Like a magnet picking up a sewing pin, the four-thumbed hand moved away from Ben's wound with the splinter easing out of his body until it floated in midair. Ssherrss moved his hand, and the metal rod thumped to the ground.

Ben hadn't felt a thing as the piece of javelin left his body. He gaped in fascination as the heat in his belly became more intense. The skin around the edge of the wound began to grow until the inch-wide hole became smaller and smaller. It was like watching water freeze into ice within seconds. When the professor removed his hands, Ben was whole again.

"The flowers?"

Ali nodded. "Yes."

Louisa had done little but worry since being marched through the night by her—what?

Are they saviors or captors?

Her new *captors*, as the realist in her would think of them until proven otherwise, left her in an eerie-dark forest with a few guards while others went to retrieve her friends. Exhausted by her ordeal, she tried to rest.

Her latest attempt to sleep ended with her own cry, startling her awake. She shuddered from the too-slow-to-fade memory of Iskur's hideous face. The bronze-skinned elf wore a devilish smile of glistening white as a thousand cockroaches crawled across her naked body. With her hands rubbing at phantom insect legs, she tried to push his evil visage out of her head.

After the breathing exercises failed, she thought of things that made her feel safe: the cliffs of her childhood, her mother's voice. Yet nothing worked until she pictured a certain crooked smile. A sense of security and safety washed over her. At once, she felt comforted and uneasy. She told herself she didn't need him, but she longed for him to be by her side.

How much longer?

Her eyes grew heavy, an off-kilter grin her only vision.

In less than a week on Aaru, Ben had been in a bona fide medieval battle, met three different races of magic-using aliens, almost become a meal for a giant rat, and fought, then chased kidnappers who stabbed him with a javelin, only to get captured by yet another strange pseudo-human race of albino immortals. No matter how crazy this last week had been, he knew it might get worse before it got better. The weapons they carried and the knowledge they possessed made them the most sought-after people on the planet.

He hoped that despite whatever happened in the next few hours, he could keep a clear head. Six hours of traipsing through a pitch-black forest on the side of a mountain didn't help the situation. After the welves surrounded the tracking party, their—*what*?

Are they captors or hosts?

Their *hosts* led them back to the rest of the group. The welves hadn't attacked them, as they had Ali's villagers, and if what they said was true, they had saved Louisa. As an optimist, he would stick to that explanation until proven wrong. With an incredible ability to see in the dark, the albinos navigated them back to the path in half the time. The welves themselves were a cornucopia of differences.

Their youthfulness, vibrant eyes, and pale, flawless skin, along with their hair, were the obvious constants. If they had red hair, they had the brightest, most luxurious red hair. No matter the color, their irises came painted with intense pigments and colors unseen among mere mortals. Blue eyes were deeper, brighter, or icier than any human blue. Then there were the ambers, violets, and pinks that no human possessed.

The ten males and four female welves Ben had seen appeared to be in their late twenties. Based on the variety of clothing types and hairstyles worn, they might have hailed from a half-dozen different cultures. Or, as it occurred to Ben, that many time periods.

After sunrise, they reunited with the rest of their party. A screen of Lancers and Lochem provided privacy while Ben sat around a sputtering campfire conferring with Jeevan, Esther, Ssherrss, and Khepri. They made sure to keep Ali very far away.

Ssherrss gave a grumpy snort to open the floor as they discussed their limited options. "They have extended diplommatic prrivilegess to uss, which on Aarru mmeanss you arre ssafe to comme and go ass you pleasse. I'mm not ssure they'll honorr it, but it doess mmean that we can keep ourr weaponss. The leaderr ssaid we would mmeet up with the ssoldierss who have Louissa and go to one of theirr ccitiess to mmeet theirr goverrnessss. Any quesstionss?"

There were none. If they wanted to reunite with Louisa, they had to follow the welves.

Ben thought through the different scenarios ahead of meeting the governess. If their hosts knew about their guns, that topic would dominate all discussions. How far would this group go to get the secrets of modern firearms? What little he knew about elves and welves, they were arrogant and not well liked. Could he trust them?

To stay in control of the situation, he would feign ignorance about being able to create bullets. He discussed this strategy with Jeevan and Ssherrss. As far as he knew, he continued to be the only person on Aaru with the chemistry knowledge to create mercury fulminate. At least, for now.

Everyone agreed to tell the same story: that the guns would be useless when the bullets they had were gone. After the meeting, they followed their hosts up the path, the way they'd been heading before the attack. As they began the trip, each welf now sported darkened lenses worn like goggles.

Can't handle the light? Ben thought. *Interesting.*

Ben set off to find Abu. Khepri said she'd seen him sulking toward the back of the column. He found the young man walking alone, leading one packhorse tethered to a second one right behind. When Abu saw Ben, his eyes drifted to the ground, and he wouldn't look Ben in the eye.

Without speaking, Ben took hold of the reins and wrapped his other hand over Abu's shoulders. The teenager leaned into him, tears wetting his face as they hiked the trail. They continued this way for a while as Ben thought about what he needed to say.

With a sniff, Abu spoke first. "I'm sorry. I didn't protect Miss Louisa."

Ben squeezed his shoulder. "I'm so very proud of you. You did everything you could in an impossible situation. Esther and Umrao might be dead right now if not for you."

"But I should have been quicker."

"Abu, I saw everything. I couldn't have done better. That hysakas waited until the last second and used magic to make her pass out. There was nothing you could have done."

Ben's voice was tinged with disgust. "It's my fault for losing them in the forest, but beating ourselves up is useless." He smiled at his son. "I want you to remember this lesson. Second-guessing is a waste of time. It can cost you more than what you lost in the first place."

Abu asked in confusion, "What do you mean?"

Ben sighed as scenes from his past popped to the forefront. "Right after something like an attack happens, you need to deal with the aftermath immediately. Don't think about what happened until you solve those issues first."

He frowned, remembering a distant night in Arkansas and a young officer who never got to learn this lesson. "An enemy will not pause for you to gather yourself. You must focus on the now. I have seen men killed because they didn't move on to the next problem. Only when you know it's safe can you examine past actions. Do that once, and then move on."

Abu lowered his head. "I try, but I keep seeing it in my head."

Ben took a chance with his next question. "You're talking about killing that man. Correct?"

Abu closed his eyes and gulped.

With a deep breath, Ben tightened his grip on his son's shoulder. "I know it's hard. I wish I could say it gets easier, but it doesn't. You had no choice. You know that, don't you?"

"Yes. I don't regret it, but it feels wrong."

"Taking a life should feel wrong, but that sonofabitch had it coming. God knows killing is sometimes justified. Killing someone trying to murder your friends is as justified as it gets. I hope you never have to do it again." Ben shook his head. "But seeing how dangerous this world is, chances are you'll need to fight again."

The horse tugged against Ben, reaching for a small tuft of grass at the edge of the path. Ben pulled hard and clucked, keeping the mare moving. "I need you to trust that God's able to guide your actions. When the time comes, you need to harden your heart to win the fight. Do whatever is necessary to keep your focus on what you need to do right then. Can you do that?"

Abu marched on for a minute, leaving Ben to his thoughts. Brow furrowed, Abu said, "When the attack started, I was so scared. What if I did the wrong thing? I was afraid for Esther. I was afraid Umrao was dead."

Ben smiled. "But that fear never stopped you from doing what you had to do. That is true courage. Next time, you'll still be afraid. I get afraid every time. But I want you to harness that fear. Use it to get mad enough to eat a horny toad backward. Okay?"

Abu shook his head. "I've never seen a frog with horns, but I understand what you mean, and I'll do it. Thank you. To tell you the truth, I'm getting furious thinking about what those elves did. I don't know why, but it helps."

Ben let go of Abu's shoulder and patted him on the back. In silence, they worked their way uphill. Ben tried to get excited about their destination. Coming face-to-face with a people and a culture influenced by the ancient Sumerians, he should be ecstatic. Yet their uncertain future made him feel nothing but trepidation deep in the pit of his stomach.

An hour later, they turned off the path into a small clearing, and the welves called for a break. Ben made his way forward to find the leader of their *hosts*.

With platinum hair and startling amber eyes, Commander Shanesha spoke with Ssherrss at the edge of the small field. Ben interrupted their Aaruan exchange, touching the welve's elbow.

In Greek, he asked, "Where is our friend?"

The welf opened his mouth to reply, but his eyes focused beyond Ben, and he shut his lips. His chin jerked over Ben's shoulder.

Ben heard Louisa's voice and turned. "Thank God. I was afraid I'd never see you again."

He grabbed his mouth and chin, wiping away a sob of uncontrolled relief as Louisa rushed out of an opening in the trees. The force of his emotions stunned him. Every graceful stride she took toward him punctuated the answer to an almost forgotten question.

I am willing.

Ben managed a crooked grin, the locks around his heart falling away.

Abu, seeing her, yelled, "Alhamdulillah! You're okay!"

Ben's smile widened as the teenager wrapped the petite Louisa in a hug, lifting her off the ground.

Louisa's songbird laugh filled the clearing. "It's great to see you, too."

As the two most important people in Ben's life twirled in circles, the dream he'd left for dead gasped a resuscitating breath. Hope trickled into his heart.

Lord, make it so.

Last in line, Ben waited until Khepri unwrapped her long arms from around Louisa. One emotion dominated as he stood in front of the woman who had caused him so many contradictory feelings.

Despite her dirt-smudged cheek and bedraggled hair, her eyes radiated happiness. She smiled, stepped forward, and on tippy-toes embraced his neck. She pressed her cheek to his and whispered, "I'm fine. Really."

Ben leaned down, allowing her heels to touch the ground, and grabbed her around the waist. He whispered back, "Please don't do that again. As big of a pain in my ass as you sometimes are, I—" His voice cracked, and he paused to gain control. He couldn't say the words in his heart for fear of driving her away. "We need you."

With a fierce squeeze, she pecked the scar on his cheek. Her face flushed as she broke their embrace, putting a foot of distance between them. With the lingering effects of her lips still on his cheek, he wondered where he'd gotten the dust in his eyes.

Her face grew serious. "What's going to happen to us?"

Eyes still locked with hers, he said, "I don't know. We have to get to the Ancients' site and find a way home."

She raised an eyebrow. "How do we do that?"

He shook his head and shrugged while holding his arms out, palms up.

"So, we're going to wing it?" She paused a beat and winked at him. "I like it."

A commotion from the trail drew Ben's gaze over her head. With a furrowed brow, he said, "Oh, I forgot to tell you."

Louisa looked over her shoulder and cursed in both Greek and French, "*Gios tou a putain.*"

Professor Ali Mousa walked toward them, a grim smile on his face.

The expletive she had just voiced echoed again in her thoughts with a bit of added oomph.

Son of a two-penny whore.

Her loud curse had turned the professor's smile into a frown as he continued strolling across the clearing.

Louisa turned to meet their nemesis, her blood boiling. As the man who called himself a Keeper of the Seba stopped in front of her, Louisa punched the professor in the face. The stocky man stumbled back, grabbing his nose and mouth.

As she pulled her fist back to begin a Kalari combination that would finish the threat, Ben grabbed the crook of her arm.

"He's with us."

She twisted to see Ben's face.

He gave her another off-kilter grin. "At least for now."

The End of *Ancient Civilizations*

Keep reading for a short story about Alexander's Lost Army.

Thank you for reading Ancient Civilizations. To continue with the adventure, buy or download Book 2, Echoes of Ancients today.

Echoes of Ancients - Amazon

If you enjoyed Ancient Civilizations, please consider leaving a review. As an Indie Author, every review is important.

Ancient Civilizations - Amazon

The Louisa Sophia prequel, *Louisa Sophia and a Legion of Sisters*, is available now on Amazon. Step into a world of daring heists, fierce friendships, and high-stakes adventure! Follow Louisa Sophia as she fights to protect her friends and outwit danger on a treacherous journey across 1870s Europe. Learn more about what made Louisa the woman she is in Ancient Civilizations.

Louisa Sophia and a Legion of Sisters - Amazon

To signup for one of my newsletters, go to LamentationsAndMagic.com, or RussellCowdrey.com.

Please follow me on Amazon, Facebook, Instagram, TikTok.

Thank you again for joining me on this journey, and remember; God's able, if we are willing.

History is Magic,
Russell Cowdrey

Compendium

Cast of Ancient Civilizations

- **Benjamin Moore McGehee** (Fictitious)—Former Confederate cavalry soldier turned engineer, then doctor, then archaeologist.

- **Louisa Sophia** (Real)—Illegitimate child of the Earl Cromer, who is the Egyptian consul-general or British citizen in charge of occupied Egypt after the invasion of 1882. Her age and almost all details of her life in this book are fictitious.

- **Abu Saqr** (Son of Falcon) (Fictitious)—Orphan from Aleppo, which at the time was part of the Ottoman Empire. Abu was unofficially adopted by Dr. McGehee at the age of thirteen.

- **Professor Ali Mousa** (Fictitious)—Born in the Valley of the Crescent, he is the associate curator at the Bulaq Museum and a professor of languages, history, and mathematics at the university in Cairo.

- **Duffadar Jeevan Nahal** (Fictitious)—Duffadar = "Corporal of the horse" or "sergeant," if referring to infantry, from the 13th Bengal Lancers. He and his twenty men are tasked with protecting Louisa. His horse is named Chetak, which is the name of a famous Indian war horse.

- **13th Bengal Lancers** (Real, although the soldiers in the book are fictitious)—Each of the names for Jeevan's soldiers was chosen because they were Victoria Cross recipients. The 13th Bengal Lancers in this book are part of a Dogra Hindu regiment from Punjab/Lahore. Indian regiments of the British Army during that time were segregated by religion. They speak Dogri (a dialect of Punjabi). The 13th Bengal Lancers were part of the 1882 invasion and would have been in Egypt in 1883. The men whose names were used in the book received their awards much later because Indians were not officially recognized as recipients until World War I. The individual soldiers in the book are a work of fiction, including their rank, age, physical description, skills, and so on.

- **Lance Duffadar** = Corporal—**Karamjeet Judge**

- **Lance Duffadar** = Corporal—**Bhandari Ram**

    - He is 5'5" tall (shortest man in the unit but lightning fast with a knife and wiry strong)

    - Guru of the forbidden martial art called Kalaripayattu or Kalari, which teaches weapons and then hand-to-hand techniques that utilize a lot of pressure points. Ram has been teaching his squadron the techniques of Kalari when no British are around.

- **Acting Lance Duffadar** = Lance Corporal—**Premindra Bhagat**

- **Acting Lance Duffadar** = Lance Corporal—**Yeshwant Ghadge**

- Rest of the sowars = Privates who might be mentioned

- **Chhelu Ram**

- **Gian Singh**

- **Darwan Negi**—He is wounded in the arm, and Ben sews him up.

- **Prakash Chib**

    - The incredible horseman

- **Ganju Lama**—Goes on the search for the temple

- **Namdeo Jadav**—The best singer

- **Richhpal Ram**

- **Lala Betigeri** (No last name given so I picked one.)

- **Umrao Singh**—Youngest and tallest Lancer at nineteen who becomes best friends with Abu

- Five more unnamed Lancers

- **Charles Chipiez** (Real)—French architect, illustrator, Egyptologist, Iranologist; Charles Chipiez—Wikipedia. All other details and conversations in this book are fictitious.

- **Major Charles Davis** (Real)—Officer in the Pennsylvania 7th Cavalry who received the Medal of Honor in 1863. None of his interactions with Ben are real, although his unit did serve in the Atlanta campaign and might have been in close proximity to the Texas 6th. Charles C. Davis—Wikipedia.

- **Charles Edwin Wilbour** (Real)—American journalist and archaeologist who was an expert in languages and parties. He did really own a riverboat but bought it a few years after the fictional events of the book. Charles Edwin Wilbour—Wikipedia. All other details in this book are fictitious.

- **Émile Burgsch** (Real)—German archaeologist and assistant curator of the Bulaq Museum in Cairo Egypt. Émile Brugsch—Wikipedia. All other details and conversations in this book are fictitious.

- **Hermine Hartleben** (Real)—German archaeologist. Hermine Hartleben—Wikipedia. All other details, including her engagement and conversations in this book, are fictitious.

- **Nashwa** (Fictitious)—Abu's first girlfriend and hostess at a Cairo restaurant that her family owns.

- **Evelyn Baring, 1st Earl of Cromer** (Real)—Louisa's father and consul-general of the Egyptian occupation. All details in the book about the earl are totally fiction, other than his station and being Louisa's father. Evelyn Baring, 1st Earl of Cromer—Wikipedia.

- **Mahdi Saqr** and **Yara Saqr** (Fictitious)—Abu's deceased parents

- **Ahmed Gerigar** (Fictitious)—Foreman at the Perdiccas tomb search site. His **son by the same name (real)** is also on the site and later would become Howard Carter's primary rais (foreman) during the excavation of the tomb of King Tut. All details in the book are completely fictitious. The name of Ahmed Gerigar's father and all other details are fictitious. The father character was created to provide an experienced Egyptian excavator who would have been active at the time of the book. Blog—Photographing Tutankhamun (photographing-tutankhamun.com).

All of the following characters are 100 percent fictitious.

- **Caesar Octavius Remus II** is the current emperor of Remus, a nation formed in 236 A.D. or 4281 An, after defeating the ripvor the previous year. The founders of Remus were a mix of Roman Legionaries and Sasanid soldiers who were fighting one another at the time of their summons. They joined forces to defeat the ripvor and over time combined their cultures and religions. Their religion now is a form of Zoroastrianism, which has combined Jupiter and Ahura Mazda into the monotheistic deity called Ahura Jupiter.

- **Aquila Magnus** is the first counselor to the emperor and the head of the Remus spy organizations.

- **Faustulus** is the slave who runs the emperor's household.

- **Bennu** is the female babiakhom interpreter for Remus II.

- **Iskur** is an elven assassin who travels with a band of two other elves, one hysaka and one babiakhom.

- **Hem-netjer Panehesy** is the Nubian priest who is accompanying Professor Ali. He was sent to use the Seba to bring a large military force back to Aaru.

- **Polemarchos Alexandria ben Zev i Hurasu** is the commanding officer in charge of the Alexandrian 4th Stratia; a direct descendant of Zev and Hurasu.

- **Qeb** is a babiakhom member of the Alexandrian army who serves as an adviser and a wind singer to Polemarchos Alexandria ben Zev i Hurasu.

- **Khepri** is a female hysaka orphan raised in an Alexandrian orphanage.

- **Dimaerites Esther ben Zev i Hurasu i Enoch** is the seventeen-year-old daughter of Alexandria ben Zev i Hurasu, the commander of the Alexandrian 4th Stratia, and Judah ben Enoch, the commander of the 2nd Stratia. She is a direct descendant of Zev and Hurasu, first ancestors of Alexandria, as well as first ancestor Enoch through her father's line.

- **Ssherrsslatigausss Quegmmexalarrr (Ssherrss)** is a stirithy metal singer who is part of the Alexandrian army and Khepri's alpha.

- **Shanesha** is the leader of a company of welven soldiers from the city of Nippur. He has platinum blond hair and amber eyes.

- **Inanna** means "Lady of Sky." She is the governess of the city of Nippur in the welven kingdom of Kutha.

- **Djoser** is a babiakhom wind singer who works for Iskur. He has used his beast master skills to have a martial eagle (a native of Egypt) and two caracals, which are his shadows. He is in it for the money but has no compunction about killing or torturing to complete his goals.

- **Shemush** is the hysaka life-singing healer/torturer that works with Iskur.

About the Author

Fueled by his love of reading, Indie Author, Russell Cowdrey introduces his audience to a new world filled with historical science fiction wrapped up in a fantasy blanket of aliens, magic, archaeology, military history, romance, and found family.

Before launching his debut series of Lamentations and Magic in 2023, Russell used his imagination to innovate software and set out to follow his dream of being his own boss.

Inspired by the success of other KU writers, Russell set out to write novels he enjoyed reading. After hours of research and an abundance of literature ideas, Russell's writing career came into focus.

Fans of Indiana Jones, Stargate, and The Mummy movies—with Brendan Fraser and Rachel Weisz, not that abomination with Tom Cruise—will love the twists, turns and diverse perspectives in the Lamentations and Magic series.

History is Magic and Research is Fun!

Alexander's Lost Army

East of Pelusium, Egypt, 321 B.C.

In the glow of the last embers of the campfire, Zev wondered about his God's sense of humor. *Merciful Adonai, keep her and our baby safe.*

Zev ran his hand along the supple, bronzed skin of Hurasu's waist as she lay on her side with her back to him. He pulled her closer. His palm moved over her flat stomach, willing his prayers to protect their child with a touch. Hurasu shuddered in her sleep and pushed back against him. Her red hair tickled his beard as he inhaled her always-present aroma of horse sweat and poppy flowers.

When Alexander had come to Jerusalem on his way to conquer Egypt, the high priest threw open the city gates and welcomed the young king as the fulfillment of a prophecy. Hundreds of years earlier, the Prophet Daniel had spoken of a Greek warrior king who would overthrow Jerusalem's oppressors, the Persians. To help Alexander fulfill his destiny, the high priest offered the Lochem as a tribute.

From that day until Alexander's death, Zev and his unit of elite Temple Guards had fought alongside the Greeks with the fervor of zealots.

But now? What are we fighting for?

For the second time, he marched into Egypt, but now, as part of Perdiccas's army, bent on taking back Alexander's body from the thief Ptolemy. Unlike his first trip, he had so much more to lose. For six years, he and the beautiful horse archer had loved and fought like they were promised nothing more. Last night, Hurasu had shaken the foundation of his world with her news.

Maybe today, maybe tomorrow, Perdiccas's army would battle Ptolemy's mixed Greek and Egyptian army. The fate of a future he had never imagined would be in the hands of a God he believed in but had never relied on more than he did his sword arm. HaShem must be laughing at him.

He leaned in and kissed Hurasu's shoulder before nuzzling close to her ear. "Time to rise, my love."

She turned to him, their lips connecting with a gentle touch. Both of her hands grasped his face, and she pulled back to look at him. Her hazel eyes burned with love and concern. "Put last night's words away. Focus on what you must do now." Her face became stern. "Tomorrow will wait."

He pulled her closer, wishing he had more time. "I will, and you do what you do best."

Her eyes widened. "Fight or love you?"

"Both."

Zev's morning started with excitement as a large contingent of Egyptian infantry and cavalry showed up on the army's right flank. Perdiccas ordered his unit of Lochem, along with another five thousand men, to engage the enemy. As Zev and his comrades formed their battle lines, the enemy withdrew as fast as they appeared. Since then, Zev and the rest of the small Greek army had been chasing the Egyptians.

Zev hopped up onto the tallest boulder atop the small hill and gazed toward the horizon. Overlooking the arid Egyptian landscape, the "mound" commanded the highest point for miles around. A cloud of dust rose in the wake of at least fifty chariots as they disappeared, one by one, into the entrance of a distant canyon. The enemy's decision to enter the canyon puzzled him. They must be planning to ambush the Lochem and their Greek comrades in the narrow passages.

"Commander Zev, what do you see?"

Zev looked down at his second in command. "Trouble, Dimaerites Enoch."

The dimaerites straightened his shoulders. "I don't like it. Why are we still chasing these Egyptians if they don't want to engage us?"

"Would you leave them to our rear? Besides, do you think it's some kind of omen?" Zev cracked.

"Hell, no. It's not an omen," his second in command fired back. "You know I don't believe in that superstitious silliness." The knuckles of his right hand, holding a spear, rapped the Shin symbol painted on his leather-bound, wooden shield.

"Have you ever considered that we are being punished because you are in love with a Saka woman, instead of a good Jewish girl?"[1] Enoch, Zev's friend and the one veteran warrior who had been at his side since the beginning, smirked. "Commander Zev, if you were going to pay for the fruit, you should have tasted more than just one date." The dimaerites looked around to make sure he had the other nearby troops' attention. "The problem is, if you had, Hurasu would have pruned your tiny figs." Enoch chuckled.

At the mention of Hurasu, Zev turned around on the rock. He looked over the heads of his waiting men toward the moving wall of spears, where thou-

---

1. The Saka were a group of nomadic Iranian peoples who historically inhabited the northern and eastern Eurasian Steppe and the Tarim Basin. They were related to but distinct from the Scythians. Like the Scythians, many Saka women fought alongside the men. Their warriors were known for being skilled cavalry and cavalry archers.

sands of Greek soldiers marched eight abreast. Their sarissas, intimidating eighteen-foot-long spears used with devastating success during Alexander's conquests, undulated against the sky like the legs of a millipede that found itself on its back. His eyes roved over the army's flanks. He dismissed the light infantry, the elite silver shields, and the other Lochem units. He sought the cavalry riding farther afield on the wings.

It took him only a moment to locate Hurasu's flowing red hair. His chest heaved, and his breath caught in his throat at the sight. She melded as one with her horse, and her gray mare pranced with pride.

The pair stood out, even among a forest of proud stallions with their own strong riders. He understood. He felt the same pride knowing that she belonged to him, and he belonged, heart and soul, to her.

Born to the saddle, she'd proved many times to be the best archer Zev had ever seen. Of course, the fierce Saka warrior thrived in battle. He prayed once again that the skills and the providential protection that had gotten them this far would allow them to survive this final campaign.

After hopping down from the boulder, Zev hoisted his shield and spear, which he had leaned against the stone. "Let's go. We need to get to that canyon before they can lay their traps."

He took off down the hill, setting a fast pace for such a blistering hot morning.

Zev adjusted the cloth hanging from his helmet to cover as much of his neck as possible. Though tired after seven hours of pursuing the enemy, he pushed that from his mind with a battle only moments away.

He half-listened as Dimaerites Enoch gave last-minute instructions. Eight hundred paces ahead, thousands of heavy and light Egyptian infantry moved into battle formation. Chariots and light cavalry stood on their flanks. The opposing forces faced off inside a large box canyon about a half-mile wide and the same long. Coated from head to foot in fine yellow-red Egyptian dust, both sets of soldiers blended into the canyon walls and the soil underfoot.

Something didn't feel right to Zev. The small hairs on the back of his neck strained to stand, despite the sweat holding them down.

Why hadn't they deployed at the mouth of the canyon?

The Egyptians could have used the terrain to their advantage where a small force could have held the Greeks at bay for as long as they had wished. Zev shuddered at the image of pushing through the narrow canyon opening and being assaulted from all sides in a funnel of death.

But to give us space and fight us on equal terms? This is madness.

He told himself to focus and prepare as the encouragements continued.

"Remember, stay with your yoke.[2] Know your role as Sword or Spear. Most of all, stay near the veterans. Zev's Flying Wolves are the best warriors in Alexander's army. We have traveled to hell and killed the devil himself."

Zev smelled fear coming from the ranks. Having so many unbloodied recruits rattled even the veterans. He pushed his own uncertainty away and settled his troubled mind by clenching and unclenching his trembling hand. No matter how many times he went into battle, the nerves came out. For the sake of his men, he suppressed his anxiety. He would be the steady voice of certainty amid the chaos.

---

2. A yoke is a pair of Lochem soldiers who fight together as a single unit. The sword part of the yoke uses a specialized khopesh short sword to snag and pull an opponent's shield down, exposing the enemy to the attack from the spear part of the yoke.

His second in command stood in front of a quivering teenage soldier and pointed at the Wolves' raised standard. A stretched wolf pelt and a snarling head topped the pole. Wings made of brown eagle feathers completed the banner.

Dimaerites Enoch yelled so the entire unit could hear. "Stand strong, and fight for your brother next to you! Remember, we are Wolves, and Wolves never fight alone!"

Zev watched his men's faces. Their fear eased away, replaced by determination as strong as steel. Confident that his men were ready, Zev scanned the enemy lines once more. His own vision took on the color of his men's battle lust. The Egyptians seemed to waver and shift behind the sand's rising heat.

In a heartbeat, everything in Zev's view grew distorted as if he were looking up from the bottom of a pool of crystal-blue water. Blinking, he tried to dispel the strange mirage.

A beam of light, brighter than lightning on the darkest night, shot up, and the sky blinked. White became his world. No more aroma of sweaty men. No more blistering heat on his skin. No more taste of dust. Nothing but white.

He felt himself falling for a long time and somehow understood he had entered an existence outside of time itself. Yet he had the distinct sensation of movement.

How long he fell within this timeless world he did not know. A sudden darkness startled him until he realized his eyes remained shut. More shocking, the fragrant smell of something akin to jasmine filled his nostrils. Forcing himself to blink, Zev stared at stalks of tall grass. The stem of each plant alternated light blue, then red, then pink, and back to blue.

Rolling onto his back, he saw two-foot-tall grass topped with little flowers in bloom. The stalks of the plants shimmered as if small jolts of different colored lightning flowed from their roots to the petals above. The flowers blazed in an array of colors, from golden yellow to dark violet with no apparent order.

Then he saw the moon at the edge of the horizon on his right. He moved his head, and a second moon appeared—*yes, that had to be another moon*. It hung high in the sky, straight above him, while the sun hovered above the left horizon. The three heavenly bodies formed a triangle if he drew a line connecting the three dots. Transecting the trinity were two silver streaks that raced across the sky.

The sound of his own exclamation took him by surprise. Others stirred, gasping, cursing, and even wailing. He struggled to his feet on unsteady legs, hoping to find his soldiers. The entire army had appeared as if by magic in the enormous field of prism-like grass.

With thoughts of the enemy, he spun around to be shocked by the sight of a huge snow-capped mountain range in the distance. At the base of the mountains, the enemy formations came into line.

"Wolves, get to your feet and assume your positions!" he bellowed without thinking.

During the next rushed minutes, Zev and his men raced to help one another regain composure. Several men were inconsolable, curling up in the grass and rocking themselves. Others looked ready to bolt, but the discipline of the veterans took hold. Once his section neared a semblance of order, his mind raced to Hurasu. He couldn't see her or any of the mounted archers from his location.

Stay safe, my love.

Everyone's attention snapped forward as three figures stepped away from the enemy lines. They made their way to the midpoint between the two armies.

"Adonai, save us!" Enoch whispered.

A dark-skinned Egyptian, dressed as a heavy infantryman, strolled to the right of a creature that could only be Anubis come to life. At seven feet tall, the giant canine stood on its hind legs, dressed in a half-tunic and the broad necklace of gold and lapis that Zev had seen on Egyptian priests. On the left walked a hairless green monkey wearing cropped pants. No other description came to Zev's mind for the five-and-a-half-foot-tall, bow-legged creature. It raised its arms to the sky, and thousands of men gasped at the creature's wings.

Giant hairless monkey bat.

Soldiers in the Greek army rattled their weapons in agitation.

Instead of an inevitable clash of iron, each man heard the following words spoken in his native tongue as if an invisible person stood nearby. "Brave warriors of the great Alexander. Welcome to Aaru. You have been summoned. The time of Lamentations draws near."

Printed in Dunstable, United Kingdom